D1496204

FICTION

GUINEVERE'S TRUTH AND OTHER TALES

GUINEVERE'S TRUTH AND OTHER TALES

JENNIFER ROBERSON

FIVE STAR
A part of Gale, Cengage Learning

Detroit • New York • San Francisco • New Haven, Conn • Waterville, Maine • London

DEC 0 3 2008

GALE
CENGAGE Learning

LIBRARY OF CONGRESS CATALOGING-IN-PUBLICATION DATA

Roberson, Jennifer, 1953–
    Guinevere's truth and other tales / by Jennifer Roberson. —
1st ed.
        p. cm.
    ISBN-13: 978-1-59414-150-8 (alk. paper)
    ISBN-10: 1-59414-150-9 (alk. paper)
    1. Fantasy fiction, American. I. Title.
PS3568.0236A6 2008
813'.54—dc22   2008031534

First Edition. First Printing: November 2008.
Published in 2008 in conjunction with Tekno Books.

3 9082 11088 0716

Printed in the United States of America
1 2 3 4 5 6 7 12 11 10 09 08

I dedicate this collection to my agent, Russ Galen, and to my fantasy editor, Betsy Wollheim, who made my dreams come true.

CONTENTS

Contents

INTRODUCTION

It was 1956, I was three years old, and my mother had taken me to visit my great-grandfather. While we waited for him to come downstairs to the living room, I discovered his typewriter. It was a huge old Olivetti that could have doubled as a boat anchor. I was fascinated by it, happily pushing down all those stiff keys with small fingers. Letters appeared! It was magic, pure and simple, and I fell head over heels in love.

I remember my mother remonstrating with me, afraid I'd jam up the keys, which was certainly a possibility in those days of temperamental manuals. But my great-grandfather, descending the creaking stairs of his big old house even as she spoke, told her it was fine if I wanted to play on the typewriter.

I've often wondered if he was prescient.

In 1982, I was twenty-eight years old and an adult college student finishing up my final semester in London on a foreign studies program. Initially I had attended college only to take specific courses I felt would help me as a writer—journalism, history, psychology, and anthropology—not to get a degree. But when I realized I had racked up enough elective hours to be within three semesters of achieving a bachelor of science in journalism, I decided to go for it. I packed all the required core classes I'd ignored into one year, attended summer school, and happily returned to electives for that last six months spent in England. The day I returned to the US, I would officially be a mid-year graduate, if a bit older than most.

As a lifelong Anglophile, the chance to study in England was heady and fascinating. Classes made up three days of each week; the other four days were ours to while away as we would. I spent those free days in museums, castles, manors, theatres, at concerts, and tromping around various famous sites and locales in England, Wales, and Scotland, busily storing away ideas for future novels. I also awaited word on whether the University of Arizona's master of fine arts program would accept me as a student. Though as a magazine freelancer I enjoyed some small success, I knew that after spending so many years writing and submitting novels without acceptance there were no guarantees I'd ever have a book published. So I set my sights on a backup plan: teaching on the college level. I'd worked as an investigative newspaper reporter, and as an advertising copywriter; those positions held no appeal for me. Mostly, I wanted to write novels. But I knew I'd also enjoy teaching, and the reputation of the MFA program at UofA was outstanding.

Alas, when my mother came to visit me in London, a letter from the UofA accompanied her announcing I was not accepted as a candidate for an MFA. (Later, I was told that my work samples were "too commercial.") The news was devastating. My plans blew up in my face. I had no career as a novelist, and now no hope of achieving a master's at the UofA. Maybe I would have to look to getting on with a magazine or a newspaper after all.

We students lived in a row house in South Kensington—I was on the top floor, up a narrow, winding staircase—and rode "the tube" on the Picadilly Line three mornings a week to Russell Square and the University of London. As the mail arrived very early, it was always waiting for us when we came downstairs to breakfast. I collected mine and discovered a telegram, which I thought a little strange; but E-mail wasn't part of the landscape at that time, and it was difficult to make or receive transatlantic phone calls because of the time difference and the fact that we had a single communal phone. But it was two days after my twenty-ninth birthday, and I decided it likely was from a friend or family member offering belated birthday wishes.

In fact, the telegram was from my agent, announcing that DAW Books had bought my first novel, *Shapechangers*. The news came twenty-six years and many typewriters after I fell in love with my great-grandfather's machine, two weeks after I learned I was not an MFA candidate.

I stared at the telegram while tears rolled down my face. Everyone at my table fell silent, certain a family member had died. It took me several minutes to finally explain that I was now a *real* author, that a novel I'd written would actually be published. I'd spent fifteen years writing manuscripts and submitting them, piling up rejection slips, and finally my dream had come true.

The telegram also asked if I could stop over in New York on my way home from England and meet my agent, and to have lunch with Don and Betsy Wollheim of DAW Books. It meant changing my plane reservation, of course, so I could stay overnight, but that was one penalty fee I didn't mind paying! So on December 18th, 1982, I landed in New York City as both a brand-new college graduate, and a real writer.

Unfortunately it had turned out that my agent would be on vacation when I arrived in New York, but he had arranged for me to meet with Barry Malzberg at the agency. Barry, an award-winning science fiction author of high repute, was one of the slush pile readers at the Scott Meredith Literary Agency, and he had passed my manuscript along to a hot young agent named Russ Galen, saying he thought it might sell. (And two months later, Russ indeed had it sold.) Barry and I enjoyed a very nice chat, though I was jet-lagged and nervous, and he gave me a rundown on the production stages my manuscript would go through on the way to becoming a real book. He then presented me with an advanced reading copy of a very fat fantasy novel set for publication in a few months, *The Mists of Avalon,* by Marion Zimmer Bradley. Marion happened to be one of my very favorite authors, and I was thrilled to have the ARC. Barry then very kindly escorted me several blustery blocks to the Manhattan skyscraper housing DAW Books. There I met Betsy Wollheim, my editor, and her father, Donald A. Wollheim, DAW's founder. Betsy gave me a tour of the DAW offices, pried her father out from behind his desk, and off we went to lunch a couple of blocks away.

It was a nice little restaurant, and we took a table by the window. Unfortunately the view was somewhat obstructed by scaffolding, and our ears soothed by the sweet percussion of a jackhammer. I promptly went into sticker shock when I saw the prices on the menu. Yes, DAW was buying, but I was a girl from the Phoenix suburbs and of a comfortable middle-class upbringing. I just couldn't stand it. I ordered the least expensive entree.

We talked books, of course. I remained incredibly nervous to be sitting across the table from the legendary *Donald A. Wollheim,* and probably blithered like an idiot much of the time. Don, who was known throughout the industry as a curmudgeon, didn't say a great deal, but interjected comments now and again. It was Betsy and I who gabbed most of the time.

At one point, I mentioned the ARC Barry Malzberg had given me for Marion Zimmer Bradley's new novel. This was possibly a faux pas, as *Mists* was being published by a competing house, but I was too tired, nervous and jet-lagged to realize it. Don just asked me what I thought of Marion, whose Darkover series was a hugely popular headliner for DAW.

As the jackhammer outside the window banged, I said: "I

adore MZB."

Don fixed me with a narrow, baleful, laser-like stare. "You *what?*"

What on earth had I said to annoy him? Rather weakly, I replied, "I love MZB."

"Oh." His expression softened. "I thought you said you *abhored* her."

Yeah, right; tell your brand-new publisher you hate his top-selling author. Thanks, Mr. Jackhammer.

With that misunderstanding straightened out, we went on to talk books a while longer, and I explained that I'd actually written most of the Cheysuli series. Betsy was very interested, her father less so. I learned later that Don, like Barry Malzberg, didn't really like fantasy; he preferred science fiction. I was, in fact, wholly Betsy's "baby"—*Shapechangers* was her first acquisition without any input from Don.

That lunch was the birth of a solid author-editor relationship. I have worked closely with Betsy for twenty-five years on seventeen fantasy novels (with five more under contract), and have learned a great deal from her. When Don Wollheim died, Betsy took over as president and editor-in-chief of DAW. Our relationship is part friendship, part (I've been told) sibling dynamics, and part business. I'm extremely fortunate that my editor is also my publisher; I never have to worry that a "higher-up" or bean-counter is going to make changes to Betsy's plans, because Betsy is the publisher. Her word is law.

The other major influence in my professional life is my agent, Russ Galen, who now heads up his own agency, Scovil Chichak Galen. I bless the day Barry Malzberg handed Russ my manuscript and said he believed it would sell, because Barry placed the book and my career in brilliant hands. A superb agent does far more than just send manuscripts to editors and negotiate contracts. He can literally orchestrate an author's career. Not as a Svengali, but as a partner. Over a quarter of a century, Russ and I have shared thousands of lengthy letter and e-mail exchanges and telephone calls, discussing all the minutiae of the publishing industry. We discuss what's hot, what's not; which ideas work, which don't; we strategize the best way to market various book proposals; we constantly look at my future, at where I want to be as an author, and sort out how best to get there. It's true that I do the writing, but Russ does the *guiding*. Without him, I would not be where I am today.

Or, for that matter, where I could be tomorrow.

In 1983, feeling slightly less intimidated because I was now an author even though my first novel wasn't out yet, I wrote my very first fan letter. It went to Marion Zimmer Bradley. I hoped, but didn't really expect, to hear back from her. I knew she had to be terribly busy, and undoubtedly received hundreds of fan letters every day.

A couple of weeks later I did hear from MZB, and she was inviting me to submit a short story to her new fantasy anthology, titled *Sword and Sorceress*. I wanted badly to contribute, but I had nothing on hand appropriate, and I was afraid to try to write something specifically for the anthology. I mean, what if I couldn't? What if I failed miserably? What if I sent utter tripe to, of all people, *Marion Zimmer Bradley?* Imposter Syndrome reared its ugly head and roared at me.

Then I recalled that many of the short stories in science fiction magazines were culled from novels, or later expanded into novels. Maybe I could do that. Maybe I could find a section in one of the Cheysuli manuscripts that, with a little noodling, would work. So I pulled out the manuscript that later became *Daughter of the Lion,* found a section I felt met Marion's requirements for the new anthology, reworked the beginning and end to make the story stand on its own, and sent it to MZB. She wrote back accepting the story, but asked if she could change the title to "Blood of Sorcery," as she felt it was more dramatic than "Keely." As far as I was concerned, Marion Zimmer Bradley could call it anything she liked!

I went on to write many stories specifically for Marion, though never again did I cull from an existing manuscript. Her preference as editor for a strong female protagonist echoed my own as reader and writer. And while there is a segment of reviewers, readers, and other f/sf writers who think theme anthologies are a complete waste of time, I always looked on these invitations as challenges. How better to engage the imagination than to demand different takes on an ongoing central theme?

In all, there are thirteen stories written for MZB included in this collection, including her anthologies and, later, her fantasy magazine. I always enjoyed writing for Marion, and with practice I learned a great deal about the shorter form. Eventually I went on to contribute short fiction to other anthologies and magazines, and to put on an editor's hat for my own anthologies.

These stories reflect the core of what the *Sword and Sorceress* anthologies were all about. Marion as an editor was innovative in requiring that the central character in each story be a woman, but the tales were neither to be feminist polemic, nor to feature Conan clones with breasts and brass bikinis. She wanted women protagonists from all walks of life, of all types and temperaments. These protagonists were specifically not to be *better* than men, but to be perfectly ordinary human beings involved in challenging, extraordinary circumstances. Women, Marion said, could have adventures, too.

The majority of fantasy fiction, in novels and in short stories, features popular legends, often Celtic; fairy tales; worlds imaginary and real, with historical settings—and wishful thinking—in the Dark Ages, the Medieval period, and countless others eras. Less is written in contemporary settings, though there is indeed a popular subgenre that relies on a very modern world familiar to us all, called urban fantasy. In our present, the juxtaposition of magic and reality, of mythical creatures and the mundane, offers a delicious cognitive dissonance, an exploration of what fascinates us even today about myths, legends, and tall tales. Mark Twain wrote about a Connecticut Yankee in King Arthur's court; other authors have brought fairies, elves, dwarves, princes, kings and queens, classic archetypes all, forward out of the ancient, imaginary Then and have woven them expertly into the fabric of the prosaic Now.

These stories are probably the most dissimilar in tone, despite all taking place in a contemporary setting, and are also time-specific and thus somewhat dated. "Mad Jack" tells the tale of an unhappy middle-aged man trying to rediscover the greatest joy of his childhood; "Jesus Freaks" offers readers a future that could almost be our present; "By the Time I Get to Phoenix" springboards from the classic highwayman trope; "A Compromised Christmas" explores the careful dance of partners in a new marriage; and "Piece of Mind" is the story of the only witness to the infamous murder of two innocent people.

I think all are familiar with the Arthurian legend. Arthur to this day remains part and parcel of our world; hundreds of academics and scientists have debated whether he really lived, whether Camelot actually existed. Excavations have been undertaken in an attempt to find ruins and artifacts that might prove the legend true. And yet the continuing lack of evidence in no way diminishes that legend. For centuries we have read novels and viewed films about Arthur, Merlin, Guinevere, Lancelot, and the Knights of the Round Table; I daresay we'll continue to do so, as will our descendents.

For many years I resisted writing in the Arthurian mythos. So many authors had done it already, and some had done it brilliantly. Mary Stewart. Rosemary Sutcliffe. Gillian Bradshaw. Marion Zimmer Bradley. I was perfectly content to read, and to love, their works.

Over time, however, the legend seduced me.

Mary Stewart's Merlin trilogy was and is a truly superb exploration of the Arthurian legend from Merlin's point of view; they are three of my favorite novels. Instead of the traditional ancient wizard of long white hair and beard, gnarled hands, and magic wands, Stewart presents us with Merlin in all ages, in all facets. He is a boy, an adolescent, and an adult, dedicated to the goal of putting and keeping Arthur on the throne of Britain. Seeing the legend entirely through Merlin's eyes affords readers a very different and refreshing take on the legend.

What Stewart did so well, I could not hope to emulate. But experiment with, yes. Carefully I tiptoed out into the shallows of a very deep and wondrous lake. Here is Merlin seen one night through a boy's eyes, in "A Lesser Working." Merlin is also in "Shadows in the Wood," freed from imprisonment by lovers who are central to another compelling legend, one I explored in two historical novels: *Lady of the Forest,* and *Lady of Sherwood.* And here, also, is Arthur's wife and Lancelot's lover, whose bittersweet story in her own words stands apart from traditional tales in "Guinevere's Truth."

One might think that when various authors write multiple-volume series, and, in some cases, *multiple* multiple-volume series, that surely they've told every tale. Except that they haven't. Sometimes characters in a novel step forward and demand a story all of their own, or a vignette niggles to be written, or a nifty-neato idea just isn't large enough to work into a book. And sometimes a short story simply appears in the author's head one day, featuring familiar characters in familiar worlds.

As mentioned, my first published short story was culled from one of the future Cheysuli volumes. When invited by MZB to submit a story to the second *Sword and Sorceress* anthology, I'd already created another world to play in with *Sword-Dancer,* though the novel hadn't yet been published. It was intended to be a singleton title, not a series, but by the time I finished the book I was having so much fun that I had to write more about the protagonists, Tiger and Del. So it was natural for me to consider writing a story set in my new universe. It would be a good introduction, I felt, to a world very different from the Cheysuli books. And so a tale called "The Lady and the Tiger" was born.

"The Lady and the Tiger" worked then because readers didn't know Tiger and Del. The twist isn't a twist anymore. But I include it here because the story features the first appearance of two characters who have gone on to be the most popular I have created in twenty-five years and three universes. Tiger and Del appear again in "Rite of Passage."

"Blood of Sorcery" was the story published in MZB's first *Sword and Sorceress* anthology; "Of Honor and the Lion" is a novelette, and though written after several Cheysuli books had been published, it is actually a prequel to *Shapechangers.* It's also a story I'll expand into a novel, as I plan to return to the world of the Cheysuli with three new books.

"Ending, and Beginning" first appeared in the *30th Anniversary DAW Fantasy* collection and introduces my most recent fantasy universe, "Karavans," home to four new novels and an ensemble cast of characters including gods, demons, devils, demigods, humans, and a mobile hell-on-earth. As of this writing, *Karavans* and *Deepwood* are on the shelves with *The Wild Road* in progress; the fourth volume, *Dragon Moon,* will follow in 2009.

Assembling this collection has given me a chance to revisit the broad spectrum of my writing from the earliest days of my career in the '80s through the latter days of the 2000s, rekindling memories of those first heady days as a "real" author. It's been a great ride, and I hope it continues for decades to come.

4

A LESSER WORKING

"Sir," I said, "won't you come into the inn?" It wasn't much, perhaps not properly an inn as others might name it, being little more than a smoke-darkened square of rough-hewn wood mortared with clay, but it boasted a sound roof and a common room men might nonetheless be grateful for in a storm such as this. "No need to stay out here, sir, when you might come inside."

"Might I?" he murmured tonelessly, as if he didn't care.

"Sir," I began again; what profit in staying beneath the weathered and leaking limbs of the lean-to currently sheltering four horses as wet as this man? "There is ale, a little mead . . . and Mam has made a stew of two hares and tubers and sage and wild onions."

"A feast." His tone was far more dry than the black hair clinging to his head.

It stung, that tone. "Better than naught," I retorted, "unless you wish to share the horses' fodder."

He looked at me then, noticed me then for what I was, not merely a voice he preferred not to hear. In the freckled illumination of the small pierced-tin lantern I carried, his face was every bit as white as his hair was dark. Thin, pale skin stretched tightly over sharply defined bones. The eyes too were dark, though perhaps the rims, in daylight, would be blue, or brown, or even winter-gray. Here, in the night, in the storm, he was all of darkness, cloaked in oiled wool that dripped onto straw and packed earth.

One of the horses chose that moment to sneeze violently, banging its nose on the wooden feed bin chewed nearly to pieces by countless teeth. The horse was startled by unexpected pain and jerked back abruptly, bumping into me so hard that I was knocked off-balance. Staggering, I dropped the lantern altogether; as I saw oil and flame spill out I immediately went to my knees to make sure no fire was started. But the roof leaked, and the straw was too damp to kindle. Oil hissed, and the flamelets went out.

A hand on my arm pulled me to my feet. With the lantern doused there was no light, for rain-laden clouds obscured the moon and stars. I could find my way back to the inn because I had countless times before, but surely the stranger could not.

He released me then and turned to the horse, even in the dark urging it toward the feed bin again. A few quiet words soothed it; though I didn't know the language, the horse apparently did. It quieted at once.

"Put your hand on my shoulder," I urged. "I will lead you to the inn. No sense staying out here in the storm *and* the dark."

"In Tintagel," he said obscurely, "there is no rain."

I blinked. Likely not; the duke's castle was undoubtedly sounder than the stable lean-to.

"Though a storm will come of it," he added.

Was he mad? He kept to the company of horses when the men he had rode in with had already dried their cloaks by the fire. Fa had sent me out after the straggler to light his way in; that he might prefer the storm had not occurred to anyone.

"A storm *has* come of it," I said tartly, and winced inwardly; Mam, had she heard that, would no doubt cuff me for it.

"Ah, but this one was not of my making," he said mildly, seemingly unoffended. "Nor the one in Tintagel; that is merely a man's lust. But the storm to come . . . well, that one *shall* be mine."

Perhaps he was made to stay with the horses because he was mad. If so, then I needn't remain. But I tried one last time. "Sir, it is too dark to see. Will you come inside? I know the way even without light."

"Light," he said, "is what I have made this night. A lamp, a lantern, a torch. A bonfire for Britain in the shape of the seed, the infant, the child who will become the man."

He *was* mad. Sighing, I made to move past him, to go out into the rain, hoping to think of an explanation suitable for Fa and Mam, but a hand came down on my shoulder. It prisoned me there, though the touch was not firm. I simply knew I must stay.

"Boy," he said, "what do you know of politics?"

"It's a spell," I answered promptly.

The grip tightened as if I had startled him. "A spell?"

"It makes men behave in ways they perhaps should not."

I had more than startled him. I had amused. He laughed briefly, but without ridicule, and took his hand from my shoulder. "What do you know of such—spells?"

"What my uncle told me. He was a soldier, sir. He came home from war, you see, and explained it to us. How men conjure politics to order the world the way they would have it be ordered, even if others would have it be otherwise."

"Well," he said after a long moment replete with consideration, "your uncle was a wise man."

"It killed him," I said matter-of-factly; it had been three years, and the grief was aged now. "The wound festered, and he died. Of politics, he said."

"It is true," the stranger said meditatively, "that politics kill men. Likely Gorlois will die of that same spell, after what I have done this night."

The duke? But what could this man have done to him? "Duke Gorlois is away from Tintagel," I said. "He and his men rode away days ago."

"Ah," he said, with an odd tone in his voice, "but he is back. Even as we speak he is home in Tintagel, sharing his lady wife's bed."

"But—he has not come this way," I blurted. "He always comes this way."

"Tonight," he said, "the duke found another way."

I did not see how. There was only one road from Tintagel, and it ran by the inn. "A new road?" I asked; Fa would need to know. "Is there an inn on it?"

The laughter was soft, but inoffensive. "There is not," he answered. "You need not fear for your custom."

Lightning abruptly split the sky. I squinted against the blinding flare that set spots before my eyes, and steeled myself for the thunder. It came in haste and hunger, crashing down over the lean-to as if to shatter it. Even knowing it was imminent, I jumped. So did the horses. Only the stranger was immune.

"I wonder," he mused, "if that heralded the seed."

"The seed?" I was busy with the nearest horse, holding the halter as I rubbed its jaw, attempting to ease it in the aftermath of thunder.

"A man's seed," he explained almost dreamily, though he spoke to himself, not to me. "And the woman believing it of her husband's loins."

Even Fa would not expect me to stay outside in a storm with a madman. I opened my mouth to take my leave, but the stranger was speaking again. And he seemed to know what I was thinking.

"Forgive me, boy." His tone was crisper now, though still clearly weary. "It takes me this way after a Great Working of—politics. I am not always fit company for others, after."

I ventured a question. "Is that why you're staying out here in the dark with the horses?"

He answered with a question. "Do you fear the dark?"

"No," I answered truthfully. "But it is difficult to tend my chores when I can't see—*ah!*"

He had caught my hand in his own. "Forgive me," he repeated. "I did not mean to startle you."

He touched the palm of my upturned hand with two cool fingertips. "Sir, what—?"

And then light flared, a spark of brilliant blue that bloomed in my hand like a fire freshly kindled. He cupped my hand in both of his and held it, keeping me from leaping back. "It will not burn, boy. That I promise. No harm shall come of it."

I stared at the light pulsing in my palm. It was neither flame nor lightning, but something in between. It was the shape and size of a raindrop.

"Now you can see," he said, "to tend your chores."

He let go of me then. His hands dropped away from my own. I stared at my hand, at the light in my palm burning steadily, neither hot nor cold. I tipped my hand, wondering if the "raindrop" would spill out and splatter against the straw, but it did not.

I looked up at him then, seeing him more clearly than I had with the light of my pierced-tin lantern. His eyes were black, but even as I watched them the blackness shrank down. The color left behind was clear as winter water.

"Are you ill?" I blurted, for this light showed me the truth: the eyes were gray, but the skin beneath them etched deeply with shadowed hollows, and the lips were white.

"Not ill," he answered. "Rather, diminished. It was a Great Working, what was done tonight."

"This storm?"

25

His pale mouth twitched in something like a smile. "Not this one."

"But—you can?"

"Make storms?" He shrugged, little more than the slight hitching of a single shoulder. "Storms are Lesser Workings, and inconsequential in the ordering of a realm. I leave them to themselves."

"Then what did you do? What politics did you conjure?"

He said, with no humor in it, "Your future."

I stared at him, wishing to name him mad to his face. But the truth burned in my hand. Not mad. *Enchanter.*

What boy, what man, would not wish to know the answer? And so I ventured the question. "What of my future, sir?"

"Your uncle went to war, you say."

"He did."

"So will you go."

I twitched with startlement. "I? But Fa has said I may not; that I must stay and tend the inn when he is old."

"And so you shall. But there is time for all: to go to war, to come home from it—safely—and to tend the inn."

My hand shook a little. The blue light danced. "Sir—do you See this?" Meaning: *In a vision?*

"I See a boy your age, discovering the truth of his begetting. I See him grown to manhood, discovering the truth of power. And I See him serving Britain *with* that power."

I licked dry lips. "Is he an enchanter, too?"

He smiled. "Not that kind of power, boy. Magic of a sort, but no more than that which lives in *your* heart."

"Mine?"

"The power to lead," he said. "The power to inspire."

"In—me?"

"You will not be king," he told me. "That is for another. But kings have need of good men, strong men, men such as you will be."

"The Pendragon?" I asked; he was king now.

The smile fled his face. "No, boy. Not Uther. Another."

"Who?"

His eyes had gone distant, as if he saw elsewhere. "The Lady Ygraine's son."

"The Lady Ygraine *has* no son," I blurted; everyone knew it was the duke's great regret.

"In nine months' time," he murmured.

"Then—will Duke Gorlois be named king? In the Pendragon's place?" How else would Lady Ygraine's son become a king?

The distance was gone from his eyes. Once again he put a hand on my shoulder. "Weariness besets my tongue; I have said too much. Shall we go to the inn? I am famished. Hare stew with tubers and sage and wild onions should suit me well."

I hesitated. "But—who shall be king? Who is this king I shall serve?"

His smile this time held no weariness, but lighted the lean-to as if it were the world. "You shall know him," he promised, "when you see him."

"I will, sir?"

"Down this very road he shall ride, and come to this very inn, and you shall see him and know him for what he is: king that was, and king that shall be." His hand guided me out into the storm. "Go, boy. Lead on."

But I hesitated. "Who are *you*, sir?"

"I? I am merely a Welshman, a man born to a mam and a fa even as you were. My gift is to see a little farther, perhaps, but no more than that."

I glanced at the glowing raindrop in my hand, then gazed at him steadily. "I do not believe you, sir."

"No?" He sighed, and his hand tightened. "Well, then,

27

perhaps a bit more than that. But not this night. I am done with all Workings this night, even the Lesser ones . . . except perhaps for this small light meant to show us the way."

"Done with politics, sir?"

He laughed, and the weariness fled. "Ah, but I shall never escape *that* Great Working. I am a meddler, you see. Men—ask me things. And ask things *of* me."

I ventured it very quietly. "What things, sir?"

He gazed over my head into the darkness beyond. "A new face," he murmured. "A new form. The wherewithal to pass beyond the guards, and to enter the lady's bed."

"Sir—"

"Come," he said firmly, and pushed me out into the rain. "Show me the way, boy, before your fa comes out to find us."

Fa would, and punish me for lagging. I preceded the enchanter as he wished, the light in my palm undiminished by the storm. It was but fourteen steps to the inn, and as I reached for the doorlatch the light flickered and died. The Lesser Working was done.

I felt so bereft I stopped short. Patiently he put his hand on mine, closing his fingers and my own upon the latch. He lifted, and so I lifted as well; the door swung open into the quite ordinary yellow light of the fire on the hearth and the lamps in the common room, where three men waited as well as Mam and Fa.

"Good lady," said the enchanter, "might I trouble you for stew?"

Sleeping Dogs

He did not so much as knock, or call out to be beckoned in. He simply kicked open the door.

It set the dogs to barking, all three of them, and the newest litter of pups to squeaking and squawling as the bitch sprang up from her nest before the hearth. Most of the cats paid no mind at all, save to stare balefully at the intruder; one or two of them fluffed tails and keened a warning, but their small noise was lost in the clamoring of the dogs.

"Sit you down, sirs," I told two of them. "And you, lady, tend your pups; I will tend this man."

I waited. The males settled. The bitch lingered longer, hackles erect, then returned to her pups. She cleaned each and every one, tumbling them like oracle bones, then lay down with a final growl. All six fastened themselves to damp nipples with manifest contentment.

I turned my attention at last to the man. "It wasn't locked, the door."

"I need you," he said. "At once."

"It wasn't locked," I repeated.

He made an impatient gesture. "Now, if you please."

I looked past him to the threshold, to the darkness beyond, searching for companions; surely he had some, being who he was. And yet he was unattended, save for the storm; rain slanted into my hut. It beat against his cloak and soaked through dark hair to his head, exposing the shape of his skull.

The cloak spilled water. A widening pool crept across the flagstones by my door to the hand-loomed carpets I had labored over too long in an effort to make the hut home. Then, it had been makework. Now part of my life.

"What is the trouble?" I asked.

"Prolonged labor." He was terse. "You are the sorceress; I want you to help her deliver safely."

Sorceress. I sighed. "Wait outside," I told him.

He stared in disbelief as water ran from hair and cloak. "Outside—?"

"And shut the door behind you."

In poor light, his eyes were black. He was wet, cold, worried, too distracted to make proper protest. He simply turned on his heel and went out, leaving the door standing open.

My lap was heavy with cat. I stroked the black silk of her spine and apologized for the upheaval, then gathered up her warm bulk and placed her on the rug with her daughter, who had kittens of her own. No one protested. The night was cold and wet; they were snug and warm.

It took but a moment to shroud myself in my cloak, to gather up my bag, and then I went out the door. The latch, I discovered, was broken—he had been overhasty—and to keep the door closed I was required to set a rock against it.

He waited nearby with two dark horses, both standing with rumps to rain, heads hanging, eyes closed. Breath steamed in the air. He had ridden hard.

"Here." He handed me rein, turned to his own mount and swung up, kicking rain-soaked cloak aside. Dim fireglow from my window sparked briefly on a spur. Graceful for a man, even in urgency. A horseman born and bred; the mounts were exceptional.

With less grace, I snugged a foot in the stirrup and mounted, gathering slick wet reins. "I am surprised you came yourself.

Have you no men to send?"

"I have men," he answered stiffly. "I came myself because she is worth it, and I wanted to waste no time."

"Commendable." And unlike him, or so they said; his reputation was for fecklessness, not solicitude.

"She is worth it," he repeated, and turned his horse from me.

Iron rang on ironwood as we rode across the drawbridge. The moat, in the rain, was gray, freckled by slapping drops. Torches hissed and guttered as wind licked into cressets. He had said nothing of the rain, but I knew it could not please him. A night-storm was not a good omen for the birth of the king's first child, bastard-born or no.

A horse-boy came running out of darkness to catch the reins to our mounts. When he saw me, he stared; he was far too young to have known me, but my story is harper-fodder. The old king had made it so to justify his actions. The young king, now dismounting, said little on his own, but denied nothing the father had claimed. I could not say if it was out of respect for the dead, or merely a form of agreement. At best, it was indolence; he gave little thought to others.

The horse-boy clutched at reins as I climbed down from the royal mount. His eyes lingered on my face; on the mark branded into my flesh, high on my left cheekbone. The king had ordered it done before he ordered me out of the castle.

No man, seeing me, could not know what I had done. To the castle, I was outlawed; yet now I was brought home. Without honor, perhaps, and certainly lacking fanfare, but nonetheless I was *home*.

The horse-boy led away the mounts. The young king, the new king, knitted black brows at me. "Come," he said impatiently. "Will you gawk in the rain all night?"

Gawk. Indeed, I gawked. Twenty years beyond the walls, and

I had forgotten nothing. Neither had anything changed.

Except the old king was dead, and his orders were no longer obeyed.

I touched a fingertip to my cheek, then drew my hood closer, as if to keep out the rain. Instead it kept in the tears.

"This way," he said.

Mercifully, he did not take me into the Hall. That I could not bear, even after so many years. Instead he took me through a side door and a quiet corridor, avoiding sycophants, and stopped at last at a door in a corner of the castle.

I went in as he lingered, holding open the door, and stopped almost at once. "I thought—" But I broke it off as he crossed the room and knelt by the bed, crooning to the occupant. Not in the way of a madman, or a man far gone in his cups, but in a way I knew so well, having my own share of the Gift.

He turned his head and stared at me, daring me to challenge his right to do as he did, to question his priorities. I dreamed of doing neither, understanding too well.

So. Not woman at all, but wolfhound. Yet worth saving all the same.

He tensed as I came to the bed. In his eyes was the fear I might startle the bitch, but the fear died as he saw the mark on my face. Something else lit dark eyes: memory and acknowledgement.

And yet he spoke of neither. "She is the best," he said tautly. "All of twelve years in the breeding, and the only one worth the time. I culled her littermates for temperament, and the sire died last year. If she dies, the line is lost."

"This is her first litter?"

He nodded. "Second cycle, of course, so as not to taint the pups. But—you see how she is."

Indeed. She was exhausted, and no puppies to show for her time. "Her name?"

"Ceara."

"Spear." I smiled. "A proud name for a king's hound."

"Deserved," he said curtly. "I will pay you well if you save her."

"We will speak of payment later." I set down my bag, stripped out of my wet cloak and dropped it, then moved close to the bed. Crooning much as he had.

The bitch rolled a dark eye in my direction, but made no sign of protest. She was clearly too weary to expend any effort past that of trying to pass her puppies.

"What will you do?" he asked intently.

"It might be best if you left," I told him quietly. "If you are here, she will think of you; she would do better to think of the task."

It whispered in his tone: dreadful fascination. "Will you use sorcery?"

Deliberately, I faced him. "How much do you want this litter? How much do you want this bitch?"

I saw the answer in his face; he saw acknowledgment in mine. He left the room in silence save for the wet slapping of his cloak, the ring of a silver spur, the click of the closing door.

The bitch whimpered. I turned to her at once, knowing it would not be a simple task to bring forth live puppies or to preserve the hound. She had spent too much time already; likely, all were dead.

I sang to her softly, giving her the history of the realm for want of a better thing. It is tone that counts, not content; she heard my voice, my promises, and listened, allowing me to soothe her. Such is the work of my sorcery; a man with patience and compassion can do as much, but few are willing to try. Midwifery, they claim, is woman's work, be the mother human or animal.

"Bright, bold girl," I whispered, putting gentle hands on the

33

wolfhound. "Bred of kings and queens to serve kings and queens . . . huge of heart, bright of spirit, unflagging in loyalty. And bought so cheaply, too—a kind word, the touch of a hand, the glint of pride in a man's eye—" But I broke it off, knowing I was treading too close to things better left unsaid.

Long of leg, big of bone, well-fleshed and tautly muscled. Standing, her shoulders would reach my hips. Rearing up, hooking front paws over shoulders, she would look a man in the eye. Running against the wind, she could strike a pace to rival a horse's.

Warhound, hunter, companion. The consummate defender, capable of taking down elk, wolf, man. Bred for the first two, trained to the third.

But now she did none of those things, being confined to the bed. The coarse silver-gray coat lacked the luster of health. The tail, thick as a tree limb, lay limply across the bed.

"The last of your line," I said. "Such a waste of blood and heritage, spilled out for a man's pride."

She stirred, whimpering, as I gently slipped my hand inside and felt for the first puppy. And I found it, grasped it, urged it out into candlelight.

Stillborn. And the next, the next, the next. Five of them, dead. The bitch whined, whimpered, strained, and passed a final puppy. As I had with each, I tore the sac at the head, carefully worked it backward, then freed the puppy entirely. Quickly, gently, I cleaned mucus and fluids from the mouth and nose, then began briskly to rub it dry with a piece of sacking. And this one began to breathe.

Too soon to rejoice. I tied the cord, cut it, dabbed an herbal paste upon it. Rubbed again, mimicking as best I could the bitch's tongue with the sacking. The puppy squirmed, whimpered, lifted a blind, seeking head.

"One pup, Ceara." I said softly. "Surely you have milk enough for one."

The bitch whined and craned her head toward me. I put the stillborn pups aside, then placed the puppy at the warm, swollen flesh of her belly. Her tongue replaced the sacking, urging the pup to suck.

I heard the door open. Spurs rang. He had come to see the results of all his years of careful breeding.

"She is weary, but should do," I told him calmly. "She passed the remains easily enough, and the last puppy. But all the others were stillborn."

"One," he said sharply.

"One. A male."

Disappointment flickered across his features. I knew he had wanted a bitch, so he could breed from her. He moved close to the bed, mouth relaxing, and spoke quietly to the wolfhound. She gazed up at him briefly with pronounced weariness and pride, then set tongue to pup once more.

"He should thrive," I told him.

The royal mouth tautened again. Dark eyes blackened. One hand stabbed toward the puppy, but I caught him by the wrist. He stared at me angrily. "*You* did it," he accused. "You put a changeling in its place!"

"Changeling!" I stared as he snapped his wrist free of my hand. "Are you mad? She bore that pup but a moment before you entered. That is no *changeling.*"

"Look at her." One finger indicated the bitch. "Ceara is of the finest line of wolfhounds in this realm. She was bred to a half-brother of the same line. Do you stand here and tell me *that* is a wolfhound puppy?"

I looked at the pup. He was short-haired, pale fawn, edged with black at muzzle and legs, tipped on ears, and tail. And I hid a smile with effort; no changeling, he. No shapechanged

35

puppy. Merely the offspring of one of the king's mastiff guard dogs.

"No," I said quietly. "I would suggest you tend your kennels more closely. Or hire men who do; your bitch has borne you a halfling."

"Changeling," he hissed. "Do you know what this means?"

I sighed, holding onto waning patience with effort. "It means, no doubt, you will have this puppy killed and tell others interested in the litter that all were stillborn."

"Of course. How else is the line kept pure?" He was impatient. "It is best to do it now, before Ceara grows too attached. . . . I will have her bred again next cycle—" His face was grim. "And I will order beaten the kennel-boy who allowed this to happen."

"Of course." I kept my tone neutral. "You are the king, and her master . . . you may do as you see fit."

He frowned. "You make no protest? I should think that being a woman—"

"—I would beg you to spare the pup's life?" I shrugged. "Would it do any good?"

He stared at the bitch, carefully tending her only living puppy. He scowled at the puppy, so clearly sired by a dog who was not a wolfhound. And something warred in his eyes. There was, I thought in surprise, a trace of humanity in him after all, and compassion, perhaps even tenderness; whatever else he was, he had his father's talent, and his mother's Gift.

He looked at me uncertainly, shedding arrogance like a cloak. "He would have to be castrated if I were to let you take him. I could not have it said he was Ceara's pup, nor allowed to sire mongrels on wild bitches."

Inwardly I rejoiced. "When he is old enough, I will see to it."

He chewed his bottom lip. "You must swear."

"Of course."

Dark eyes narrowed. Uncertainty was replaced with suspicion. "For a sorceress, you are over-accommodating."

"Am I? What do you know of sorceresses? What do you know of me?"

Brows snapped together. "All I need to know. They tell tales of you, madam. How anyone with a sick or injured animal need only take it to you, and you cure it with sorcery."

I lifted one shoulder. "If that is true, would you not agree it is a benevolent power?"

He looked again at the wolfhound and her offspring. The arrogant mouth tightened. "I said I would pay you for the safe delivery of my bitch. Sorcery or no. I keep my word."

I laughed. "I am no more a sorceress now than I was when I bore the king a son twenty years ago."

His head snapped up. "We do not speak of that here!"

"Do we not?" I lifted brows. "Then you are dead, my lord—or do you simply conveniently choose not to hear the harper ballads, the whisperings of your servants, the tales in the village—"

His color was bad. "My father told me the truth, madam. How you were barren until you turned to sorcery. How your spells conjured a son without benefit of bedding."

I drew in a quiet breath. "If that is true, what does it make you? Demon-begotten, conjured man, witch's poppet come to life?"

His hand flashed out to fetch me a blow across my cheek. A ring caught flesh, tore it; blood spilled down my cheek.

He stared. Dilated eyes were fixed on the blood, and on the mark branded into my face. "He said you were a *sorceress.*"

"What I touch, I heal. It is a true Gift, and I use it; call it sorcery if you like."

"He said—"

"—many things, I am certain, and with good reason." Something twisted inside. "He came to resent my Gift, because

37

it could not heal him."

"Heal *him!*" He stared. "What do you mean, madam?"

"I mean that in one thing, my Gift failed. I could not heal him." Blood trickled down to my chin. "He was incapable of siring a child. A spear wound, festering, rendered him unable. It was a secret between us and never spoken aloud. But the time came when he required a son. And so his lady wife, desiring to give her lord that son, turned to—"

"—sorcery."

"No." I shook my head. "My Gift had failed, so I sought another way. I turned to another man."

Color flamed. "Harlot."

"No more that than sorceress." Weariness descended upon me so suddenly it was frightened. "An old tale, my lord, and not worth the hearing. Now, if you will give me leave to go, I will take Ceara's misbegotten son and return to my home." I would be spending many waking hours feeding the puppy goat's milk.

"That hovel."

I bent, retrieved my wet cloak from the floor, slipped it over shoulders. The pup I would wrap in sacking and carry in my bag; the ride was not so far.

His tone was steadfast. "You were turned out for *sorcery.*"

"I had to be turned out for something."

Breath hissed through his teeth. "Then why not for the *truth?*"

I hesitated. "You are perhaps too young to understand, but the king loved his queen. She was innocent of men when they married, and loved him as much as he loved her. When he was no longer able to bed her, she swore it did not matter; that it would change none of her feelings for him." I swallowed with difficulty. "And it did not; in that she told the truth. But he required a son. It was destroying him, as king and man, that he could sire none. And so his lady wife, seeking to assuage his anguish and fulfill his needs, gave him that son."

He sat down awkwardly on the bed, spurs tangled together.

"An adulterous queen is executed," I told him. "He loved me too much for that."

"And—so—" He shivered. "He named you sorceress and cast you out."

"Everyone knew I was a healer. Healers, when patients die—or others sicken—are often accused of sorcery." I sighed. "It was a greater kindness than having me executed."

His eyes locked on the bloodied brand. "But if they thought I was begotten through sorcery—"

"No. Not that. The charge of sorcery came for the healing, not your conception—there could be no taint cast upon your birth, or your worthiness questioned."

"Then why did the king bother with this mummery?"

"Ambition," I said quietly. "The head kennel-keeper wanted more than he had, having bedded a queen. And so he sold the truth to a high-ranking nobleman who also desired more power, and knew how to go about getting it."

He recoiled in horror. "*Kennel*-keeper!"

I nearly laughed. "You would prefer nobility? Ah, my apologies, but I knew him best of all. I spent much of my time in the kennels, training the hounds. I bred your Ceara's great-great-granddam."

But Ceara was not, at that moment, his concern. "And so the king accused you of sorcery, to turn attention from the truth."

I caught a drop of blood on my fingertips. "The truth could have fueled the fires of rebellion. To put down rebellions, kings make sacrifices."

His tone was colorless. "You."

"As I made my own: *you*."

Dark brows knitted. His hair, like mine, was still damp but drying, curling against his neck. He had my coloring, but his father's bones, strong and bold and striking. "What happened to him? My—" He paused. "The kennel-keeper."

"He was murdered."

His mouth opened in outraged shock.

"Not by the king. By the nobleman who paid him gold for the truth; having spoken, he offered no more."

The mouth closed slowly. His eyes were full of memories, recalling a childhood of safety and security; the promise of eventual power. Now he had it. And now also the truth.

"Did it hurt?" he asked.

I made a move to touch the brand, withdrew my hand when I recalled the cut. "It healed. So will this."

His tone was steady. "No. I meant, did it hurt to give up your title, your place, your life? All for a lie?"

"Not so much as it hurt to give up my son."

He flinched, recoiling from comprehension. He hid himself behind a veil of dark lashes, masking himself to me.

Then at last he rose, speaking forcefully. "I will have you back. Too much time has passed; no one remembers."

"Everyone remembers." I shook my head. "If you recall me to the castle, all the songs will be sung, all the tales will be told. And the truth will do its damage by stripping you of your title."

"I am king, madam. Bred and trained for it, as a hound is bred and trained."

"You are the son of an adulterous queen, called sorceress, and the king's kennel-keeper," I told him plainly. "Noblemen are not impressed by such. The truth will affront them and everything they uphold; you will damage fragile self-importance and nonexistent honor. Mongrel, they will call you, baseborn son of a tender of hounds—" I drew in a breath, made myself speak more quietly. "They will haul you down from the throne and cast you out. They will cull you as a *mongrel*—and replace you with the nobleman who survives the battle for power. Is that really what you want?"

Fiercely, he answered, "I want things put right."

"They are as right as they can ever be, after so much time. After so much anguish." I forced a smile. "Sleeping dogs, left to lie, never bite their master."

He was king enough to know it, and to acknowledge it. But now, after so many years, more than merely king. He was also a mother's son. "Did you mean never to tell me?"

"It was for you to come to me."

A muscle ticked in his jaw. "I came for Ceara's sake."

"It brought you. Does it matter?"

"I may come again. For my sake, now."

A soft flutter filled my chest, of hope and anticipation; of gratitude for all the petitions answered. "The hovel will welcome you."

He smiled. It was the first of his I had seen, and so reminiscent of his father, whom I had not loved, but liked, for his empathy with the hounds. "Then you desire no change in your lifestyle."

"Sleeping dogs, my lord."

Ceara shifted on the bed. The pup, sated, slept snugged against her belly. She looked at her master, whined, slapped her heavy tail against the coverlet. It brought him to her at once.

He bent to thread fingers through the coarse, wiry coat, to stroke her head and scratch her ears and find the place at her throat that dropped lids over her eyes and transformed her to slack-jawed satisfaction.

He touched the puppy gently, stroking the velvet fawn-and-black baby coat. In the silence of the room I heard the muffled grunt.

He turned abruptly to face me. "I will keep the pup," he said firmly. "For Ceara. But also for *you*."

"For me?"

Fierceness returned, accompanied by self-condemnation.

"Why strip him from her, or ask her to give him up merely to placate a man's pride and sense of self?" He came forward and touched the blood on my face, smiling faintly. "I am old for lessons, madam, but I think you will teach me many."

"Old dogs, young men." I pulled my cloak closed. "Come whenever you can; when the noble dogs lie sleeping. And bring the pup, as well. It will be interesting to watch what he becomes."

My son grimaced disgust. "With *that* breeding, who can say?"

"Mongrels are often the best," I told him serenely, "in dogs *and* kings."

It was the only gift I could give him, after so many years. But as he laughed aloud, I knew it was enough.

MAD JACK

Lush, undulant countryside, verdigrised by summer into gilt and gold and green. By train the view was fixed, bound by iron rails; by bus as bound but freer, to curve and sweep and angle, to undulate with the countryside like a serpent's tail, undeterred by such transient barricades as stone, as steel, as water.

He smiled. *Nor am I.*

Else he would not now be here, traveling by bus through the lush, undulant countryside of a land not his own, of a people not his own save they bore perhaps more patience with such as he, who understood the secrets of that land. Their secrets, Scottish secrets, though even they might not know this one.

He smiled again, from inside as well as out, aware of the warm clenching of his belly, of anticipation, of excitement.

Maybe this time. . . . Maybe this time it would be true.

But maybe not. It had not been true in all the other journeys, though the smile had been the same inside and out, the warm clenching of his belly. And the anticipation.

"Hope springs eternal?"

But it was *his* hope, his eternal hope springing from deep inside, always, pushing out the fear, the vicious disbelief of his time, of his people, who refused to see such possibilities. To admit there were things in the world that were not *of* the world.

It was so easy to lose belief, to dismiss trust, to deny such things as he had once believed and now needed—very badly—to believe again. Others cloaked it in runes and rituals designed to

43

destroy fancy and replace it with fact, to label it myth, magic, fantasy: not true, not real, due no place in the world of reality, of responsibility.

He had been real. He had been responsible. The world had closed upon him, and he had welcomed it because it was as they told him it should be. There was no room, no time for fancies, for fantasies; he was a man, an adult; in the parlance of childhood: a *grownup.*

And he had lived among them in the real world, acknowledging and accepting responsibilities of his own making and not; of such small needs as delivering garbage to the curbside, of such larger requisites as delivering a dying child to the hospital.

He had been real, had been responsible, had like a squire embraced the duties of manhood—and yet such dedicated service to that knight had earned him only grief.

—gilt, and gold, and green—

Divorced. An ugly word, a filthy word, a word wrought of the power to alter so many lives, too many. But another word was far worse. And that word was death.

His own he could have dealt with, save for the child he would leave behind. Instead, the child had left him. Had left father, mother, all the detritus of a young life as yet filled with myth, with magic, with fantasy—and now was no more than a statistic. A child, asleep in his bed. A car, driving by. And a shot, a single shot: Was it dare? Was it duty?

A sleeping child dying; dead by the time his father carried him into the hospital, where they said it was too late.

And the woman he once had loved, who once had loved him, was cruelly unkind in the ravages of her grief.

His own was unslaked. But he had learned how to ward it away, how to stave it off. A task. A quest. The ultimate fantasy.

His coworkers expressed understanding; his boss called him mad. His friends said he should go for it; the dead child's mother called him mad.

He supposed he was. But it gave him a task, a quest. It gave him leave to do what he felt he had to do, to justify his survival. Savings, unsaved. Portfolio plundered. None of it mattered. There was no child who might benefit from his father's fiscal conservatism, who would attend college without the nagging fear there might not be enough money, or that he would, when he graduated, be in debt for a decade as he labored to pay back what was borrowed.

Instead, what was borrowed had been the decade that comprised the child's life, and the debt had been repaid in the guise of a single bullet.

So many places. So many hopes. So much anticipation, and all as yet for naught. His quest was undertaken but the task remained undone.

The bus slowed. He felt his muscles tighten in familiar anticipation; despite all his travels he had never gained the patience of those who knew debarkation at ten *of* the hour—or after—made no difference at all in the ordering of the world.

In his world, it did.

It might.

It *would*.

Please God, it had to.

The bus stopped. He said, "Let it be here."

Each time, the litany. And each time: disappointment.

"This time," he murmured. "*This* time. Yes."

The door folded open. He had little but himself and one small bag. He and the bag got out of the bus and began the ending of his journey. Yet another journey. Another beginning. Ending. In between, he walked.

"Let it be here," he murmured. "This time. Yes."

Lush, undulant countryside, verdigrised by summer into gilt, and gold, and green. He ate of berries on the bushes beside the asphalt roadway, curving and sweeping through the hills like a serpent's tail, undeterred by such transient barricades as stone, as trees, as water. And water there was aplenty.

Jack studied it as he walked. So many legends told of this water, of its secrets, of its truths. And yet to look upon it offered no answers, merely the fact of its being.

"Let it be here," he said.

This time. Yes.

Not so long a walk; he had walked farther. And a castle at the end of it, the ruins of a castle, mortared, mossy stone tumbled in heaps and piles, the remnants of its walls. Grass clothed it now where stone gave way, verdigrised by summer; and beyond it the water; beyond that the sky.

"Here," he said.

They had come as he had come, the others, but not for this reason: these folk laughed in many languages, carried many cameras, called to the water as if it were a dog to come lalloping up to them and collapse upon their feet, panting loyalty.

The water would not come. And what they believed was in it, what they *wanted* to believe, would not answer to such fools as they, and perhaps not even to him.

Let it be here.

The castle skirted the shoreline, but did not quite encroach. He left them all behind, the laughing strangers camera-weighted, reading aloud of legend, and walked down to the shore. It was a lake fully cognizant of what it was, and what was said of it; he saw it in the cool, quiet confidence, the certitude of its presence and its place in the world.

He set down his bag but did not divest himself of shoes and socks; despite the season, he was born of warmer weather. And it was not in him to pollute the water with his presence.

He waited, and eventually the last bus of the day came and collected the others, and he was left alone. He sat upon a cluster of granite and made himself very still.

"This time," he murmured. As he had murmured every time. And took from his pocket a handful of dross, that was to him gold.

"Here I am," he said. Beyond him stretched the summer: *gilt and gold and green.* "This time," he begged. As he had begged before.

But this time was different. This time he did not think of the dead boy but of the other boy, the only boy, the lonely boy; who was, he supposed, very much like the dead boy, but wasn't.

Although perhaps he *was* dead, if in a different way; the kind of dead that happens when a boy becomes a man, when myth and magic and fantasy are replaced by the sword blade of reality, the knife called responsibility.

That boy too was dead, albeit his heart yet beat. That boy too was dead in heart, in soul, in mind; but his death needn't be permanent. His day to be buried in the cold, broken ground had not yet come upon him.

"Mad Jack," he murmured; what would they say of him now, to see him like this?

He laughed. But very softly.

And the water laughed back.

At first he could give it no credence. But then he removed himself from reality, despite his physicality, and listened more closely, more deeply, to the voice of the water, the rhythm of its silence.

Wind chafed his scalp, lifting grief-grayed hair. Wind slewed by his ears, seducing like a lover: here, there, another where, then back again to kiss.

And his head was filled with the elusive fragrance of fantasy, the subversive mélange of myth.

"It *was* true," he said. "Once. Before I permitted the world to make me blind, to fill my ears with the cacophony of a life I

47

never aspired to."

But no. He had aspired. As all the others aspired, as they had been shaped to aspire, and also to desire.

Bound by shore, by hills, by trees, the water stretched before him: slate and steel and silver. Summer now was banished in the setting of the sun.

"Let it be here," he begged.

And the water acquiesced.

With a hiss of froth on sand, with the tumult of wave on stone, it ran up the shore to his feet. He tensed, but did not move. And when it engulfed his shoes, when it soaked his feet, when it stole away his treasure of strings and sealing wax he did not curse, but rejoiced. Displacement was necessary: water giving up so much required itself to submit, to permit such contained upheaval as the beast, as if it sounded, shouldered through the pale between surface and the air.

It came, did the beast, like a hound to its master's hand, a hand too long denied by far too many years. It came not because he called it as the others had called, but because he had need of it, because his spirit recalled what joys had bound them once, what adventures they had shared, when kings and princes bowed; when pirate ships lowered sails.

Up from the water it came, shaking wing-clad shoulders, snorting through flaring nostrils. The great opaline eye rolled within its socket, beneath the incongruity of delicate, wire-like lashes tempered to gold in the crucible of sunset.

"Oh," Jack breathed. "Oh, but I'd *forgotten*—"

Forgotten everything that now was recalled, and cherished for the memories as much as he grieved for loss.

Fine arched toes broke free of the shoreline froth, and each nail glistened. The scales of the flesh were tightly closed to shed water, sun-heated in the decay of the day like iron within the furnace, an argent heart shining in it ocher and amber and bronze.

The scales of his flesh: *gilt, and gold, and green.*

The glistening verdigrised haunches remained in water; there was no room for more upon the escarpment of shore. And the tail, the serpent-like tail, curved itself across stone, sliced determinedly through sand to touch a shod foot, to drape in blissful familiarity as a dog's paw, wholly undeterred by such transient barricades as a man's shoes, and his tears.

Through them, Mad Jack laughed.

Not Nessie. Never.

"Hello, Puff," he said.

THE LADY AND THE TIGER

"Tiger," the girl said, "you aren't paying any attention."

Oh yes I was. Just not to *her*. Not anymore. I slid her an absent sideways glance and smiled without any real enthusiasm. "More aqivi?"

She tipped her wooden mug to show me hers was mostly full. Much of what sloshed in the cup was probably water; cantina girls learn real quick how to water their aqivi so they stay sober while the patrons get drunk enough to spend all the coin in their pouches.

I sighed. She was suddenly tiresome. Especially when I saw the lower lip creep out to jut forward in a childish pout that did not become her young-old face. But I couldn't really blame her. Competition had just walked in the front door.

Competition was a tall, lean, fair-skinned, blue-eyed Northern blonde gorgeous enough to make my eyes water. My mouth was already salivating. Hurriedly I swallowed, got better control of my innards and managed some semblance of dignity. It wasn't much—I don't have much to start with—but it was enough to stiffen my spine and make me watch in narrow-eyed appreciation.

She moved with a liquid grace. Her hair was loose and hung past her shoulders, rippling as she glanced around the cantina. She wore a white silk burnous that only enhanced her fairness even as it hid her charms, but somehow I had no doubt that what lay beneath the fabric was the finest I had ever seen.

Every other male in the cantina knew it as well as I did. Conversation stopped dead as she entered, then started up again and eddied abstractedly, circling and bobbing and going nowhere because no one was listening to what anyone was saying. Everyone was watching the girl.

She knew it. She shook back her hair and lifted her chin a little. Those glacially blue eyes slid over every man in the place. I wondered if she found us all lacking to some degree, for her expression didn't change one bit. She merely looked at the purveyor of local spirits a long moment, seemed to discern some form of acquiescence in his face and nodded once. He smiled weakly, dazzled as a baby, and shrugged.

The girl planted her sandaled feet, arms hanging loose at her sides. She didn't have to raise her voice over the din of the cantina because everyone stopped talking at once.

"You men," she said in an accented voice, "I have business with you." Briefly amusement flickered in her eyes. "A different sort than you are used to from a woman, perhaps, but business all the same." Her eyes were judgmental; her mouth pursed a little in contemplation of her audience. A faint line appeared between her pale brows. "I have need of money. But I wish to get it fairly, without selling my body."

One of the men hooted. "What else have you to offer, my girl? A smile? Those are free in this place."

Her eyes fastened on him at once. She did not smile, as if unwilling to barter away something she could very well sell. A smile from that mouth would be worth the gold.

"Afterward," she said, "the smile may cost you nothing. But you will have earned it, then."

The jokester hooted again. He made an obscene witticism that elicited knowing laughter from several men, but most said nothing. Like me, they watched her.

Her mouth tightened. "You are betting men, are you not?

51

Willing to wager a few coins in a worthwhile game? Well, I have such a game to offer." Her eyes swept the room's denizens again. "Most of you wear swords. Some of you may even be adequate with the blade. I challenge one of you, or two—or even three—to a sword-dance."

My brows shot up. A woman challenging men to a sword-dance? Unusual. As a matter of fact, unheard of. Here in the South only men carry swords; women are veiled and guarded and treated softly. None of them would consider touching a dainty finger to a sword hilt, let alone lifting one against a man. Yet this beautiful Northern girl had challenged the entire cantina to a sword-dance.

That rankled. For one thing, a woman has no business meddling about with a man's concerns.

For another, the sword-dance is nothing to take lightly. It requires skill, strength, endurance, intelligence . . . well, to be perfectly frank it isn't the sort of thing just anyone can do. Those who do it are generally professionals, men who make their living hiring out their swords. Like me.

I scowled at her. She didn't see it; I was in a far corner tucked into a niche with a small knife- and sword-hacked table in front of me. Somehow I had managed to slide most of my impressive length underneath the table so that I sat on the end of my spine, and what little of me showed was not arranged to draw her attention. Especially with the sulky black-haired cantina girl seated hard against my right side.

For a long moment no one, absolutely no one, said a word. She stood there in white silk with her slender hands showing at the ends of her loose sleeves and her sandaled feet at the hem of the burnous. The hood hung from her shoulders, mostly obscured by the gleaming curtain of her hair. And those blue, blue eyes bored a hole into every single face in the cantina.

"Well?" she asked. "Have I come upon a nest of eunuchs?"

I winced. I didn't particularly want to see all that beauty ruined by an angry male. If she kept up with the insults she might find herself in a real sword-dance, and there was no doubt she would lose.

Mutters made the rounds of the room. I saw some smiles and raised brows, but no one seemed to take her seriously. I marked the tension in her body even beneath the enveloping silk; anger was in her eyes. The chin thrust upward again.

Before she could resort to insults again I spoke up. "Show us your weapon, bascha." The Southron word was a compliment, but I didn't know if she realized that. "We might take you more seriously if we knew you had more than just a well-honed tongue with which to fight."

The pale brows lanced down, wrinkling the skin between her eyes. It was a half-glare, half-scowl she cast in my direction, but she followed my suggestion. Sort of. Before I could push myself into an upright position—the better to appreciate the results of my suggestion—she'd stripped the burnous from her body and stood before us all in a sleeveless brown leather tunic that hit her mid-thigh. Blue stitching edged the borders—some form of runic glyphs—but I didn't pay much attention to them. I was too busy checking out the scenery.

She had legs a mile long. I'm tall, topping most men by a head and a half, but I was willing to bet the crown of her head came up to my shoulder. Her arms were long as well, slender and fair, and taut with subtle muscles that slid beneath the flesh. Criss-crossing her chest—equally admirable—was a supple leather harness, and over her left shoulder peeked the hilt of a sword.

She tapped the hilt with her right hand. "Now," she said, "who will join me in a circle?"

She wasn't joking. She really did want a sword-dance. Sword *fights* are common enough in the South, but the ritualistic—and dangerous—sword-dances are not. Her words rang false in my ears.

"You said you needed money," one man called out. "What are you wagering, then, if you have none?"

She didn't miss a beat. "My smile," she said. "And a little of my time."

I wet my drying lips and swallowed heavily.

"What do *we* put up?" another man shouted. "Our good looks?"

She didn't smile. She waited for the laughter to die down. "Your gold," she said coolly. "It will cost you a gold piece—or its equivalent—to step into the circle with me."

That silenced a lot of them. This cantina isn't the best—it isn't the worst, either, but it comes closer to that than the best—and most of the patrons don't have gold to wager. Not even gold to drink on. But a lot of us, looking at her, reached into our pouches and fingered the weight of our coins.

Eventually, of course, someone found the required amount. Amid much joking and loud raillery he got up from his table, executed a clumsy bow and tapped the sword hanging at his waist. Already I discounted him; a man who carries a sword at his waist is always an amateur. Professionals go in harness.

Automatically my hand went up to my own. It snugged against my chest beneath the green burnous I wore. Singlestroke reared his heavy hilt above my left shoulder through the slit in the seam of the burnous. Of course sitting slumped the way I was, the blade was hardly in the best position for a quick unsheathing, but then I had no plans to show Singlestroke's edge to the patrons. Or the blonde.

She draped her white burnous over the nearest table, then flicked her fingers in a come-hither gesture. I saw the light in her eyes and realized she relished what she did. And yet she was cool. I saw no hint of anger or pride or the sort of emotion that could get a sword-dancer into trouble; more often than not the man who loses his head in the circle will be carried out of it. Frowning, I scratched at the claw scars on the right side of my face and waited.

Almost at once the cantina floor was cleared. Tables and stools and benches were dragged out of the way; the patrons stood in groups wagering among themselves, ringing down coin against the tables and tossing bets to others. I did not doubt that most of the bets were going against the girl. Maybe all of them.

She waited. Her arms still hung at her sides. I saw her shake her hands a few times, loosening her limber wrists; her feet were spread slightly, one a little in front of the other. She did not stand high on the balls of her feet; not yet. I thought it might come to that when the sword-dance began.

But it was not a dance. It was a travesty. No sooner had she whipped the sword from its sheath across her back than she had torn the man's weapon from his hands. It clanged against the wooden floor with the dull thud of poor tempering; there was the hint of a smile in her eyes but she did not look at the sword as it lay before them both.

The man's hands clenched three times. His face was red with embarrassment and shame. I saw the idea pass through his eyes to call foul or some such thing, so he could pick up the sword and go again, but he didn't do it. I think he understood what she was about, for all he did was toss down the gold coin so it rang at her feet.

Not a muscle twitched in her face. Instead she remained silent, watching as he bent and retrieved the sword. Then, with only the ghost of a smile, she flicked some hair behind her back. "Who is next?"

She did not pick up the coin. It emphasized her contempt for her first opponent better than I could have done with a single word. All eyes strayed to the gold glinting against the wine-soaked wood, then went back to her. If she didn't pick it up, no one else would either. The loser, churlish and childish, had hurt himself more than her.

The next man fared little better. Oh, he kept his hands wrapped around the hilt of his sword a little longer, but in the end she twisted it out of his grasp with a subtle maneuver and stepped back as he bellowed his surprise. But he, at least, was a better loser; he handed her his gold and then retrieved his sword with a bow in her direction.

She said nothing. Words from her would underline his failure and she owed him better than that. Already the collective masculine pride in the place was smarting; comments from the victor would worsen matters. She knew that much of us, at least; I wondered how she had learned it.

I saw the odd wiggle of her fingers. Come hither, it said. For a moment I considered doing just that, then decided against it. It would serve no good at all to destroy the reputation she was building. She stood no chance against me. And I was enjoying her dance; I had no wish to end it so soon.

A third man stepped into the center of the cantina, crossing over the imaginary line into the circle. In sand the circle is drawn; a sword-dancer stepping outside the boundary loses at once. But inside a cantina, with no circle upon the floor, the dance is changed. A subtle change, but evident. Every man there knew exactly where the boundary lay. So did she.

I saw her eyes narrow. For a brief moment there was a flicker of consideration in them, though her face remained calm. Then I saw the harness criss-crossed over his chest and back and realized he was a sword-dancer. I didn't know him—the South is big and even I can't know them all—but it was obvious he was a professional. There were no unnecessary twitches and shift-ings and fidgetings from him. He stood quietly before her, waiting politely, and I saw the beginnings of a smile on her face.

"Have you seen enough?" she asked.

"Enough to know better than to discount you."

"For that, my thanks."

He smiled. "Save your thanks for when I have allowed you to leave the circle alive."

It wasn't bluster. He meant it. He was a professional and would behave as one. In the circle it's hard to do otherwise.

It wasn't a true sword-dance. For one, they began with swords in their hands. In close quarters it's common enough—there is no room for a true dance—but it does change the parameters. It means, usually, the thing can be ended with the first thrust, because the circle is too small for the customary variations. I wondered how he would end it. I wondered if he would leave her alive.

Anyone else would. She had wagered herself to the winner. But to a sword-dancer the dance is a serious matter. In such a challenge as this generally the dance is friendly enough, an exhibition of skill more than anything else, but occasionally you'll find it to the death. He was within his rights to kill her. She had claimed herself a sword-dancer—heresy enough, in view of her sex—and her death in the circle was well within the rules.

Still, I doubted he'd kill her. He was all male and she magnificently female. It would be more of a courtship rite.

The swords swung up. Clashed. Rang as they twisted apart and meshed again. He was taller and stronger than the girl, but she was quicker. I saw it almost at once. Before she had held back, winning quickly because she saw no need to tease and bait the others. Now she danced. Now she twisted that supple body, blond hair flying, and danced.

He led, she followed. Changed. She dominated, then faded, feinting, ducking a swipe of the blade that would have chopped a ragged hole in her shining blond hair. She followed that with a trick of her own, pricking one of his bared ribs with the tip of her sword and then sliding away as he blinked at her in surprise. She could have had him then. But she leaped away, circling warily, as if she could not believe it herself.

I swore. She moved well and handled the sword with more skill than I could have imagined in a woman, but she was sloppy. Unprofessional. She had let her man go free. Had it been *me*, I'd have chopped him down instantly.

"Fool," I muttered. "Even boys know better. . . ."

A moment later the sword-dancer had drawn a crimson line across one flashing thigh. I saw the frown in her face and the shock in her eyes. I thought then the thing would end; I had seen apprentices lose all their skill and aggression the moment blood flowed, even so much as a prick. No doubt the scratch stung, but it was hardly the thing to concern a professional.

But she wasn't one. She was a woman, and suddenly everyone remembered it. Including the man she faced.

He stepped back at once. He did not lower his guard but neither did he follow up his advantage. He stood pat, waiting for her shock to pass, and in that moment she had him.

Her blade flicked out and caught him once on each forearm, then across his knuckles, and as he swore at her she slid the tip beneath one of his thumbnails. Blood fell and so did his sword.

The thumb went into his mouth. Then out of it. He wore an incredulous expression that warred with the pain in his eyes. Then he swore again and stared at his bleeding thumb, at a loss for what to do about it.

My own thumb ached in response. But my pride didn't. He deserved to lose. No man should ever discount his opponent in the circle, not even a woman.

And *I* didn't intend to.

I felt it almost at once. Faces turned in my direction. Whispers started up. I heard the mutters, though none were clear—just bits of "Sandtiger" and "sword-dancer." Slowly I straightened up on my bench and rested one shoulder blade against the wall. I waited. And eventually, of course, someone came over to see if I was interested.

I was. But I waited until the price was right. Then, lazily, I uncoiled my long legs and rose, letting them all see my height and the considerable width of my shoulders. And Singlestroke, hiding coyly beneath my burnous.

"I'm a fair man," I told them all. "I don't want to cheat anybody. You know that; you know *me*. But there is something at risk here." I waited a beat, then grinned my lazy grin. "My reputation."

It brought the expected laughter. Relief sped around the room and suddenly the patrons were boisterous again, rowdy and happy, positive I would uphold the pride of the male sex against this woman. Even if she *had* bested three men—and one of them a professional—none of them had been the Sandtiger. None of them had been that legendary sword-dancer.

She stood in the center of the invisible circle, clutching the coins in her hand. Her other held her sword. I saw the color standing high in her face and the anger in her eyes; all to the good. This was a grudge-match no matter how you looked at it.

"You deserve something for your trouble," I told her. "What do you say to a ninety-ten split? Ten to you if you lose." I thought saying "if" showed some sensitivity on my part; I could have said "when."

"Winner take all." It was clipped off, strangulated by her Northern accent.

I grinned at her. "That means all of you *and* the money . . . when I win." This time I couldn't bypass the truth.

She turned around, marched to the bar and slapped down the coins. Two gold pieces. The first coin still glinted against the floor. When she spun back around the color was brighter in her face. *"Winner take all."*

"Fine with me." I glanced around at the intrigued audience. "What about a purse? Put up some coin for your enjoyment. Let's have something worth dancing for."

It had the desired effect. Someone passed around the pouch and by the time it had made a circuit of the room it was nearly full. Not all of it was gold, of course, but it was still a substantial amount. They would all make something on their side bets, and the girl or I would take home the spoils.

I grinned at her. "Last chance for a decent split."

"You heard my offer." Her face was perfectly blank.

I sighed. "Still, I refuse to hold an unfair advantage over you. Unless, of course, you *know* who I am."

"An overlarge, somewhat drunken man," she said distinctly. "What more?"

I scowled at her. "I am not drunk."

She eyed me consideringly. "That, the circle will discern. . . . Very well, who are you?"

"My name," I said, "is the Sandtiger."

I saw it go home. She was a Northerner and therefore a stranger, but she'd been South long enough to hear of me. Most people have. My reputation gets around.

"Sword-dancer." She said it softly, rolling it over on her tongue. "Are you truly the Sandtiger?"

Idly I stroked the claw marks on the side of my face. "Call me Tiger for short."

She took a deep breath that did wonderful things to her frontal anatomy. But when she let the air out again I knew her decision was made. "We have an agreement."

"You're sure?"

Her eyes swept the waiting faces. "I have no desire to dash the hopes of all these men who wish to see me skewered by the greatest sword-dancer of them all." An ironic smile was in her eyes. "Dance with me, Tiger."

"Outside," I said. "Let's make this a proper dance."

She tilted her head a little, then nodded. And we took it outside.

The Southron sun is very hot. It bakes the sand until you want to scream with it, but you don't. You haven't got the saliva for it. You learn to live with it. Or you die with it.

This time of year the heat is not so bad. Just hot enough to make a sword hilt warm in your hands and your feet flinch away from the heat that bakes through your sandals. Almost at once I shed my burnous and faced her in my brief leather dhoti. Then I stripped out of my harness and dropped it on top of the pile of silk, once I'd drawn Singlestroke, and I waited while two men drew the circle.

The grip fit my hand in a perfect intercourse of hard flesh and beaded metal. Early in my apprenticeship I had experimented with wrapping leather around the grip to cushion my palms, but I had learned I was better without it. My hands were so thickly callused I hardly felt the grip and the heat was only a faint underscore to the brightness of the gold. Sunlight ran down the blade like light against a mirror. I smiled.

We paced to the center of the circle. I put Singlestroke in the precise center and measured her blade with my eye as she set her sword down. It was a big blade for a woman, but it was no match for Singlestroke. Not many swords are.

"Luck, bascha," I said.

"I make my own." She turned her back on me and marched to the edge of the circle. I saw her mouth move and realized she had begun her song.

She had not used it inside. Perhaps she had thought her opponents unworthy of the honor, for honor it was. Even the sword-dancer she had bested had not elicited a song from her. I frowned at her, trying to sort out her motivations, and then I shrugged and scuffed through the sand to my own portion of the circle. The two blades, side by side, glowed in the sunlight.

I felt the familiar tautening of my muscles and the knot of tension forming in my belly. Almost instantly it loosened, dispelling the familiar sensation of anticipation. I was cool and calm, untouched by the heat or the moment; I waited, and so did she.

I heard her song. It was sung very softly, privately, and yet it carried to my side of the circle. She meant me to hear it. I couldn't understand it—it was sung in her Northern dialect—but I understood its fundamental meaning. It wasn't a death-song but a lifesong, a salute to her opponent, a commendation of the skill yet to be displayed and a celebration of the dance. Whatever else she was, she was professional after all.

I smiled. "Winner take all—" And we were running.

I am big but I am quick. I reached Singlestroke first. I snatched the sword out of the sand, letting the hot grains slide away as I settled my hands, and made the first move. But she caught me by surprise.

I knew she had less energy than I; she had spent some of it in three previous dances. But she threw herself down into the sand, rolling, grasping, and coming up in a single fluid movement. From underneath her blade slashed upward, grating against Singlestroke as I brought my sword down. I saw the sinews tighten in her forearms clear to her shoulders; she held the posture long enough to break my momentum, then twisted and danced away. I was caught flat-footed in the sand, untouched but definitely lacking her finesse.

I scowled across the circle at her. The dance would take longer than I thought.

She didn't laugh. She circled and watched, coolly professional with no more come-hither effects. She balanced on the balls of her feet, always moving; her shining hair was shoved behind her ears and hung past her breasts as she bent forward in a subtle crouch. She had stopped singing, but she didn't need to anymore. The purpose had been served.

Our blades met again, shrieking in contrapuntal song. I nicked her forearm twice, then felt a stinging across two knuckles. That she had slipped past me at all, even for that much, was miracle in itself.

I was barely aware of the audience. A hum of voices surrounded us, forming a second circle. I heard shouts and comments and laughter, and the clink of coin as more bets were laid.

The girl smiled. "Dance with me, Tiger."

We danced. The sand flew and the swords flashed and the sweat ran down our flesh. I blinked stinging salt out of my eyes and felt the dry pain lodged in my throat. Again and again Singlestroke flashed out to parry or strike down her blade; again and again she came back with her own counter-moves. Where I was tall and strong, she was supple and quick; where my reach was longer, hers was more subtle; where my skill was more obvious, hers was unexpected. And it was all to her advantage.

Finally, having grown tired of the inequities of such a dance, I decided to end it. She was good. She was much better than I expected. But she was the woman and I the man.

And the Sandtiger never loses.

I grinned at her, though it was a rictus of exertion. "Good dance," I said. "But tonight I desire a different sort of battle. . . ."

"In bed?" she scoffed. "First you have to win."

And I did. Of course. I leaned on her a little, let Singlestroke taste a little more of her pale flesh, and knocked the sword from her hands. I stepped on it before she could lunge to grab it up. "Enough," I said charitably. "The dance is won."

Cheers and applause broke out. Backs were slapped, coin was

exchanged and drinks were offered by the management. But I didn't go in at once. I watched as she faced me, filmed with sweat, empty-handed and proud, and saw her force a smile.

"You are indeed the Sandtiger."

I tapped the string of curving black claws hanging around my neck. "Did you doubt these?"

"No. Nor those marks on your face." She sighed and pushed an arm across her forehead, shoving damp hair away from her eyes. "But I hoped I might win."

"The first time I lose will be the last," I told her. "Did you want to kill me so badly?"

"I *have* killed," she said defensively.

"That isn't what I asked."

She grimaced. "No. I didn't want to kill you. I just wanted to beat you."

"Because I'm a man. . . ."

The pale brows lanced down. She stared at me in genuine puzzlement. "No . . . because I wanted to *win.*"

I bent and picked up her sword. The audience, for the most part, was heading for the cantina, but a few well-wishers remained behind. As I handed back her sword I smiled my sandtiger's smile. "We'll dance again, bascha . . . tonight in bed. This time maybe I'll let you win."

"*Let* me!" she flared. Anger leaped into her eyes. "What I do, *I do!* No one *lets me!*"

The well-wishers laughed. It shut her up immediately, as if she had no desire to be thought a poor loser, or worse: a frustrated woman. But I saw the scarlet flags high in her cheeks as she turned to walk into the cantina.

I put out a hand and caught her shoulder. "For what it's worth, you danced well."

"For a woman?"

"For anyone." My fingers squeezed lightly as I saw the

interested onlookers. "Come inside and I'll buy you a drink."

"With my gold?" She smiled crookedly. "Well, I did lose it. Fairly. And I always pay my debts." I felt her sidelong appraisal. "Maybe it won't be so bad."

I smiled. "I'm the Sandtiger, remember?"

She laughed. "So you are."

We retired inside the cantina and spent the rest of the afternoon swilling aqivi.

She drinks as well as she dances.

In the soft, small hours when even the rats were quiet, I felt the warmth of her breath against my ear. I opened one eye, then both. "What is it?"

"How much?" she asked. "How much was in the pouch?"

I grinned. "You mean, how much did you lose?"

"That is only one way of putting it."

I shifted over onto my back and thrust an arm beneath the pillow. The other arm slid down to cradle her head against my shoulder. The smooth, lean length of her was warm against my body. "Enough to last us a month, at least. If we are not terribly vulgar about spending our wealth."

"I am never vulgar."

"I thought you might be this afternoon, when I nicked you on the arm."

She harrumphed. "You would have deserved it, cutting me that way. Why did you do it?"

"You were careless. You'd already let that sword-dancer draw blood. I just wanted to wake you up."

"Was it worth it to see me bleed?"

I set my mouth against the mass of her hair. "I wanted to slit him open from guts to gullet, Del. But you took care of him for me."

She sighed. "Tiger . . . we can't do this forever."

"No. They'll catch onto it soon enough, and we'll have to come up with another scam."

She was silent a moment. The room was dark and I could hardly see her, but her hair was a dim glow against the shadows. Then she sighed. "I did not become a sword-dancer to trick stupid men out of their coin."

"Neither did I, Del. But for now, until we find an employer, it's all we've got."

"I know that." She moved closer. "I think I'm just tired of having to lose."

I grinned. "*You* know these Southron males would never bet as much coin if they thought a woman might win. That isn't part of the game."

Silence was her eloquent protest.

I rolled onto my side and leaned over her. "Besides," I said drily, "you and I both know you can cut the legs out from under me in the circle. I wouldn't stand a chance if you *really* decided to dance."

She smiled. And then she laughed. Just once, but it was enough.

What else can you say to the truth?

SPOILS OF WAR

All around her the arrows sang. It was a sibilant song of death, she thought: whining, humming, buzzing . . . the percussion of iron on wood . . . the crescendo of human screams. But the melody did not please her.

The wood was alive in her hands. Its touch was security, nameless progenitor of satisfaction. It was not *pleasant* to kill a man, but if she missed he might kill her.

Carefully she wound fingers around the leather grip. Four years before the fingers had been callused, the hands of a competent archer; now they were soft and white, the hands of the mountain lord's lady.

Right-handed, she cocked the red-fletched arrow. The shaft was banded black-on-red-on-white, the colors of her husband; the colors of the lord. The arrows singing by her were fletched in white, with triple bands of black. The colors of the enemy who sought to take the castle.

Four years. But she had not forgotten how.

Stone merlons warded either side, cutting off the angles. But to sight she needed room; to kill she needed sight. And so she stepped away from the merlons and stood before the crenel that reached her hips but no higher; she was an easy target now, in her lord's tricolor tunic. Black-on-red-on-white.

All around her, the arrows sang.

Unsmiling, she chose her target: a man in black and white. Unsmiling, she loosed the arrow . . . and it sang, how it *sang*, slicing through the sky . . . she heard the distant crescendo; she heard the archer's scream.

She took an arrow from the quiver; nocked, sighted, loosed; heard the song and heard the scream, enjoying neither of them. Knowing that even the death of one enemy might save the life of a friend. Might save the life of her lord.

A step. She knew it. She knew the hand that touched her own as she reached for another arrow; the fingers that closed on her wrist and drew her behind a merlon. And knew the voice as well; in bed, it whispered love words.

"Enough," he said. "Enough. This is no place for you."

Black-on-red-on-white. But the silk of his tunic was torn, baring silver ringmail. She looked into his face and saw blood and grime and enduring strength; in dark eyes, determination. He had slipped the ringmail coif and she saw sweat-damp hair pressed flat against skull except where the weave of the links had formed a pattern.

Fingers lingered against her hand. "Enough," he said again. "I see what it does to you."

Her hand tightened on her bow. "Do you send me down from the wall?"

He was grim, but also gentle. "I must. I must. For my sake as well as your own; I fear that I might lose you."

An arrow sang beside them and shattered against the stone. Neither of them flinched. "Will you strip me of my honor?"

Now he did flinch; her tone was truer than the arrow. "This is not a question of honor . . . it is a question of life."

"*You* risk yourself."

He said nothing, knowing better; he had said it before, and was made to suffer for it. And yet he knew, as she did, there was no need to speak; between them lay the words: *War is made for men.*

"Go down," he said. "Remember that I am your lord."

She did not move, though she thought the bow might break. "Will you strip me of my honor?"

The tension sang between them.

His dark eyes were fathomless. "I do not wish to lose you."

"If you send me down, you will."

He could be harsh, but now he was not. In his face she saw regret commingled with admiration. "You are a willful woman."

"You knew that four years ago."

Surprising her, he laughed. "Oh, aye, I did . . . it was why I wanted you."

"And now you fight a war."

Grimly, he said, "I keep what is mine. Cattle, castle, wife." Seeing her face, he smiled. "In no particular order."

She took an arrow from her quiver. "I will not go down from the wall."

Over the crenel, he looked at the enemy. And then he looked at his wife. "I will let you keep your honor if you promise to keep your life."

Unsmiling, she nocked the arrow. As he watched, she loosed it, and listened to its song.

They came to her at sundown and said the war was done. They told her the lord was dead. The enemy had won.

"Yes," she said; her quiver was empty. For her the war *was* done.

They took her to his body. Around it stood other men—black-on-red-on-white—warding their lord against arrows. But one had been enough. Through an eye, it touched the brain.

She knelt. She laid down her bow for the first time since dawn. She touched his face and knew him gone, his spirit had flown free. In silence she closed his other eye, and then she rose to face his men.

"The lord is dead. The war is done. The enemy has won."

She looked into their faces. "Put down your weapons and open the gates; the victor is now the lord."

One man stirred. "Lady, what of you?"

She did not smile. "I am part of the spoils; it is the way of war and women."

As one, they looked at their lord. And went to open the gates.

The victor came before her in the hall of the castle keep. *His* hall, now; no more was it her husband's. All around her the candles blazed as she waited on the dais.

He was not old, but neither was he young. Years of warfare and its trappings had ruined the hair on the top of his head so that he wore a graying, grizzled cap where the coif had rubbed him bare. Ringmail glittered; his tunic was black and white.

In silence, she waited. She was not a meek woman and gave him no meekness now; proudly, she waited. Watching the man who had killed her husband; who had taken cattle, castle, wife. In precise and particular order.

He halted before the dais. He was armed, as a victor should be, with knife and sword and pride. "He fought well."

His voice was a hoarse rumble: bellowing orders ruined a throat. "Yes," she said, "he did. He did not care to lose me."

Something moved in his eyes. "I saw you on the wall."

Unsmiling, she lifted her chin. "How many did I kill?"

"How many arrows loosed?"

"Thirty," she told him clearly, "banded black and red and white."

He nodded once, unsmiling. "Thirty of my men."

It did not please her to take the life of a single man, but she knew, if she had to, she would be willing to do it again. In war, it was simply practical; the *im*practical did not survive.

"The lord is dead," she told him formally. "This castle and

all its holdings, including inhabitants, are yours to do with as you will."

He did not move, but faced her. "Was he kind, or was he cruel?"

"Both and neither," she told him, "as all men are dependent upon their needs."

"Have you children?"

"None, my lord," she said steadily. "It was his greatest regret."

"And did he beat you for it?"

"No, my lord. He did not."

His voice was very quiet. "Did you love your husband?"

She swallowed tightly. "Once, I hated him, when he stole me from my father, who taught me what honor was. But my father *also* taught me there is no honor in hatred, and so I let it go. No more did I hate my lord, but neither did I love him."

"Four years," he said hoarsely, and she saw the tears in her father's eyes.

She went to him. She took his battle-scarred hands into her own and kissed them tenderly. "I swear, it does not matter. I knew you would come one day."

PIECE OF MIND

In the Los Angeles metro area, you can pay $350K-plus for a one-bedroom, one-bath bungalow boasting a backyard so small you can spit across it—even on a day so hot you can't rustle up any sweat, let alone saliva. And that's all for the privilege of breathing brown air, contesting with a rush "hour" lasting three at the minimum, and risking every kind of "rage" the sociologists can hang a name on.

But a man does need a roof over his head, so I ended up in a weird little amoebic blob of an apartment complex, a haphazard collection of wooden shingle-sided boxes dating from the '50s. It wasn't Melrose Place, and the zip wasn't 90210, but it would do for a newly divorced, middle-aged man of no particular means.

Interstate 10 may carry tourists through miles of the sere and featureless desert west of Phoenix, but closer to the coast the air gains moisture. In my little complex, vegetation ruled. Ivy filled the shadows, clung to shingles; roses of all varieties fought for space; aging eucalyptus and pepper trees overhung the courtyard, prehensile roots threatening fence and sidewalk.

I found it relaxing to twist off the cap of a longneck beer at day's end and sit outside on a three-by-six-foot slab of ancient, wafer-thin concrete crumbling from the onslaught of time and whatever toxins linger in L.A.'s air. I didn't want to think of what the brown cloud was doing to my lungs, but I wasn't motivated enough to leave the Valley. The kids were in the area.

Soon enough they'd discover independence and Dear Old Dad would be relegated to nonessential personnel; until that happened, I'd stay close.

Next door, across the water-stained, weather-warped wooden fence, an explosion of sound punched a hole in my reverie. I heard a screen door whack shut, the sound of a woman's voice, and the cacophony of barking dogs. She was calling them back, telling them to behave themselves, explaining that making so much racket was no way to endear themselves to new neighbors. I heartily concurred, inwardly cursing the landlady who allowed pets. She was one of those sweet little old widow-ladies who was addicted to cats and spent much of her income on feeding the feral as well as her own; apparently her tolerance extended to dogs, now. Dogs next door. *Barking* dogs.

Muttering expletives, I set the mostly-empty beer bottle on the crumbling concrete, then heaved myself out of the fraying webwork chaise lounge with some care, not wanting to drop my butt through *or* collapse the flimsy aluminum armrests.

The dogs had muted their barking to the occasional *sotto voce* wuff as I sauntered over to the sagging fence, stepped up on a slumping brick border of a gone-to-seed garden, and looked into the yard next door. When they saw me—well, saw my head floating above the fence—they instantly set off an even louder chorus of complaint. I caught a glimpse of huge ears and stumpy legs in the midst of hurried guard-dog activity, and then the woman was coming out the back door yet again to hush them.

I saw hair the color some called light brown, others dark blond, caught up in a sloppy ponytail at the back of her head; plus stretchy black bike shorts and a pink tank top. Shorts and tank displayed long, browned limbs and cleanly defined muscles. No body fat. Trust her to be one of those California gym types.

She saw me, winced at renewed barking, and raised her voice. *"Enough!"*

73

Amazingly, the dogs shut up.

"Thank you," she said politely, for all the world as if she spoke to a human instead of a pack of mutts with elongated satellite dishes for ears and tails longer than their legs. Then she grinned at me from her own wafer-thin, crumbling, three-by-six concrete slab. "They'll quit once they get used to you."

"Those are dogs?"

Her expression was blandly neutral. "Not as far as *they're* concerned. But yes, that is what their registration papers say."

"They're not mutts?"

"They're Cardigan Welsh Corgis." She made a gesture with her hand that brought all three of the dogs to her at a run, competing with one another to see who'd arrive first. "I work at home much of the time, or I'm not gone for long, so I'll try to keep them quiet. I'm sorry if they disturbed you."

I didn't really care, but I asked it anyway because once upon a time small talk had been ingrained. "What do you do?"

Abruptly her expression transmuted itself to one I'd seen before. She was about to sidestep honesty with something not quite a lie, but neither would it be the truth, the whole truth, and nothing but the truth. "Research."

And because I had learned to ignore such attempts, and because it would provoke a more honest response, I asked her what kind.

Across the width of her tiny yard, the twin of mine, and over the top of a sagging fence that cut me off from the shoulders down, she examined me. A wry smile crooked the corner of her mouth. "You must be the private detective. Mrs. Landry told me about you."

"Mrs. Landry's a nosy old fool," I said, "but yes, I am." I paused. "And I imagine *she* could tell me what kind of research you do."

Unexpectedly, she laughed. "Yes, I imagine she could. But

then we met when she hired me, so she ought to know."

"Hired you to do research?" I was intrigued in spite of myself; what kind of research would a little old widow-lady want of my new neighbor, who looked more like an aerobics instructor than a bookworm?

"In a manner of speaking," the neighbor answered. She eyed me speculatively a moment, as if deciding something. "Do you have any pets?"

"A cockroach I call Henry."

She studied my expression again. Something like dry amusement flickered in brown eyes. "Sorry, but I don't do them." And with that she went into her shingled, ivy-choked box along with her three dogs and let the screen door whack closed behind her.

I was morosely contemplating the quaking clothes dryer from a spindle-legged chair when the Dog Woman arrived. She lugged a cheap plastic clothes basket heaped with muddy towels. Mrs. Landry's apartment complex hosted a small laundry room containing one dryer, one washer, and three chairs. Most everyone drove down the street to a Laundromat, but I'd always felt the Landry Laundry was good enough for me. Apparently for the Dog Woman, too.

She glanced at me as she came in, noted the washer was available, and dumped her load inside. I watched her go through the motions of measuring detergent and setting the washer dials. Once done, she turned to face me. "I hope the dogs haven't bothered you lately."

I shook my head. "You were right. Now that they're settled in, they don't bark much." I couldn't help but notice she was bare-legged and bare-armed again, this time in ancient cutoffs and a paw-printed sleeveless T-shirt. I hadn't seen her in weeks, though I did hear the screen door slam from time to time, and her voice in conversation with the dogs outside. One-sided.

"You think a lot of those critters."

My neighbor's eyebrows arched. "Sure. They're good company. Smart, interactive. . . ." She stopped. "You're not particularly interested, are you? Don't you like dogs?"

I sighed. "They're okay."

Her eyes examined me. "Mrs. Landry said you were divorced."

"Yeah. So?" I wondered if she was considering hitting on me. Then decided it was a pretty stupid thought: I didn't look like much of a catch.

"I'm sorry," she said. "I know it's difficult."

I grunted. "You divorced, too?"

"No. Never been married." Something in my expression must have told her something. "And no, I'm not gay. It's just not always easy meeting an understanding man in my line of work."

"Research," I said neutrally.

She shrugged. "More or less."

Unless she was some kind of sex surrogate, I couldn't see what kind of research might scare a man off. She wasn't hard to look at. "Maybe it's the dogs," I muttered.

"What?"

I hadn't meant to say it aloud. "Well, some men don't like dogs."

"And some dogs don't like men." She smiled as I glanced up sharply. "What goes around—"

"—comes around," I finished, and pushed out of the chair. My load was done drying. It was a simple thing to pull clothes out of the hot barrel and dump them into my plastic basket. Why fold?

"Mrs. Landry told me you used to be a cop."

My jaw tightened, but I kept stuffing clothing into the basket. "Yep."

"But now you're a private detective."

"Just like *Magnum*," I agreed; too often I watched the reruns on daytime TV. " 'Cept I don't look much like Tom Selleck, and I lost the Ferrari in the divorce."

That did not elicit a smile. "She said you told her you walked away after a bad case. Quit the LAPD."

It was a night I'd downed far too many beers, and Mrs. Landry had knocked on my door to ask if I could help her with a leaky pipe underneath her kitchen sink. I'd managed to get the leak stopped, but in the meantime I'd talked too much.

"It was time," I said dismissively.

Brown eyes were very serious. "It must have been a difficult decision."

I grinned crookedly as I gathered up the brimming basket. "You don't know the half of it."

She waited until I was at the door of the tiny laundry room. "Then maybe you should tell me."

I stopped. Turned. "What?"

"The half I don't know."

"Hell, lady, *I* don't know the half of it. I just knew I had to get out."

Her eyes drilled into me. For some reason I couldn't move. Her voice sounded odd. Pupils expanded. "She said you saw in black and white. Your wife."

I stared at her, stunned.

Her tone was almost dreamy. "That you had no imagination."

I wanted to turn my back, to walk away. But couldn't.

"That you lived too much inside your head."

Finally I could speak. "Among other things." My voice was rusty. "Are you one of her women-friends?"

She smiled oddly. "I've never met her."

"Then how in the hell do you know what she said?"

She blinked. It wasn't one of those involuntary movements,

like a heartbeat, but something she did on purpose. As if she flipped a switch inside her head. "Have you ever had any pets?"

It broke the mood. I shrugged, turned to go. "Not since I was a kid."

"*Wait.*" The crack in her voice stopped me. I swung back. She was staring at me fixedly again, pupils still dilated, and said in an eerily distant voice, "Your father killed your dog."

I felt a frisson slide down my spine. "Listen—"

"Your father killed your dog."

"Because the dog had been hit by a car," I said sharply. "He was badly hurt, and in pain. My father had no choice."

"So were you," she said. "In pain. You knew what he was feeling. You *felt* what he was feeling. The dog. You saw the accident."

I shook my head. "I wasn't there."

"Yes, you were."

"I was on my way home from school. I didn't see it."

The color had drained out of her face. She put out a hand to steady herself against the washing machine.

"Are you sick?" I asked sharply. Or on drugs.

Even her lips were white. "You don't see in black and white."

I lingered in the doorway, caught on the cusp of wanting to go and wanting to stay. "What are you talking about?"

"You see in color. *Too much* color."

I dropped the basket and made it to her before she collapsed. I hooked the chair with a foot, yanked it over, put her into it. She was all bones and loose limbs. She muttered an expletive under her breath, then bent forward. Splayed fingers were locked into light brown hair.

"What are you on?" I asked.

She shook her head against her knees. "No drugs."

I stood over her. "This happen to you often?"

She muttered another expletive.

"Look, if you feel sick, I can get the wastebasket."

"No." She shuddered once, words muffled. "No, it doesn't take me that way."

Alarms went off in my head. "What doesn't 'take' you *what* way?"

She heaved a sigh, sat up, pulled fallen hair out of her face. Her color was somewhat improved, but a fine sheen of sweat filmed her face.

I'd been married; I couldn't help it. "Hot flash?"

She grimaced. "I wish. No . . . no, it's just—something that happens." She closed her eyes a moment, then looked up at me. "Would you do me a favor and help me to my apartment? I'm always a little shaky afterwards."

"Is this a medical problem?"

Her hands trembled on the chair arms as she pushed herself to her feet. "Not medical, no."

I hooked a hand under her arm, steadying her. "Come on, then. We'll take it slow."

She nodded. It looked for all the world like a rag doll's head flopping back and forth.

I took her to her apartment, pushed open the door, and was greeted by three highly suspicious dogs. I wondered uneasily if I was about to lose my ankles, but she said something to them quietly and they stopped barking. The trio stood there at rigid attention, watching closely as I got her to an easy chair.

"Thank you," she said. "Would you . . . would you mind getting me some iced tea? There's some in the fridge already made."

The dogs let me go to the kitchen, but only under close supervision. I hunted up a glass, found the pitcher of tea in the refrigerator, poured it full. The liquid was cloudy, and lemon slices floated in it. I sniffed suspiciously.

"It's sweet tea," she called from the other room. "No drugs, I promise."

I walked back into the front room with the glass. "You

psychic, or something?"

She glanced at the dogs who clustered around my legs, and reached out for the tea. "You're a detective. Detect."

A chill touched me at the base of my spine. "We worked with one or two psychics in the department. I never believed there was any merit to them. Their claims. Their *visions*. I never solved a single case using them."

She drank tea, both trembling hands wrapped around the glass. The sugar left a glistening rim along her top lip. "It's a wild talent," she explained. "It comes and goes in people. Very few can *summon* a vision at a given time, so it's not surprising cops don't believe what they say, if they can't perform on command." She looked at the dogs. "We're not a circus act."

"Research," I said dubiously. "Paranormal?"

She drank more tea, then smoothed the dampness from her lip with three steadying fingers. "Mrs. Landry asked me to read her cats. That's how we met."

"*Read* her cats." If she heard my doubt, she gave no sign. "Two of them were with her husband when he died. He was at home, you know. Mrs. Landry was out grocery shopping. She always worried that he was in pain when he died, that he was terribly afraid because he was alone." Shoulders lifted in a slight shrug. "I did what I could."

I kept my tone as neutral as possible. "You read her cats."

"It was very sudden, his death. There was a moment of pain—he died of an aneurysm—but it passed. He was gone very quickly. He didn't have time to be afraid."

"The *cats* told you this?"

"No." She set the drained glass down on the table next to the easy chair. "No. They showed me." She saw the look in my eyes. "The same way your dog showed you, when he was dying. On your way home from school."

I opened my mouth to reply, but found myself unable.

"You don't see in black and white," she said. "You see in color. Or did. Very vivid color, in a much broader spectrum than anyone else. They are the colors of the mind. But you've shut them down. I think you must have done it that day, because it was too painful to see from behind your dog's eyes. Or else you said something, and your father told you it was just your imagination. Parents often do that, when they don't understand what the child is saying."

I murmured, "My wife says I don't have any imagination." Then I caught myself. "*Ex*-wife."

"Most of us don't get married. Or don't *stay* married." Her tone was dry.

" 'Us'? You're counting me in with you?"

"Of course." She leaned back against the chair, slumping into it. "Thank you. The sugar helped. But I need to rest now."

"You *read* me back there? In the laundry room?"

"No. I can't read humans. Not—clearly. But there were edges . . . pieces." The bones stood out beneath the whitening skin of her face. "I'm sorry. I have to rest now."

One of the dogs growled. Very softly. Almost apologetically.

I didn't have to 'read' him to know what he meant. I took myself out of the apartment and back to my own, where I opened the bottle of single malt I kept for special occasions. The first and only time I'd availed myself of it was when the divorce papers arrived in the mail.

Outside, I sat in the fraying chaise lounge and drank scotch, remembering a dog, and a car, and the unremitting pain that ceased only when my father ended the dog's life. But before that, in the final moment, I had felt the unflagging trust in the canine heart: *the human will save me.*

I swore. Downed scotch. Fell asleep—or passed out—as the moon rose to replace the sun.

★ ★ ★ ★ ★

My neighbor opened the interior door just as I knocked on her screen door, and stared at me through the fine mesh. She wore nice slacks, silk blouse, a well-cut blazer. Hair was neatly brushed and shining, hanging loose to her shoulders. Makeup told the story.

"You're going out," I said inanely.

One hand resettled the purse strap over her shoulder. "I have an appointment."

"Reading more cats?"

"As a matter of fact, no. It's a Great Dane."

"Should you be doing it so soon? I mean, it was only yesterday that you nearly passed out in the laundry room."

"I'm fine." Her eyes were cool, her tone businesslike. "Is there something I can help you with?"

I found myself blurting, "You can let me go with you."

"I'm sorry," she said, "but that wouldn't be a good idea."

"Why not?"

"Because you don't believe what I told you. You want to go only to prove to yourself I'm lying."

I opened my mouth to deny it. Closed it. Shrugged. "Maybe so. I guess you *are* psychic."

"Not really. This particular gift goes far beyond that."

"But you told me—"

She interrupted. "I told you what you wanted to hear. You said you worked with psychics when you were a cop. What I do is different."

"But you said 'us'. As in, you and me."

"Because it's in you, too. Buried very deeply under years of denial, but there."

"You can't know that."

Her tone was tinged with humor. "Of course I can." Then abruptly she pushed the screen door open one-handed and stepped back. "Are you coming in?"

"You have an appointment, you said."

"Appointments can be rescheduled."

"But—"

"You came here for a reason."

It was very lame, but I offered it anyway. "Cup of sugar?"

She smiled dutifully, but the eyes remained serious. "Come in."

"Won't the Great Dane be offended?"

"The Great Dane would just as soon be a couch potato." She stepped aside as I moved past her. "It's his owner who believes the dog knows something."

"And it doesn't?"

"Probably not. Sometimes dogs are just—dogs. But this *is* California, home of the Great Woo-Woo, and some people identify a little too much with their pets." She slipped the purse from her shoulder and put it on the console table behind the sofa. "I got over feeling guilty years ago. If it makes the owners feel better, it's not wasted money."

"You mean they hire you even if there's nothing to read?"

"There's always something to read." She gestured to the sofa, then sat down in the easy chair. "But sometimes what I read is merely a cat's inarticulate longing for food, or a dog's annoyance with the fly buzzing around its head." She smoothed the slacks over one knee. "What can I help you with?"

I glanced around. "Where are your dogs?"

"Outside, basking in the sun." Her eyes were steady. "Well?"

"Can you read something that belonged to an animal?" I asked. "Like a—a food dish, or something?"

"Sometimes. Is that what you want me to do?"

I drew in a breath, released it. Then dug down into the pocket of my jeans. I pulled out the collar. "This."

She looked at it in my hand. A simple braided nylon collar,

tan, stained dark in spots, the kind called a slip-collar, with a metal ring at each end. You threaded the nylon through to make a loop, and slipped it over the dog's head.

I watched her eyes. The pupils went pinpoint, then spread like ink. Her hand came up, lingered; but she dropped it back to the chair arm. "Wait a moment. Please."

She pulled a cell phone from her purse. Ten numbers were punched in. In a moment she was explaining quietly that something had come up and she'd have to reschedule; and, likely in answer to what was said, explained it was very important. Then she disconnected, dropped the phone back into her purse, and leaned forward.

Her hand hovered. I pushed the collar into it. Her fingers grasped it, closed tightly—and then spasmed, dropping it.

She was standing. Trembling. *"My God—"*

I looked at the collar lying on the carpet. Then at her.

"My God—" she repeated. "Do you know what that is?"

"Do you?"

"*Yes* I know what that is! But—" She broke it off, bit deeply into her lip, drew in a shuddering breath, then took a visible grip on her emotions. "If I do this—and yes, I know what you want—then you have to come with me. Put yourself behind the dog's eyes."

"Me? But I can't do—"

"Yes, you can." We stood three feet apart, stiff with emotion. The collar lay between us. "Yes. You can."

I felt saliva drying in my mouth. "You think I didn't *try?* Hell, we were all ready to try anything by then! I took that thing home with me, practically *slept* with it, and never saw a single thing. Never felt anything." I sucked in a breath and admitted it for the first time in thirty years. "Not like with my dog when I was a kid."

She shook her head. "I can't do this alone."

"I don't know how. I shut it away, just like you said. My parents told me I was imagining things . . . that I'd had a shock, and they understood, but I couldn't let it upset me so much." I made a gesture of futility with empty hands. "I don't know how to do it."

"I'll help you. But you have to agree to come with me. All the way." Her eyes were unexpectedly compassionate. "You were a cop once. You'll have to be one again."

After a moment, I nodded. "All right."

She sat down on the carpet and gestured for me to do the same. The collar lay between us. "We will reach out together, and we will pick it up together."

"Then what?"

"Hold it," she said simply.

"How will I know if it's working?"

"You will."

"What if it *doesn't* work?"

"It will." She saw something in my face. She extended her left hand. After a moment I closed my right around it. "Now," she said.

I saw our free hands move out, move down, then close upon the collar. I felt the braided nylon, the slightly frayed strands where something had rubbed, the cool metal rings.

And tasted—

—*blood in my mouth. Blood everywhere. It splattered my legs, matting fur together; drenched my paws. Leathery pads felt it against the sidewalk, slick and slippery, drying to stickiness. I smelled it everywhere, clogging nostrils, overwhelming my superior canine olfactory sense.*

Movement. The scent, the sharp tang of human surprise, fear, panic. Hackles rose from neck to the base of my curled tail in a ridge of thick, coarse hair. I heard a man's voice, a blurt, a bleat of sound, shock and outrage. Another man's breathing, harsh and rasping;

smelled the anger, the hatred, the cold fury that overwhelmed any comprehension of what he did beyond stopping it, stopping them; ending it, ending them; ending HER—

—crushed grass, leather, torn flesh, perfume, aftershave—

—aftershave I knew—

—had lived with—

—it was him, HIM, the man, the man I knew—

Knife. Long blade, red and silver in the moonlight. A woman on the ground, slack across the concrete, pale hair a tumbled mass turning red and black and sticky.

—I know the man, the murderer—

—the man who once fed me, walked me, petted me, praised me—

HIM. But what is he—

So much blood.

Everywhere.

Blood.

—and the other man, falling. Bleeding. Breath running out. Two bodies on the ground.

Blood is everywhere.

I lift my voice in a wailing howl.

In the moonlight, I see him turn. In the streetlights, I see him look at me. Black face. Familiar face.

Knife in his hand.

Blood on the knife.

Blood is everywhere.

He turns. Walks away. Back into the darkness.

I bark.

But he is gone. Two bodies on the ground.

I bark and bark and bark—

I yanked my hand away from hers, let go of the collar. Felt rage well up. "That son of a bitch!"

She was white-faced and shaking. Like me, she had released the collar. It lay again on the carpet. "That poor woman."

"And the kid," I said. "Poor guy, wrong place at the wrong time, like everyone said." I closed my eyes, then popped them open again as the memory, the *smells,* threatened to overwhelm me. "I was the dog."

"Yes."

"We saw what *he* saw. The Akita. That night on Bundy."

"He was the only witness," she said, "except for the murderer."

"That son of a bitch. . . ." I rocked back, clasped hands on top of my head. Breathed noisily. "And it's not admissible."

"Double jeopardy," she murmured.

"But I know, now—*we* know. . . ." I squeezed my eyes shut.

Her voice was very quiet. "You left the department after the trial. That was the case that went bad."

I opened my eyes. "After the Dream Team of lawyers got through with us, I had no heart for it anymore. We *knew* we had the evidence. But they played the department. Played the media. Cherry-picked the jury. And played the race card."

Tears shone in her eyes. "You took the Akita's collar home. To find out the truth."

I grimaced. "I was desperate. I knew even if it worked, even if somehow it worked, no one would believe me. Are you kidding? But I thought maybe it would give me a lead, if I could put myself there that night, behind the dog's eyes—find something we missed, something no one could manipulate. . . ." I shook my head. "Nothing. I couldn't do it. I didn't have the—*magic*—anymore."

She smiled. "Is that what you called it?"

" 'Magic'? Yeah, as a kid. Hell, I didn't know what it was—I *still* don't. . . . It's as good a word as any."

"I'm sorry," she said.

I nodded. "Yeah." Then the world revolved around me, began to gray out. "Whoa—"

87

"Lie down. I've got some energy bars in my purse . . . lie down, Mr. Magnum."

"Mag—" Then I got the reference. Laughing, I lay down as ordered, sprawled on my back. Heard the rustle of torn paper peeled away. Felt the nubbly surface of a granola bar shoved into my hand.

"Eat it. Then eat another. In a few hours you may feel like getting up. It's just backlash, from the energy expenditure. It's always best to do this on a full stomach, but, well . . . sometimes it doesn't work out that way."

I bit off a hunk of granola bar. "What about you?"

Her words were distorted. "I'm already eating mine."

I lay there a moment, chewing. Contemplating. "Will my life ever be normal again?"

"Nope."

"Didn't think so." I finished the first bar, accepted a second from her. "It's a curse, isn't it?"

"Sometimes. Now you know what happened that night in front of the condo, when two people lost their lives because of an ex-husband's jealousy. You will never be able to forget it. But it's a gift as well."

"How is it a *gift,* when you can experience something like that?"

"It's a gift when you can tell a frail, terrified old woman who's had nightmares for years that her beloved husband did not die in pain, and wasn't afraid because he was alone. It's a gift when you offer peace of mind." Her smile widened. "A *piece* of mind."

I considered it. "Maybe that'd be all right." I sat up slowly, steadying myself against the floor. "I need to leave. But I want to come back . . . talk to you more about all of this."

She watched me stand up, noted my unsteadiness. Refrained from suggesting I wait. "Where are you going?"

"Cemetery," I said. "There's someone I need to visit. To tell her I know the truth." I glanced back. "That *we* know the truth. Finally."

She nodded. "Peace of mind."

I paused in the doorway, stretching open the screen door. "Never found a man who could understand you, huh?"

"Not yet."

"Yeah, well . . . my wife didn't understand me, either. Maybe it's better if we stick to our own kind."

"Maybe," she said thoughtfully, climbing to her feet. She paused in the doorway, caught the screen door from my hand as I turned to go. "Excuse my bluntness but, well. . . ." She plunged ahead. "You're bitter and burned out, and dreadfully out of shape. Now that you know what you are inside, what you can do, you need to clean up your act. It takes every piece of you, the—" She paused, smiling. "—magic. You need to be ready for it."

I grimaced, aware of my crumpled shirt, stubbled face, bloodshot eyes, the beginnings of a potbelly. She wasn't ultra-fit because she was a narcissistic gym rat. It was self-preservation in the eye of the hurricane.

I turned to go, grimacing. "Yeah."

"My name, by the way, is Sarah. Sarah Connor."

I stopped short and swung back. "You're kidding me."

Color stole into her cheeks. "I take it you saw *The Terminator.*"

"Hell, I *own* the movie. On DVD."

She thought about it. "I guess if your name isn't Arnold, we'll be okay."

I laughed. "No, not Arnold. That I can promise you."

"Well?" she asked as I turned away again. "What is it?"

I threw it back over my shoulder as I reached my little sidewalk. "Clint East—"

"No!" she interrupted, wide-eyed. "Really?"

"Just *East*," I said. "But the guys in the department, well. . . ." I grinned. "They called me Woody."

Sarah laughed aloud.

As she closed her door, still grinning, I stuffed hands in my pockets and went whistling next door to mine, feeling good about myself for the first time in months.

SHADOWS IN THE WOOD

Awareness stirred. Then stilled. Stirred again, weakly; was like a weary man struggling to open eyelids grown too heavy for his will. Opened. Closed. Awake, then asleep.

He had lived in darkness so long he did not at first believe such a thing as light existed. But it sparked at the edges of awareness, kindled fitfully into life. A very quiet life it was, timid and halting, but incontrovertibly life. *He recognized it as such. And in that recognition, he acknowledged sentience. Victory at last over the enemy.*

At last? For all he knew, it had been no more than the day before now, this moment, that he had been defeated. Enspelled. Entrapped. But with sentience and awareness came also understanding that such imprisonment as his had been conjured to last a lifetime, or a hundred lifetimes of men older than he. For time out of mind.

But he was not . . . man. *That he knew. The body, the soul, remained imprisoned. Only the mind, the barest flicker of awareness, bestirred itself out of the long, enforced lethargy.*

He wondered what had awakened him. Here, there was no scent, no sight, no sound. He tasted nothing, because he had no mouth. He merely was, when before, for time uncounted, he was not.

Was not.

Now, again, all unexpectedly, he was.

Astonishment. Relief. Exultation.

Alive. Not as men marked it, for he, in this place, was nothing approaching human. He had no heart to beat, no mouth to speak, no eyes to see; neither ears to hear, nor nose to smell. No body answered

91

his will. No pulse throbbed in his neck. But for now it did not matter. Something in him sensed, something in him knew, *release after all was possible.*

Someone is coming.

No more than that.

Someone is coming.

It was his comfort. It was his joy. It was the light against the darkness, the shield against the spear.

Someone. Someday.

For now, it was enough.

ENGLAND, 1202

She felt the morning fog drift down and settle, a cool caress of dampness upon her face and hair, insinuating itself beneath the peaked hummock of rough-spun blanket draped across one shoulder. She burrowed closer into the blankets and hides to the warmth that was male, to the Crusade-scarred body grown precious years before; beloved before even they met in carnal congress beneath the roof of the tiny oratory built onto her father's manor at her mother's behest.

All dead to her now: father, mother, brother; even the manor, which now was held by the Crown, embodied by a man she knew as heartless. John Lackland. John Softsword. John, King of England. Who refused to return to her the hall into which she had been born, in which she had found a worthwhile living even after she knew herself the only one left of her blood. A man, a king, who listened instead to another man she named enemy: William deLacey. High Sheriff of Nottingham.

The warmth, the body beside her sensed her awakening and began its own. He turned toward her, drawing her nearer, wrapping her in his arms and legs. One spread-fingered hand cradled the back of her skull, tucking her head beneath his chin.

He stroked the black strands escaped from her braid. "Cold?"

She felt more than heard the words deep in his chest, and smiled. "Not *now*."

The prickle of unshaven jaw snagged her hair as he shifted closer. " 'Twill be winter soon."

"Too soon," she murmured, twining her limbs more tightly with his.

One hand wound a strand of her hair through his fingers. "I had hoped to offer you more than a rude cave, and a bed upon the ground."

Of course he had. And would have: wealth beyond imagining, power, title, castle. But he, as she, was denied that legacy, stripped of all his father had labored to build even as hers had labored, even as hers was stripped, albeit in death. Her father had been a mere knight, his a powerful earl, but it mattered little to sheriff or king. Knight and earl were dead, and the heirs of both, through royal decree, lacked such claim as would put them beneath the roofs their fathers had caused to be raised.

She gazed upward, blinking against moisture. The only roof now they called their own was the canopy of trees arching high overhead, their hall made of living trunks rather than hewn pillars; windows not of glass but built instead of air, where the leaves twined aside and permitted entry to the sun. Such little sky to see, here in the shadows of Sherwood, where their only hope of survival lay in escaping the sheriff's men.

She and Robin—formerly Sir Robert of Locksley, knight and honored Crusader, companion to now-dead Lionheart—took such privacy as they could find in the depths of the woods, laying a bed some distance from the others, friends and fellow outlaws, screened by the latticework of limbs and leaves, of bracken and vine. A pile of small boughs, uprooted fern, an armful of hides and blankets spread upon the hummock. Some would call it rude, a peasant's crude nest. But so long as he was in it, she would call it home.

Yet Robin was right. Already autumn's leaves fell, cloaking the ground and everything upon it, including themselves. They would soon have little warmth, and less foliage to hide behind. It was close on time to go to the caves.

But not just yet. His hands were upon her, and hers upon him, finding eager entrance into clothing beneath the blankets of cloth, of hide, of fallen leaves. As dawn broke upon them, sluggish behind the fog, they affirmed yet again beneath the vault of tree and sky what had been obvious to their souls, obvious to their hearts, from even before the beginning that night in the oratory, with illumination banished save for lightning's fitful brilliance.

Robin set his shoulder against the bole of a broad-crowned oak and gazed down the road, one hand wrapped around the grip of a strung bow that stood nearly as tall as he. A leather baldric crossed from left shoulder to right hip; from a quiver behind the shoulder sprouted a spray of goosefeathers, and a sheaf of straight-hewn shafts a full clothyard long. He wore hosen and tunic as any peasant, woven of crude cloth, but also boots upon his feet—boots once fine, now scuffed and soiled—and a brigandine taken from a man he himself had killed. Once accustomed to weighty armor, he found the shirt of linked rings to be no burden.

In the Holy Land, on Crusade, stealth was not an issue. He had ridden with an army headed by three sovereigns and many high lords. But Sir Robert of Locksley had returned to England a very different man. And that man, now stripped of his knighthood, his earldom, and his home by the Lionheart's brother, lived among the shadows in the company of outlaws instead of kings and queens.

Robin in the Wood, Robin in the Hood. Robin Hood. Whose entire life, now, was defined by stealth.

He listened for hoofbeats. Then knelt, pressed a palm against the beaten track, and felt for the same. He heard, and felt, nothing. There was no prey upon the road.

Once awake, awareness did not slide again into sleep. The tiny spark he recognized as himself, in spirit if not embodied, continued to glow brightly, slowly gathering strength until he had no fear it might be snuffed out. He remained bound, bodiless, with no recourse to escape, but he was awake, aware, and alive. He understood this too was a part of the spell, that to know oneself trapped for uncountable days was as much a torture as a lash upon bare flesh—as if betrayal such as he had known were not torture enough. But he rather thought not. These happenings seemed unplanned, and unforeseen, by the enemy who had enspelled him.

He recognized—something. Nebulous yet, wholly unformed, but his senses comprehended what his body could not feel.

Someone is coming.

Awareness coalesced, compacted, then spasmed in recognition. In comprehension of—opportunity.

He lacked a mouth, but the words, the plea, formed nonetheless. Oh, come. Come soon. Come NOW.

Marian had grown accustomed to living among the trees, naming the forest her hall. She had arrived at a compromise with the results of such surroundings: the damp soil that worked its way into her clothing, the stains of vegetation, the litter of crumpled leaves, the occasional thorn punctures and scratches. So long as no true hurt came of such importunities, she could suffer them in silence, except when a broken thorn stuck fast beneath her flesh, in which case someone—usually Robin, or Much with his quick, deft hands—dug it out for her.

She had, three years before, cast off the binding skirts of a lady's embroidered chemises and went now clothed more like a man, in heavy woven hosen, tunic, and boots. Over it all she wore a surcoat belted around her hips, the sleeveless, open-sided length of cloth invented on Crusade to beat back the blow of the Holy Land's sun on metal armor. But hers was not made of fine cloth with the red cross of Crusade on her breast or shoulder; hers was leather, cut to her size, and offered more maidenly modesty than hosen and tunic alone.

Though at that, Marian smiled. She was no more a maiden, being too often titled *whore* despite the fact she and Robin had married a few years earlier. And her modesty had been shed years before that in the oratory.

But the part of living as an outlaw among the trees and deadfall that she most detested was packing to move the camp. They had all taken to heart the lessons learned of keeping safe from the men who would capture them. They claimed no true home except what they made for a day or a night, though occasionally they settled some few days longer in a place deemed safe; no tables, no stools, save for the trunks of fallen trees, a tumble of moss-laden stone. But there were such things as iron pots, a tripod for the fire, bowls, mugs, bedding. Not to mention the swords, the staffs, the knives, and the invaluable bows Robin had taught each of them to use with frightening accuracy, from Much the simpleton boy and the giant, Little John; to Will Scarlet, the minstrel Alan of the Dales; and even poor Brother Tuck, preferring to trust to God rather than to the bow, but learning it nonetheless. An English longbow, Robin had explained, was a more powerful weapon even than a Norman crossbow with its deadly quarrels, for a clothyard arrow could punch through armor from long distances, with the archer well-shielded behind trees and brush.

Marian had cause to know. She had herself learned how to use a bow years before, but now knew also how to fletch the shafts with goosefeathers, to tie on and seal the deadly iron broadheads with sinew and glue. A few of the sheriff's men had been wounded by her arrows, by the accuracy of her aim that might have, could have, killed them, had she chosen to do so. One day, she knew, she would choose, would be brought to the choice. She did not wish to make it. But so long as such men as the sheriff set upon them desired the lives of men she cared for, Marian would not shirk the task of preserving those lives at the cost of their own.

Now Robin came back from the High Road linking Nottingham to Lincoln, a byway that afforded them opportunity to improve the lot of the poor while inconveniencing lords and wealthy merchants who protested the loss of coin and ornamentation. He slipped through the trees and foliage as if born to the life, making little sound. When he saw what little was left to do before departure, he smiled at her in accord. They knew one another's thoughts. Knew one another's habits.

"Anyone coming?" Will Scarlet asked, picking idly at his teeth with a green twig. "Any rich Norman rabbits for our stewpot?"

Robin shook his head with its cascade of pale hair. "No one."

Little John reached down for his pack. "Gives us time, then, to make some distance."

Alan of the Dales was making certain his lute case rode easily against his shoulders. "We'll have to take a deer once we reach the caves, or go hungry tonight."

"And tomorrow," Tuck put in, patting his ample belly. "No doubt I could go without, but—"

"But we dare not risk it," Scarlet interjected, "or we'll be hearing your complaints all night!"

Tuck was astonished. "I never complain!"

"Your *belly* does," Little John clarified pointedly.

"Oh." The monk's expression was mortified. "Oh, dear."

"Never mind," Robin told him, grinning. "We'll take our deer, and feast right well."

Marian swung her own pack up and slid her arms through straps. It was a matter of less effort, now, to arrange pack, bow, and quiver about her person without tangling anything. Outlawry and privation had trained them all.

Much, grown taller than when he had joined them but still thin and hollow-faced, doused the small fire. He could not fully hide its signs, or that people had gathered around it, but his job was to make certain none of them could be identified. The sheriff's men might find a deserted clearing, but there would be no tracks to follow, no indication of who had camped there. Sherwood housed innumerable outlaws. Not every fire, nor every campsite, hosted Robin Hood and his band.

Robin's hand fell on Much's shoulder, thanking him in silence. Next he glanced at Marian. She nodded, drawing in a breath. Then they turned as one to the trees and stepped into the shadows, fading away as if their bodies were wrought of air and light, not formed of flesh and bone. In such meager human sorcery lay survival.

He sensed impatience, and feelings and emotions that had been dead to him for days, years, decades. He sensed urgency, and yearning; he tasted the promise of power, the ability once again to make a difference in the world.

Kingmaker. Widowmaker. Reviled, and beloved. But he knew only one path. Impediments upon it were to be overcome.

Hurry, *he wished.*

He wished it very hard.

The outcry echoed in the trees. Robin spun around, gesturing sharply to the others strung out behind him on the deer track. Even as all of them dove into foliage, separating to offer more difficult targets, a second cry rang out, a different voice now, followed by shouts in Norman French. He held his breath, listening; now it was possible to also hear the threshing of men running through the forest, and the louder crashing of horses in pursuit.

Robin, grimacing as he dropped flat behind a downed tree, swore in silence. Poachers, likely, or even known outlaws, had been spotted by one of the sheriff's patrols. It was sheer bad luck that those pursued were heading straight toward him and his party.

He raised his head slightly and searched over his shoulder. Save for the last fading movement of stilling branches and waving hip-high fern, there was no hint that a woman and five men were hidden close by. He wished he could see Marian, but if she were invisible to him, neither could the Norman soldiers see her.

More crashing through underbrush. Now he could hear panting, and wheezing, and the blurted, broken prayers of a man who would do better to hoard his breath. Not far away another man cried out, and then a triumphant shout went up from the soldiers.

Underbrush broke apart in front of Robin. The second outlaw was abruptly *there,* his arms outstretched, his batting hands attempting to open an escape route through hanging vines and low, sweeping branches. Robin briefly saw the scratched, agonized face, the staring eyes, the open mouth. And then the man teetered atop the very trunk Locksley took shelter behind.

Growling oaths behind gritted teeth, Robin reared up, grabbed the man's tunic, and yanked him off the tree. The outlaw came down hard and loose, limbs splayed; a knee caught Robin in the side of the head hard enough to double his vision. "Stay down!" he hissed, as the man lay sprawled belly-down on the ground, sobbing in fear and exhaustion.

A soldier on horseback broke through, blue cloak flapping. He wore the traditional conical Norman helm with its steel nasal bisecting his dark face. Robin ducked as the horse gathered itself and sailed over the tree—sailed, too, over two men seeking protection in its meager shelter.

Robin turned on his knees, shouting a warning to the others. More soldiers were crashing before him now, spreading out. The Norman who had jumped the log was calling to his fellows in French, wheeling his horse even as he raised an already spanned crossbow, quarrel resting in its channel. But Robin had had more time; his own arrow was loosed, flying, and took the soldier through the throat.

Now he focused on another—*how many are there?*—as he deftly nocked a second arrow.—*so many*—There was no time to think, to plan. Only to react.

He stood. Pulled the bowstring back to his chin. Sighted, and let fly.

The Norman flew backward off his horse as if a trebuchet stone had struck him in the chest.

But others had broken through. They had spotted new prey now, shouting positions to one another. Even as Robin nocked a third arrow, someone clutched at him. "Don't let them catch me!" the rescued man cried. "They'll cut me hand off!"

His aim spoiled, the arrow went wide. Cursing, Robin caught a glimpse of flared equine nostrils, the gape of equine mouth, and the flash of a sword blade swinging down at his head.

"Get *off*—" he blurted, diving for the ground.

But the blade sheared through hair and flesh, and the sharpened tip slid across his skull.

Marian was well-hidden until Robin's arrow took the first soldier through the throat. The Norman tumbled limply off his mount, but one booted foot caught in the stirrup long enough to spook the horse, who responded with great lunging leaps sideways. Marian, directly in the animal's path, attempted to scramble out of the way. But the horse, panicked, wheeled around, and the body, coming loose at last, was swung out sideways in a wide arc.

The impact of the mailed body colliding with her own knocked Marian off her feet. She was aware of weight, disorientation, her own startled outcry—and then she went down hard against the ground, sprawled on her back, pinned by the weight of the soldier.

She had heard the term "dead weight" before. She had not truly known what it implied. Now she did.

Breath was gone. She gulped air as fear crowded close. She could not *breathe*—

Panicked, she shoved at the body, trying to dislodge it. Her struggles did nothing but waste what little breath remained in her lungs.

A dead man could not kill her.

The thought stilled her, calmed her, permitted her to draw a normal breath again. Air came in with relief, and then she became aware of more than the soldier's weight, but his stench as well. Bladder and bowels.

And blood. Blood in her mouth, running into her throat. She choked, coughed, felt the spray leave her mouth. She turned her head and spat, not knowing if it were dead man's blood or her own.

The body muffled sound, but she heard shouting. And then abruptly the terrible weight was lifted, dragged aside. Someone was grunting with effort.

"Lady . . . Lady Marian—" Tuck. His hands grasped one of her arms, dragged her up from the ground. "They're distracted—you must go now!"

She was dizzy, blinking at him woozily as she put a hand to her mouth. Blood filled it again.

"You're swifter than I," Tuck wheezed. "You must go on.

Take Robin, and go!"

That got through. "Robin?"

"Injured." Tuck yanked her to her feet. "Can you stand?— good. Here. . . ." He pulled her to a downed tree. She saw Robin then, slumped against the trunk as blood sheeted down the side of his face. "Go, both of you." Tuck pushed her. "The others are leading them away. Waste no time. 'Tis Robin they want more than any of us."

She knelt beside Robin. He was conscious, but clearly in pain. She put a hand to his face and realized they both bled badly.

"Up," Tuck insisted. He yanked Marian back to her feet, then pulled Robin from the ground. "Go on. Get as far as you can."

"Caves," Robin said between gritted teeth, weaving in place.

Tuck nodded. "We shall meet you there when we can."

Marian spat blood again. Hers, she realized, not the dead man's. She had cut her mouth. "Can you walk?" she asked Robin.

Through the blood, he managed a twisted smile. "Given a choice between that, or hanging?" He closed her hand in his own. "Say rather I can *run*."

Robin pulled her over the fallen tree, and then both of them were running.

Awareness encompassed more than he had expected ever to sense again, to know, to feel. It was nearly tangible now, coming closer, closer. If hands were his to use, he could nearly touch redemption. Nearly know release.

Come—

Robin's lungs were afire, but even that pain did not match the pounding in his head. His right hand clutched Marian's left; otherwise, he would have pressed it against his temple in a fruitless attempt to dull the pain. To halt the blood.

Head wounds. He had learned on Crusade how badly head wounds bled, even if they were not serious. And he believed his was not; the pain was immense, but no worse than anything he had felt before. He remained conscious and on his feet, albeit those feet were clumsy.

Marian's breathing matched his, ragged and whistling. Together they stumbled through the foliage, attempting to put distance between themselves and the Normans. Tuck had done them a huge service, Robin knew; it was possible he and the others were captured by now, some of them even killed. But the monk had gotten *them* away from such danger, and if they were careful they might yet be worthy of his sacrifice. He did not know where they went, merely that they ran. They left behind them deer trail and fought to make a new one, raking aside with outstretched hands impediments such as vine and undergrowth.

"Wait—" It was barely the breath of a sound expelled from her bloodied mouth. "Stop—"

He halted, catching a hanging vine to hold himself upright. Marian released his hand and bent over, sucking air noisily. Her long black braid was disheveled, strands pulled loose by branches as they ran. A bruise was rising on her face, blotching one cheekbone. She wiped her mouth free of blood, studied the slick hand dispassionately, then looked at Robin, still panting.

"—head?" she asked.

"Attached." It was all he could manage, clinging to the vine.

Marian nodded vaguely, attempting a smile. She straightened, then turned and staggered toward a great old oak, roots thick as a man's thigh where they broke free of the soil in a tangle akin to Celtic knotwork. She drooped against the trunk, pressing her forehead into bark.

Robin loosed his grip on the vine and made his way across to her, wincing against the renewed pain in his head. With care he avoided tripping over the oak roots, but when he reached the trunk he nearly fell. He caught himself with one outstretched arm, then turned and set his spine against the trunk, sliding down until he sat on the ground, cradled between two twisted roots.

With gentle fingers he explored the side of his head. Fortunately the sword blade's motion had mostly been spent. It had sliced into the flesh above his right ear, but had not cracked the skull beneath. That skull would no doubt house an abominable headache for a day or two, but he was mostly undamaged.

He shifted his position to a more comfortable one. Breath came more easily now. Marian's surcoat swung as she turned; then, like him, she sat down amidst the roots. She looked aside, spat blood, then blotted her mouth against her tunic sleeve.

She studied the soiled sleeve critically. "Stopping, I think."

Robin stretched out his arm, slung it wearily across her shoulders, and pulled her close. "I think we are out of danger." He paused. "For now."

Marian didn't answer. She was staring around, frowning. "Where are we?"

Robin glanced into the shadows, noting the trees seemed almost uniform in size, shape, and placement. Mistletoe clustered in branches, foliage crowded the ground, but the huge trees took precedence over the rest of the forest.

He felt at his head again. "When I was a child, my mother told me there were oak groves planted by Druids in Sherwood. That they were the oldest part of the forest, and sacred. But she was always telling me stories. I never knew which were true."

"These are oaks," Marian said. "And—" She broke off sharply. "Robin . . . there are *faces*." Alarm chilled him. He sat bolt upright, preparing to gather his legs under him until she waved him back down. "No, not Normans—at least, not living ones. Look! Do you see?" She gestured. "Look at the trunks."

He looked, and saw nothing.

Marian got to her feet and crunched through fallen leaves to the oak closest to the one Robin leaned against. "Look here." Her blood-smeared hand touched the massive trunk, tracing a shape. "Here are the eyes, the nose—and the mouth. See it?" She looked back at him, waiting expectantly.

He rolled his head in negation. "A trick of light and shadow."

"On *all* of them? Look around, Robin." Marian's outstretched arm encompassed their surroundings. "This is an oak grove, one far older than you or me . . . or even, I daresay, our fathers' fathers. Just as your mother told you." She moved to the next tree, intent. Once again her hand traced a shape. "Eyes, nose, mouth . . . and here is the chin."

He made a noncommittal sound.

Marian's expression was sympathetic, but clearly she was certain of what she saw. He closed his eyes and rested as she walked from tree to tree, murmuring to herself. He was nearly asleep when she reached his tree, circling it. He heard her stop, heard her startled blurt of sound, and then abruptly she was attempting to haul him to his feet.

"Come and see," she ordered.

His remonstration made no headway. She dragged him around to the backside of the huge old tree, took his hand in hers, and pressed his fingers against the wood.

"Feel it." She moved his hand, tracing something. "Here, see? The brow, the bridge of the nose, the cheekbones—this one is much clearer than the others. Do you see it?"

He did. This time, he did. There in the bark, no longer merely a trick of light and shadow, was the shape of a face. It was much clearer than those in the other trunks. Sightless eyes stared.

"It's a man," Marian said quietly.

And then, beneath their bloodied hands, the wood began to move.

The spell attenuated, began to shred, broke. He felt it fail, felt the last minute particles attempt to bind themselves together once more in order to also bind him, but it was too late. Awareness melded with spirit, merged with comprehension, joined with the power that had been held too long in abeyance. He tapped it, called it, welcomed it; felt it bound joyously back to him like a hound to its hearth. One moment it was absent, the next, present.

With a roar of triumph, he ripped himself free of the tree, woodchips flying; banished the clinging aftermath of the long, dreamless sleep and stepped into life again, into the world again, into his body. Flesh, blood, and bone. And power incarnate.

The empty tree screamed.

As the body tore itself free of the massive trunk, shredding strips and chips of wood, Marian blurted a sound of shock and hastily backed away. A root caught her and she went down hard. Even as Robin bent to help her up, he halted, arrested in mid-motion. Both stared at the stranger who had wrenched himself out of living oak.

He was wild-eyed, breathing hard. From the tree he went to his knees as if in supplication, or perhaps weakness. Splayed hands pressed against the layers of leaves, elbows locked to hold himself upright. Shoulder-length hair, dark save where it was frosted with the first touch of gray, tumbled around his face. Marian could not see his expression now as he knelt, but she heard the rapid, uneven breathing; saw the shuddering in spine and shoulders.

For all she and Robin were stunned, the stranger seemed to be more so.

She let Robin pull her to her feet. They put a cautious

distance between themselves and the man, but did not flee. Instead, they stared at one another in blank astonishment, then turned as one to the stranger. Robin's sword chimed as he unsheathed it.

When the man looked up, Marian saw gray eyes clear as water, black-lashed, and pale, unblemished skin. His beard was short and well-tended. He wore a blue robe of excellent cloth, and pinned to his left shoulder was a red-and-gold enameled brooch, dragon-shaped, of Celtic workmanship. When he brought his hands out of the loose, powdery leaves, she saw he wore a gold ring set with a red cabochon stone she believed might be a ruby.

"Robin." She kept her tone carefully casual. "Is this a trick of light and shadow?"

Equally casual, he replied, "This appears to be flesh and blood."

"We are awake, are we not?"

"As far as I can tell, we are awake." He tugged her litter-strewn braid sharply. "Feel that?"

"Yes," she said crossly, putting a hand to her scalp.

"And I still bleed a little, so this must be real." He paused. "And my mother apparently told me the truth."

Marian was amazed at how calm he sounded. She didn't feel calm. She felt—oddly detached. Somehow distant from what she had witnessed, and what she was witnessing now. And yet every noise she heard sounded preternaturally loud.

Should I not be running? Or, if she were a proper woman, fainting?

But then, she had not been proper since meeting Robin. Still, Marian wondered why she felt no urge to run. It wasn't fear that the stranger might harm her if she tried; she wasn't certain a man who had been trapped in a tree trunk moments before *could* harm her. But she found herself immensely curious to know what had happened to him—and to be quite certain she had truly seen him tear himself out of a living tree.

Still on his knees, the man looked over his shoulder at the tree. Except for a hollowed gouge in the trunk, the oak appeared no different. It was simply a tree. But a glance at other oaks still bearing likenesses of other men emphasized the truth of his own presence.

He turned back to face them. With hands now grown steady, he pushed heavy hair away from his face and bared a narrow circlet of beaten gold. He was, Marian realized, only ten or twelve years older than she.

She wondered what Robin was thinking. A quick glance at his face showed grimness, and skin drawn taut beneath the golden stubble and smeared blood. He seemed at ease; but then he always looked relaxed, wholly unprepared to strike when but a moment later the enemy was down. They had lost their bows along the way as they ran, but were not unarmed; they had a meat-knife, quiver, and arrows, and Robin the sword.

Oddly, she wanted to say, *"Do not harm him,"* which made no sense. She knew nothing of the man save he had, to all appearances, been a resident of a tree. A resident *in* a tree.

The stranger's eyes fixed themselves on Robin's sword. A sudden light came into them, an expression of sharpened awareness and understanding. Abruptly he stood up. Sharply he asked something in a language neither of them knew.

Robin said something in fluent Norman French. The stranger frowned, plainly impatient, and tried several different languages in swift succession. In each there were words that sounded vaguely familiar to Marian, but he remained a cipher until a final try.

"Latin!" Marian exclaimed. "Oh, where is Tuck when we need him?"

This time when the stranger spoke, his words, though twisted, were in an accented English they could understand. "When is it?"

Robin began to ask a question of his own, something to do with a carved man turning into flesh and stepping out of a tree, but the stranger overrode him.

"When is it?"

When. Not where. Perplexed, Marian said, "The Year of Our Lord 1202."

The gray eyes widened. "So long? I had not thought so—" His tone took on bitterness. "—when I had mind again to think at all." He looked more closely at Marian, then at Robin, inspecting them.

Marian became aware of her disheveled clothing, a braid half undone, bits of leaf and twigs caught in her hair and the loose weave of her hosen beneath the surcoat. Her chin itched from drying blood, and her face stung from scratches. Then the stranger turned to the tree again and put out a hand, feeling the bark. When he brought it away, smeared streaks of red crossed his palm.

"Blood," he murmured. "Surely she did not foresee this, or she would have prepared for it. But who would have expected the blood of two Sacrifices to commingle in the Holy Grove, let alone upon the walls of my prison?"

" 'Sacrifices?' " Robin demanded. "Are we meant to die here, when somehow all of your companions are let out of *their* trees?"

The stranger ignored the question and looked at Marian. "The Year of Our Lord, you said." She nodded. "You mean the man Christians called the Nazarene?"

Marian blinked. "Of course."

" 'Of course.' " He sounded rueful. Then his expression altered. His eyes were once again fixed on Robin's sword. "There is a task before me. It was mine to do before the enchantment, and no less mine to do now that I am free of it, regardless of how long it has been. Will you aid me?"

"Aid you?" Robin echoed. "Perhaps you should aid *us* by explaining what just happened."

The stranger smiled. "I see power is no more understood now—whenever this time may be—than it was then." Absently he touched the brooch on his left shoulder. "Vortigern meant me to be the Sacrifice when his walls would not stand; instead, I gave him news of the dragons under the water. When the red defeated the white." His pupils had swollen, turning eyes from gray to black. "He is dead. The red dragon of Wales. And so the task lies before me." His eyes cleared and he looked at them both as if seeing them for the first time. "Forgive me. Perhaps it will all explain itself upon introductions. I am Myrddyn Emrys." He gave it the Welsh pronunciation, tongue-tip against upper teeth. "Men call me Merlin."

"Merlin!" Robin blurted.

The stranger nodded. "And the task is to find a sword, and give it back to the lake."

"Merlin," Robin repeated, and this time Marian heard adult disbelief colored by a young boy's burgeoning hope.

Merlin had spent his entire life being—*different*. People feared him for it, distrusted, disbelieved; some of them were convinced he should be killed outright, lest he prove a danger to them. But that life, that time, was done. He faced a new world now, a different world, and far more difficult challenges. In his time, magic at least had been acknowledged if often distrusted; here, clearly, no one believed in it at all. Which somewhat explained the inability of the young man and young woman to accept what had happened.

An enchantment, he had told them as they knelt to wash their bloodied faces at a trickle of a stream, a spell wrought by Nimue, the great sorceress. He did not tell them his own part in the spell, that he had allowed himself for the first time in his life to be blinded by a woman's beauty and allure, to permit her into his heart. Once she had learned enough of him, enough of his power, she had revealed her true goal: to imprison him for all time, and thus remove the impediment he represented to the new power in Britain.

A Britain without Arthur.

He grieved privately, letting no one, not even Nimue, recognize the depth of his pain. Arthur he had wrought out of the flesh of Britain herself, a man destined to unite a world torn awry against the threat of the Saxon hordes. And so he had for a time; but then other forces took advantage of a childless king and a queen in disrepute, dividing Arthur's attention when it was most needed to settle an uneasy court. By the time the Saxon threat became immediate, Arthur had lost too many sup-porters among the noblemen—and too many knights. The advent of a bastard got unknowingly on his own sister had sealed his fate. Merlin, in retirement, had done what he could, but Ar-thur died and Britain was left defenseless.

A Britain without Arthur could not survive as Merlin had meant her to, safeguarded by the one man empowered with the natural ability to keep her whole. Thousands of years had passed since Arthur's death, and even now Merlin had only to look at the man kneeling at stream's edge, with his fall of white-blond hair and pale greenish-brown eyes, and his height, to see that the Saxons had triumphed. And so the man agreed when asked, explaining that Britain's people were now called 'English,' born of 'England,' that once had been 'Angle-land.' The land of Angles and Saxons.

Marian, however, was not. It was clear when Merlin looked upon her. She was small, slight, and black-haired, bearing more resemblance to the people of his time in her features, despite the blue of her eyes. She called herself English, but her blood was older than Robin's.

And now England—Britain—had fallen again. To a people called the Normans, Robin explained, who refused even to learn the language of the people they conquered. A people who had a king whose excess of temper was legendary, along with the greed and turbulence of his reign.

"Then we should waste no more time," Merlin told them. "Arthur is dead, but his legacy may yet be realized."

"By finding the sword," Marian said dubiously, rebraiding her hair.

Robin's smile, even as he felt at the clotted slice in his head, was very nearly fatuous. "Excalibur."

"The sword belongs to the lake," Merlin said, "now that Arthur cannot wield it. Britain's welfare resides in it. Arthur, with Excalibur, drove away the Saxons once, but Mordred and his faction kept him from completing his task. You have told me of other invasions. To keep Britain from ever being invaded again, we must find the sword and return it to the lake."

"That will be enough?" Marian asked. "No one ever again shall invade England?"

"No one."

"You are Merlin the Enchanter," Robin said. "What use would we be to *you?*"

"You will recall that it was you who got me out of the tree," he reminded them dryly.

They exchanged glances, still perplexed.

"You are the Sacrifices," Merlin explained gently. "Just as Arthur himself was."

And as he saw the confusion deepening in their eyes, he realized that with the years had disappeared the knowledge that was beginning to die out even in his time.

He gestured back toward the way they had come. "That was a Holy Grove, sacred to the Druids. It was Nimue's conceit to imprison me there—and, apparently, others as well." His expression reflected regret that he, Marian, and Robin had been unable to free the others. "There are men and women born into the world who are meant to be Sacrifices for their people, for their times, to keep the land strong and whole. They need not be killed upon an altar, though that was done once, but merely die in defense of their land and ideals. To die serving the greater whole."

"We are outlaws," Robin said. "We are fortunate if we can feed ourselves each day; what service can *we* offer England?"

"Hope," Merlin answered. "Have you not told me you give over to peasants most of what you take?"

"Because the king is taxing the poor to death," Marian declared.

Merlin nodded. "And so you steal from those who have wealth to spare, and divide it fairly among those who have none." His eyes were unwavering. "At the risk of your own lives."

He had made them uncomfortable. They neither of them fully understood what they represented to the folk they aided. Perhaps they never would. It was the nature of Sacrifices to do what was required without acknowledging the selflessness of it, because they saw only the need and simply acted. Arthur had not been raised to be a king per se, but to be a decent, honest, fair man of great ability, capable of leading others to the goal he perceived as worthy, because it served the people.

Arthur had come into privilege and kingship because it was the position needed to guide Britain. Robert of Locksley and Marian of Ravenskeep had been stripped of their privilege because that loss led them to the position of aiding the poor, when no one else in England appeared willing to do so.

Who else was worthy of aiding him in his task?

"We had better go," Merlin said.

"Wait." Robin's brows were knit beneath raggedly cut hair. "Do you even know where the sword is?"

Merlin smiled. "Do you expect a quest? To be a knight of the Round Table, searching for the Grail? But the answer is disappointing, I fear: Nimue *told* me, as my body was turned to wood."

Robert of Locksley, born the son of an earl—albeit last, and was thus inconsequential—wanted very much to say he disbelieved the nonsense the stranger told them. He recalled too vividly the beatings meted out by his father, wishing to purge what remained in his sons of anything fanciful, such as stories of Arthur and his enchanter, Merlin. But Robin's mother had told him to believe as he wished, that stories were good for the soul as well as the heart. And so he had learned the stories, and loved them, and believed them, until he grew up and joined a Crusade that took the lives of innocents as well as warriors. He could not say when he had come to understand that there were stories and there were truths, with a vast gulf between the two, but he knew that Merlin, Arthur, and all the others of the legend were not real.

Except that Merlin was—*here*.

The part of him that wished to believe wondered why Merlin did not simply conjure a spell that would move them to wherever it was he wanted to go, without benefit of walking. The rational part of him believed in no such ability, that the stranger was nothing but a madman. But he remembered all too well the sight of the tree disgorging a man. Still, Merlin did not do so; he said he could not.

They slept little, ate less, and followed whatever it was that guided Merlin. The enchanter pronounced himself stunned by the changes that had overtaken England—no, Britain—and yet admitted there was much that had not altered. He seemed unimpressed by the fact that he had been entrapped in a tree for hundreds of years; if anything, he considered it quite natural. Such things as sorcery were expected by Merlin, while Robin found it impossible to accept that fanciful stories, no matter how beautiful, no matter how entrancing, were grounded in fact.

But when at last they walked out of the forest and saw the wooded hill rising before them, surrounded by a ring of grassy lowlands, and Merlin sank down as if in prayer, murmuring in a language neither he nor Marian understood, Robin knew more was at work than fancy or folly.

From his knees, Merlin said, "Avalon."

Robin started. "No!"

"It was an island," Merlin persisted. "Look you, and see how it might have been. The shore here, the water there—and the isle beyond."

Robin looked upon it. An expanse of land stretched before him, and a high hill above it, swelling out of turf. There was no water, no shore, nothing to cross save grass.

"It is much changed," said Merlin, "but not so very altered that a man of my begetting may not recognize it."

A man of his begetting. A chill prickled Robin's spine.

Marian gazed upon the hill. "Women ruled there."

"For time out of mind," Merlin agreed. "It was the goddess's place, and that of her servants. Men were occasionally tolerated, but never truly welcomed."

"You?" she asked.

His tone was dry. "Tolerated."

"And the sword?" Robin inquired.

Merlin seemed to have drifted away from them. "There is a grave upon the island," he said. "A man sleeps in it. But also an ideal. He and others embodied—and yet embody—it. The sword is there." He looked at Robin. "Come nightfall, you and the goddess's daughter must climb what is now a hill, but once was an island."

Marian's brows rose. "Goddess's daughter?"

"In your blood," he answered. "In your bones. But those who remain will attempt to stop you regardless." He smiled as they exchanged a concerned glance. "Just as the sheriff attempts to stop you from robbing the wealthy and poaching the king's deer."

That put it in perspective. Robin sighed. "What do you want us to do?"

"Find the sword," Merlin answered. "I am known there, even by the stones that outlive us all; I cannot go. It is for you to do."

"I am a man," Robin said. "Will I be—what did you say? Tolerated?"

Merlin inclined his head in Marian's direction. "Because of her, yes."

Marian's tone was implacable. "We go nowhere, and do nothing, without knowing what we may expect."

"Resistance," Merlin told her.

Suspicious, Robin inquired, "What *kind* of resistance?"

The enchanter spread his hands. "That I cannot say. It may take many forms."

Robin remained suspicious. "But you will not accompany us."

Merlin shook his head. "If I go, the task cannot be completed. And it must be, for Arthur's sake and the welfare of Britain."

Robin laughed. "You have a way with words, Myrddyn Emrys. Perhaps that is the secret of your sorcery. You convince others to do the work for you."

Merlin said, "So long as the work is done, it matters not who has the doing of it."

Marian continued to gaze upon the hill. "How will we know to find the sword? Is it standing up from a stone?"

Robin's laughter rang out. The enchanter was mystified, until the story was explained. Merlin frowned. "It was not like that at all. There was no such drama. It was—"

Marian halted him with a raised hand. "Please. Let it remain as we know it. Tales and legends are akin to food when there is little hope in a poor man's life."

Merlin's smile twitched. "This is as much as I know: the grave and the sword are on the isle. Where, I cannot say."

It felt like a challenge. Or even, after all, a quest. Marian looked at Robin. "The moon will be full tonight. Shall we go a'hunting?"

He put out a hand and brushed a strand of hair away from her eyes, smiling. "Let us make a new legend."

Moonlight lay on the land as Marian and Robin crossed the grass Merlin claimed had once been a lake. She wondered if it might possibly be true, as its appearance was so different from that of the forest behind them, and the hill before. There were no great oaks, beeches, and alders, no tangle of foliage, no stone outcroppings. Merely grasslands, hollowed out of the earth.

A faint wind blew, teasing at their hair. Robin's was awash with moonlight, nearly silver-white. The metal of his brigandine glowed and sparked. The light was kind to his face, for all his expression was serious; she wanted abruptly to stop him, to kiss him, to vow again how much she loved him, but something in the night suggested such behavior would be unwelcome. She felt urgency well up into a desire to find the sword for Merlin and return to him as soon as possible. Nothing in her wished to tarry.

Beside her, Robin shuddered. He felt her glance and smiled ruefully. "Someone walked over my grave."

Fear sent a frisson through her. "Say no such thing. Not here."

He glanced around, rubbing at the back of his neck. "Perhaps not," he agreed.

Before them lay the first incline of the hill, a ragged seam of stone curving into the darkness, and a terrace of grass above it. Here vegetation began, clumps spreading inward, ascending the hill. The trees stood higher yet, forming a crown around the summit. She and Robin climbed steadily upward, until he stopped short just as they entered the outer fringe of trees.

The look on his face startled her. "What is it?"

"I am not supposed to be here." He worked his shoulders as if they prickled with chill. "Merlin was right—men are not wanted. But—" He broke off, feeling gingerly at the cut on his head.

"But?" she prodded.

"But I in particular am not wanted. Or so it feels." He studied his fingers. "Bleeding again."

"Let me see." She moved around to his other side, turning his head into the moonlight. "A little, yes. . . ." She peeled hair away, saw where fresh blood welled. Moment by moment it ran faster, thicker, until even her fingers could not stop it. "Perhaps we should turn back."

Robin's expression was odd. "He said there would be resistance."

Marian frowned as she drew her meat-knife and commenced cutting a strip from her tunic. "You believe you are bleeding again because of that?"

"I believe . . . that on a night such as this, it may be possible." He winced. "And the ache is returning."

"Bend your head." Marian tied the cloth around his head. "Do you believe what he says? That there even *is* a sword, and if we find it, it may guard England?"

Robin sighed, fingering the knot she had tied in the makeshift bandage. "I am not certain what I believe. But if there is truth to it. . . ." He shrugged. "What harm if we try?"

"An aching head."

"Ah, well, I daresay I can stand that." Robin looked at the vanguard of trees springing up around them. "The stories say Arthur was taken away by nine queens, and given secret burial rites. If this *is* Avalon—what remains of it, in any case—it is possible his grave is here. And what else is there to do but bury the king's sword with the king's body?"

"Give it to his son," Marian answered promptly. "Save that no one of Arthur's court would wish to see a bastard, a patricide, carrying it."

"Merlin was not there when Arthur died," Robin went on thoughtfully. "He may have meant to give it back to the lake on Arthur's death, but if the women of Avalon took it away with the body—"

"—they would have brought it here." Marian gazed up the hill to where the trees thickened, choked with undergrowth. "But all of it is merely a story. . . ."

"Is it?" Robin asked. "Stories are changed over time, embellished the way Alan embellishes his ballads, but what if the kernel is true? What if that man back there, whom we witnessed come out of a tree no matter how much we wish to deny it, truly is Merlin?"

"Then Arthur's grave is up there."

"And the sword," Robin said. *"Excalibur."* He reached out a hand to her. "Shall we find it?"

Marian put her own in his. "Alan would make a fine ballad of this."

Robin's teeth gleamed in a wide grin. "Oh, that he would! He would have us being beset on all sides by unseen enemies, battling evil spirits, making our way up a hill that crawled with the shades of long-dead men."

"Well," Marian said dryly, "of such fancies are legends born."

With every step he took ascending the hill, Robin felt oppressed. Heavy. As if his body gained the mass and weight of stones, ancient under the sun. Breath ran ragged. His head ached. It took all of his strength to put one foot after the other and continue climbing.

He knew Marian was concerned. He saw it each time she halted a step or two above him, looking back to find him toiling behind her, expending effort merely to keep moving. The bandage around his head stilled most of the blood, but a stubborn trickle dribbled continuously down beside his ear. His shoulder was wet with it, where the blood had fallen.

They were nearly to the crown of the hill when he drew his sword. He could not say why it was necessary, save to know it was. In his years upon Crusade, and more years yet as an outlaw in Sherwood, he had learned to trust his instincts.

Just as they crossed beyond the last line of trees and stepped out onto the rocky summit, Marian stopped short. Her eyes, he saw, were stretched wide, unblinking; trembling hands moved to cover her ears. The sound she made was like nothing he had ever heard from her, a combination of whimper, protest, and astonishment.

He reached out to touch her, to put his hand upon her shoulder, but found such resistance in the air that he could not. His hand stopped short of her body, unable to go farther. "Marian?"

"I hear them," she said.

Robin heard nothing.

She drew in a breath. "Their souls are still here."

"Whose souls?"

"The women—the women who lived here. Those who worshipped the goddess." She closed her eyes then, intent upon something he could neither see nor hear. "They knew peace here, in life and death. Not Christians, but reverent in their own way, following their faith." She removed her hands and looked at him. "Merlin was right: he could not come here. Nor do they wish you to be here."

"And you?" he asked.

Marian smiled crookedly. "I may or may not be descended from women who lived here in Merlin's day. The power has faded, but there is memory here. I will not be chased away." She closed her eyes again. He could see the lids twitching as if she slept; her mouth moved slightly. The words she quoted were nothing he had ever heard, from her or anyone else.

"Marian—?"

This time it was she who reached out to him. Resistance snapped. He felt her hand on his, smooth and warm, as she led him to the center of the hilltop.

"He is with *me*," she said, and the world made way.

There were voices in her ears. Nothing she could make out, not words she understood, but voices, women's voices, calling out. Was it her help they desired, or her absence? Marian could not tell what it was they wanted, merely that they existed, that they filled her mind with sound and her heart with yearning.

His hand was warm in hers, but she was barely conscious of it. She led him without hesitation to the center of the summit, to the place where stacked stone had tumbled into ruin, from graceful lines into disarray. Most were lichen-clad, moss-grown, buried in soil and groundcover. Some had cracked wide open, broken into bits by frost and sun. Nothing here resembled a place to live, but live they had. She could feel it in her bones, sense it singing in her blood.

"Here," she said.

Robin stopped beside her. "The grave?"

121

She turned her face up to the moon, squinting at its brilliance. "No. The women worshipped here."

He was silent. Marian sensed his unease. She turned to him, to reassure him that she was welcome here, that so long as he was her Consort he would be tolerated—but she forgot the intention as something came down between them. A hissing line of light lanced out of the sky, so cold it burned. They broke apart and fell back, guarding their eyes. In the flash of illumination Marian saw Robin's drawn and hollowed face, the grimness in his mouth. The bared blade of his sword glinted in the darkness.

She was Christian-born and -bred, not a goddess-worshipper. But something within responded to the place. She, a woman, had a right to be here. None of the women of Avalon had ever turned away one of their own, though not all had remained. What remained of them would not turn her away. Still, she was uneasy.

Resistance, Merlin had said. Robin had spoken of unseen enemies and evil beings. Marian sensed neither here, merely the memories of women who had left the world of men to make their own way, to find their own faith. That memory could make itself tangible did not, somehow, strike her as unusual. Not here. Not this night. Nor that the souls of the women, tied to the stone and soil of Avalon, would be present still. They had not known a heaven such as Christians did. They had worshipped another way.

Blasphemy, the priests would say. Heresy. It was not Marian's way, but she could respect that women before her might seek another road. A woman's life was difficult, with or without a man.

Her man stood beside her.

Marian looked into his eyes. Blood yet ran down his jaw to drip upon his shoulder. She reached up, touched his face, felt the warmth of his flesh beneath the beard. Felt the stickiness of blood.

In her heart welled a strange, strong fierceness. *We have come at Merlin's behest,* she said, *not to disrupt, not to dishonor, but to set to rights what has been perverted. England—Britain—must prevail, but she cannot without your aid. Allow us to be the vessels of this aid. Let us have the sword.*

A moment later, the answer was given.

Marian smiled. "I know the way."

His brows arched. "To the grave?"

She gestured. "Look."

She waited for him to see it, to find it, to remark in satisfaction. But he did none of those things. He looked, but was blind.

"Here." She took his hand again, led him to the stone. Beneath a scattering of dirt, encroached upon by groundcover, lay a flat, crude slab of weathered stone half the length of Robin's height.

"This?" he asked. "This is—nothing."

The answer was immediate. "If men knew Arthur slept here, they would come. And if they came, they would undoubtedly expect a monument to the king. But that is not what the women, or Avalon, wished. Only peace. And that they offered Arthur."

He was dubious. "How can you be certain this is his grave? Surely others have died here."

She shrugged. "I can give you no explanation. I just—know." *Because they have told me.*

Robin closed his mouth on his next question and squatted down. He set aside his sword, then leaned forward. One hand went out to the stone, to touch its surface. He ran his fingers over the stone, and stopped. His expression abruptly stilled.

"What is it?" Marian asked.

He traced the stone again, feeling more carefully this time. She saw the pattern: down the length of the stone, then across.

" 'Tis carved here," Robin said. He motioned her to kneel down, then took her hand and pressed it across the stone. "Do you feel it?"

Marian shook her head.

"Wait. . . ." He guided her hand up, then down, then across. "Do you feel it?"

She frowned. "Some kind of carving, I agree. But I cannot make it out."

Robin retrieved his sword from beside the stone and set it atop the pitted surface. And Marian understood.

She said, "Merlin came out of the tree. Out of wood."

Robin nodded. "And this is stone."

With the touch of our blood. She stared at the sword as it lay atop the slab. Then slowly she bent and took it into her hands. Her right she curled around the leather-wrapped grip. Her left she closed upon the blade, closed and closed, then slid it the length of the blade.

"Marian!" His hands were on hers, freeing the sword. He swore under his breath as he saw the blood flow.

"No," she said as he searched hastily for something to stop the blood. "Wait." She reached up, touched the side of his head with its soggy strip of cloth, brought her other hand away. Carefully, she pressed both against the stone. In the wake of her touch, she left bloody handprints.

"Marian." He caught her now, trapped her hands, wrapped around the left the cloth he had cut from his own tunic. She allowed it, watched his eyes as he tended her. In this moment he thought only of her, not of what they wrought atop Arthur's grave.

When he was done, she looked at the stone. "There," she told him.

Robin barely glanced at it, more concerned with her welfare. But when he looked again, his eyes widened.

He stood up abruptly, stiff with shock. Of utter disbelief.

Marian smiled through her tears. "Take it up, Robin. Excalibur was never meant for a woman's hands, any more than Avalon was meant for a man."

But for a long time he stood atop the hill, moonlight bleaching his hair, and did not touch it.

Smiling, Marian rose. In her hands she carried the other sword, the blade that knew its home in the sheath at Robin's hip. She began to walk away, back to the trees cloaking the shoulders of Avalon's crown.

"Marian."

She held her silence. And when he joined her, when he came down the hill to walk beside her through the trees to the shore on the verge of grass, not water, he carried Arthur's sword.

Merlin saw it in their faces as they came up out of the grasslands below the hill. He had seen it many times before, hundreds of years before, in those who served Arthur: the acknowledgment that they were a part of something greater than any man might name, though he could not explain it. Goddess-touched, god-touched, God-touched; the name did not matter. What mattered was that they had, this night, become a part of the tapestry others long before Merlin had begun to weave. A tapestry made of living threads, dyed in the blood of the Sacrifice.

He smiled. The Nazarene, too, had been a Sacrifice.

He waited in silence as they came up to him. Marian carried Robin's sword. The other, the one Merlin himself had been given by the Lady, rested in the hands of a man who would have, had he been born in an earlier time, aided Arthur with all the loyalty in his soul.

As he aided him now.

Merlin smiled. "It is well done."

Robin's expression was solemn. "What would you have of us now?"

"Your part is finished," Merlin answered. "This is for me to do." He took the great sword from Robin, held it almost reverently. "In the morning, you will go back to Sherwood, to the life you have made. I thank you both for your time, and your aid. I promise you this much in recompense, because I have seen it: you will not die for years and years. No one so petty as the Sheriff of Nottingham will cause your deaths; time will take its toll. But where I go now, I go alone."

"To the lake?" Marian asked.

"We could follow you," Robin threatened mildly.

Merlin laughed. "But you are there already."

He turned then, put his back to them, took three steps away from them. Even as he heard each begin to ask what it was he did, he sent the sword spinning into the air. Moonlight sparked and glinted. Not meant to fly, eventually the weapon came down. It struck the ground soundlessly, too far for them to hear.

"Now," Merlin murmured.

Beneath the sword, the earth opened. From it swelled water, bursting free to spill out onto the grasslands between forest and hill. Satisfied, Merlin watched as it ran and ran, as it filled and filled, more rapidly than a man could clearly see, until at last the water stilled. Lapping at his feet were the wavelets of a lake. Rising from the waters, shrouded in mist and moonlight, was the isle of Avalon.

"Lady," Merlin said, "I give it back to you. I give *him* back to you. So both may guard Britain."

After a moment he turned to them both. He marked the pallor of their faces, the stillness of their bodies, the blood upon their flesh. Smiling, he stepped close. He set each hand to the backs of their skulls, and, such as it was in him to do, blessed them both even as he healed their hurts.

Robin said, baffled, "It was on Avalon already."

Merlin nodded. "The women safeguarded it, not knowing it was the Lady who entrusted it to me until Arthur came of age. But it was never of earth. It was for no one to keep, not even the well-intentioned."

"Why us?" Marian asked. "Why not you?"

"In the old ways, a woman ruled. But never alone. She had a Consort. She made the Great Marriage. And it was sealed with blood." He smiled at them both. "The times have changed. No need for the Consort to die, but the blood of the Great Marriage remains sacred. I had none to offer." He saw the frowns in their eyes, the uneasiness with the idea of ancient rituals. "Go home," he said gently. "You have served Britain well. She will not fail for time out of mind."

Tears stood in Marian's eyes. "What about you?"

"The same," he answered. "I go. This is not my time. This is not my place. I belong—elsewhere."

"Where *will* you go?" Robin asked.

Merlin smiled. He indicated a shadow upon the water, stretching out from the island. "They are sending a boat for me."

"But—you said you were not wanted there," Marian said.

"I am tolerated," Merlin answered, "now and again." He looked over their heads at the forest beyond. "Make a bed among the trees. There is an oak grove there that will serve you well—and I promise there are no faces in the trees, nor captive enchanters." He nodded. "Go now."

They were reluctant to leave but did as he bade, slowly walking away. He watched the man reach out for the woman's hand; watched the woman reach out for the man's. Their fingers entwined, then locked, and they walked together toward the trees.

The boat bumped quietly against the shore. Dark shapes were in it, shrouded in such a way he could see no faces. He stepped into the boat, found his balance, nodded. The boat began to move.

Merlin looked back at the shore. In the moonlight he saw them, and then they stepped into darkness, became shadows in the wood.

He turned away and took his seat in the boat. He stripped off the circlet, the ring, and the dragon brooch. Without regret, he tossed them over the side into the water. Payment rendered.

For want of conversation, he said to the wraiths of Avalon, "They will be legend themselves, one day. Just as Arthur is."

Then the mists came down around him as Avalon disappeared, and the Lady took him home.

IN HIS NAME

My mother had learned long ago how to make a mask of her face. She wore it now. I did not know when she might put it off again, unless it be alone in the dark in her chambers where no one might see the truth of what the woman was.

I listened. One always listened to my mother. One knew better than to turn any part of one's attention away from my mother, lest there be punishment for it.

When she had finished explaining what it was she wanted done, what she wanted her daughter to do, the daughter herself felt the cold coils of fear thread themselves through her bowels.

She would win, of course. She always won, my mother. And I would lose. Always.

And Aristobulus? Would he lose as well?

Or would I lose *him?*

My mother's eyes glittered. Long eyes, eloquent eyes, tawny of iris but very black of pupil, engorged and expanding in the pallor of my room gilded ocher and amber and ivory in the light of dying lamps. She wore deep, bloodied wine swathed about her body. As she moved, as she breathed, she clattered of gold and glass.

She breathed fiercely, breasts thrusting against the fabric weighted down by ropes of necklaces. She stood very straight, shoulders thrown back, skull held high on her neck, so that I was put in mind of a spear in place of a woman.

"It will have to be you," she said, as if she wished it otherwise so she could take pleasure of it.

Me. Again, me.

The spear wore a mask; the mask was cold and inhuman, and all too plainly my mother. "It *shall* be you," she declared, and her nostrils flared like a stallion's scenting mare, or challenge. "You will do me this thing."

I had done so many things to please my mother. But Aristobulus . . . *Aristobulus was for me.* To please myself.

My mother had made no objection when the marriage was proposed, but it was less likely that she wanted to please her daughter—who was herself nonetheless pleased—than that she was simply distracted by her own predicament and the politics of the city.

And that predicament—or perhaps I should say its resolution—now depended on me.

"If you want your marriage," my mother said plainly, "you shall help me make mine."

I protested the only way I knew would be construed as flattery, rather than refusal. "You are the most beautiful woman in all of the city. The king himself says so."

My mother studied me closely, examining my phrasing, inflection, and then she smiled. There was little of humor in it; the mask was no longer cold and lifeless but blazed with ferocious focus. "I *was*," she said simply, "and the king is besotted by lust, which somewhat hinders the truth. No. This is for you to do."

"Aristobulus," I blurted, thinking of the shame in what she would have me do.

My mother gestured impatiently. "I will see to it he is not present."

"But—the king. . . ."

"It is for him this shall be done."

No. For *her.* Always for her.

Abrupt epiphany: "This is because of *that man.*"

Her smile slackened, then stretched into a flat, vicious compression of pomaded lips. " 'That man' is nothing to me."

But he was. Why else would she do this?

Why else would she feel the need?

"The king will not change his mind about marrying you," I said. "Not even because of that man who cries out against the marriage."

"The king is the king before he is a man, before he is a bed-mate. Such men can be persuaded by political concerns."

"But—you said yourself he is besotted!"

Her tone was exquisitely dry. "In private, kings are besotted. In public they must be ruthless."

"And magnanimous," I countered. It was why she wanted me to do what she told me to do. In magnanimity he would give her what she wanted, though innocent of her presence behind the asking of it.

My mother laughed deep in her throat. "Indeed, I am *counting* on his magnanimity!"

So she would. She had to.

I shut my eyes. The serpents knotted my bowels.

"Brush your hair," she said. "Do not bind it back. Nothing more is needed. There is enough of me in you, as I was when I was young."

Nothing more needed than courage. Than the guile bred into her bones. But only her bones lived in me. Guile was not my portion.

"He is only a man," I said. "A disaffected scoundrel seeking attention. No one listens to him."

"They listen. The *king* listens."

"No one pays mind to his words."

"Some do. More will. I know it." The eyes in the mask glittered. "You will do this thing."

Had I a choice? Had I ever a choice?

I stared hard at bitten nails.

"Brush your hair," my mother said, "then go to the king and his guests. And when he offers you a gift, say you must think on it, and then return to me."

Desperately I said, "What if he offers no gift?"

"He must. It is his birthday. He would be thought weak and selfish if he did not share his wealth with another on this day of all days."

I looked up from ruined nails. Challenged as much as I could, as much as I had ever dared with this woman. "And if I ask for *me?*"

So cold, so hard a mask. "Then Aristobulus shall be told to find another wife."

And so the challenge was vanquished. Of course. What else? My mother understood that when there was only one thing of importance in a person's life, the promise of its withdrawal can cause even kings to fall.

This king would not. But another man might.

My mother picked up the brush I had set down on the table and put it into my hand. "I will wait for you here."

I did as my mother asked. I went before the king she wished to marry, who wished to marry her; I went before his aides, before his army officers, the great men of the city. And I danced.

For Aristobulus, who was not present. For *me,* who was.

Not for my mother, my dancing, though she would benefit. Not for the king, *this* dance, though the result would be his command. Not for the men who stared with avid eyes; whose breathing quickened even as the dance; whose hands trembled on winecups; whose bodies tautened and swayed in minute echo of my own; whose minds were rapt on the dancing of the daughter of the woman who might become queen.

Who *would* become queen, had she to kill to do it.

And they say men are ruthless, to shape the world as they will.

For Aristobulus, I danced.

The king was pleased. "A fine gift!" he cried as he motioned me to rise from the floor where I ended the dance. "The finest of all gifts: a beautiful young woman dancing homage—and seduction!—before her king!"

Homage, no. Seduction, yes. For Aristobulus. Even for me, that I might yet be his wife.

Around the room, as I rose, white teeth gleamed in dark faces. I shut out the words, the murmurs; shut out all but the king himself, to whom I went as he gestured me forward.

"Indeed, a fine gift. And so I shall offer *you* one: Ask, and it shall be yours." Now his teeth gleamed as well. "Even if it be half of my kingdom, ask and it shall be yours. I vow it so, here before the others!"

Aristobulus, I told him silently. He is worth half a kingdom.

But I said nothing of that. I blushed, as the king expected, as my mother no doubt anticipated. And it made him more generous yet.

"Ask!" the king cried. "Be not shy. You are deserving of a great gift. But if it would please you better, go and think upon it. Come back when you are certain."

It was dismissal. There were other concerns for him to attend, and my time was done.

For now. Until the woman told me what she wanted of the man, what I must ask because he offered me even so much as half a kingdom, and would not stint the request.

I returned to my mother.

She was, as expected, pleased by my success. Behind the mask long eyes gleamed. She examined me critically: marked the sheen of sweat on my body; the shrouding of the fabric drawn close by the humidity of my flesh; the wilderness of my hair, left free of adornment or binding. At her request.

"Yes," she said finally. "It was a wise choice. Only you might have accomplished it; I am an aging woman, and my flesh shows the marks of my children."

So would mine show the marks of my own. Aristobulus' children.

My mother smiled. "Change nothing," she said. "Go as you are now, so he will be no less enamored. And tell him what you desire, that I shall tell you now."

What I desired? Half of his kingdom, that Aristobulus might rule—and I as his queen.

But of course that was not what my mother desired. She desired to marry the man who already ruled a kingdom, and I was not the woman she wished to be its queen.

"Go," she said, "and tell the great king *this*."

I listened as she told me. The serpents writhed in my bowels. Despite the sweat on my flesh, I shivered as she spoke.

"Ask it," she said. "He will not deny it to you."

What pleasure I had offered would be vanquished by what I asked. But she would not suffer for it. It mattered little to her that *I* lost favor; I was dispensable.

My mother picked up from my table the tray that had held my meager collection of cosmetics and perfumes. She pressed it into my hands. "Do not fail me in this, or you fail yourself."

And Aristobulus.

I nodded. I left her.

Before the king, before them all, I put down the tray on the tile. And I asked, as my mother had bid me. I used her words, her inflections, even her mask. Before the palace aides, before the army officers, before the great men of the city, I asked the king for my gift.

It was not half a kingdom. But by the color of his face, by the recoil in his eyes, he would have been more content to divide what he ruled than to give me what I requested.

The room fell into the kind of silence that is loud in implication, filled up by the cacophony of busy thoughts, of acknowledged repercussions. I had created this silence, and it cramped my ears now as well as my bowels.

"So," he said, sounding less a great king than a weary man. "So, you will have this of me."

The mask—her mask?—sat tautly on my face. "If it be within your power." That, too, she had told me to say. It was blatant challenge.

Color rushed back to his face. "Oh, I think so. I do indeed think so, as my armies have made it so." He flicked a glance at the men: officers of the armies who secured his kingdom, and the rich men of the city who funded his wars.

I wanted very much to shred a fingernail, but there were none of them left to chew. Instead I pressed my trembling fingers against the fabric of my clothing, drying now to my body.

"Very well," he said. "I have promised you." He turned to a soldier-bodyguard and murmured to him. The man bowed, took up the tray from the floor, and left the hall. The king turned back to me. "It shall be done," he said, "as you have asked it."

To a person in fear, to a person in dread, to a person who suffers there is no measurement of time. Time simply exists, passes, divides itself into various fragments of days, portions of the nights. To maintain the mask I had borrowed I counted the fragments and portions, until at last I heard the sibilants of many men remarking, in varying degrees of shock, distaste, and pleasure, on the return of the soldier.

Pleasure, yes. For some of them. This was a political thing.

My mother had said it: *"In public they must be ruthless."*

135

Now I was ruthless.

"He can be persuaded by political concerns."

Now I was political.

For Aristobulus.

The king motioned the soldier forward, to me. He brought me the weighted tray, set it into my hands, stepped away from me.

The king said, "You have what you wanted."

No, I said in my head, I have what *she* wanted.

"Go," the king bid me. "Do as you will with it."

I knew what I would do. I knew what I *had* to do. For Aristobulus.

Before me, in my room, my mother's mask cracked. She saw the gift I had asked—the gift *she* had asked—and shattered the mask of her face.

Or perhaps I had stolen it for myself; my face was stiff and cold, remote from any emotion.

"So!" she said. "There shall be no impediment now! Phillip's widow shall be permitted to marry Phillip's brother!"

No one would speak of that now. Not *now*. They would speak of something else. They would speak instead of me: of what I had asked the king, of what he had given me in the name of a dance.

The deed was and would be mine. Forever. They would forget even my mother's name, who had wrought this for herself.

She saw me trembling, and laughed. She took the tray from my shaking hands and lifted it high in the air. And she danced, did my mother, though with little of grace or beauty while holding so high a tray and taking infinite care it did not spill its grisly bounty.

Droplets flew, but did not besmirch her. No blood on her hands, ever. Only on mine.

I looked at them now, empty. Bitten nails, bloodied. Awkward hands, bloodied. Clothing sodden with it.

My mother laughed and danced. Her name would be forgotten. Mine—and his—would not.

Salomé. And John, called Baptist.

I bit deeply into my lip. *For Aristobulus.*

A Wolf Upon the Wind

"—bitch-begotten whore—"

She had bitten him, bitten him hard, catching his bottom lip within her teeth; and now blood painted his chin, was channeled by saffron-hued beard into crimson ribbons that streamed against soiled tunic. He spat more ribbons, more blood aside, then smiled grimly and spat it also into her face.

She did not know why a man was honored for defending his life, while she was called names as she defended hers. Or why a man was granted a clean death, a warrior's death, taken up to Odin's Valhalla, while a woman, equally victim, was degraded. Abused. And killed without honor, or died of *dis*honor, because the body gave up hope.

She would not, and did not—and so he was forced to take it from her: her body, and thus her life.

Bitch-begotten whore, he said—because she was *not* a whore, and therefore fought to preserve that which another honored: virginity, modesty, a quiet demeanor. But he took all from her, this man, this warrior; raped her soul as well as her body, and the demeanor others honored was now vilified because she sought to change it, to preserve what had been hers, was *meant* to be hers, until she chose otherwise.

First with himself. Then with his ax hilt.

"Bitch-begotten whore."

What did he think she should do? Let him do as he would without protest?

Permit him to do such as *this?*

He bore wounds of her now, though she doubted any would scar. Bitten lip, clawed face, before the nails broke, before her fingers were crushed. Before teeth and jaw were shattered with a single great blow of his hand.

So much broken, now. Inside and out.

He used her again, slick now with her blood as much as spilled seed. And complained of her, that she no longer fit. But that was his fault, too; the ax handle had torn her.

Little time left. No glory, she thought; no battlefield song of a warrior's honorable death. Just—*death*. Without glory, honor, song. A woman, apparently, merited none.

No Valhalla for *her*. No Valkyrie come down from the heavens to carry her from the field. There was no provision for slain women in the honor of Odin's hall.

No hope either, now, for reparation. Revenge.

She gave nothing. He took it. Took it all, including her life.

"Bitch-begotten whore."

The last words she heard.

Vision was a red haze of sunset, of blood. He squinted, blinked, twitched his head in a tiny, wayward motion meant to rid his eyes of the veil so he might see again. There was much to see, he knew: the battle was ended. There was a victor, and also a vanquished.

He was uncertain which he was.

By the hand of Tyr, god of war, had he lost? Had he won? *Was* he lost?

To either side, he might be lost. Might be dead. How they counted him, lost or won, was wholly dependent on which side was victor. He did not know himself.

Wind howled down the field, whipping a frenzy among the dead, for what rode upon the wind was a vanguard of beasts and steeds come down to collect the souls. The living saw nothing save the remains of the battle, the aftermath of war.

He felt it then, felt the wind, heard its song, saw the vanguard stoop out of the darkening sky, riding friezes of lowering clouds. A Brisingamen of beasts strung like monstrous ornaments torn from Freya's throat, adornment for the dead.

Ah. He *was* dead, then. Or dying.

His old name was as dead. He bore a new one, now: *einheriar*. A warrior dead in battle, bound for Valhalla.

He felt no pain, neither of body nor soul. There was glory in life, glory in battle, glory in death. He would go to Valhalla, bow to Odin, eat of the great boar, Saehrimnir, roasted by Andhrimnir, Odin's own cook; and drink of the mead from out of Heidrun's teats, Odin's sacred goat—and he would never be alone, never lack a woman. Never truly be dead within the hall of Odin.

A red haze, a smear against his eyes, bloodying the world. It obscured his vision of those who came to claim him, to gather up fallen heroes. He heard them still, fleet steeds and panting beasts; felt it still, wild wind wailing down the field. And welcomed them all, for he knew what rode them.

Valhalla, and Valkyrie.

She came down then, upon a storm-gray wolf. Was it Freki? Geri? Was it one of Odin's pets come to honor him? He saw its amber eyes, slitted as if it laughed; saw its perfect teeth in a snarl that was also leer. And the woman upon it.

Flags of wheat-gold hair whipped back in the haste of her journey. She was made of the songs they sang over mead, the glories told of *Valkyrien* over roasted boar. A woman for each of them, claimed the warriors; as many as could be had by an inexhaustible man, for what was Valhalla but perfection in a male, and reward for an *einheriar*'s valor? Warm hall, fresh mead, well-tended boar, and women for every warrior.

Oh, by one-eyed Odin, death was no distress. Not when it promised *this.*

He would have stood for her, but the ax blow had shattered a leg. Would have sat for her, save ribs were splintered to fragments. Would have bowed his head to her, but for the hole where his throat had been.

None of it mattered, now. She was as he had been promised, as they each of them had been promised, and his foretold future was infinitely preferable to his painful present.

Fierce maiden, fierce smile, baring perfect teeth in a leer that matched the wolf's. Hair settled now from her ride, whipped no more by the wild wind. She wore a cloak of it; as she bent to him it spilled down over shoulders to drift across his face, to mingle with his beard. He feared his blood would sully it.

She saw it in his eyes: distress that he would soil her. And laughed. Nothing of him could soil her, nothing of blood, of viscera, of the produce of battle. She was one of Tyr's blessed maidens, and thus inviolable.

"Einheriar," she said, "will you come with me?"

At her voice, the wind rose. The wolf—Freki? Geri?—shook storm-hued pelt, and panted.

When he spoke, no voice issued; he had nothing left of his throat save a sliver of bloodied bone. But she heard him. Knew the words: *indeed, come,* and *gladly.*

"Then come," she said, and put out her slim, strong hand.

His body trembled. Fingertips barely touched. Behind her, the wolf growled.

"Come," she said, impatient. "Are you not worthy of Valhalla?"

How *dared* she question it?

Fingertips touched. Clawed. With effort, he gripped her hand. With no effort, she gripped his.

"What are you?" she asked. "Hero?"

141

Einheriar! Had he not died in Tyr's name? How could he be other?

His turn for impatience. Still the wolf growled.

"More," she said. "Oh, indeed, more than hero—or less. I think you are not worthy to be hosted in Odin's hall."

Fury kindled.—*bitch-begotten whore*—

The Valkyrie bared perfect teeth. Lightnings were in her eyes, and thunder in her laughter. "This is what I am. Now see what I *was*, when you were done with me."

And there was nothing of beauty in her, nothing at all save the truth he had made himself in the woman he had killed: flattened nose, shattered teeth, broken jaw unhinged. And ax-born blood flowing down her thighs to mingle with his own.

He knew her then, *knew* her, and wept with fear.

She bent to his torn ear. "You gave me to Tyr," she said. "Now I send you to Hel."

A Compromised Christmas

"Jane," he said. Then, when she did not answer; when she did no more then go on walking as if she didn't hear him, or as if she chose *not* to hear him (though that wasn't Janeish at all), more emphatically: "*Jane!*"

And Jane turned, clearly startled, dark brown hair curling this way and that in the thin, constant drizzle—a "soft day," she'd called it happily, claiming it was an Irish saying (and wasn't he sick of hearing of Irish this and Welsh that; and now Scotland, to boot)—and stared at him in surprise, as if it did not occur to her that *he* did not care for the drizzle, the day, and most particularly their destination.

"What is it?" Jane asked, pausing long enough in her single-minded striding for him to catch up.

And then he felt ashamed, because despite the cold-born blush in her cheeks and the bluish-pink hue of her nose, she was patently unconcerned about the miserable weather conditions. In fact, he thought suspiciously, she appeared to *glory* in them.

"Jane," he said more gently, not meaning to squash her spirit, "honeymooners *are* supposed to walk as a couple. You know, like in the cruise and resort commercials: hand-in-hand in the sunset against a tropical backdrop." In fact, he wanted nothing more just now than to *be* on one of those cruise ships in the Caribbean somewhere—even in the Bermuda Triangle, for Crissake!—if it meant they might be warm and dry instead of

143

cold and damp.

But Jane had picked Scotland.

In December.

On Christmas Eve.

Jane laughed, expelling a rush of vapor like a dragon blowing smoke; in fact, he harbored suspicions that she had practiced for that very reason. "Oh, Joe, I'm sorry. Am I neglecting you?"

Yes, of course she was. She had struck out along the track like an Amazon—or whatever such a woman might be called in Scotland; he doubted it was an Amazon; weren't they Greek, or something?

He laughed a little himself, dismayed to hear how hollow it sounded; he didn't really want to mimic a pettish child. "It's only I'm not as fit as you," he told her, sending forth his own plume of dragon's breath. "I lead a pretty sedentary lifestyle, after all . . . writing ads doesn't prepare you for hiking into the wilds of Scotland."

Jane blinked. "The wilds? This? The road is right *there.*"

And so it was: a two-lane blacktopped road all of four or five feet away. So close, in fact, he might have suggested they at least walk on level asphalt to improve their footing rather than beat their way through a thin trickle of track hedged by tangled strawberry and blackberry bushes. In fact, he *had* suggested they rent a car in Inverness, but Jane had wanted the bus; now they had forsaken even that for foot-power.

So, no, he supposed it wasn't really the "wilds," not *truly* the "wilds," but it was close enough for him. "Jane—"

But she cut him off by stepping close, very close, and made him temporarily uncognizant of the damp, the day, the destination, by kissing him.

Joe kissed her back, thinking inconsequentially of Judy Garland and ruby slippers; if he tapped his booted heels together, would Scotland go the way of the Emerald City? (Please?)

No. Scotland remained. So did he.

Jane punched him lightly. "It's not so bad. This is not Glencoe, after all, and I'm not making you climb the Devil's Stair. This is only a bit of a stroll—"

"A *stroll!*"

The light died out of her face. "Oh, Joe, it's really not that much farther."

A single step more was altogether too far for his peace of mind. But he had humored Jane, compromising, giving in to her crazy dream of honeymooning in Scotland, even though *he'd* wanted the Caribbean cruise, or maybe Hawaii—

"It's so beautiful," Jane said. "Just look around, Joe."

It was cold, and damp, and depressing. He was a man for sidewalks and multilevel parking garages and skyscrapers without a thirteenth floor—even if there really *was* a thirteenth floor and they just called it something else.

Scotland was Jane's idea. December had been his, and Christmas, *before* he'd known about Scotland. "Jane—"

Gray eyes were bright and hopeful. "Don't you think it's romantic? The air fairly *reeks* of romance!"

The air reeked of a rain that lacked the odors of oil, gasoline, human waste; lacked what he was used to. He smelled dirt and stone and tree. It was not an aroma he knew; it was *certainly* not an odor he equated with romance.

But romance had brought them here; he did love Jane.

Joe smiled. "I suppose."

She caught his gloved hand in her mittened one, tugging him close to her side. "It's not so much farther," she said. "I promise."

"We can't stay long," he warned. "I don't want to miss the last bus back to Drumroll."

Jane's laughed kited joyously. "Drumnadrochit!" she cried. "Not Drumroll, or Drummer Boy—just Drum-na-drock-it. And I don't care if we *do* miss the bus; we'll just walk back."

He'd been afraid she'd say that. "One-way on foot is enough, Jane. We can climb all over your castle if you insist, but I want to *ride* back to town."

She arched a dark brow. "And all the way back to Inverness?"

"My God, yes! I don't want to walk to *Inverness.*"

Jane laughed and tugged him along. "No, no—I don't want to walk that far, either. I only meant you sounded as if you're sorry you're here at all."

Well, yes. In a way. "I know you've always wanted to come to the British Isles, sweetheart, but there is such a season as summer even in Scotland." He grimaced. "I think."

Jane shook her head decisively. "That's when all the tourists come."

"Possibly because they don't like the cold and wet any more than I," he chided gently. "I'm a warm-blooded mammal, after all—"

"And so am *I,* but this isn't so bad!" She pulled him along without respite. "For heaven's sake, you're swathed in layers of wool and down . . . it must be like a sauna in there." She snagged his parka zipper and made as if to pull. "Let me see—"

He caught her hand and grasped it, squeezing her fingers into immobility. "No. I don't want to be any colder than I already am."

"This isn't the North Pole, Joe. It's not *that* cold. And the drizzle's not much more than a mist."

"Do you know that in Australia right now it's summer?"

She laughed. "Yes. But why do what's easy? I wanted a honeymoon I could remember forever."

"I'd remember Australia," Joe said. *And the Caribbean. Hawaii. Any number of warmer places.*

"I didn't want to do what everyone else does. You know—like a cruise." Jane grimaced, bending blackberry out of her path. "Those sorts of things always seemed so *sterile,* somehow."

Joe thought she might have selected another descriptive word and gotten her point across as effectively. "I know lots of people who have had perfectly good honeymoons on board a cruise ship."

"Any of them still married?"

"Well—" He sighed. "No."

Jane laughed. "You see? Scotland is good for the soul."

"I doubt Scotland has anything to do with whether a marriage survives."

"No," Jane agreed. "That has to do with making compromises." She cast him an eloquent smile. "I know you didn't want to come here, Joe. Thanks for humoring me."

And so she made it all right without effort, which eased him a little in the matter of his annoyance. The stress of writing ad copy to deadline for multimillion dollar accounts didn't leave much room for compromise. Jane seemed to understand it. She made life easier.

He pulled her close, kissed her ear through tangled damp hair—Jane had left off her woolen hat (so the clean Scottish air would clear the city fog from her head, she'd said)—and told her he loved her.

"Me, too," she said, predictably; but it was a comfortable predictability. Then, "There! You see? Urquhart Castle!"

Ur-cut, she called it; not the Ur-cue-heart *he'd* called it the first time, when he'd seen the name in print; when he'd looked up in a travel book just where Drummer Boy was and the castle on the loch. Not *lock*—lochhh, with a breathy gargle in the throat. Or so Jane said. She had an ear for such things.

He had an ear for a jingle, a catchphrase, a *hook;* Captain Hook, they called him, in the early days before imminent burnout sent him running away from long-legged blondes in sleek, burnished sports cars to a serene, uncomplicated young woman who worked contentedly in a library and read historical and fantasy novels in her spare time.

Jane was—*different;* that's what his friends told him, verging on condescension, touching on implication without committing themselves. And she was, and he loved her for it; he knew that, for her, *he* was different. And so she had, in her very Janeish way, undertaken to overhaul his spirit, to restore his equilibrium and his priorities in life.

In *Scotland,* of all places!

Urquhart Castle, perched on the edge of a loch: piles of brickwork, a tower, a few open-air rooms, some grass-swathed mounds. As castles went, he supposed it was better than most, because much of it remained fairly intact; or so Jane had read out of a guidebook. Very romantic indeed, if your idea of romance was huddling up in goosedown, nylon, and wool, wishing for a ceramic heater—except at Urquhart, in Scotland, there were no outlets, and he didn't have his converter, either. It was back in the hotel in Inverness.

A muffled motorized roar behind Joe caused him to swing around in his tracks. "The bus!"

Jane spared it a passing glance. "So it is. But we're not even there yet, and I want to spend some time soaking up the atmosphere. . . . We'll just walk back to Drumnadrochit later."

Atmosphere. Joe sighed. He envisioned himself in a warm, packed pub swilling stout with the natives, or maybe Glenfiddich or maybe even plain old brandy; *something* to warm his bones!

The bus crept on by them, turned off the blacktop onto the gravel next to the entrance gate, and waited.

Bastard, Joe thought. *He'll wait long enough to tease me, then roar off just as I make up my mind.*

Oblivious to the bus, Jane dragged him on through the untenanted gate—no fee due in December; Joe decided not even the Scots were foolish enough to hang about waiting for romantic-minded Americans (on Christmas Eve–day, no less!)—and down the gravel pathway toward the stone piles of Urquhart Castle. Joe could not believe anyone ever actually *lived* in such a place, but he supposed at one point in time there were roofs over the rooms, and fires, and lots of wool kilts and plaids and sheep. Anything to cut the chill.

"Scotch," he muttered. "This is why they invented it."

"Come *on,* Joe!" Jane urged him into a faster walk. "You say you're not in shape—well, this is a way to get *into* shape!"

"Climbing around a pile of old rocks?"

"Joe." Jane swung to face him. He stopped short even as she did, so as not to step on her boots. "Joe, you're an advertising copywriter. You sell *dreams,*" Jane said earnestly. "Can't you see what this is all about?" She thrust out an encompassing hand. "This is history, Joe. It's a million miles away from yours or mine, but it belongs to real people, people who lived and died protecting this loch. *Look* at it, Joe. Can't you imagine the walls whole again, and the roofs? Can't you make believe the people live again inside these walls, looking eastward across the loch for the Christmas Star?"

"No one was here when the Christmas Star appeared—*if* it appeared; there's some doubt as to that—"

Jane cut him off. "I didn't mean at *that moment,* Joe. I meant other people like you and me, just starting out, standing here on the banks of the loch painting pictures against the sky—"

Joe grinned, hooking an arm around Jane's shoulders. "I'm just an old fuddy-duddy who's cold and wet and thinking about taking you to bed instead of climbing all over a ruined castle."

"Castle first, bed later."

He arched eloquent brows. "Makes a man wonder about his

place in your scheme of things."

"My scheme of things is perfectly normal," Jane retorted. "Since you're no' a braw, bonny Scot wi' naught bu' a kilt o'er his ballocks—" She grinned as he winced, dropping the thick Highland burr. "—I doubt you're much interested in stripping down here in the wet grass during a cold Scottish sunset."

"No," he conceded, shivering.

"Then we'll do the castle first, bed later." And she was off like a dog just let free of the lead, darting to the tower. "Joe— come *on.*"

Dutifully he came on, just as the bus behind began its laborious about-face on its return to Drumnadrochit.

"Bastard," Joe muttered.

Eventually, Jane gave in to his pleas to stop investigating each and every single stone—all of which Joe said were absolutely identical and therefore not worthy of her continued scrutiny— and sat down with him on a wooden bench (not a relic of Urquhart's era, but a modern convenience placed there for tourists; Jane disliked the anachronism) to stare across the loch.

Jane sighed and leaned close. "All it wants is a clansman on the hill piping down the sun. Maybe 'Amazing Grace' or an old Christmas song. A Gaelic Christmas carol."

"All *I* want is a warm bed, my wife in it, and a lock upon the door." The drizzle (mist?) had at last let up, but the temperature was no warmer; in fact, Joe was convinced it was colder than ever. "We could freeze out here."

Jane snuggled a little closer. "No. Not really." Her head tilted against his shoulder; rain-curled hair tickled his cheek. "We'll start back soon; the walk will warm us up."

"Then let's go ahead and—"

"Not yet. A little longer."

"I'm getting hungry, Jane."

"There are crackers in my pocket." But she didn't move to fish them out. She stared across the rippling waters of the loch, gray as her eyes. "I feel it in my bones. History, Joe. I can almost hear the cannon fired to fend off invaders there in the loch—"

"What about me?" He set his lips against her ear. "Hear this?"

Jane stiffened. "*Joe.*"

It was neither a shout, nor a cry, nor a blurt of shock. What it was, he decided, was a whisper of sheer fascination. *If I could get that tone across in an ad—*

"Joe, *look.*"

Joe looked. And laughed; but softly, so as not to hurt her feelings. "It's just a log, or marsh gas."

"I don't think s—"

"Come on, Jane, you can't expect me to believe that *we'd* see Nessie when all those scientists never could track her—*it*—down."

"Joe—"

"You spent too much time at the Monster Museum, Jane."

"*Shut up, Joe!* Just look!"

He shut up. And looked.

Marsh gas. What else?

Jane's breath was audible: a long, low sigh of infinite wonder and satisfaction.

No, Joe declared to the Inner Hairy Man. *I'm not seeing ANY of this.*

But he was. He just *was,* despite his disbelief, despite his skepticism, despite evidence to the contrary; far more evidence against than there was *for;* after all, there was no such thing as a Loch Ness Monster.

Jane whispered his name. Joe didn't answer.

It was a long, slow, seductive roll, a displacement in the water; paler gleam of pale winter sun on loch-painted scales, dozens

151

and dozens of scales, glistening like crystals, like diamonds, like black Australian opal. Water ran from a glossy pearlescent hide (skin? coat?) as it lifted itself to the surface: undulant spine (spine?) and a condescension of snout. It (he? she?) blew water from delicate flaring nostrils as Jane had blown dragon breath, then broke the surface with more than snout, feeding into the sunset a long, fluted head, then burgundy-colored throat, then the swell of serpent shoulders clad in filmy pewter-hued gauze, a gossamer web spun between the delicate birdlike bones that unfurled from against the body to catch the setting sun. It was sea-horse, dinosaur, dragon, a kraken of Loch Ness, rising like a whale to taste the death of the day.

I don't believe th—

Expelling spray and wind, the monster turned and blew eastward a mournful, eerie call (a winding horn? the belly-deep moan of a lion announcing the commencement of evening?) on the pale, fading edges of a day transmuting itself to dusk.

An elegant beast—and then Joe shook himself, laughing silently; to append such a term to a *monster!* "Here be dragons," he muttered, voicing the warnings on ancient maps.

The sun dipped low in the west. In the east, against deepening dusk, a new light was born, as if dawn came too quickly. A single point of light far brighter than manmade illumination, or a trick of the sun off metal. And a brief, brilliant burst as if it spent itself too quickly, then paled away into smoke. Only the burned edges of light danced in the corners of Joe's vision.

The beast-call came again. Then the ribbed gossamer webbing folded itself against damp-dappled scales and the massive serpent body slid beneath still gray waters.

"Jesus Christ," Joe whispered.

Tears shone in Jane's eyes. "I think—that was the point."

"Jane—" But he broke it off. For the first time in his life there were no words in his mouth, to disparage or deny; to condescend with glibness. There was only a terrible wonder, a consuming comprehension that he had witnessed—magic? Or maybe miracle.

From the hill behind them, hard by Urquhart Castle on the shores of Loch Ness, came the faint drone and wail of bagpipes played very softly, like the low moaning tribute of loch-beast to Christmas Star.

Joe didn't turn to look. To do so doubted the moment, and that he would not risk.

His wife leaned harder against him. "Merry Christmas," she whispered.

Of Honor and the Lion

I swear, I have never been so weary . . . of fighting, of killing, of running, of walking; even, I think, of living. But I do not dare do otherwise; dying serves nothing, and no one, and I have made promises.

One foot . . . one foot, step by step . . . one foot in front of the other . . . keep walking . . . keep running—stop for nothing and no one, not even the child you carry—

I squeezed my eyes tight-shut. If only I could rest—

But I knew better.

I had known better all along, but still I ignored it, foolishly hoping and praying that for once, if only for once, *he would be man instead of Mujhar.*

Aloud, I told the child, "I should have known better."

It kicked; did it agree? I clutched helplessly at my belly.

"Not yet," I panted, tasting the dust of the road. "Wait you only a little—at least till we reach Mujhara . . . until we see the Lion. . . ."

I

The wolfhound bitch, asprawl on a rug near the firepit, wearily suckled nine squalling pups. Her ghost-gray mate paced the length of the hall to the marble dais, toenails clicking, tree-limb tail swinging. A man was seated there; more than a man, a king, embraced by the cavernous throne. He watched me, saying nothing. Absently fondling the wolfhound's ears, waiting for what I would say.

And so I said it: "No."

He stared, fingers arrested. Then he pushed the wolfhound away to give me his full attention.

"No," I said again.

Still he stared, gray eyes glittering. I have seen that look before; he meant me to give in. Often, too often, I did. This time I would not.

He sat very quietly in the throne all acrouch upon the dais. The Lion, Hale called it: the Lion Throne of Homana. My father was Mujhar. Worshiped by his subjects, served by the Cheysuli. By one in particular: Hale, liege man. Who, whenever he chooses, wears the guise of a fox.

So quietly he sat within the Lion's embrace, nothing at all astir, save gray, glittering eyes. Not the feral yellow of Hale's; my father is Homanan. He claims no Cheysuli blood.

Neither does his daughter. All she claims is a Cheysuli, who heats her Homanan blood.

Moving not at all, until he spoke my name. In a tone of subtle command, expecting me to give in as so many others give in, knowing nothing else but perfect service to the Mujhar.

"*Lindir,*" he said.

Now I shook my head.

He moved then, but slightly, shifting forward a little, as if he feared the Lion's mouth, obscenely agape above his head, would somehow swallow my words, warping the substance of what I said, meaning something else.

He would come to know I did not.

Candlelight glittered off gemstones and gold. It weighted fingers, banded brow, stretched from shoulder to shoulder. He had adorned himself for the feast at which he had planned to make the announcement.

Now I stole the chance, tarnishing pride with my defiance.

"You will," he told me gently. "The arrangements have been made."

"*Un*make them," I said. "I will not marry him."

There, the words were said. And plainly, he thought me mad. All he could do was gape, mimicking the Lion. Unattractive on my father; his flesh was made for better things.

Color congested his face. Slowly, but it came, creeping in, ignoring his rank, shapechanging paternal sanguinity into sanguinary red.

His voice now was thickened, lacking customary timbre. "You are a term of the accord."

"I was never asked if I *wanted* to be a term."

Patent astonishment: "Why should you be asked?"

It was all I could do not to shout at him, though unsurprised by his reaction. And half expecting it; kings and fathers are accustomed to obedience in their children. Certainly mine was; I had always given it freely. But this time I could not.

Quietly, carefully, I drew in a breath, and answered. "Because I am not a cow, to be bred for milk at her owner's pleasure. I am not a mare, matched to the fastest stallion to produce fleeter offspring." I glanced briefly at the wolfhound bitch, sprawled on the rug with her pups. Then met his stare again, matching its intensity; I have my father's eyes. "Neither am I a bitch, suckling puppies twice a year whether I want to or not, having no choice in the matter." I lifted my head a little. "I am a woman . . . I am *Lindir.* I will not be anything else. Less *or* more."

Now he sat back in the Lion. I had, all unknowing, given him a weapon. And now he would use it. "Ah, but you *are* more," he said. "You are Lindir of Homana, daughter to Shaine the Mujhar. It gives you value, my girl, whether you like it or not."

The taste was sour on my tongue. "Value," I said in disgust. "Is that how I am judged?"

"Aye," he answered softly. "For the blood in your veins, my girl, and the children you will bear."

Frankness, at least; no more prevarication. The truth was disconcerting, though not really a surprise. It was just that my father had never said such before, to me, couching his words in kindness and courtesy, avoiding things of substance.

"So," I said in bitterness, "when you did not get a son on my mother, you decided to use me. One day, some day, when I was grown . . . is that why you have not let me marry before now?" I fought down rising anger. It was not because I had not wed before now, but because of the requisites that govern girls of royal birth. "Men have asked, I know: princes, and kings for their sons. As you say, I am Shaine's daughter . . . surely *someone* wanted me."

"Ellas, Erinn, and Caledon," he agreed, naming kingdoms. "And I said no to all of them, saving you for something more."

The word was ash in my mouth. "Solinde," I said flatly, naming another kingdom.

"Ellic," he confirmed. "Bellam's only son, and heir to everything."

Loss of control would accomplish nothing. I bit back frustration and helplessness, taking solace in secret knowledge. I had a weapon, too, thought I hoped I would not be forced to use it.

"Did Bellam ask? Or did you offer?" I paused. "Who *made* me one of the terms?"

"It is often done," he said. "Sons and daughters are wed to insure alliances."

So, he had offered; it did make a difference. To my actions, as well as my pride. Quietly, I said, "I have always been an obedient daughter—"

"Until now."

"—until now." I drew in a breath for patience. "But as it is I who am most inconvenienced by this marriage, I think—"

157

"*I* think you are a spoiled, selfish bitch."

It stopped me short with its brutal bluntness, as he meant it to. Shocked into silence, all I could do was stare. He had never spoken so to me, *never,* only to those who crossed him, who threatened pride and authority; both were absolute. Too stunned to breathe, to speak, to cry, I stood completely still. Feeling my flesh turn cold. Knowing I would lose.

My father rose. He stood before the Lion, weighted with gold and gems and the manifest power of king. He explained to me my place, then cruelly put me in it.

"Ellic of Solinde," he began coldly, "is of an age with you, which is more than most girls get when war plays matchmaker. He is battle-proved. He is sound of limb and soul. He has six bastards to credit his manhood." Behind the line of graying dark beard, I could see the set of his mouth. Hard and cold and unyielding. "He is all of that, Lindir, as well as heir to the throne of Solinde. And you *will* be his queen."

I threw his pride back at him. "He is the son of the enemy!"

"Solinde and Homana are at peace." His tone was deceptively gentle. "No more are we enemies, Lindir, after centuries of warfare. A peace has been made at last . . . *and* you *are one of the terms!*"

He might as well have been the Lion, the roar reverberated so. As before, I could only stare. My lips were very dry, but I did not dare to wet them.

His shout had dissipated. He spoke very softly again, but with no less intensity. "I have given you everything, and you have taken freely. Now it is your turn to give."

I hated myself for crying. More than I hated him. But not as I hated Ellic. "I do not desire to wed him—"

"—no more than he, you," he told me curtly. "Ah, I see you are shocked." Briefly, he smiled. "Thinking only of yourself, Lindir, you neglected to think of Ellic. He wants this marriage no more than you. He has been suckled on war just as you have, and on hatred for the enemy; his has been Homana. Do you expect Bellam's Solindish son to desire Shaine's Homanan daughter any more than she desires him?" He shook his head slowly. "He is as bound as you are, but he understands his duty. He will bear his burden."

I struggled to speak clearly, knowing anger or tears or desperation would make him ashamed of me. A man ashamed of his daughter will turn away, not listen. "And I Ellic's children?"

His mouth was very taut. "More than your mother bore me."

It was, I knew, a bone of contention between them, and had been for years. No son for Homana, only a single daughter. And she was not enough. The Lion demanded a male.

I drew in a very deep breath. "Have I no say at all?"

"You have had it already." Then his tone softened. "Lindir, surely you understand—I must have an heir. Your mother will bear me none; the Lion is dry of sons." His expression, too, had softened. I saw appeal in it now. He wanted understanding. He desired my compassion for the man who had no sons. "Bear Ellic two sons, or even three, then give one of them to me. Give one of them to the Lion; Homana has need of a prince."

I looked him straight in the eye. I summoned all my strength, all my control; hid away humiliation. "Do you want me to beg?" I asked.

It shocked him deeply. It stripped away all his magnificence and left him with death mask and shroud.

And then, abruptly, *alive,* he came down from the Lion, down from the dais, and caught me, grasping my arms, holding me tightly, gripping with all his strength.

"You will beg for nothing!" he cried. "Nothing. Never. From no one. Do you hear? Do you hear? You are my daughter, *my daughter,* the flesh and blood of kings and queens—" He broke it off abruptly, as stunned as I was by his vehemence, but it did not stop him. Not entirely. He took his hands from me only; held me in place with ferocious pride. "You will beg for *nothing.*"

Numbly, I nodded. "I understand, my lord."

He heard what he expected, what I intended him to hear, nothing more. Nothing of what I felt. "Then I dismiss you, Lindir, to your chambers, where you may be attired as befits a princess on her betrothal day." He smiled, tracing back from my face a fallen strand of rose-gold hair. "Ellic will be astounded."

I took my leave and departed. Behind me, he spoke to the wolfhound. More gently than to me.

The child was heavy within me. Uneasily, it shifted, disturbed by my activity, my bid for a final rescue. Nothing else was left. No one else was left, save the man who was my father; who was death as well as life, offering both in abundance.

The child. Always the child, once nothing more than a word, now the future of a realm, the future of a race, and neither of them the same.

Kicking, twisting, shifting, protesting my exertions. I hugged my swollen belly, trying to soothe the child, promising relief, bribing it with lies.

All in the name of pride. In the name of injured honor.

I nearly laughed aloud, still hugging my too-large belly. "Pride," I said to the child. "Pride and honor. More powerful than magic— more enduring than love—more destructive than weapons . . . and I think they will kill us both."

In answer, the child kicked. It nearly brought me down. I laughed raggedly, wiped sweat out of my eyes, considered what they would say; the heir of the Lion brought into the world in the heat and dust of the road? No, it would not do.

Gods, but my back hurt. "Not so far," I told it gently, stroking my squirming belly. "I promise, not so far . . . you have only to wait a little."

But it had waited nine months. Now it demanded freedom.

If I died, the child died. If it died, Homana died. Homana and the Cheysuli.

I staggered down the road, making promises to the child. Promises to a dead man: I will give the Lion a child.

II

In my chambers, where my father had sent me, I dismissed the women who had come to dress me as befits a princess. Startled, they stared, but went, knowing better than to ask questions. I shut the door on them all.

And as I had known he would, he came in through the antechamber. With him was his fox.

An honored, honorable man, warrior-born and bred, sworn to serve my father. And so he had, for years. For all the years of my life: eighteen of them.

He had a wife, Raissa; *cheysula* in the Old Tongue. He had Finn, a son of his own, and a foster-son, Duncan, born to his wife's first husband. He had a pavilion in the Keep, where the Cheysuli lived. But he also had a home here in Homana-Mujhar, my father's palace; a man divided, serving his lord and his race by performing an ancient custom sacred to his people. Liege man to the Mujhar. Father, brother, son; indistinguishable and distinct.

And I knew, looking at Hale, that could my father do it, he would leave Homana to him.

But the Homanans would never accept it. He was Cheysuli: shapechanger. A man who becomes a fox at will, with an animal's habits and appetites. More yet than that: a man born of the race that had once ruled Homana, that had tamed a wild land, that had the blessing of the gods. Children of the gods; it was what *Cheysuli* meant.

Once purely Cheysuli, Homana was now Homanan, because the Cheysuli had stepped aside, forsaking the Lion freely, giving it over to the Homanans as a gesture of good faith, of proof that their sorcery was not evil; that they were a benevolent race. Serving the new aristocracy with all the honor they could offer.

For centuries they had served. Homana was now my father's, but with no son to succeed him.

Instead, he would name a grandson born of his Homanan daughter's loins, bred of Solindish Ellic.

I looked at Hale. "You know him as well as I—" But I broke it off, shrugged, tried to sound unconcerned. "Better by far than I; you have known him longer."

"Aye," he said gently. "Since before you were born."

Helplessly, I asked, "How did it come to this? How did it come to *this?*"

"A man and a woman are but children of the gods." A Cheysuli saying, though he quoted it in Homanan. And then he quoted in the Old Tongue, in lyrical Cheysuli, making a fluid, scooping gesture that left his right hand palm-up with fingers spread. *"Tahlmorra lujhala mei wiccan, cheysu."*

I knew it so well: The fate of a man rests always within the hands of the gods.

Abruptly, I was angry. "Will you do nothing but mouth such things? What good are they to me? What good are they to Shaine's daughter, who must wed the enemy to provide *two* realms with sons for their thrones?" Tears ran down my face; before him, I could cry. "Is it so easy for you? Will you stand beside my father and say nothing as I am bartered away? As I am *sold* to Solinde: a term of the accord."

A muscle ticked beside one eye. A distinctly yellow eye, feral as a wolf's.

"He must have told you," I said. "Surely my father told you.

You are his liege man; he tells you everything." Then my breath ran ragged. "You were there," I said numbly. "You were there, were you not, when my father offered me? To Bellam. To his son. To Solinde, as a term. . . . You were there—you *must* have been—you are always with him in Council—" Now I could hardly speak, shivering in shock. "Was it you who *suggested* it?"

The light was fierce in his eyes. "Do you think," he said coldly, "that I would give up my children and *cheysula* for a woman I would suggest be bartered away?"

"Give up—" I echoed blankly.

The anger peeled away, showing the nakedness of his need; Hale, who said so little. Who showed so little of himself, resolved to being a shadow to his lord in everything. Quiet, unobtrusive, even in emotions; a proper liege man.

Who loved his lord's daughter.

And a man who knew better.

They are a proud, prickly race, bound by honor codes more stringent than any I have known. Loyal, steadfast, dangerously single-minded when it comes to serving sovereign. But more so yet when it comes to serving their *tahlmorra,* their eternal destiny, the fate that rules their souls. Bound by ancient gods and self-imposed honor codes, they are not like other men.

Hale was like no one else. He had never been, for me.

But until this moment, I had not quite known what I was to him.

"After what we have shared," I said, "do you think I can marry Ellic?"

Again the muscle ticked. "No more than I can go back to the Keep."

I could not believe he meant it. Not Hale. Not the loyal liege man, sworn to a blood oath. I must have misunderstood him, or read into his statement the thing I most wanted to hear.

Carefully, I said, "It is easier for you. You have said it before:

in the clans, a warrior may take *cheysula* and *meijha*—wife and light woman—while giving honor to them both."

His tone was very steady. "Raissa bore me a son. I owe Finn more time, and Duncan, though he needs less of me." His mouth hooked down a little, but in wry affection. "Duncan needs no one but himself, I think, being self-possessed for a boy . . . but Finn—" He sighed a little. "—Finn will need more than most."

Aye, I had misheard him. I had hoped too high.

I drew in a painful breath. "You, of all people, understand what it is to serve, sacrificing personal desires in the name of a greater thing. But I lack your strength. All I want to do is run."

"And give up your heritage?"

"My heritage is myself." Bitterness crept in. "My father bequeathed me stubbornness, if little else, and determination. Spoiled, selfish bitch, he called me; well, perhaps I am. But I will not marry Ellic. I will not bear my sons for Solinde."

His voice was very quiet. "What of for the Lion?"

It fanned my anger again. "Am I to be nothing more than a broodmare, then, parceling out my sons? One to Solinde, one to Homana—"

"—one to the Cheysuli." Now he moved, for the first time since he had entered, coming to me, to take my hands and hold them, but doing no more than that. "Lindir, we are all governed by the gods. Cheysuli, Homanan, Mujhar and liege man . . . even the Mujhar's daughter. You say you will give no children to Homana, but I say you will. I have it on good authority."

"The prophecy." I said it without heat, though I think he knew what I felt. I am not overfond of the prophecy, a distinctly Cheysuli thing, born of Homana's ancestors, ruling today's descendants. The prophecy claimed one day a man of all blood would unite, in peace, four warring realms and two magical races. It foretold the coming of the Firstborn, Homana reborn again in the blood of the ancestors, united in one man. A man with power incarnate: shapechanger, healer, sorcerer, all dedicated to good. "Your prophecy says *my* son will rule?"

"A child of your loins will beget the first Cheysuli Mujhar in nearly four hundred years."

"And Ellic's," I said bitterly.

His hands tightened on mine. "Ellic is not Cheysuli."

"No, no, of course not," I agreed impatiently, "but what does it matter? If I am wed to him and I bear him a son, your prophecy is proved right."

"Is it?" Hale smiled. "I think it is more likely you will bear a Cheysuli child."

"Oh?" I arched my brows. "And do you intend to come with me to Solinde, to *serve* me there?" Purposely, I was crude. "I think it might discompose my husband."

Now he let go of me. I saw in his eyes the feral glint usually masked by civility. But a Cheysuli is not quite human, no matter how human his shape. He *thinks* differently, no matter how human his words.

His tone was intense. "What did you tell your *jehan?*"

"That I would not marry Ellic."

"And did he use his wiles to change your mind?"

I smiled, a little. He knows my father so well, unsurprised by anything. There was irony in his tone, compounding the bitterness.

I shrugged. "You know him. You know me. Whom do you think won?"

For the first time, Hale grinned. Incongruous on his predator's face, but fitting all the same. He lit up my chamber. He lit up my heart. He set my world ablaze.

"Shaine thinks *he* has won; you would make certain of that, if you intended to thwart him still. I know *you*, Lindir."

Laughing, I nodded. "I left him with that impression."

165

"And what is the truth of the matter?"

The laughter spilled away. I had asked the question often, of myself; as often had answered it. And now I answered him. "I will have to go away. I would sooner live the life of a croftwife in Homana than the life of a queen in Solinde."

"Oh?" Black brows rose. "You have a crofter in mind?"

I laughed again into his face, suddenly emboldened by my decision. The weight was gone from my shoulders; I had said what I would do. "My father's arms-master has always been very kind to me. Torrin has a brother whose croft is not so far from the border between Homana and Ellas. I could go there, and stay, until I decided my next step. My father would never suspect Torrin, nor would he think such a thing of me."

His expression was serious. "Better yet," he said, "come into the forests with me."

Oh gods, how I had hoped—"But you cannot," I told him. "You are liege man to the Mujhar. What of your honor, what of your oath . . . what of children and *cheysula?*" Even as I asked it, was aware of duality. I wanted so badly for Hale to take me from Homana-Mujhar, from my father's authority, so I could live with him in freedom. But I knew, in doing it, he would abdicate half of his soul; Cheysuli oaths are binding. He would abjure his honor.

He did not look away. "An oath is binding so long as it serves the prophecy. This one no longer does."

I stared. "Are you saying this was *meant?* That one day—someday, somehow, regardless of everything else—I would bear a child to you?"

"A child for the Lion, who will beget a Cheysuli Mujhar."

Suspicion was a serpent. "You are more honorable than any man I know, even other Cheysuli . . . the prophecy, to you, is more binding, I believe, than even the link with your *lir.*" *I* glanced at the vixen, Tara, sitting so patiently at Hale's side. It was all I could do to look back, to see the beloved face. Gods, but it hurt. "Then there is nothing at all between us save your service to your gods."

His mouth was taut and grim. "Honorable?" he asked. "I have lain with my liege's daughter, winning from her that which is due her *cheysul*." Relentlessly, he went on. "I have left my woman and my children, my Keep, my clan, in the name of what is between us." His eyes were very fierce. "If that is not enough for you, you are not worth the sacrifice."

Gods, I wanted to be. I wanted to be worthy of *him*.

"How will we go?" I asked.

"I will be a fox." He smiled. "You shall be a servant."

Laggardly, I stirred. "I will require proper clothing; nothing I have will suit."

"Already done," he told me, and with that he sealed our fates as he sealed the fate of Homana.

I knew the guard no more than he knew me. He was young, younger than I, and shocked to see a woman so far gone with child demanding he open the gate, to be let into the great palace of Homana-Mujhar.

"Lady," he said gently, so courteous, so kind; seeing my distress, my distended abdomen, "Lady, I beg you, go back where you came from; there is no one for you here."

I knew what he was thinking: that I intended to claim my child the Mujhar's, in hopes of gaining a coin, a gem, a place in Homana-Mujhar. It nearly made me laugh. I might have laughed, too, had I dared unlock teeth from bleeding lips.

Into his hand I put Hale's golden earring, shaped in the form of a fox.

His eyes widened. No woman desiring something of the Mujhar offered such a thing; now he was confused. "Lady—" he began.

"Show him," I said tautly. "Show the Mujhar." It was all I could

manage, now, having come so far down the road.

He went. He came back. With him were others, including Torrin, my father's arms-master, who had always been kind to me. To whose brother I would have fled, had Hale not taken me.

Through my pain, I smiled. "He wanted a child from me, a son for the Lion, though admittedly he might have preferred a different sire." I wanted to laugh, but could not. I drew in a deep, shaking breath, aware of hands reaching out, steadying, gently urging me onward, toward the rose-red palace. "Well, now he will have it." Blackness loomed so near. "Is my mother here?"

It was Torrin who answered quietly and gently into the sudden silence. "No, lady," he said. "Your mother died within a year of your departure, of a wasting disease."

I caught my breath on a contraction. "But—Homana has a queen. I have heard it said—" I tried to stifle a cry as they led me forward. "I have heard—"

"Lorsilla," Torrin told me gently. "The Mujhar's second wife."

Second wife. "How long?"

"Nearly seven years."

"Wasted no time, did he?" Bitterly I looked at Torrin, quiet, competent Torrin, whose face was ashen with shock. "But no son, has he? That I would have heard."

"No son," he told me. "The Queen of Homana is barren, having borne a boy who died in childbirth."

I laughed aloud as they held me. And as I laughed I felt the waters break and gush down my thighs, soaking my homespun trews. Man's clothes I wore. No more the Lady Lindir.

"Gods," someone whispered, "she will birth the child here—"

"No," Torrin said, "she will birth it where she should. In her own chambers, beneath her own roof."

"The sky is my roof—" I mumbled. "—for eight years, my roof, with Hale at my hearth—"

Torrin scooped me up. "Your roof is here, Lindir. In the House of the Lion."

In my child's house.

III

In huddled shadows, we watched the sun go down. Hale said nothing, being locked away within himself, stroking his *lir* instead of me; was he wishing himself back? Did he regret what he had done, leaving kin, clan and king for the sake of a Homanan woman?

No. More than just for that; for the sake of Homana herself, and the Cheysuli race.

"He will be angry," I said.

Hale bestirred himself, setting aside the fox from his lap and reaching out instead to touch a lock of my hair, fallen over one shoulder.

"Angry," he agreed, "and hurt very deeply. It is a wound that will not entirely heal, not ever; we have done the unthinkable."

I moved closer to him, pressing against the flesh of his bare arm. Through my cloak, my tunicked overblouse, I felt the hard, carved metal of his *lir*-band, solid gold, clasped about his arm above the elbow. He wore another on his right, and an earring in his left lobe, all shaped to look like his vixen. Gold, heavy gold, bright Cheysuli gold, a symbol of the *lir*-bond; of a powerful, unflagging pride.

I touched one long-fingered hand, threading mine through his. "Had I gone without you, he would have sent you to find me."

Fallen hair, sweeping forward as he bent his head, shielded most of his face. In profile, I saw wide brow, straight nose, pronounced cheekbones, clean jaw, all carved by a master's hand. Bronze of skin, black of hair, eerily yellow of eyes. They are a handsome race, the Cheysuli, shaped of glorious angularities and smooth, taut skin. And an economy of motion that makes every movement count.

"To find you, to bring you back." His tone was crisp; he was still liege man, in his heart. If he could no longer serve his Mujhar, he would serve the Mujhar's daughter.

"And?"

"To give you over to punishment, for wanting a Cheysuli instead of Solindish Ellic." He lifted his head, looked at me, there was acknowledgment in his eyes, of what we had done, the two of us, and what would become of us both in the face of my father's wrath. "It might have been better had you gone to Torrin's brother. Sent, it would have made more sense. . . . I could have simply disappeared, and you, and they would say evil had befallen us, instead of making up stories." He shook his head once, mouth crimped hard, he blamed himself only, giving me no portion. "I meant to say so, in your chamber, but there you were, afire from anger and anguish, afraid of what might happen, and I could not. All I could think to do was take you out of there with me, admittedly in disguise, but at least not separated. Not torn apart, as Shaine would have done, once he had seen what was between us."

"What will he do?" I asked.

"Send men to find us, to *take* us . . . to bring us back to Homana-Mujhar."

"What comes then?"

The muscles of his arm shifted beneath my hand, tightening, knotting, upstanding beneath his flesh. "He will send you to Solinde, if Ellic will take you still. Me he will dismiss." His eyes were fixed distances. "And I will be *kin-wrecked*, left with no one . . . no clan, no links to anyone save my *lir*, not even *cheysula* and children."

I drew in a painful breath, knowing he had lost far more than I had ever known. "But—you are without them now. No clan.

No children, and no *cheysula.*"

He turned his head. He touched me, stroking the line of my jaw, threading fingers through my hair. "With you, I have enough."

With him, I thought, I had everything.

The child would not be born. Having tasted the promise of life without a womb, it turned back, refusing, clinging to what it knew.

I opened my mouth and screamed.

"Gods," someone blurted, "the child will be the death of her."

Someone else answered. All women now, here; no men, who would profane the labor with ignorance. "So long as it is born, so long as it is a boy, the dying does not matter. So the Mujhar has said."

Gods, he hates me so. But a practical man, my father; he needed a boy for the Lion, and if I gave him one he would gladly accept it. Perhaps he would even love me again, for giving him his heir.

The first voice sounded appalled. "You wish the lady dead?"

"She started a war," the other said. "Ended peace with Solinde, and began the war again."

"But I heard the shapechanger stole her for himself, that the lady had no choice. She was compelled, they say, through the force of his sorcery."

The second voice was grim, unrelenting, contemptuous. "They say what they are told."

I knew what my father told them. What he took pains to tell, so as to soothe his wounded pride and repair his battered honor. Lies, all of them. Every one, told again and again, with embellishment, to justify what he did in the name of his vanished daughter.

One: that Hale had stolen me.

Two: that the Cheysuli had cursed the House of Homana, depriving it of sons.

Three: that each and every Cheysuli worked to throw down the House of Homana, to steal the Lion for themselves.

Qu'mahlin, *Hale called it. The annihilation of a race. The expunging of a people from the land they had made out of what their gods had given them, as ours had given us.*

Exiles in their own land. Prey of the man they once had served with a perfect loyalty.

My father was slaughtering the Cheysuli. Every year, every month, every day. As many as he could find, indiscriminate of age or gender. He sent men out to kill them, and that is what they did.

Once, overcome, I had told Hale it was all because of me. That I was to blame for the deaths, and all the hatred.

He had told me no: Because of the prophecy. That we were merely tools.

I opened my mouth and screamed.

IV

They came upon us without warning, slicing the air with swords. Mounted on plunging horses, clad in Mujharan livery. My father's men, of course; a few had found us at last.

One of the men wore a crimson captain's baldric slashed across his chest. He saw us, cursed us, called us spawn of demons, as bad as the Ihlini. And then he looked, and then he *saw* us, and realized who he had.

"By the gods!" he cried. "The traitor and his whore!"

Whore, was I? And Hale named a traitor? Neither. *Never.*

Cursing the captain in terms as elaborate as his own, I thrust myself from the underbrush and leaped to catch the horse's bit. I know something of horses; I yanked down on the shanks, then slammed my fisted free hand into his soft muzzle as hard as I could.

"Lindir!" It was Hale, reaching for me, catching an arm and jerking me away, nearly off my feet. I was pushed, ungently, back into the brush, back into the trees. "Run," he told me curtly, as the others began to gather.

"What of—"

"*Run.*"

I ran, but not far, only far enough to put myself beyond the sword's reach. I crouched down in underbrush, clawing thorns away, tearing flesh and not caring, thinking only of Hale.

His *lir* was a rusty blur, yapping, snapping, nipping at fetlocks to make the horses dance, keeping the swords at bay. I saw Hale, still in human form, jerk free and throw his knife. I saw it flash and fly home, buried in crimson baldric. No more would my father's captain call either of us names.

But there remained six of them, and Hale's knife was gone. His warbow was on the ground, and quiver; we had stopped to eat, to sleep, to lose our cares in one another, if only for a moment. Now we might lose our lives.

I scrabbled forward, crabbing across the ground, unmindful of nettles and briars, pausing once only to tear my hair free of thorns. And then I had it, Hale's bow, and the quiver full of arrows.

Gods, they will kill him—

I nocked and loosed the arrow, feeling the pull of the bow, the tremendous power, so at odds with its compact appearance. It was made so purposely.

One man tumbled from his horse, crying out in shock. The fletching stood up from his chest as the sword fell from his hand.

I nocked and loosed again.

Seven men, then six, now only five . . . four converged on Hale. I nocked, steadied, prepared to shoot, but none of the targets was still. And Hale was in their midst.

Abruptly, he was not. Not the Hale I knew. No longer a man but animal; beast, some would say.

It makes me queasy, the blurring, the void, the absence of substance in place of a man. I blinked, holding the bowstring

173

much too tightly for accuracy. Hale had tried and tried to break the habit in me, but it was too firmly ingrained. I had grown up seeing the shapechange, but the emptiness always made me ill.

That a man can reshape himself—

My father's guardsmen were young, those who remained. Too young to recall the days when Cheysuli walked the streets of Mujhara freely, and the halls of Homana-Mujhar. Too young to recall that in addition to the shapechange, Cheysuli also could heal. Certainly too young to have witnessed a warrior trading human for animal, losing nothing of his humanity, his awareness, merely putting on a new shape as a man puts on new boots.

Old enough only to know that Cheysuli were worth the killing, because that is what they were told.

Much too young. They looked at Hale the man; at Hale, now the animal. They looked at him and screamed.

Two foxes laced the horses' legs like embroidery, yapping, snapping, nipping. Driving the mounts into a frenzy, kicking, squealing, hopping, trying to rid themselves of tenacious irritation. And the men, still astride their horses, found it impossible to put a sword into either fox, for fear of striking fellow guardsman or plunging mount.

"Run," I muttered, *"run—"*

And so they did, the two of them, having driven the horses half mad. Two ruddy foxes, streaking through the brush, black-tipped brushes bobbing behind them as they ran.

My turn now.

With exceeding care, I nocked each successive arrow. One by one I took them down. One by one they died.

"Traitor?" I cried. "Whore? Better than any of you? *Better than my father—"*

Hale's hand was on my shoulder, a human hand with human empathy. He took the warbow, the arrows, then closed my mouth with gentle fingers. "They were doing what they were told."

"To murder us, and others—?"

"That is Shaine's guilt, not theirs." His face was streaked with blood. Horse's, I wondered, or man's? "You must recall, Lindir, their honor depends upon an abiding obedience. And the welfare of Homana."

I scooped tangled hair from my face. "They might have killed us both."

"No. The child is not yet born."

"The *child!*" I cried, half-sobbing. "Always the child, with you! Have you forgotten, then? I have miscarried two of them already . . . this one, too, perhaps. What then, Hale? What then of the Cheysuli? What then of the Lion?"

"The child will be born. If not this one, another."

"How many more?" I cried. "How many nights of pain and grief, pouring out your half-formed seed onto the ground, the thirsty Homanan earth, crying out for blood?" I was shaking now, and crying, released from the requirements of survival into a reaction that stripped me of my dignity, but not of humanity. "How much longer, Hale? Nearly eight years now . . . how much longer will it continue?"

"Until it stops," he said, and turned me toward the deeper forest. "And it may, sooner than you think. . . . Shaine has more than shapechangers to think about. Now he has Ihlini."

A ripple ran through my flesh. "Tynstar has joined Bellam?"

"Tynstar joins no one. He uses those he requires . . . for the moment, it is Bellam. And Solinde will pay the price." His tone was grim. "One day. When Bellam is not looking."

"And my father?" I asked.

"Of a certainty."

I thought of my father. I thought of Bellam. But mostly I thought of Tynstar, called the Ihlini, and all the others like him.

The man born of a race of sorcerers who serve Asar-Suti, the god who made and dwells in darkness, who rules the nether world.

I shivered. Once, Homana could have withstood Ihlini sorcery, for in the Cheysuli she had a share of her own. Now, without them, there was nothing but men to halt Tynstar's magic.

And I knew men were not enough.

"It will not be born," someone said. "The child refuses."

In my extremity, it was all I could do to whisper. "Perhaps because it knows it will find no welcome in the house or heart of its grand-sire."

Through slitted, greasy lashes I saw them, the women, exchanging glances of shock, guilt, acknowledgment. I knew none of them: it had been eight years since I had left Homana-Mujhar, and my father saw fit to deny me anyone I might feel comfortable with. Even as I bore the child who might well become the heir to Homana, he desired to punish me.

If I bore it.

If I lived to bear it.

"Hale," I said aloud. "If Hale were here—" But I broke it off, knowing what the outraged gasps portended. They would go and tell my father that even now I called out for the shapechanger who had freely broken his oath, that I desired the traitor even in extremity. In eight years my father had pulled a blanket over the eyes of his subjects, blinding them all, so that new generations would consider the Cheysuli evil, and kill them with impunity.

Older people would know better. Men like Torrin, a Mujhar's man, yet fair, who knew Hale nearly as well as I, or had; who knew me better. Women like my mother, who had given thanks to the gods that a man like Hale could keep her small daughter safe against all odds . . . and still did, though now the mother was dead and the daughter no longer small.

But the others would not admit it, if they knew. Blind obedience of the Mujhar, shutting away the light from their minds.

My lord Mujhar, you are a fool . . . and, I think, a madman—

V

Hale's face was ashen. I said his name once, twice, thrice, but he ignored me. He had gone beyond me into grief, into shock so binding that nothing so tame as his *meijha* calling his name would touch him. For no matter how much a warrior loved his woman, the *lir*-bond took precedence.

And now that bond was broken.

"Tynstar," he said emptily. "Tynstar and his *godfire,* the blood of Asar-Suti."

It set the hairs to rising on my arms. There is much I do not know of Ihlini, save they, like my father, desire the destruction of the Cheysuli. But *godfire* I do know, the cold, purple fire that eats through flesh and bone, even through hardest stone. The blood of Asar-Suti, issuing from the netherworld.

Tynstar had barely touched Tara. Caressed, she was nearly consumed.

There was little left of the *lir* except a parody. Legs were curled obscenely, crisped into twisted sinew. Fur was blackened, charred, stinking of sorcery; even I could smell it. The Ihlini had killed Hale's *lir* and stripped me of my warrior.

I touched his arm gently. "Hale—if we stay, Tynstar will find us as well."

He seemed not to see Tara as she was now. He seemed not to see me. Only the loss of his heart, his soul, his life.

His voice belonged to someone else. "You know the price, Lindir."

Aye, I did. A warrior deprived of his *lir* by death was constrained by custom to leave clan, kin, life; to give himself over to an obscene rite called the death-ritual. Because, I had been told, a warrior without a *lir* was only half a man, having no magic, no shapechange, doomed to a slow, certain madness. That, no Cheysuli would countenance. And so warriors like Hale, lacking a *lir,* walked out of life into death, however it happened to take them.

"If we stay here—"

"Then go." His eyes were oddly unfocused. Clearly, he was in pain. More than grief and anguish, but also pain of body. Not being Cheysuli, I could not begin to comprehend. But I saw the agony in his eyes, the emptiness of his soul. He was not the Hale I knew.

"Will you let Tynstar kill us as well?" I set broken nails into his flesh and pulled, trying to force him up, to run, to *go.* "Gods, Hale, think of something more than Tara's death. . . ." My hand dropped to my belly. "Think of your *child,* who may inherit the Lion, or sire the child who will—"

He threw me off easily. "Go," he said. "Run, then; save yourself, and the child. But I can do nothing more."

"Except die?" I wanted to strike him, to batter down his unexpected implacability. "Are you a fool, to throw away life because Tynstar has killed your *lir?* I know what you have said about the death-ritual, but surely it is more myth than truth." Frenziedly, I caught at his hand. "After taking me out of Homana-Mujhar to live like a fugitive for eight years, killing to stay alive, you now refuse responsibility? You tell me to go and turn your back—Hale, it is *your child* I carry! Are you blind to that? To what your prophecy demands?"

He spun faster than I could have predicted, catching my wrists and holding them against his chest, trapping me easily. "Lindir!" he cried. "Nowhere in the prophecy does it say I live to see the child!"

I gaped at him. "And you will let *that* make your decision?"

Bitterly, I shook my head. "You fool, you yourself have said not all of the prophecy was recovered, that bits and pieces are missing. . . . Without full knowledge of what the gods intend, you are sentencing yourself to death." I tried to twist free, could not. "I am sorry Tara's dead, but it does not have to mean *you* must die, too! Gods, Hale—"

And abruptly, he was in my mind, shutting off my thoughts, my words, my feelings, shunting all of them aside to replace them with his own. It is yet a third gift of the Cheysuli—the shapechange, healing, compulsion—and now he used it against me.

"You will sleep," he said. "For an hour, two . . . by then it will be over. By then Tynstar will be dead, or I will. And you will be safe, and the child, so that you can go home to Homana-Mujhar, to bear the child in safety and security. For Homana and the Cheysuli."

He kissed me, lay me down amidst the brush.

Was gone.

Out of terrible pain I reached, snagged a sleeve, caught it, gripped it, dragged the arm it encased toward me, until it stiffened, and I could pull myself up a little.

"—Tynstar—" I gasped. "It was Tynstar—it was the Ihlini—"

I sagged, fell back, felt the texture of the velvet crusted with gems. And I knew.

In eight years, graying hair was grayer still, and beard. But the glittering eyes were the same. That, and the pride. The powerful arrogance that drives a man to madness all in the name of injured honor.

"It was Tynstar," I repeated. "Not you after all, my lord Mujhar . . . though the gods know you tried."

Beneath the beard and mustache, his lips were tight and flat. But they parted as he spoke. "I am glad," he said, "because now I know it

179

was painful."

My own pain was suddenly bearable; the child was quiescent, as if it knew my father. Recognized the blood, the corrosiveness of the hatred, the virulence of the anger.

I took my hand from his sleeve, desiring not to touch him. Weakly, I asked, "What did he do to you . . . what did he do to you that was worth the extermination of a race . . . the destruction of a realm?" I drew in a difficult breath, willing the child to remain quiet. "Surely Ellic would have been satisfied with another bride . . . surely you are strong enough, resilient enough, to live your life without a liege man at your side . . . you are Mujhar, are you not? The Lion of Homana, save in human form. . . ." Again, I sucked in air. "You have shapechanged your humility into arrogance, your humanity into obscenity. . . ."

"Enough!" he cried. "Enough! What I did was for the good of Homana, for my realm . . . for the good of the Lion, so dishonored by a man, a shaperhanger—" He broke it off, clearly walking the edge of the sword of sanity and near to falling off. "Your suffering is deserved," he said plainly, "and I will relieve you of none of it."

"Once, I loved you," I told him. "More than I loved Hale, and the child I carry. But you have made that impossible. You have stripped me of everything you gave me, even that—"

"Enough!" he cried again. "You will bend your will to birthing that child, not wasting your strength on lies."

I nearly laughed at him; would have, had I the strength to do it. "You want this child so badly . . . a son for the Lion." Heavily, I swallowed, feeling pain washing in again, cramping breasts and belly. "But what if it is a girl? What if, after all these years, this pain, I give you a girl? Will you begin again, my lord? Will you use her for marriage bait, measuring the bidders one against the other, until you find the one you want? Like Ellic. Like Bellam—" I stopped, because if I tried to speak I would scream.

Hoarsely, he swore. "If this child is a girl I will give it to the beasts. The father was one—let the daughter know what it is!"

Hot tears ran down my temples, dampening hair already soaked with sweat. But I could not speak to deny him.

VI

Hale was already dead when I found him. And alone, so alone, lacking life, lacking *lir* . . . all he had now was the knowledge that he would never see the edge of madness, nor walk it, nor slip over to the other side, where Cheysuli as Homanans are stripped of dignity and humanity, becoming little more than brittle shells housing an absence of soul.

Once he had told me Cheysuli do not grieve, not as Homanans do, keening aloud for their loss. Cheysuli are an intensely private people, showing little of themselves except when it is necessary. For death, it was not; in private, they grieved, but rejoiced also, because the soul without a shell was now at home in the afterworld.

So I would not grieve aloud. But neither could I rejoice.

One of the women stirred. "My lord, the child is coming."

My father left the chamber.

VII

"Promise me," I begged. "Promise me you will see it to safety if the child is a girl."

Torrin's face was gray as he carried me through the corridor within my father's palace. Dampness trickled down my legs, staining the trews I wore.

"Promise me," I begged. "He will keep a boy—he *needs* a boy—but I fear for it if it is a girl. . . . I swear, I think he is mad enough to kill it."

Still Torrin said nothing to me, speaking quietly to others, sending them all ahead.

"You *know* him," I said. "You know he will do it."

"No," he said at last. "The child is in no danger from Shaine. I swear, Lindir, that if he so much as *threatens* to harm the child, I will take it for my own."

I bit into my lip. "He will dismiss you."

His tone was very grim. "I will dismiss myself."

Tears ran down my face. "I want Hale," I whispered.

"So do I, Lindir. And so, I think, does Shaine, though he will never admit it. Not to kill, but to embrace; they were brothers in all but birth."

"Until I took him away."

"He took himself, and you. And no one, who had seen him with you, was surprised. Only Shaine. Only Shaine."

The pain was getting worse. "Is Lorsilla kind?"

"Aye, Lindir, she is kind. And I swear, she will help me. If the child is a girl, the queen will help me take her."

"And if it is a boy?"

Torrin's voice was grimmer yet. "I will stay, if only to see that he is worthy of the Lion."

Through my pain, I smiled. "You sound like a Cheysuli."

"We are one and the same, I think. Shaped of Homanan clay, fired by the gods. Shaine is a fool to think differently."

"Will we lose the war with Solinde? Bellam has Tynstar, now . . . Tynstar and the Ihlini."

His arms were tight around me. "I think we will lose the war."

It was almost a relief. "Well, if we do—" I broke off, sighing; so weary, now, of speech. So weary now of thinking. "Hale would say it will pave the way for the man who will win it back . . . and the man after him who will become the first Cheysuli Mujhar in nearly four hundred years."

Other voices swam nearer, saying things to Torrin. Things I

did not know, drifting on tides of pain.

He put me down on the bed. Women were shooing him out. "You have my promise, lady. Now, it is time you bent your will to bringing forth a healthy child."

"For the Lion?"

"For us all."

He might have said something more, but the women had their way and chased him out of the chamber.

Leaving me to bear the child of prophecy: Hale's daughter, or his son.

I heard the infant's cry. Felt the blood gush out, hot, too quick, smelling sweet and thick. No one moved to staunch it.

"A girl," someone said. "Not a boy, a girl."

"Torrin!" I cried.

"The Mujhar will be angry."

"The Mujhar must be told."

Silence.

Then, "Who will tell the Mujhar?"

Too much blood . . . not so long now. . . . "Torrin," I whispered. "Let it be Torrin who tells him."

The silence was disapproving.

I summoned up my strength. "Would you rather have it be me?"

The women knew better. So, I think, did I; the dead do not speak.

One of them held the girl, all sticky and smeared with blood. Sound of limb and lungs. The downy fuzz was dark; her eyes I could not see.

Not so long now . . . I stretched out a hand toward her. "I want—"

FAIR PLAY

Half-grown, half-starved, and only half a woman; he reckoned her twelve, *possibly*. With the eyes of a desperation more appropriate to the dying.

At the door, resolution wavered. Her hands remained on the rough sacking tacked up to keep out the road dust; wood was too dear for doors. She lingered there, clutching tightly, until a man came in behind her and tore the fabric away, swearing at the impediment. The man wanted ale *immediately*. And a whore, probably sooner.

A second glance, and briefly: then the man was pushing by, muttering of girl-babes just quit of the breast wandering unasked into men's affairs.

The girl bit into her lip, staring blindly after him. Then the tears faded. The small chin firmed. Resolve blazed in dark eyes. She moved stiffly aside from the entrance and stared hard at each man. The room was full of them: ten, twelve, maybe twenty. She looked at every man, weighing each in his turn, until she came to *him*, and saw him staring back. Weighing even as she did.

Color waned, then returned, tinting the dusky skin. He looked back dispassionately, contemplating the girl: disheveled dark hair spilling over narrow shoulders; the curve of brow and cheek, too young yet for coarseness; the fingertip cleft in her chin. Beneath the dust, behind the hair, without the disfiguring bruises, she promised one day to be pretty. *If* she lived that long. For now, no one knew it; it was her only hope.

But in her the hope was extinguished. She knew the world too well.

She came, as he expected. Crossed the room from door to corner, to stand beside his table. Trembling violently, and hating herself for it.

The tapster also came, to shoo away the pest.

"No," he said softly.

The tapster was shooed instead.

The girl stared at him, trying to tame her trembling. Her torn, knee-length tunic matched the door sacking. The stains of it matched the table: drying blood, and spilled wine.

"Well?" he asked quietly.

She reached to the bottom of her tunic and untied the dirty knot. Something glinted briefly. Then she set it down on the table, where he could see the cross-hatching that denoted its worth, and snatched her hand away.

"A three-piece," he observed.

She bit into her lip, then licked it. The words spilled out in a rush. "Is it enough?" she asked. "For that, will you do a thing?"

He smiled without giving offense. "Enough for *some* things, certainly. What one do you want to buy?"

A sheen of tears in her eyes, then a mocking glint of contempt. "A man's death," she declared, and spat onto the floor.

"Ah." Lightly he touched the blood-stained coin with a sensitized fingertip. Metal was not so conductive as fabric or flesh, but neither was he an apprentice. He read the coin easily; he also read the girl. "Ah," he murmured once more.

She was fiercely adamant. "Is it *enough?*"

Idly, he turned the coin over. On the back, the three crosshatches; on the front, the High King's seal: a hawk stooping on a hare.

"The king's copper," he remarked, "is not easily come by."

"I'm not a *thief!*" she flared. "And I'm not a whore, either . . . but it's what he *wants* me to be." Dusky cheeks burned dark. "That coin bought my mother's death. She hid it, and he killed her. Now he wants me in her place, to earn a living for him." The notched chin rose. "I'm not a thief," she repeated thickly. "And I'm not a whore, either."

"No," he said quietly. "And *I* am not a killer of men."

Swollen lips parted slightly. Nostrils flared, and quivered. Dark eyes lost their passion. "But—you are *here.*"

He understood her. *Here* was a hovel posing as a tavern. The thatching was black and greasy, the packed dirt floors fouled. The common room stank of bad wine, old ale, burned meat, and the stench of unwashed bodies.

"I am *here,*" he answered quietly, "because it was the only room I could find. I am only passing through."

A grimy hand darted out and recaptured the coin. He trapped it on the way back and held it in his own.

She tested him once, then went very still. In her fist was the three-piece coin, the High King's own copper. But the fist was in his hand; the dirty, callused hand with bleeding, ravaged nails. And her world in the touching of it.

"*Ah,*" he said softly. "Now I understand."

The delicate chin trembled once, then was stilled. "*Do* you?" she challenged thickly. "You are a man. How *could* you?" And then the dark eyes dulled. "Unless you want me to—"

"No." He released her fist. "Take me to him, Safiyah."

She stared. "You *know*—?" But she bit it off. Clutching the coin, she stared. "Just like—so?"

He rose quietly. "Just like so."

"But. . . ." Nonplussed, she bit her lip. "I thought it would be in secret. At night. In the dark."

"Would you say it lacks the doing, that it can wait so long?"

"No!" she hissed, then gulped. "But—now? And with me there?"

He touched her head gently. "And is it not for you it is done?"

She bared teeth. "For my mother."

"Your mother is dead, Safiyah. This will not bring her back. Therefore it is for *you*."

"Then *yes*," she hissed. "For me."

He smiled very faintly. "Then I think it is worth the doing."

She gripped the coin in her fist. "Do you want payment after?" And then realization flared. "It isn't *enough*, is it? You're only lying to me, to make me go away!"

"Have I not asked you to take me to him?"

Now she was confused. She held out the coin again.

"After," he said quietly.

For the moment, it sufficed.

A hovel, as expected. And the father much the same: foul of clothing and habits, but free with his daughter's body if that body bought him wine.

The father was, at first, overjoyed to see his daughter complying with his wishes: that she take up her mother's trade. The misunderstanding was soon dispelled.

Blood muddied the dirt. But the body was no longer present. "You murdered your wife."

The father's eyes were dark and drugged with wine. He bared rotting teeth. "She stole from me and hid it."

"Coin she earned by whoring. Whoring because she had to; you beat her, otherwise."

Dull dark eyes flickered. "A man does as he will with his woman."

"If nothing else, bad business. A dead whore earns nothing."

The father pointed briefly. "I got *her* for that."

"And if she refuses? Will you beat her, too? Perhaps even kill her, when she does as her mother did in hopes of running away?"

Sluggish belligerence: "A man does as he will with his *daughter,* same as he does with his wife."

"Even to raping her? As you have just raped Safiyah?"

Safiyah's father spat at the stranger's soft-booted feet. "*That* for your words! The woman was mine, as *she* is; I do as I will with them all!"

"Ah," the stranger murmured. Then looked at the girl beside him. "Go outside, Safiyah."

She stared back blankly. Then comprehension flared in her eyes. She fled her father's hovel.

When it was done, he stepped outside into the clean sunlight, deftly straightening one rune-bordered linen cuff just escaping the suede sleeve. As expected, the girl was waiting. In an agony of curiosity and a stricken, sickened anguish.

She stood before the hovel, hugging her hollow belly. "Did you do it? Did you *do* it?"

He squinted slightly against the sun, then lifted a shielding hand. On the back of it was a mark: a blue crescent moon. "I did what was required."

"He's dead. . . ." she murmured dully.

And then the scream came from the hovel: a keening wail of shocked discovery; of disbelief, comprehension, denial.

"*Not* dead," she blurted, and stared up at the man. "You said he was *dead!*"

"No," he answered gently. "I said I did what was required."

Her father ran out of the hovel. His clothing was torn away to display his despoiled body: full, dark-nippled breasts; slim waist curving into hips; the furred mound beneath.

"A *woman!*" her father screamed. Man's voice. Man's face. But beneath it a woman's body. "*Look what you've done to me!*"

"Mmmm," the stranger answered, then looked down at Safiyah.

"Look what you've done to me!"

Safiyah's stare was glazed. The stranger reached down and took her cold hand. He warmed it with a thought, then led her away quietly. Behind them the father sobbed as he fell to his knees: *"Look what he's done to me. . . ."*

He knelt, still holding her hand. Her expression was dulled by disbelief; by the shock of what she had seen.

He still held her other hand. Gently he pressed his thumb against thin skin, feeling the fragile bones. He said a single word. Then, "Be free of it," and took his hand from hers.

Safiyah stared at it. On the back of her hand was a mark: a blue crescent moon. *"What—?"* she began.

"Be free of fear," he told her. "Do you not know the crescent moon?"

Safiyah trembled. *"No. . . ."*

"Ah." He smiled gently. "No more than the High King's mark on the three-piece coin." He displayed the back of his hand. "Do you see? We match."

She stared at the mark. "But—what *is* it? And why did you do it?"

"I did it because you are a woman alone in the world. Honest, decent work is hard for a woman to find when she has no man to tend her . . . and even a man is no guarantee of a safe life, as your mother discovered." He tilted his head toward her father, from whom issued hoarse sobbing. "He will leave here, because he will not be able to bear what he is when others knew what he *was*. You, too, must leave, so you can begin anew. But your way is not his. I have given you safe passage."

Her eyes were huge and wary. "I don't understand."

"Show your hand to a man with bread, and he will give you meat. Show your hand to a cloth merchant, and he will give you silk. Show your hand to a mule-trader, and he will give you a horse." His tone altered subtlety. "It is for survival. Until you can find honest, decent work. But if you attempt to use it for wealth, the mark will disappear."

She stared at the blue crescent moon. "Will I have it forever?"

"Only as long as you need it. But a strong woman such as Safiyah will not be in need for very long; eventually, she will *do*. She will change the world around her. She will remake it to fit her ideals."

"*I* can do that?"

"You must. Women are worth far more than what your father believed. His kind have ruled too long. Now it is for you."

Comprehension brightened her eyes. Then, distracted, she reached out, hesitated, then touched his own crescent moon. "What is it? How did *you* get it?"

"The mark of the High King's mage." He paused. "I was born with it. It was how the priests knew."

She nodded vaguely, uncomprehending; to her it was a word. To her, he was a man. "What about him?" she asked, staring at the woman. "What about my father?"

"Turnabout is fair play." The High King's mage smiled. "He must whore for himself, now."

That, she understood. Safiyah began to laugh.

GARDEN OF GLORIES

Feidra surveyed the courtyard garden with a practiced eye. But it was a soft eye, not seeking now to find fault; she had found fault already, had corrected it, and thus was given leave to take pleasure in what she had wrought.

"Magic," she said, and grinned. "Merris would laugh."

Merris would. Merris was like that. She said what she would say, laughed when she would laugh, ridiculed against her taste that which was another's.

It did not disturb Feidra. Merris was Merris. Feidra was—Feidra. Her pleasures were her own, if predictable; her powers insignificant among those others counted as real, as worthy, as meaningful within the context of their lives. Small lives, she thought, if painted with bloodier colors; hers was far more fruitful, the subtlety more peaceful.

Fruit. Feidra's smile broadened. The courtyard would offer its bounty in good time: oranges, sweet and juicy; lemons for their tartness; grapefruits for her breakfast. For now the trees bloomed, buzzing with bees; Feidra loved the sound. Let others have their shouts, their war cries, their songs of steel and death.

Rank upon rank of terraced, brick-bordered gardens formed stair-steps up the hand-smoothed walls. As militaristic, Feidra thought, in their arrangement as Merris was in war. Foliage matched hue for hue, for texture, for height; the colors and size of petals delicate as often as blatant. But the militancy of her gardens ruled with perhaps more kindness than the sere desert scape of Merris' life; a spirit found peace, not warfare, in the ripe beauty of Feidra's garden. A different kind of glory than that Merris courted.

She closed her eyes. The sun was warm on her face, wholly seductive, suggesting refuge in indolence, in irresponsibility after too much time spent in work; and it was due her, she felt, after ministrations. All the importunate weeds pulled, the untamed roses checked into order out of rank chaos, the upstart vines coaxed to the challenge of new trellises, the hummingbirds welcomed with a little sugar and water set out in a clay bowl rimmed in crimson glaze. The bees would water there, too, drawn by the sweetness, but Feidra did not mind. Let them share as they would. Or not. It was the way of the world.

Spring yet, but warming toward summer. For now the days were temperate, seductive in full measure after the cold of winter. She knew of few people who could ignore the days, the warmth, and the erotica of the season, to keep within their homes.

She was barefoot. Clay tiles beneath her feet warmed in the sunlight. Damp earth dried on flesh, turning to crusted mud that would flake off as she walked. She did not doubt her face bore testament also to her offices, and did not care.

Merris, of course, would laugh. Merris would toss her a damp cloth and say, with excess irony, that she should clean her face; that the daughter of their father was required to be clean, so she might catch a man.

But Feidra had caught a man. Like a fish she had hooked him, and brought him home to dinner. Like a fish, he had rotted, offending her home, her garden, and she had eventually put him out of both, disposing of him, his things, like a fish left out of water too long now reeking in the sun. Unwanted under her roof.

Feidra smiled. Her face was dirty and she did not care. She

had caught a man, as her father had wanted. And she had let him go.

Merris would not believe it.

The corbies crowded, stealing the breath from Merris. But better breath than blood; there was too much blood in the grass for them to deal with hers, still mostly in her body, and she had bound her wounds. None so bad as to die from; she would be well enough. But the spirit, knowing loss, bled yet, and would, until she fashioned in her mind a victory out of defeat.

It would require time, and healing. Time Merris had aplenty now, for the victor had picked the spoils, stealing from dead and dying what wealth could be judged to spend; a silver pin, a ring, boots, a fine-hilted knife. They were soldiers, not merchants; there was little to fill a purse save what commerce would result from the aftermath of war.

They had believed her dead, and she had not disabused them of it. She had made no sound, offered no resistance, as they tore the pin from her tunic, worked the boots from her feet, pulled the ring from her finger. A poor ring, worth little, save in its giver; but Kendig was dead, and what she had of him was muttered over by enemies for its lack of value, but put into purses regardless.

What she had of him, too, was the heart that yet beat in her breast, and that she could not forget. Forgive, perhaps, someday; she had hoped they would die together when the day came for it, pledged like man and wife at the pulpit of battle, but he had died without her. And left her to live after all, so she could feel his blood drying into the weave of her tunic, crusting on her face.

Feidra, she thought, would bring her a bowl of cool citrus-scented water and a cloth to be sopped in it, to wash the blood away while she let Merris brood. It was what she did so well, did Feidra: ministering to others when lured out of her garden; and brooding was, always, what Merris was better at.

Brooding. And battle.

The corbies crowded. She lacked a pin, boots, a ring; had lost sword and knife as well. But she lived, and would; it was for her to survive, to recover, to fight again at need.

Feidra would grieve for Kendig. Feidra did not know him, but would grieve nonetheless. Her gift was to make things live. Her curse was to watch them die.

Feidra would grieve, as well, for the sister who spurned men who looked on women as weakling, but who had found a man nonetheless who treated her as his equal in battle as well as in bed. He was hard to come by, was Kendig, and harder to keep; Feidra had had her choice among the men who came to call, but Merris never knew it. Nor had wanted it.

She shifted, biting her lip. He was heavy, was dead Kendig; they had learned to fit themselves to one another in all the ways a man and woman could, but they had not planned for death. They had not teased death, mocking its aspect, its ascendancy, and now Kendig's body, all the stilled parts of his body, was manifestly heavier, more awkward than imagined.

Merris cursed the corbies as she dragged herself from beneath the butchered body. It was the price of war, was death; she and Kendig had challenged death aplenty, yet never courted it. They had not loved it that much, offering only respect as soldiers did.

But death was blind to the difference, to the semantics of their lives. Death loved Kendig, too. Merris, death ignored.

The bench was warm beneath Feidra's buttocks clad only in loose-woven linen. Unlike stone, wood caught and imprisoned the sun until it turned away its face, and so Feidra, shut-eyed, catlike, reveled in it: bare muddy toes against spring-warmed stone clad in its raiment of petals; the buttocks, so nearly naked, content upon the wood, her spine equally pleased to rest against a wall. Near her ear a bee buzzed its office: to lift from the blossom the nectar that would give life to another plant; that would, in its bounty, give flavor to the honey.

The world was livid crimson beyond the fragile lids. A sorry shield, she thought, made of flesh and lashes, not at all like the studded shield Merris carried in war to turn back the blades, the arrows, the stones of the enemy. If Feidra raised *her* shield, no enemy would come to call; only the brilliance of the day, and the promise of the season.

She knew her garden, her courtyard. She knew its sounds, its smells. She knew the moment someone arrived at her gate. The day altered its song, the shadow muted sunlight.

"Come in," Feidra invited, not raising the fleshly shield. "Share the day with me. It is too glorious to waste."

"Glory," Merris said, "is dependent on one's taste."

Feidra stood up all at once. The sun, let into her eyes, dazzled her a moment, so that all she saw was a figure at the gate with a hand upon the iron as if it could not let go.

She took inventory of her sister as she did of her garden. Weeds to pull, she thought, and thorns to cut back, and dry soil to water so Merris might bloom again, restored from the hostility of a long season left untended, the sterility of drought.

Merris was, had always been, the less beautiful of them, in the ways a man counted. But Feidra, who knew better, counted beauty in the spirit, in the strength of a stubborn will. Merris was thin, severe, honed keen and clean by battle; as sharp in tongue and wit as the steel of her blades. But as true, also, if less kind than some might prefer.

Feidra blinked. Blades. Gone.

Merris, come home again. With no weapons at all.

"You lost," she said abruptly.

Merris did not flinch. "This time, yes. Next time, we will win."

"We?"

A shrug, quickly accomplished: a casual hitch of a shoulder. "Whoever I take service with. Whoever will have me."

Feidra no longer felt the warmth of the clay tiles as she crossed the courtyard. The callused hand still gripped the iron. Feidra put hers upon it. Callus upon callus. One hand wielded a sword, the other a trowel.

"Come in," Feidra said. "Do you expect ceremony?"

The edged smile was faint. "If I did, I would not have come. I know the woman who lives here."

Feidra smiled. She wanted to laugh, but could find no heart for it. Merris cherished honesty, as cruel as it was kind. She stepped back and unlatched the gate, iron grinding on iron. "She lives here yet," Feidra said, "if alone."

Merris stilled into stone. "Is he dead, then? Edvik?"

"Oh, no . . . not so far as I know." She knew it was not the sort of answer Merris expected. "When last I saw him, he was quite alive."

"Ah. Drinking again, is he?" Merris stepped through the gate into the courtyard. "A pretty place for a man, no? He need do nothing but enjoy your bounty as well as your body. And no earning of it, no right to either."

Feidra shut the gate again. "He had right. Once. The priestess bound us."

"Father wanted you *un*bound," Merris said dryly, "and immediately. Of all the men who came, you chose him."

"He was pretty," Feidra said, repeating to her sister what she had said to herself so often. "He was all the things I believed I wanted. And, for a time, did want." She set the latch again, smiling to herself as Merris stilled into silence. The courtyard and its glories did that to a soul. "There are men, and there are men. Some are worth the trouble."

"Not Edvik," Merris muttered.

"No, not Edvik. But what is life for, save to make mistakes so we may learn from them?"

Merris cast a wary eye upon her. The scar beside it lent a wicked glint. "Philosophy, from you? Father would despair."

Feidra laughed. "Father despaired of me the day I wed Edvik."

Merris' mouth hooked wryly. "His despair of you was of markedly shorter duration than his despair of me."

"Your choice," Feidra reminded. "Will you come into the house?" She thought so. Merris found little beauty in the glory of her garden. Beauty, to Merris, was steel freshly honed, and the vulgar harshness of the army. There she thrived, even as Feidra would not.

"No," Merris said. "No, let it be here. I detest roofs."

"Ah, but there is a roof even here," Feidra pointed out, glancing at the array of overhead lattices bent beneath ivy and the trailing limbs of roses. They required shoring up; it was her next project.

"A singularly more attractive roof than tile and timber," Merris demurred. "And closer to hand than the table inside."

Feidra saw why such was important as Merris moved to the bench. She had lost the lithe elegance of her step, the understated power that was her personal gift. "You are hurt."

"*Was* hurt," Merris corrected succinctly, seating herself with care upon the sun-warmed bench. "Mostly healed; I took time for it before setting out."

But there was tension in the line of her shoulders, and Feidra was not fooled. "Well, then. Shall I bring refreshment? Would your pride countenance care?"

As a child, Merris had been serious. But now she smiled. It puckered the scar by her eye. "My pride, just now, countenances much. Bring out what you will, and sit. It will do me well just being still a while."

Feidra agreed wholeheartedly, but said nothing of it.

Merris was still and took relief of it, but the courtyard was not. It was a living thing, if judged by context other than that of warfare; she had not looked upon a garden as anything but time wasted, effort expended, and fair prey to an army bent on seeking good ground. Too many times gardens had been broken apart by a siege, or beaten beneath hooves and boots. Feidra's folly, she thought, to believe a life could be governed by the shapeshifting of the seasons. What governed life was death, and a soul's avoidance of it. Better to die of a purpose than to justify one's life by the color of a flower.

But it was warm in the garden, and redolent of citrus. The hard green knobs depended already in clusters from bee-beleagered blossoms; they would swell, alter color, and ripen— and one day she need only pluck an orange from a tree to have juice in her cup, or the sweet fragile pulp bursting to flavor within her mouth.

It was a long way from war, here in Feidra's garden. A long way from the world Merris had made her own. What could she tell her sister? What *should* she tell her sister, that Feidra might understand? That any woman could, who was raised to different needs.

Merris smiled. Her skull found purchase against the wall of Feidra's little house. Ivy importuned itself within the strands of her hair, finding little lattice; she cropped her hair man-short so as not to interfere in the practice of her trade.

She had described to Kendig once the house they had grown up in, alone but for their father. How Feidra, in her youth, acquired her mother's habits without knowing how; their mother had died when they were very young. Their father had believed his wife returned to them in the small ways of the household, and sought physical pleasures elsewhere if not another wife. He had Feidra for all but bed. For a son, he had Merris.

Except she was born a woman.

The smile died away from her mouth. How he had misunderstood. How he had shouted, and threatened, and beaten, though with a lighter hand than most. Had cajoled, had pleaded, and thundered. But she had stood firm amidst the wreckage of what had been their love. Her duty, she said, was different; he had Feidra for his household, and Merris for a war.

But a man would change that, her father assured her. She need only look to a man, and once she had one she would set aside foolish thoughts and comfort herself as a woman should: pleasing a man, tending a house, bearing his children.

Until one day it killed her, in spirit if not in body. But he had not said that. It was not necessary. She had known it from the beginning.

In war, all unexpectedly, she had found a man. And in war she had lost him. Unexpectedly.

A clink of pottery, and Feidra came through the door with cups in one hand and a pitcher in the other. It was too early for citrus, but watered wine would do. Grapes were another of the things Feidra tended.

Feidra poured in silence, handing the cup to Merris. Merris accepted with grave thanks, invoked the Goddess's blessing briefly in soldier's argot, and drank. It slid down her throat as it always did when made of Feidra's grapes: sweet and smooth and soothing.

"Edvik did not drink you dry, I see."

Feidra smiled and sipped from her own cup. "No," she answered. "But he had little time for it, once I told him to go."

A slow stirring of anger on her sister's behalf. "And how long this time?"

Feidra arched elegant, eloquent brows.

"How long before you open the gate to him as you opened it to me?"

"Oh," Feidra said, "that is done between us."

It was casual, lacking defense, stripped of explanation. It was Feidra's way.

But Merris snorted disbelief. "Done, is it? You and Edvik? He must be dead, save you deny it."

"He may be dead. But I think not; someone would come to tell me." Feidra settled beside her, sharing the warmth of the day.

Merris frowned. "How can it be done? Unless. . . ." She paused a long moment, considering offense unintended but nonetheless real. But they were sisters, and honest; sometimes to a fault. "Is there another, then? Have you come to your senses at last?"

Feidra shrugged. "No other."

"For you, I mean." And dryly, "I would expect it of Edvik."

"No, there is no other for me. For Edvik, perhaps, but that does not matter. . . ." Her sideways glance was amused. "Is it so difficult to believe I might at last be a woman without a man, and content?"

"*You?*"

Feidra laughed. She sipped. She enjoyed the moment.

"Not you," Merris declared. Then, "Oh, but it will not last."

"Perhaps. Perhaps not. I am not counting the days." Feidra sighed and persuaded ivy to disassociate itself from her ear, where it courted her curls. "How many times have you told me a woman requires no man to be whole. To be accepted for herself?"

"Many times," Merris answered, "but not so many of late. It has been three years since I was last here."

Feidra frowned. "And two since I put Edvik out."

It astounded Merris. "Two years? Alone? You?" She paused. "Are you ill?" she asked severely.

Her sister smiled the smile of a cat. "You mimic Father, now. He should live again, to hear you."

"But. . . ." Merris shut her mouth; it displeased her to know she claimed any part of him. "Feidra—surely others have come to call."

"Of course they have," Feidra said matter-of-factly. "But I am content."

"Alone."

"Alone." She glanced at her sister. "You, of all people, should know the pleasure of that."

"Pleasure? I would say: necessity." And thought then of Kendig, knowing herself a liar even to herself.

"You've always been so strong," Feidra said reflectively. "You stood up to Father, refused to be what he expected you to be. And went off to make your own way. I envied you that strength, that freedom . . . I had so little of either."

"But—you *wanted* to get married!"

"Of course I did. I regret none of it."

Merris twisted her mouth. "Not even Edvik?"

"Oh, I might have wished later I had been wiser in my choosing, but I *did* the choosing. In fact, I found my strength and my freedom. Father gave in at last."

The irony was habitual. "Probably because he feared his only remaining daughter would follow her elder sister."

"Oh, no, he knew better." Feidra grinned. "Can you see me on a battlefield taking to task a soldier for crushing the grass beneath his boots?"

"And trying summarily to restore it?" Merris grinned back. "You should hire on to those who have lost their gardens to war; you would be rich in short order!"

"Perhaps I should," Feidra said, but Merris knew she would

not. Her work was here. Her strength, her magic, was rooted in her courtyard.

"So, for two years you have lived without a man." Merris scratched at the healing scar beside her left eye. "I would not believe it had anyone else said so."

"Nor did Edvik, at first. He came back twenty-one times."

"And on the twenty-second?"

Feidra's expression was serious. "There was no twenty-second. He believed me, then."

"Or was too drunk to care anymore."

"He says not. The townfolk say not. But it no longer matters," Feidra said contentedly, "I tend my house for me."

Merris grunted. "For now."

"For now. I swore no oath. I am not opposed to men, you see, only to curtailment of the spirit." She paused. "But you know about that."

"I know," Merris said, and felt hollow inside.

"And so now I understand what it is you tried to tell me, so many years ago. That a woman should be what she is, and not what men—fathers, brothers, or husbands—would have her be."

Quietly Merris said, "But there is compromise."

"*You* say so? You?" Feidra laughed. "You are the most uncompromising soul I know!"

Merris made no answer.

"Merris—you let no man dictate what you should be."

"No."

"You follow your own desires."

"Yes."

"And are happy for it!"

Merris sighed. "Sometimes. Sometimes—not so happy."

"When are you not?" Feidra challenged, then amended her tone. "Oh, I am sorry . . . surely you do not find happiness in war. In—killing."

"No, not happiness. Competency. Control." Merris cradled the pottery cup in both palms, scraping baked clay against the horn of her hands.

"A feeling of worth, that I can do what I am best at, and be honored for it."

"Killing."

"Fighting," Merris corrected. "Earning my pay in service to another."

"And do you believe in them all? These lords you serve, these causes?"

"I am not a whore," Merris answered, knowing it would hurt her. "If there is peace won before a battle, it pleases me. But all too often there is not, and I am left to fight."

"Do you shock the enemy? Do you win because of that?"

Merris smiled briefly. "I win because I am good."

"At killing."

Merris set down the cup. "I am not made for gardens," she said, "any more than you are made for war. Kendig understood."

Eventually Feidra asked, "Who is Kendig?"

"Was," she said tautly. "My swordmate. My bedmate. The only man I have ever been able—and free—to love." She waited for no blurt of shock, no comment of disbelief, but looked straightly at her sister. "I came because I knew you could offer a child more than I. That you *would*."

Color fled from Feidra. The blossoms behind her were made lewdly lurid by the pallor of her face.

"I know it grieved you," Merris said gently, "that there would be no children. I could not perceive it; war is no place for a child, nor a mother who kills men. A warrior's mind does not shape itself to think of bearing children. And so I did not. And then there was Kendig. And now—there is a child."

Feidra's breathing was ragged.

"What else is there to do?" Merris asked. "Our magic is alien to one another. I am dark, and you are light. I am death, and you are life."

"Merris."

"The child will be what it is meant to be. But I am less forgiving, less tolerant than you. The first time my daughter restored a boot-crushed flower, I would ridicule her for it. And I refuse to be my father."

Sharply: "And on the day your son picks up a trowel and wields it as a sword?"

Merris smiled. "It need not be a son."

The cup fell from Feidra's hands and shattered against the tile. "Oh . . . oh, Merris. . . ."

"This is your gift," her sister declared, "this magic you have wrought here in your courtyard. A child should have a choice."

"But—you need not go! You need not leave it to me!" Spots of livid color blazed in Feidra's cheeks. "You need not desert your child!"

"I am a soldier," Merris said. "It is all I know."

"But you could live here, with me! Or—" Feidra made shift to repair the potential schism. "—or not, if you prefer; there are *other* houses—"

"But no gardens such as this." Merris bent down and picked up, one by one, the shards of shattered cup. She set the pieces into her sister's lap, into cool, sun-bleached linen. "She—or he—will thrive in Feidra's garden."

Feidra stared blindly at the little pile of clay. One by one she picked up the shards and pieced them, like a puzzle, together again. In her palms the cup was whole—and did not break apart when she set it onto the bench between them.

"You see?" Merris said. "Kendig knew what I was. He loved me for it. I know what you are, and love you equally." She set one hand into her sister's curly hair, cupping her skull, and leaned her scarred forehead against Feidra's milky brow. "This is your glory," she whispered. "It has no weakness, but strength; it is different, that is all." She swallowed painfully. "Permit my child to have a chance to know it. To know and respect the difference."

In silence, when she could, Feidra nodded. And the tears that dampened her cheeks also dampened her sister's, falling at last to stain the spring-warmed, petal-clad tile beneath their dusty feet.

JESUS FREAKS

"Jesus Christ!" she shrieked.

Ho-lee shit. It's not supposed to be like this.

She slapped one hand to her heart, buried somewhere beneath the synthetic—no, faux—tiguar coat she wore. "Jesus—" But she broke it off, scrabbled inside the glitterbag slung over a shoulder, and came up with something that looked like a cross between a handgun and one of those dollar-store phaser-toys featured on an old '60s science fiction TV program Gabe had showed me. The original series.

Not a gun. Not a toy. Mike had called it a zap.

"Don't get zapped," he said. "It won't do any permanent damage, but the effects aren't pleasant."

I believed him. Mike knew about these things, since he worked in Medical. And besides, the shape I was in, I didn't feel much like dealing with anything that might scramble more of my circuits.

Meanwhile, this woman. . . .

"Wait," I croaked, holding up a bare-palmed hand, my right one; the left was splayed against the ground to keep me upright. If I moved it, I'd fall over in a heap. Okay, Gabe, where'd the scotty cough me up this time?

She was just about the last thing I'd expected. Mike had done a pretty good job of bringing me up to speed from the last gig, but maybe Medical had passed me along too fast. I was wobbly from the scotty, which was frustratingly idiosyncratic, and distinctly disoriented. Everything I owned ached. Some of it was supposed to, to trigger the proper responses, but this time I felt like hell.

Except right now what bothered me most was the girl—no, the woman; I'd been briefed on old-style Women's Lib—gaping inelegantly.

I tried a harmless smile, but she wasn't buying. Shock altered to suspicion; she felt safe enough with the zap in her hand to challenge. "Where'd you come from, anyhow? You weren't here a minute ago—I checked my sweeper. I ain't stupid enough to walk into a dark alley without checking, first. Light flashed green. . . ." A quick toss of her head rid her eyes of the tangle of purple-dyed ringlets. "—so how'd you get here?"

She wouldn't believe the truth; I didn't bother to explain. I just squinted painfully, trying to focus. *Gabe, you promised it would work the way it's supposed to. . . .* The scotty had been debugged since the last time, but I've learned the hard way not to believe everything they tell you.

It was night, as usual. A dark alley. A dark, narrow, debris-strewn alley that reeked of Pop knew what (He is omniscient, after all; a knack I hadn't inherited), and most of it very dead, or the detritus of the dead. And it was wet, to top it off; not raining now, but the crumbling patchwork of decaying plasphalt was puddled with oily water. " 'S okay—" I mumbled. "—promise."

Wan moonlight illuminated her face. The skin underneath gold glitterstars and tiny CZs glued high on oblique cheekbones was a warm, smooth brown. A fine line of perspiration stippled her upper lip. The zap's nose—or mouth; or anal orifice—didn't waver. "Yeah. Right. I heard that before."

"Not from me." I gathered legs, aware of cramping, and thought about dragging myself upright with the wall's help. I could feel blood running down my side; more dribbled into my eyes. "Can I just—?"

An explosion of light cut me off. She squinted, thrust a hand skyward to block the flash, swore. "Those damn rockets—cops oughta shove 'em up their ass to see where their brains are, 'steada botherin' people like me. . . . Hey." The light died out slowly. She stretched her eyes wide to improve her dazzled vision. "They steal all your clothes? Or you just run like that?"

I wasn't running anywhere. My feet hurt too much. "This is all they left me." It was all they ever left me.

She considered it. "That thing you're wearing, that diaper-thing . . . you look sorta like that guy I saw an old vid about once. Gander? Gondy? Something." She hitched a mostly-naked shoulder; meanwhile, the zap still stared me down. The light was nearly gone, leaving only an afterglare that painted the landscape of her face in angles of gray and black. CZs and glitterstars sparked fitfully. "Hey. You're bleeding."

"Shit happens." A lot. Too much. But that's the thing about a loop: you just keep replaying it. Mike and Gabe saw to it there were certain variations—so I wouldn't get bored, they explained—but the blood and pain was a constant. To keep me humble, they said.

A crock, if you ask me.

She'd dyed her ringlets purple, but the eyebrows were black. In bad light they formed a shelf across the shadowed sockets of dark eyes. "This ain't the way you usually run?"

I generally avoided running. Getting caught was part of the plan.

But she meant something else. "No."

"Hunh. Thought so." She edged a little closer, still gripping the zap. "Lemme see your wrist."

"My wrist?"

"Lemme see. Like this." She held up her left wrist, hand bent back, and displayed the mark. Looked like a brand, or a tattoo.

I couldn't see the details. Just a blotch.

Dutifully I held up my left wrist and mimicked her, displaying the wound that was neither brand nor tattoo.

"Shit," she said, "they lazed you! Lazed out your number, didn't they? Those asshole Jesus Freaks. . . ." She came forward, tucking the zap back into her glitterbag. Hostility toward me was banished, though she'd locked onto another target; well, I work fast when I have to. Not a lot of time. "All this shit about it being the Number of the Beast . . . they don't care lazing out the mark'll get us killed. . . ." She bent, closing fingers around my arm. "Here. I'll give you a hand. We gotta stick together, people like you and me—who else'll give us a break?"

Everything was fuzzy. Medical had passed me along too fast—next time, I'd insist Mike give me extra shore leave before sending me out again.

"What else they do besides laze out your number?" she asked, levering me up with effort.

I grunted, bending over to catch my breath. "A few things here and there. They nailed me pretty good."

"Christ on the cross," she sighed. "They have their way, they'll run us all out of business. Asshole Jesus Freaks—whyn't they leave us alone? Some guy wants a good time, who're they to say no? Guy's got the card, he gets the ride . . . but those JFs think they can preach to everybody how we oughta live." She urged me forward. "Come on, it ain't too far. Can't stay out here—once a rocket goes up, the cops ain't far behind. And they'll bust you for no license. You don't want that—trust me! Ever since the chief got religious. . . ." Her tone altered. "They do you pretty bad, huh?"

"I'll live." For a while. Long as it took, as always, before Mike and Gabe pulled me out.

"They laze your feet too, huh? Bastards. Lucky they didn't do your balls."

I swiped the back of my hand across my forehead, swabbing blood. "Yeah, well, some people might argue I don't have any, or was—am—too chicken to use them."

She grunted. "Don't put it past 'em, chico. Some of those JFs are pretty dedicated . . . they'd as soon laze off your balls as let you use 'em in Sin and Perversion." A pressure on my arm, turning me to the right. "Here. Up the stairs. Two flights; lifter's broken." She held her tattooed wrist up to a glowing sensor. "Don't know how much longer the Eye'll work—last week some JF fundie lazed off a guy's arm and lugged it to the nearest cribhouse, just to fool the Eye with the dead man's license number. Got the JF in, all right . . . luckily, they caught him before he could set off the bomb."

"Bomb?" I asked fuzzily.

"Yeah." The door slid open. She guided me through, made sure the door shut again behind us. "He said he was going to root out the nest of serpents."

"Shit," I muttered. "It's worse than we thought."

She aimed me toward the stairs. "Worse than who thought?"

I sagged elaborately. The decoy worked.

"Gotta climb," she muttered. "I can't carry you."

I wasn't that bad. Some of the disorientation was fading. But it wasn't wise to let her see it; not yet. I faked a few stumbles to make it look good, but did what I could to keep most of the weight off her. She was a tiny little thing.

"Here's the door." She flashed her wrist at another sensor, and the door ratcheted open. "Noisy SOB. Gotta get that fixed." Breathing heavily, she guided me through a small cube-shaped front room into the tinier cube beyond. "Think you can stay awake long enough for me to patch up those cuts?"

I mumbled an affirmative.

"Okay. Stay put. I'll clean you up, then let you crash. Chow's in the kitchen, through there. . . . I'll be gone when you wake up."

I blinked owlishly, then collapsed onto the edge of the bed.

She grimaced a little, saying something about bloody prints on her floor and stains on her sheets, but she didn't seem to mean it. "Stay put." She was back before I could do much more than scrub blood out of one eye. She had a dish of water, cloth, a bottle of dark red liquid. "This is gonna hurt."

"Always does," I muttered.

She grimaced. "Happen a lot, huh? Those damn JFs. . . ." She let it go, settling down to the task at hand. Carefully she sponged away blood, talking all the while. "They're like sharks, y'know. Once they smell the blood. . . ." She peered again at my face, pushing matted hair aside. "Don't look like a knife did this."

"Didn't." The scent she wore was thick and musky. She had used it liberally. Not that she needed it. Mike would say Pop had blessed her in the pheromone department.

"They crowned you good."

I grinned. "Yeah."

A purple ringlet dangled over one brown eye as she worked intently. She was hispania, or maybe afri/spania; I'd even heard the slang term afri/spic. "Don't look so bad, once the blood's wiped off—just some roundish scratches . . . they go all the way around?" I winced as she peeled hair from the back of my head. "This is weird. . . ." She let the hair flop down, pushing her own tangled ringlets aside with the back of her tattooed wrist. "Then again, they were JFs . . . who's to say what they'll try on us, next? You were just damn lucky they left you in one piece. . . ."

Well, very nearly. There were other cuts, and bruises; the stab wound in my side. She dabbed the red liquid on each of the raw spots, grimacing as I hissed. "I know—stings like hell. I figure that means it's working . . . now, as for this cut in your side—"

She broke it off, swearing. "Those damn jackals—they really tried to snuff you!"

I summoned a weak smile. "Too far from my heart to kill me."

"—deep," she murmured, touching gentle fingers to bruised flesh. "You need a Medic for this—but how in hell can we get one? No mark, no Medic . . . and those fucking Freaks'd be waiting outside the door for when the hospital kicked you out."

"So I guess that leaves you."

Residual anger blackened her eyes. "I'm no Medic—"

"You can patch me up."

"Have to." She hitched at the drooping CZ-studded strap of her top, hooking it absently over an otherwise bare shoulder. The matching stretchskirt she wore was nearly nonexistent, displaying lean legs sprinkled with CZs and glitterstars all the way down to steep gold heels. How do they walk in those things? "Just don't you go dying on me."

Dryly, I promised, "I'll do my best."

She flicked me a glance. Purple-dyed hair straggled down one cheek. "You think it's funny the JFs did this to you? You think it's funny they're doing this kinda thing to anyone who don't meet their standards?"

"No."

It mollified her, though her eyes still flashed. "They're screwing up everything, those Freaks. Tellin' people how to live, what to read, what to watch on the vid-plate. . . ." But she let it go, kneeling to get a closer look at the stab wound. Then, chewing her tongue, she pressed the red-soaked cloth against my side. "Cuss all you want."

But I've never been a man for taking names in vain. Pop taught me manners. "What's your name?" I figured it would take my mind off the sting.

"Ria," she murmured, holding the pad still even as flesh twitched.

It hurt—"—what do you do, Ria?"

She snorted. "Whaddaya think, chico? You know that part of town."

"Actually, no."

She flashed me a glance under knitted brows. "Maybe you don't." A one-shouldered shrug freed the strap to droop again. "The JFs would call me the Whore of Babylon. Me, I call it a job." She pressed the cloth more firmly against my side. "Hold that. I'll get some tape and gauze, try to make up some butterflies. Probably needs stitching, but I never was Suzy Homemaker—you'll have to take what I got."

I wondered how long it had taken her to cultivate the vulgarity of her manner, her dress; the cheapness of her speech. She hadn't been born this way. Nobody was. Pop had been plain: people make themselves.

She went off to get supplies while I applied pressure to the wound in my side. I wanted to tell her it didn't really matter, that I wouldn't die from it, but one thing you can't do in this job is tell the truth, the whole truth, and nothing but the truth— unless you have to. I'd probably have to sooner rather than later, but to someone other than Ria.

She bandaged me, taped me, then dug jockeys, jeans, and a chambray shirt out of a closet.

"Brother's?" I asked dryly.

She snapped gum, grinning as she turned around. "You're cute, you know? Real wise guy, aren't ya?"

"Let he who is without sin. . . ." I shrugged. "I just figure I shouldn't jump to conclusions."

"Why not? Everybody else does." She slanted me a bright glance, tossing ringlets out of her eyes. "When they ain't jumping *me.*"

"Cute," I said, "real cute. Anybody ever tell you that?"

"Alla time." She dumped the clothes onto the bed. "I had a boyfriend, once. A real boyfriend, not a baptist."

I blinked. "Baptist?"

"You know. A john."

I laughed, then caught my breath as my side protested. "Pretty good, Ria."

"I'm better than pretty good, chico . . . I'm damn fine." She cocked a hip and perched a hand upon it, baring the smooth length of her dusky throat. "Finer than you've ever known."

I laughed again, ruefully. "Without a doubt."

"So look, I gotta go out—gotta go to work, you know? So crash, eat—'cator's in the kitchen—shower . . . the vid-plate's in the other room, disks on the shelf." She shrugged. "Whatever you need."

"You seem pretty sure I'm harmless."

"Ain't you?" She snapped gum again. "I seen what the JFs done to you, chico—it takes a lot outta you. . . ." She displayed her tattoo. "Besides, with no number, Dios wouldn't let you out of here if you trashed the place and tried to run."

I stared. "Dios?"

"Dios. God. Big Sister." She jerked a thumb toward the other room. "Mon-i-tor. By the door."

"Ah."

"I won't be back tonight; that is, if some baptist gets lucky."

"A Baptist might."

"Small 'b,' " she ellucidated. "Capital 'B' means trouble."

"JF?"

"Most of 'em. 'Course now they've split into so many bits'n pieces it's hard to keep 'em all straight: Southern, Northern, Mason-Dixon, Manhattan, . . ." Ria yanked up the glittering strap. "Where you been, you don't know this? The White House?

Or did they laze your brain too, damn 'em; I wouldn't be surprised."

It was far too easy. "I am a stranger in a strange land."

"Yeah. Ain't we all, with the JFs tryin' to run things." She picked up her glitterbag and threaded an arm through the strap. "Sleep tight." She flashed a grin. "Dream of me."

"Would—Dios—let me out of here if I needed to go somewhere?"

"Sure, so long's you don't have anything of mine stuffed into your pockets. Everything's chipped."

"What about these clothes?"

"Not mine, chico; different code. Dios won't squawk."

"Ah."

She frowned. "But where would you go?"

"Church."

"Church!" The gum nearly fell out of her neon-painted mouth. "Jesus Christ, you mean to slamdance right in and get in somebody's face over what they did to you?"

I shrugged. "I usually turn the other cheek. Depending."

"Churches on every corner, mostly. Can't miss 'em. Mickey C's."

"What?"

"Mickey C's. MacChurch. They're everywhere." She scowled. "You after a special flavor?"

I grinned. "I'd like to go to the john."

She got it. "Huh." Gum popped in her mouth. "I'd have said you looked more Jewish."

"Don't judge a disk by its color."

"Never." Ria grinned. "But I can't pass up the purple ones." She flicked a ringlet dangling against a bare shoulder. "You like purple, chico grande?"

I jabbed a chin in the direction of the other room. "Dios doesn't discriminate, does—he? She? It?"

215

"It's pronouced shee-it." Beneath the glitterstars and CZs, her skin glowed dusky-rose. Well, I had pheromones, too. "Get it?"

"Hah," I said dutifully. "Yes, I like purple. . . . I like all colors, all shapes, all sizes. It's how I'm programmed."

She froze. "You're not—? Christ, don't tell me you're a fucking cyboy. Damn it, chico. . . ." Her eyes were huge. "Are you?"

"Would it matter? Are we not all one in the Eye of Dios?"

"Damn you—"

"Now, now. That's not polite. What if it stuck?"

"What if what stuck?"

"Damnation."

"Can't."

"How do you know?"

"Because if you're damned, you go to hell. And there ain't none."

"How do you know?"

" 'Cause if there was one, I'd be in it. So would a lot of us. The Jesus Freaks would see to that; they damn us alla time." She scratched carefully at her cheek, deftly avoiding glitterstars and CZs. "You'd be there too, I guess."

"Not a chance."

Ria laughed, good humor restored. "Snowball's?"

I pondered it. "If there is no hell, a snowball would not be at risk."

Ria squinted. "Kinda like the 'if a tree falls' question, ain't it?"

"Kinda."

"Well, they ain't solved that one, yet, either . . . and likely they never will. JFs don't much care for philosophy. They figure all the questions are answered. All you gotta do is look 'em up in that damn Book—" She waved at me violently. "Yeah, yeah, I know—we're back to hell already."

"Some, yes," I agreed mildly. "But the Doghouse isn't all that bad."

"Doghouse?"

It was my turn to grin. "Dog spelled backward. . . ."

"Christ." She waved again, cutting me off. "I give up. I'm millering."

"Millering?"

"I'm outta here. Later." She was gone only briefly, then poked her head back around the door jamb. Her expression was impish as she aimed a finger toward the monitor. "Vaya con Dios."

"Hey."

She turned back. "Yeah?"

"What's 'Ria' short for?"

She shrugged. "Old hispania name. A real mouthful, traditional-like, which I'm not. I cut it to Maria, then Ria." Her mouth twisted. "Something different."

"Ah." Okay, Gabe. I owe you. "Thanks for cleaning me up."

"Sure, no problemo." She hesitated. "If you go out . . . well, you comin' back here tonight?"

"Won't you be—busy?"

"Not here. This ain't my crib; it's home." Ria arched an eyebrow. "I let the baptist buy a cube."

"Then maybe I'll be back, if it's okay."

Something fizzed in her eyes. "I'll reprog Dios to let you in on your voiceprint. It's on file now. Just say your name at the door." She paused. "What is your name?"

Same as always. "J.C. Carpenter." I picked up the jeans. "Thanks again. I owe you."

Maria Magdalena shrugged. "So St. Peter can punch my ticket at the pearlies."

I waited until she was gone. Triggered the link. *Pete?*

Yeah?

She in?

Whaddaya think, chico grande?
I grinned. *Thanks, Pete.*
No problemo.

I slept off the scotty-lag overnight, showered, repatched my side, ate replicated bread and olives washed down with goat's milk. Ria wasn't home yet; some baptist had gotten lucky. I had Dios let me out, then went hunting the first Mickey C's I could find. It wasn't difficult; as Ria'd said, there was one on every corner. All I had to do was look for the golden crosses.

The vid-plate in the door glowed cool blue. White Scripture scrolled across it continuously in a multiplicity of languages; indeed, Pop's kids had been exceedingly fruitful. It was a real task to play shepherd now; too many far-flung sheep bleating in tongues.

"Yo," I said. "Dios?"

The screen blanked. No multi-lined Scripture, save for a single continuous crawl across the bottom, like a sports score. In hispania. Password time. I sighed. "Repent ye sinner?"

The crawl shifted mid-word to English.

New file. Try sporting events. "John 3:16?"

Nada.

"What's the deal?" I asked. "Little hard to minister to the masses if they can't get in the front door, don't you think?"

The crawl continued.

Scotty-lag's gone. Time to get into the swing of things and do the job I came for. I thought about Ria's instructions concerning Dios. "Voiceprint," I said. "Jesus Christ."

The screen blanked entirely. Then a muted, tasteful chime sounded from the invisible speaker, followed immediately by an equally muted, tasteful voice. "Praise His name, for only through the Son of God shall you discover Him."

Loosely translated from the original. "Praise the Lord," I

murmured obediently, in fatuous self-flattery. The door hissed aside and tucked itself away into hidden pockets. I grinned irreverently. "All things shall come to he who believes."

As I crossed the threshold the door whispered closed behind me. A man waited for me on the other side, hands folded together just below his waist. He wore a simple but well-tailored navy suit, a quiet synthsilk tie in muted burgundy-on-cream, a single modest ring, and a professional smile. "How may we serve you, my son?"

"Cut the crap," I said. "You don't look a thing like my Father, and you don't have the faintest idea how to serve Him. Just take me to the jerk who runs this joint."

His smile didn't slip; he was probably used to abuse. "This is a house of worship," he said quietly. "We seek no confrontation—"

"You seek confrontation all the time, my man. That's what videvangelists are all about: preaching the Word to he who doesn't give a rat's ass where he's going when he's dead." I got up into his face. "Does that compute?"

His mouth compressed only faintly. Blue eyes reflected no hostility, only a pinched kind of contempt. "Reverend Guy is very busy. Do you have an appointment?"

"He claims to know me very well," I told him. "Matter of fact, I hear he invokes my name a lot."

His face closed up. His mouth now was little more than a retentive seam. "I'm sorry—"

"So's Pop. He's mad as—well . . . let's just say He's not going to take it anymore." I flicked a nonexistent speck of dust off his immaculate lapel. "How about it? Do you take me to the reverend like a regular stand-up sort of guy, or do I perform a miracle and walk right through a wall?"

"I beg your pardon, sir—"

"Never mind." I stepped right by him and stared hard at the

blank wall. "No voiceprint. No retinal scan. How's about this?" I pressed the inside of my wrist against the smooth surface. The wall was Red Sea to my Moses and slid apart into pockets, displaying a handsomely appointed office lush with leather and living plants, not synthsilk. A massive desk stood paramount; on the faux brick wall behind it glowed three golden crosses. The office was empty, but I had no doubt some kind of Dios watched from somewhere.

"Sir!" Navy Suit's face was white. His hands trembled minutely. "Why didn't you say you had been blessed? You had only to tell me!"

I drew a blank. Gabe does the best he can, but he doesn't know everything—and Pop's too busy a lot of the time to explain the mysteries. "Blessed?"

His fingers touched the half inch of snowy cuff showing at his wrist. A gold cufflink glinted. "The Stigmata. So few of us have been privileged. . . ."

"Oh." The light went on. "You mean I've been pre-approved?"

"Sir." His expression was severe without quite bordering on blatant rudeness; I no longer fit into any of his pre-conceived slots, and it made him nervous. He wanted to throw me out, but no longer knew if he had the authority. "Forgive me if I don't respond to your levity, but we take matters of religion very seriously."

"You're forgiven. . . ." Such a small matter when you know the trick. "Now, define 'religion.' "

He stared.

"Well?"

"Sir, there are many definitions."

"Tell me yours."

He was nonplussed, but did his best. Unctuously he began, "Religion is a system of belief . . . a code of ethics, a philosophy—"

I knew Mike and Gabe were listening through the link. They get a kick out of semantics. *Okay guys, here we go.* "Philosophy? But I thought you shunned philosophers because they ask the kinds of questions that the Book doesn't answer—the Book being, I'm assuming, the Bible." He nodded; what other Book could there be? "So. How come you worship something you abhor?"

I was getting to him. "But we don't—"

"But if religion—in your own words—is a system for belief, a code of ethics—quantified, I presume, according to the dictates of a quorum—and yet is also a philosophy, how then can you deny that you worship that which you abhor?"

He breathed rapidly. He shot pristine cuffs once again with trembling fingers. "Sir—I think you should speak with Reverend Guy."

About time I got some service around here. "Please."

He gestured toward the office. "Through there. He will be with you in a moment."

"Thank you."

He stepped back hastily. The door/wall whispered closed between us, leaving me in alone in the office.

Well, maybe not entirely alone. Yet another door slid open. "Number Three," I muttered as a man stepped through. He'd obviously been listening, to arrive so promptly.

He moved purposefully to a position that put the desk between us, but he did not sit. "I'm Reverend Guy. How may I be of service?" Just the faintest suggestion of a drawl. Southern, then, or Mason-Dixon, according to Ria's labels. He wore an exquisitely tailored suit of charcoal-gray synthsilk, cream shirt, and a handpainted, multi-hued tie. His white hair was thick and vigorous, brushed into stylish quiescence and lightly moussed. Good teeth—maybe his own; probably recapped—good smile. Sincere. Grooming was immaculate, and the diamond in the gold pinky ring was of tastefully moderate size.

"Tell me something," I said. "Is it a requirement for videvangelists to have big hair? I've never yet seen a bald Bakkerite."

His smile froze. Sincerity altered to wary suspicion. "Bakkerite?"

"Don't know the term?"

Suspicion was answered. His manner now was clipped, almost
curt; he'd be asking his frontman how in the world I'd gained
admittance. "Of course I know the term. It is an insult. We do
not condone its use."

"Then how about Swaggart-stick?"

His nostrils pinched. "I think perhaps you should leave. James
made a mistake in admitting you."

"James didn't have much choice." I lifted my right wrist and
flashed him the wound. Then the left one. "He really had no
choice—but then, he didn't know that. Now you do."

He didn't bat an eyelash. "Stigmata can be falsified."

"I imagine a Bakkerite would know that."

"If you expect me to accept that at face value—"

"Do you doubt the Lord, Reverend Guy?"

"I do not doubt that Jesus Christ will return one day—"

"He's *heee-ere.*"

"—to relieve the world of its suffering—"

"And of those who mean to lead it astray. Even the elect.
Remember your Revelations?" I placed my palms flat against
the glossy surface of his desk and leaned on braced arms.
"Depending on which version of the Bible you use. . . . Pop
only knows who's reinterpreted the latest translation for the
hundred-thousandth time." I turned and hitched one buttock
up on the edge of his desk, swinging a bare foot idly. "You ever
think about that? Translation? Interpretation?"

Reverend Guy was silent.

"Translation isn't an exact science, you know. Think about it.

222

Translation has a huge margin for error; it has to, because it's solely dependent upon the skill and knowledge of the translator. And no matter how good your translator might be, he's human. He's mortal. He is flawed." I paused. He still maintained a silence bristling with outrage. "And when the text he's working with is a translation of a translation of a—well, you get my drift." I shrugged. "Your Book was written in a whole raft of languages long dead. It's a regular Babel, reverend . . . and I find it unlikely—no, impossible—that any man on earth, no matter how erudite, could literally translate what a whole series of men—no women, just men—with very different agendas wrote nearly twenty-two centuries ago."

Reverend Guy sat down with rigid grace. His expression had gotten stuck in I-have-to-listen-because-I-have-no-choice-but-I-don't-believe-a-word-of-it mode.

Time for hardball. "Did you know King James was bisexual?"

The flesh of his throat darkened perceptibly. Slowly the wave of color crept up into his face. "We no longer use that version."

"Because you discovered the truth. Some historian 'outed' the king."

He worked hard to maintain an even tone. "There have been many versions since the King James—"

"The copyists who worked from bootleg translations—remember, back in James's time not many were permitted to own a printed Bible; maybe a means to maintain control?—were nothing but hired labor. They worked for good old King Jim, who was the one who determined what stayed in, and what got thrown out." I shrugged. "The 'divine right of kings.' Except he wasn't. Divine. Neither are you."

He peeled his lips apart. "Why have you come?"

"Haven't you read your Bible lately?"

His face quivered. "Which version?"

I laughed. "Very good. But then most Bakkerites are pretty

quick on their feet, or they'd all go to prison." I displayed my teeth; I'd had good dentistry, too. "I have come to set things to rights."

Congestion drained away. He was dead white and coldly furious. "If that is true—if for the sake of argument I accept your presumption—"

"Devil's advocate?"

"—and agree that you are whom you claim you are, why do you come to the house of God? WE do not need to be set to rights! THEY require it!"

"They?"

"Out there, in the streets." He gesticulated. "Everywhere. Sin runs rampant; have you not seen it? In our cyberbooks, on vid-plate, on the disks, in art, photography—even in our software! My dear Lord—"

"Thank you."

"—everywhere we walk we are accosted by sin! Whores ply the streets, children are suborned—"

"Rock music?"

"He comes in a bewildering array of guises: in art, in games—"

"Who does?"

"The anti-Christ."

"Oh. Him. Or—her." I grinned at his thunderstruck expression. "It is sexist to believe the anti-Christ must be male."

"Sexism! Sexism! Do you see?" He rose up from his chair. "Women have shunned their true roles as helpmeets to put on the raiment of men—"

"Fig leaves were unisex."

Reverend Guy trembled with righteous indignation. "I will have you taken from this place. This is a house of God—"

"This is your house. You built it with the money you scammed out of innocents hoping to purchase peace." I shook my head.

"Pop's never been here. There isn't room for Him here."

He was completely nonplussed. "Room?"

"Egos." I paused. "He's got one, you know. He'd have to. Not everyone can pull off Creation in only seven days."

"Six," he corrected mechanically. "On the seventh day He rested."

"Seven. He cheated. He forgot the crossopterygian. Had to make it from scratch and drop it in the soup."

He blinked twice. "Soup?"

"Primordial." Now the poor soul was really confused; being a chip-carrying Creationist, he'd neglected his science studies. "Remember what I said about interpretation? Well, Pop never meant everyone to assume He created man as man . . . I mean, with two legs, arms, eyes, ears, a nose, beer belly and repairman butt. Let's face it, Adam and Eve weren't apes—"

His turn. "Thank you."

"—they were fish. Sort of. Pre-fish, maybe; it's a hard concept to get a handle on."

"This is outrageous." But he wasn't very convincing. By now he was fascinated, if still locked in denial.

"The truth is stranger than fiction," I agreed. "But truth is truth."

"I know the law." He drew himself up. "To be true, truth must be provably true in a court of law."

"So you want proof." I pointed toward a carafe sitting on his credenza. "Is that water?"

He didn't look. "Yes."

"Try again." I shrugged. "White Zin went out in the '80s. I made it a cab-shiraz. Arizona grapes, with California gone bye-bye."

He looked, then twitched his head back to me. His eyes now were like marbles, hard and cold and steely. "You have hacked the church computer and put a virus in the replicator software.

You'll go to prison for this."

"Afraid I might find the proof I need to bring you up on charges?" I shook my head. "Not worth the effort. You'll answer to a Higher Authority."

"You are a clever man, but you cannot fool me."

"Never con a con man."

His right hand hovered near the front of his desk; computer controls, of course. "This has gone far enough. I shall have church security escort you off the premises."

"You want proof? I'll give you proof." I chewed my bottom lip. "Do you watch old shows in the vid-plate?"

It was so inconsequential a question he answered immediately and without prevarication. "Of course. Old shows were cleaner, more wholesome."

"Not that old. No—there was a show on fifty years or so ago about this guy who went bopping around in time. Nice guy, with a holographic pal. Quantum something. Quantum Hop."

"Leap." Then he flushed, as if embarrassed to admit he knew the show.

"Hop, leap; who's to know?" I shrugged. "But they had this waiting room for the people who got taken out of their bodies when this guy hopped—leaped—in."

Reverend Guy stared. "What does this have to do with blasphemy?"

"Not much. I'm just trying to prepare you for the scotty."

"Scotty?"

I keyed the link. *Gabe?*

Here.

Ready for this guy?

Any time.

I smiled at him. "Vaya con Dios. I'll be waiting for you."

Gabe didn't keep the good reverend long. He never does. It's against the House rules to play too many body- or head-games; the scotty's a rough ride even for me. But by the time Reverend Guy was back, I'd settled into his chair with my feet up on his desk, leaving smudged heelprints all over the polished surface.

He wobbled a little on materialization, but steadied himself with a hand pressed against the front of the desk. I smiled. "We call it the Second Going, euphemistically speaking. Kind of appropriate, though."

Reverend Guy shuddered. "My God—"

"Everybody's." I drank wine, decided to go for a favorite instead and altered it to scotch. Single malt, in fact, quite old, with nice peaty flavor that lovingly bathed my tongue—but never mind that. " 'A rose by any other name. . . .' " I pointed to the chairs set discreetly aside for visitors. "Have a seat. Scotch? Or wine. Beer?"

"Nothing." He groped for the chair, pulled it up, collapsed into it. His mouth worked a few seconds before a voice emerged. "Why . . . why. . . ."

"Somebody once told me that if you posed that question to a computer, you'd knock it into a loop and get it stuck there. My feeling was, if I were that computer I'd come back with 'Because.' " I grinned. "Or 'Why ask why?' "

He swallowed heavily and tried again. "Why here?"

"My here isn't always here," I said. "Sometimes it's there. Or somewhere else entirely."

"I don't understand."

"It's not a Second Coming, reverend. It's more like a twelfth, a twenty-first, a fifty-third . . . shoot, I've lost count. I just go where I'm needed."

"—go?"

"Hop. Leap. Scotty. I'm just the meat, not the mind. I leave that stuff to Gabe and Mike."

"I met—" He paused; it was difficult. "—Gabe."

I grinned. "Gabe's a good guy. Got a great sense of humor."

"Gabriel."

"We're pretty informal." I sat up, pulling my feet off his desk. "What's this I hear about some nut trying to bomb a whorehouse?"

He reddened. "They are abominations."

"Bombs are, yes."

"Whores."

"They're women making a living. And all it is, really, is the law of supply and demand . . . if you want it to end, why not look at the men who seek out such carnal traffic?"

"The whores lure them."

"In some cases, I suppose. But I figure it's usually a guy looking for a good time. He'll take what he can get."

He swallowed visibly. "You condone prostitution?"

"It's the second oldest profession, reverend. That goes a loooooong way back."

He was less condescending now—the scotty is pretty humbling all on its own, and then there's Gabe—but remained intransigent on the subject of women. "It should not be permitted."

"Who says?"

"The Bible says—"

"Which version? Whose translation? Good ol' King James?" I grinned as he winced. "Only one man can say what is and is not permitted—and I don't notice the streets are gridlocked due to a massive influx of salt pillars."

"A low-sodium diet is better for you."

I blinked. "Is that a joke? Did you make a joke?"

He passed a hand over his face. "This is—quite unbelievable."

"I hear they call you Jesus Freaks."

Silence. But confirmation pinched his eyes.

"Not much better than Bakkerite or Swaggart-stick, is it? Slugs you right in the gut, doesn't it?"

"We are trying to make the world a better place."

"By trying to force the world to live by your rules?"

"We live our lives according to the Word of God."

Good humor evaporated; well, I'm not perfect. Just forgiven. "You live your lives according to the will of whatever man—or woman—is articulate, imaginative, smart, and charismatic enough to assume the mantle of leadership."

Two livid spots of color burned high on his cheeks. "You could say that very thing about Jesus Christ Himself. *Your*self."

I applauded softly. "Bravo. So is the man deafened by his own tumult eventually restored."

His color faded again as he acknowledged my observation. "But—I—" He plucked his glossy synthsilk handkerchief from his breast pocket and blotted his upper lip. "I have questioned—"

"You're supposed to question. Pop gave you a brain."

"But. . . ." He blinked three times in rapid succession. "I must never question. We must follow the Word of God."

"Or the word of Reverend Guy."

Desperation was setting in. "I am an instrument of my God!"

"Really? You're going to stick to that after where you've just been?"

His face matched his suit. "You cannot expect me to renounce my faith—"

"Ah. Faith. That's a different story. Faith is a whole different kettle of fish."

"Crossopterygians?"

I applauded again; he really was loosening up. That's half the battle; men and women like this guy are so anal-retentive. "Faith and religion are not synonymous. In fact, I view them as oxymorons."

"I don't understand."

"Religion is a ritual. People trust ritual. It's easy. It keeps them from having to think for themselves." I shrugged. "Smoke and mirrors. Mumbo-jumbo. Sleight of hand. Dog-and-pony show. Just a few definitions of organized religion."

"But—faith is—"

"—entirely different. Faith is belief. Faith is a pure and unquestioning belief in God . . . whatever His Name or Guise might be. Pop likes masquerades." I studied my scotch. "Ritual is power. The individual who conducts the ritual is the instrument of that power. If he—or she—is clever enough, the people forget the instrument is nothing more than that, and begin to put their faith in the human vessel instead of in the—entity—for whom the ritual is performed." I looked through the glass and saw his face warped by curvature. "You and people like you are fucking up the world."

He recoiled. "I will not have that word spoken in the house of God!"

"He invented it."

"It is filth."

"It's ugly. It's meant to be. It's meant to shock. But it's overused, and now it means nothing except to those people who are truly offended." I wasn't smiling now. "You offend me. You are abomination. In the name of my Father—in *my* name!—you try to remake the world and everyone in it by dictating how they should live." I had his full attention now. "There are Christians in the world who believe as strongly, but in their own quiet way. These poor people are getting tarred by the same brush. Some of them are hesitant to admit they were born again because you've made it a dirty word." I shook my head. "Face it, reverend—you and JFs like you are giving the rest of us a bad name."

"But you dictate how people should live! The Bible—"

"—is a book. Do you believe everything you read?"

He was trembling again. He was a con man, perhaps, but the most dangerous kind; he truly believed what he was doing was for the common good. He lived the party line. "I must believe. I must put my trust in God."

"It's a great how-to manual," I said quietly; no more need for bombast or fancy semantics. "There's a lot of good stuff in there. But it's kind of like an instruction booklet in a foreign language: you can make out enough of the words to get the gist of it, but there's always a part left over." I smiled and set down the glass. "Pop quit on you once. He hit the delete key, except for one small file called Noah. He swore never to do it again. But things were getting more and more screwed up . . . so He sent me. Again. And again. As many times as it takes."

"Different times?"

"Different times, different places, different races. I've got a trunkful of passports."

"Why. . . ." His feet were flat on the floor. He smoothed damp palms down his trousered thighs. "Why come to me? Why not to the president?"

"Presidents come and go. Bakkerites usually have greater longevity." I stood up. "It only takes one man. One woman. That's all."

He was alarmed. "There is too much to do . . . one man couldn't possibly do it all!"

"I only had thirty-three years," I reminded him. "And we didn't have vid-plates, or the 'net, or any of the conveniences you take for granted. All I had was myself, and a certain knack for the language." I grinned. "You know—the parables."

He stared back in incomprehension.

I ellucidated. "Communication is a two-way street. People hear, and people learn, if the language—if the imagery—jibes with their frame of reference. You know. Fiery chariots, the great red dragon with ten horns and seven heads, and all like that; it's easy to remember. Vivid imagery is the best way to plant an idea."

He nodded slowly. "I think—I think I'm beginning to understand."

"Look," I said, "let the kids play their fantasy games. Let the people read their cyberbooks, sing their songs, paint what comes into their heads. They're telling stories . . . painting parables . . . exploring the greatest gift Pop ever gave to mankind." I tapped my head. "Imagination. Creativity. The people of this country have fought long and hard for the freedom to simply be. Don't strip that away from them."

His hands were trembling. "I meant well."

"You all mean well. All you fundie Jesus Freaks."

He had the grace to wince. "I'm sorry."

"You've told me. Now tell the guy in the navy suit. Tell your congregation. Post it on the vid-plate on your door. Get it out on the 'net."

"They won't listen."

"One day at a time, chico."

He swallowed heavily. "What happens now?"

"To me? I leave. I've got two days, still—it's always three days."

His handkerchief was crumpled. He dried his hands, then stuffed it into a trouser pocket as he rose. "Tomorrow is Sunday. Will you come to the service?"

"We'll be there."

"We? Oh—you mean Gabe."

"No. Pretty little chica name of Ria."

It shocked him. "You're with a woman?"

"Don't worry," I said, "it's strictly platonic." I walked around his desk and clapped him on the shoulder. "Keep the faith, guy. I'm millering."

On the street again I blinked into brilliant sunshine. One of Pop's best days.

I keyed the link. *Gabe?*

Yeah?

A day or two extra?

You know the rules, J.C.

She's a great girl, Gabe.

She is every time, J.C. And every time the answer's the same. Three days.

Yeah. I know. I glanced back at the vid-plate. The Scriptures were gone, replaced with a notice that said the screen was temporarily out of service and would be reprogrammed soon. *Gabe?*

Still here, J.C.

Tell Pop I think it'll work.

I think He knows, J.C.

Millering, I said. Gabe shut down the link.

RITE OF PASSAGE

The woman moved like a dancer. Her feet sluffed through the warm sand with the soft, seductive sibilance of bare flesh against fine-grained dust. Wisps rose, drifted; layered our bodies in dull, gritty shrouds: pale umber, ocher-bronze, taupe-gray.

But the shrouds, I thought, were applicable; the woman could kill us all.

I watched her move. I watched the others watch her move. All men. No women here, at this moment, under such circumstances; never.

Except for Del.

I watched her move: detached appreciation. Admiration, as always. And pride. Two-edged pride. One: that the woman brought honor to the ritual of the dance within the circle, and two: that she was my right hand, my left hand; companion, swordmate, bedmate.

Edged? Of course. Pride is always a two-edged blade. With Del, the second edge is the sharpest of all, for *me,* because for the Sandtiger to speak of pride in Del is to speak also of possessiveness. She'd told me once that a man proud of a woman is too often prouder of his possession *of* her, and not of the woman for being herself.

I saw her point, but . . . well Del and I don't always agree. But then, if we did, life would be truly boring.

I watched Del and the men who watched her as a matter of course, but I also watched the man she faced in the circle. I saw the signature pattern of his sword flashing in the sunlight, Southron-style: dip here, feint there, slash, lunge, cut, thrust . . . and always trying to throw the flashes and glints into her eyes. With precise purpose, of course; ordinarily, a shrewd ploy. Another opponent might have winced or squinted against the blinding light, giving over the advantage; Del didn't. But then, Del was accustomed to manufacturing her own light with that Northern sword of hers; the Southron one the man used was hardly a match for her own.

He was good. Almost quite good. But not quite. Certainly not good enough to overcome Del.

I knew she would kill him. But *he* didn't. He hadn't realized it yet.

Few men do realize it when they enter the circle with Del. They only see her: Del, the Northern woman with blond, corn-silk hair and blue, blue eyes. Her perfect face with its sun-gilded flesh stretched taut across flawless bones. They see all of that, and her magnificent body, and they hardly notice the sword in her hands. Instead, they smile. They feel tolerant and magnani-mous, because they must face a woman, and a beautiful woman. But because she is beautiful they will give her anything, if only to share a moment of her time, and so they give her their lives.

She danced. Long legs, long arms, bared to the Southron sun; Del wears a sleeveless thigh-length leather tunic bordered with Northern runes. But the runes were now a blur of blue silk against dark leather as she moved.

Step. Step. Slide. Skip. Miniscule shifting of balance from one hip to the other. Sinews sliding beneath the flesh of her arms as she parried and riposted. All in the wrists, with Del. A delicate tracery of blade tip against the afternoon sky, blocking her op-ponent's weapon with a latticework of steel.

Del never set out to be a killer. Even now she isn't, quite; she's a sword-dancer, like me. But in this line of work, more often than not, the dance—a ritualized exhibition of highly-trained sword-skill—becomes serious and people die.

As this man would die, regardless of his own particular skill. Regardless of how many years he had apprenticed with a shodo or how many skill levels he had attained. He still danced, but he was dead.

She is simply that good.

I sighed a little, watching her. She didn't *play* with him, precisely, being too well-trained for such arrogance within the circle, but I could see she had judged and acknowledged her opponent's sword-skill as less than her own. It wouldn't make her smile; not Del. It wouldn't make her careless. But it *would* make her examine the limits of his talent with the unlimited repertoire of her own, and show him what it meant to step into the circle with someone of her caliber.

Regardless of her gender.

"Sword-dancer?" The question came from a man who stepped up next to me outside of the circle, slipping out of the crowd to stand closer to me than I liked. "Sandtiger?"

I didn't take my eyes from the dance, but I could see the man. Young. Copper-skinned. Swathed in a rich silk burnous of melon orange, sashed with a belt of gold-freighted bronze. A small turban hid most of his hair, but not the fringe of dark brown lashes surrounding hazel eyes.

"Sandtiger?" he asked again, hands tucked into voluminous sleeves.

"Sandtiger," I agreed, still watching the dance.

He sighed a little and smiled. The smile faded; he realized my attention was mostly on the circle, not on him. For just an instant, anxiety flickered in his eyes. "My master offers gold to the sword-dancer called the Sandtiger."

Well, Del could win without me watching. I turned to face the young man at once. "Employment?" I asked smoothly.

A bob of turbaned head. "Of great urgency, my lord Sandtiger. My master waits to speak with you."

I didn't answer at once. Too much noise. All the indrawn breaths of the onlookers reverberated as one tremendous hiss of shock and disbelief. Well, I could have warned them. . . . No doubt he was too overcome by the fact he danced with a woman, even a woman who was quite obviously dangerous. No doubt he grew lazy. Or desperate. And now he was plainly dead.

I glanced at Del, automatically evaluating her condition. Her face bore a faint sheen of sweat. She was sun-flushed, lips pressed together. Blond hair, disheveled and damp, hung around her shoulders. But her breathing was even and shallow; the Southroner had hardly pressed her at all.

She turned and looked at me. The Northern sword, blood-painted now, hung loosely in her hand. She hunched one shoulder almost imperceptibly—a comment; an answer to my unspoken question—and then she nodded, only once; an equally private exchange.

I turned back to the turbaned messenger. A servant. I thought, but not just any servant. Whoever his master was, his wealth was manifest. And in the South, wealth is synonymous with power.

"Well?" I suggested.

The hazel eyes were fixed on Del as she cleaned her sword of blood. The onlookers huddled and muttered among themselves, settling bets; none were winners, I knew, except for the one wise man who knew the woman better than most. Many drifted away from the circle entirely; away from the woman who had killed one of their number in a supremely masculine occupation with supremely "masculine" skill.

Sword-dancing isn't for everyone, any more than assassination is. The profession carries its own weight in legend and superstition. And now Del, once more, turned Southron tradition upside down and inside out.

I smiled a little. The servant looked back at me. He didn't smile at all. "A *woman.*" Two words: disbelief, shock, a trace of anger as well. Underlying hostility: *a woman had beaten a man.*

"A woman," I agreed blandly. "About that job . . . ?"

He pulled himself together. "My master extends an invitation for you to take tea with him. I am not authorized to inform you of the employment he has to offer. Will you come?"

Tea. Not one of my favorite drinks. Especially effang tea, gritty, thick, offensive, but customary in the South. Maybe I could talk the man into some aqivi. . . . "I'll come," I agreed. "Where to?"

The servant gestured expansively, one smooth hand sweeping out of its silken sleeve. "This way, my lord Sandtiger."

And so I left Del behind, as I so often had to when we rode the Southron sands, and went with the servant to see what the master had to offer.

Damp hair tumbled over her shoulders. Her skin glowed apricot-pink from the bathwater's heat. Dressed in a fresh tunic—this one bordered with crimson silk—she sat on the edge of the narrow cot, bending to lace sandals cross-gartered to her knees. "Well?"

Del was never one to waste her breath on two words when one would do. But then, she knew she didn't have to, with me. Enough time spent together in deadly situations had honed language down to only a few necessary words.

I shut the door behind me. The inn wasn't the best; we'd spent the last of our coppers a couple of weeks ago searching for the man Del had just dispatched in the circle. Since then our only income had been wagers won from unsuspecting Southron men betting against the Northern woman. Hoolies, the only way we could pay *this* bill was to use all the bets I'd just won, leaving us no extra. That's the lot of a sword-dancer: rich one day, broke the next.

Today was a rich day, thanks to the job I'd just accepted.

"I said I'd have to check with my partner," I said, "but, frankly, we need the money, and I didn't dare tell him about you."

One shoulder moved in a negligent shrug. "We agreed I'd keep a low profile while we were in the South, Tiger, to make things easier." She didn't so much as glance at me as she said it, but her even tone was eloquent; in the South, women aren't due the respect men are. Women bear children, tend the man, tend the household. They don't enter business. They *certainly* don't enter the circle.

"Yes, well . . . um, this was a little different."

She waited in silence for the explanation.

I sighed. "It's like this," I told her. "Our employer is a *khemi.*"

Del merely frowned.

I sighed again, heavily, "It's a religious sect. An offshoot of the Hamidaa faith. Hamidaa hold majority here."

She nodded, but the frown didn't fade.

"*Khemi* are zealots," I explained. "They take the word of the Hamidaa'n—the sacred scrolls of the Hamidaa—rather literally."

"And what does the Hamidaa'n say?"

"That women are abomination, unclean vessels that should not be touched, spoken to or allowed to enter a *khemi*'s thoughts."

"Pretty conclusive," Del observed after a moment. "Can't be too many *khemi* left, if they don't have congress with women."

She was taking it better than I'd expected. "I imagine they've figured out a few loopholes, since the job involves a son. Ordinarily I'd have turned it down, of course, since I do have *some* sensibilities, after all, but we really *do* need the money."

"Just what *is* this job?"

"We are expected to negotiate the release of this son, who was kidnapped two months ago."

"Negotiate." Del nodded. "That means steal back. Who, how and when?"

"Name's Dario," I said. "Soon as possible."

Del combed slender fingers through damp hair. Her attention seemed divided, but I knew she listened intently. "That's the who and the when. What about the how?"

"Haven't gotten that far. I wanted to leave something for *you* to contribute."

She smiled briefly. "I imagine this *khemi* had an explanation for the kidnapping."

"Says a neighboring tanzeer had the boy taken to force trade concessions."

Pale brows slide up. "Trade concessions? Tanzeer? That means—"

"It means our employer is the tanzeer of *this* domain, bascha, and he's more than willing to pay handsomely." I pulled the leather purse out of a pocket in my russet burnous and rattled the contents with pleasure. "Half up front, half after. *This* is enough to last six months, depending on how extravagant we feel once the job is done. Imagine how rich we'll be when we're paid the *other* half."

"You and your gold. . . ." Del's attention was mostly on the sword she unsheathed and set across her lap. "Sounds easy enough. When do we leave?"

"About a half hour ago."

Rez. Small enough town, was Rez, capping a domain not much larger. No wonder the tanzeer had deemed it necessary to go to such dramatic lengths as kidnapping to get concessions from Dumaan's tanzeer. Dumaan had been a rich town, rich domain.

Dumaan had wealth to spare.

Some of it was in my purse.

Del and I did a careful reconnoitering of Rez, locating the puny palace and paying strict attention to the comings and goings of palace servants. It is the servant population that forms the heart of any tanzeer's palace; subsequently, it is the servant population that forms the heart of any city, town, village. You don't see a tanzeer without first seeing his loyal servants, any more than you break into a tanzeer's palace without first figuring out how to get past his loyal servants.

A day spent loitering outside the ramshackle walls of the dilapidated palace with the rest of the bored petitioners did get me a little information. I now knew one thing was certain: Rez's tanzeer didn't subscribe to the same religion Dumaan's did. Or there wouldn't be female servants on marketing expeditions. And there *certainly* wouldn't be harem girls.

It was Del who came up with the idea. I mostly watched the silk-swathed women spill out of the palace gates, giggling among themselves like children. Hoolies, for all I knew they *were* children; the silk burnouses hid everything save hands and sandaled feet, and the hands clutched at bright draperies eagerly, as if unwilling to share with the petitioners what the tanzeer saw anytime he wanted. They were accompanied by three men in correspondingly bright silks and turbans; eunuchs, I knew, judging by bulk and Southron custom.

As I watched, Del considered. And then she dragged me off into the labyrinthine market stalls and made me listen in silence as she explained her plan.

Since she wouldn't let me talk, I did what I could to dissuade her. I shook my head repeatedly, vehemently rejecting her suggestion.

Finally, she stopped and glared. "Have you a better idea? Or *any* idea at all?"

I scowled. "That's unfair, Del. I haven't had time to think of one."

"No. You've been too busy ogling harem girls." A hand plastered across my mouth kept me from replying. "Wait here while I get the things we need." And she was gone.

Disgruntled, I waited in the shade of a saffron-dyed canvas awning, out of direct sunlight. The Southron sun can leach the sense from your head if you stay out in it too long; I wondered if it had finally gotten to Del's Northern brains.

She came back a while later lugging an armload of silks and spent several minutes laboriously separating them until she had one suit of masculine apparel and one of feminine. And then I began to understand.

"*Delilah*—"

"Put the clothes on." She plopped a creamy silken turban down on top of the pile in my arms. "We're going into the palace as soon as we're dressed."

"You want me to masquerade as a *eunuch*—?"

"You can't much masquerade as a harem girl, can you?" A smile curved the corners of her mouth. "Get dressed, Tiger— we'll be in and out in no time with Dario in tow."

"The *khemi* may have the right idea about you women," I muttered in disgust, staring at the clothing in my arms. "How does a eunuch act?"

"Probably not much different from the Sandtiger." Her words were muffled behind the multitudinous robes she was bundling herself into. "Ready?"

"I haven't even started."

"Hurry, Tiger. We have to insinuate ourselves into that flock of Southron sillies. And they're due to come by here about— *now*. Tiger—come *on*—"

Silks whipping, tassels flying, Del hastened after the women as they bobbed and weaved their way through the narrow stall-ways on their way back to the palace. Hastily I jerked on my eunuch's robes, slapped the turban on my head and went after her.

As always, the fist clenched itself into the wall of my belly as I passed guard after guard on my way into the palace. Del fit in with the other girls well enough—though a head taller than most—but *I* felt about as innocuous as a sandtiger in a flock of day-old goat kids. Nonetheless, no one paid much attention to me as we paraded down the corridors of the musty old palace.

I wasn't certain I *liked* being taken for a eunuch so easily.

I watched as Del in her rose-colored robes allowed the other girls to move ahead of her. Now we brought up the rear. I saw Del's quick hand gesture; we ducked out going around the next bend and huddled in a cavernous doorway.

"All right," she murmured. "We've passed four corridors—Dario's supposed to be in a room off the fifth. Come on, Tiger."

Sighing, I followed as she darted out of the doorway and headed down the appropriate corridor at a run. I *didn't* run, but only because I decided it was not in keeping with a eunuch's decorum.

I caught up to her outside yet another doorway. This one bore a large iron lock attached to the handle. "Dario?" I asked.

Del shrugged. "The women said it was. No reason not to trust them."

I glanced around the corridor uneasily. "Fine. *You* trust them, then. But did they slip you a key as well?"

"I already had one." She displayed it. "I borrowed it from the same eunuch who donated his clothing to you."

"Borrowed" key, "donated" clothing. Borrowed *time,* more like. "Hurry up, Del. Our luck can't hold forever."

She turned and inserted the key into the lock. Iron grated on iron; I wished for a little fat to oil the mechanism. But just about the time I was opening my mouth to urge a little more care, the lock surrendered and the door was ours.

Del shoved; nothing happened. I leaned on it a little and felt it move. Rust sifted from all the hinges. But the door stood open at last.

The room, as we'd hoped, was occupied. The occupant stood in the precise center of the little room—cell, really—and stared at us anxiously. He was, I judged, not much past ten or twelve. Dark-haired, dark-skinned, brown-eyed, clad in silken jade-green jodhpurs and soiled lime-colored tunic; two months had played havoc with all his finery. He was thin, a little gaunt, but still had both arms, both legs, his head; Rez's tanzeer, it appeared, didn't desire to injure Dumaan's heir, only to arrange a more equitable trade alliance.

And now the leverage was gone.

"Here, Dario." Del, smiling encouragingly, reached under a couple of layers of silken harem robes and pulled out more clouds of the stuff. Orange. It dripped from her hands: a woman's robes. "Put these on. Use the hood and modesty veil. Walk with your head down. Stay close to me and they'll never know the difference." Her warm smile flashed again. "We're getting you out of this place."

The boy didn't move. "Hamidaa'n tells us women are abomination, unclean vessels placed upon the earth by demons. They are the excrescence of all our former lives." Dario spoke matter-of-factly in a thin, clear voice. "I will touch nothing of women, speak to no women, admit nothing of women into my thoughts. I am *khemi.*" His eyes ignored Del altogether and looked only at me. "*You* are a man, a Southroner; *you* understand."

After a moment of absolute silence in which all I could hear were the rats scraping in the wall, I looked at Del.

She was pale but otherwise unshaken. At least, I thought she was. Sometimes you can't tell, with her. She can be cold, she can be hard, she can be ruthless—out of the circle as well as in. But she can also laugh and cry and shout aloud in an almost childish display of spirits too exuberant to be contained.

She did none of those things now. I thought, as I watched her looking at the boy, she had never met an opponent such as this son of the Hamidaa'n.

And I thought she was at a loss for what to do and how to answer for the first time in her life.

Slowly I squatted down in the cell. I was eye to eye with the boy. I smiled. "Choices," I said casually, "are sometimes difficult to make. A man may believe a choice between life and death is no choice at all, given his preference for staying alive, but it isn't always that simple. Now, something tells me you'd like very much to get out of here. Am I right?"

His chin trembled a little. He firmed it. "My father will send men to rescue me."

"Your father sent *us* to rescue you." I didn't bother to tell him his *khemi* father had no idea my partner was a woman. "A choice, Dario. Come with us now and we'll take you to your father, or stay here in this stinking rat hole."

Something squeaked and scrabbled in the wall behind the boy. I couldn't have timed it better.

Dario looked down at his bare feet sharply. Like the rest of him, they were dirty. But they also bore torn, triangular rat bites.

"Choices, Dario, are sometimes easy to make. But, once made, you have to live with them."

He was shaking. Tears began to gather in his eyes. Teeth bit into his lower lip as he stared resolutely at me, ignoring Del altogether. "Hamidaa'n tells us women are abomination, unclean vessels—"

He stopped talking because I closed his mouth with my hand.

I am large. So is my hand. Most of Dario's face disappeared beneath my palm and fingers. "Enough," I told him pleasantly. "I have no doubts you can quote scripture with the best of them, *khemi,* but now is not the time. Now *is* the time for you to make your choice." I released him and rose, gesturing toward Del and the silks.

Dario scrubbed the heel of a grimy hand across an equally dirty face. He stretched the flesh all out of shape, especially around the eyes: an attempt to persuade imminent tears to go elsewhere immediately. He caught a handful of lank hair behind an ear and tugged, hard, as if hoping that pain would make the decision itself less painful. I watched the boy struggle with his convictions and thought him very strong, if totally misguided.

Finally he looked up at me from fierce brown eyes. "I will walk out like *this.* In *these* clothes."

"And be caught in an instant," I pointed out. "The idea here, Dario, is to pass you off as a woman—or at least a *girl*—because otherwise we don't stand a chance of getting you out." I glanced sidelong at Del; her silence is always very eloquent. "Decide, Dario. Del and I can't waste any more time on you."

He flinched. But he made his decision more quickly than I'd expected. "*You* hand me the clothes."

"Oh, *I* see—from my hands they're cleaner?" I jerked the silks from Del's hand and threw them at Dario. "Put them on. *Now.*"

He allowed them to slither off his body to the ground. I thought he might grind them into the soiled flooring, but he didn't. He picked them up and dragged them over his head, sliding stiff arms through the sleeves. The silks were much too large for him, but I thought as long as Del and I stuffed him between us, it might work.

"Now," I said to Del, and as one we each grabbed an arm and hustled Dario out of the cell. The brat protested, of course,

claiming Del's touch would soil him past redemption; after *I* threatened to soil him, he shut up and let us direct him through the corridors.

We reached the nearest exit. I leaned on the door and it grated open, spilling sunlight into the corridor—

—and came face to face with four large eunuchs.

Armed eunuchs.

For a moment I thought maybe, just *maybe*, we might make it past them. But I don't suppose my face—stubbled, scarred, lacking excess flesh—looks much like a eunuch's. And although I claimed the height, I had none of the customary bulk. At any rate, they each drew a sword and advanced through the door as we gave way into the corridor.

"Hoolies," I said in disgust. "I think our luck just ran out."

"Something like," Del agreed, and parted the folds of her silken robes to yank her own sword free of its harness and sheath.

I shoved Dario behind me, nearly grinding him into the wall in an effort to sweep him clear of danger. Like Del I had unsheathed my sword, but I wasted a moment longer tearing the no-longer-necessary silks from my body.

Four to two. Not bad odds, when you consider Del and I are worth at *least* two to one when it comes to sword-dancing, probably more like three to one. Sword *fighting*, however, is different; it showed as the first eunuch lumbered past Del to engage me and discovered discounting Del was as good as discounting life. He lost his.

I heard Dario's outcry behind me. I spared him a glance; he was fine. Just staring gape-mouthed at Del in shock. Grimly I smiled as Del engaged another eunuch while the remaining two came at me.

When involved in a fight that may end your life at any moment, you don't have much time to keep tabs on what anyone else is doing. It is deadly to split your concentration. And yet I found mine split twice. There was Dario, of course; I was certain the eunuchs wouldn't hurt him, but it was entirely possible he might not duck a sword swipe meant for *me*. But there was also Del. I knew better than to worry about her—Del had proved her worth with a sword already, even as she did again—but a partnership is precisely that: two or more people engaged in an activity or form of commerce that should profit both or all. If it's a *good* partnership, none of the parties involved bothers to wonder what makes it that way. It just *is*.

So I didn't *worry* about Del, exactly, but I did keep an eye on her just to make sure she wasn't in any trouble. I'd learned that was all right in the parlance of our partnership; often enough, and even now, she did the same for me. It's an equality two sword-dancers *must* share if they are working together in the circle. Ours was an equality fashioned by shared danger and shared victory, in the circle and out of it. And I'd learned that in the circle, in the sword-dance, because of Del, gender no longer mattered.

Simply put: you're good, or you're dead.

Two men. My blade was already bloodied; I'd pinked one man in the arm and the other in the belly. Neither wound would stop either guard. So I tried again.

Behind me, I heard Dario breathing noisily. In pain? A quick glance: he seemed to be all right, just shocked and frightened by the violence.

Beyond the eunuchs, I saw Del in rose-colored robes. I heard the whine and whistle of her Northern sword as she brought it across the corridor in a two-handed sweep intended to relieve her opponent of his head. She is tall. She is strong. I have seen her do it before.

I saw her do it again, although it was only in a series of disjointed glances; I had my own head to concern myself with at the moment. It remained attached, but only just; one of the eunuchs parried my sword while his partner slashed at my neck. Braced, I jerked my head aside and leaped sideways even as I used the strength of my wrists to smash aside the other sword. My size is often a blessing.

My shoulder rammed into the corridor wall, sticky, smelling of blood. As I pushed off the wall, I realized I also was sticky and smelled of blood; the beheaded body had drenched me.

"Son of a dog!" one of the eunuchs shouted at me.

He'd have done better to save his breath; Del, working contrapuntally against my own sword-song, killed the man with the mouth while I took out his fellow guard.

Four dead, two standing: Del and I.

And one more slumped against the wall in shock, brown eyes nearly as wide open as the mouth: Dario.

I spat blood. Mine; I'd bitten my lip. But the blood splattered across Del's face as well as mine—Dario had been missed entirely—belonged to the beheaded man.

Del reached out and caught a handful of the silk swathing Dario. "Come." She dragged him toward the open door.

When she takes *that* tone, no one argues with her.

We stumbled out into the sunlight, blinked, squinted, determined our precise location in relationship to the palace entrance; once determined, we started running. Even Dario.

Without Del's help.

No more fluttering past the gate guards like a clutch of color-ful hatchlings. But there were only two of them, after all; Del took one, I the other, and a moment later we were running again, Dario in tow.

Horses waited for us in the market, but only two. I sheathed my sword and threw Dario up on the rump of Del's horse even as she sheathed and swung up, then jumped aboard my stud and headed him through the winding alleyways with Del—and Dario—in the lead. Hooves clicked against stall supports; I gritted my teeth and waited for the anticipated result—

—and heard the shouted curses of the angry merchant as voluminous folds of canvas collapsed into the alley.

Ahead of me, Dario was an orange bud against Del's full-blown rosy bloom. Silk snapped and rippled as she took her gelding through the alleys at a dead run, putting him over hand-carts, bushel baskets, piles of rolled rugs and water jugs. Dario, clinging, was engulfed in clouds of silk. But somehow, he hung on.

Hung on to a *woman*.

We stopped running when we left Rez behind and entered the desert between the two domains. We stopped walking when we reached the oasis.

"Water stop." I unhooked foot from stirrup and slid off my stud, unslung the goatskin bota from the saddle and headed for the well. "Can't stay for long, Dario—drink up, now."

The boy was exhausted. His stay in the dungeon hadn't done much for his color or spirits, no matter how hard he tried to show us only fierce determination. Del, still in the saddle, of-fered him a steadying hand as he tried to dismount; he ignored it. And I ignored his startled outcry as he slid off the horse's rump and landed in the sand on his.

Del unhooked and jumped down. Sunlight flashed off the hilt of her Northern sword. I saw Dario staring at it as well as at Del. No more shock. No more gaping mouth. Consideration, instead. And doubt. But I didn't think it was *self*-doubt.

Del was at the well with her own bota. Dario still hunched on the sand: a gleaming pile of orange silk. "You're burning daylight," I told him as I levered the bucket up. "Do your share, boy—water the horses."

"*Woman's* work." He spat it out between thin lips.

"*Boy's* work, if he wants to drink."

Dario got up slowly, tore the offending silks from his bedraggled body and marched across the sand to the well. He snatched the bucket out of Del's hands. An improvement, I thought, in willingness if not in manners. But as he tipped the bucket up to drink, I took it out of his hands.

"Horses first."

He was so angry he wanted to spit. But, desert-born, he knew better; he didn't waste the moisture. He just marched back to the horses and grabbed reins to lead them to the well.

That's when I saw the blood.

"Hoolies, the boy's *hurt*—" I threw my bota down and made it to Dario in two steps. Startled, he spun as I grabbed a shoulder. He lost the reins, but the horse smelling water, only went as far as Del and the well. "Where are you cut?" I asked. "How badly?"

"But—I'm *not*—" He twisted, trying to see the blood. "The man she killed spurted all over the corridor—"

"But not all over *you*," I said flatly. "Dario—"

"Leave him alone." Del was at my side. "Tiger, turn your back."

"What—?"

"*Turn your back.*" Almost without waiting for my response, she locked her hands in the waistband of Dario's jodhpurs.

"*No!*" Dario screamed it; I spun around with Del's name in my mouth as I heard the jodhpurs tear.

"A *girl*," she declared. "*A girl*—"

Dario clutched jodhpurs against belly. He—*she?*—was yelling vicious *khemi* epithets at Del. Also at me.

"Del—" I began.

"I *looked*, Tiger, and unless the *khemi* have taken to mutilating their boys, *this* boy is not a boy at all." She glared at the quivering Dario. "How in hoolies can you spout that *khemi* filth, *girl?* How do you justify it?"

"I am *khemi*," Dario quavered. "The Hamidaa'n tells us women are abomination, unclean vessels placed upon the earth by demons. They are the excrescence of all our former lives." Tears spilled over.

"*That* is no excuse—" But I wasn't allowed to finish.

"Tiger." Del cut me off with a sharp gesture. Her expression had altered significantly. Gone was the anger, the shock, the outrage. In its place I saw compassion. "Tiger, it *is* an excuse—or, at least, a reason for this masquerade. And now I want you to go away. There is something Dario and I must attend to."

"Away—?"

"*Away.*"

I went to the far side of the well and sat down to wait.

It didn't take long. I heard the sounds of silk being torn, low-voiced conversation from Del, muted responses from Dario. He—*she*—had undergone a tremendous change in attitude.

Well, I might, too, if someone discovered *I* was a woman instead of a man.

Especially at my age.

"Water the horses," Del told Dario, and then came over to the well and motioned me a few steps away.

I went. "He's—*she's*—not hurt?"

"No. Not hurt." She was more serious than usual, almost pensive. She hooked sunbleached hair behind one ear. "Dario is not a boy; neither is Dario a *girl*. Not anymore. Her courses have begun."

I opened my mouth. Shut it. "Ah." I said after a moment. There seemed to be nothing else left to say.

Del dug a hole in the sand with a sandaled foot. Her jaw was rigid. "When we get to Dumaan, I'm going with you to see Dario's father."

"Del—you can't. He doesn't know you're a woman."

Her head came up and I looked directly into a pair of angry

blue eyes. "Do you think I care? His beloved *son* is a woman, Tiger!"

I glanced over at Dario, patiently holding the bucket for two horses in competition for its contents. But I could tell by the rigidity of her posture that she knew full well we were discussing her. It would be hard not to, in view of Del's shout.

I looked back at Del. "There's a chance we won't get paid if you come with us."

"What has been done to Dario transcends the need for money," Del said flatly. "At least—it does for me."

I sighed. "I know, bascha; me, too. But—Dario seemed willing enough to spout all that nonsense."

Del's smile wasn't one; not really. "Women do—and are *made* to do—many strange things to survive in a man's world."

"Like you?"

"Like me." She unsheathed her sword with a snap of both wrists and automatically I moved back a step. "I want to go with you to see Dario's father because I intend to put him to the question."

I looked at the sword uneasily. "With that?"

"If necessary. Right now, I intend only to tell Dario how I learned to kill."

"Why?" I asked as Del turned away. "So she can learn, too?"

Del's answer was whipped over her left shoulder. "No. Because she asked."

Del came with me as I took Dario back to her father. I hadn't bothered to argue the point any longer; Del's mind was made up. And I was beginning to think she'd made Dario's mind up for *her*.

It wasn't easy getting in, of course. The palace servants were men, naturally, and the sight of Del striding defiantly through their halls was enough to make them choke on their prejudice. I imagine the sight of *any* woman might have done the trick, but Del—beautiful, deadly Del—was enough to fill their *khemi* nightmares with visions of blond-haired demons.

Dario walked between us. In a complete change of gender allegiance, she'd turned away from me on the ride to Dumaan to give Del her exclusive attention. Poor girl: all those years spent in a *khemi* household with no women—*no* women—present to answer questions.

At first I'd wondered if Dario had even known she was female rather than male; when I'd asked the question, she told me only that a sympathetic eunuch had admitted the truth of her gender only after swearing her to eternal secrecy. It was a *khemi* rite to expose female children at birth, thus removing all excrescence from the Hamidaa faith.

"But you exist," I'd protested. "Your father bedded a *woman* in order to get you!"

"A son. A son." She'd answered me very quietly. "Once a year a *khemi* lies with a woman in order to get a son." Brown eyes had flicked sidelong to mine. "*I* am my father's son."

"And if he knew the truth?"

"I would be taken to the desert. Exposed. Even now."

I hadn't said much after that. Dario's muted dignity moved me. All those years. . . .

Now, as the three of us walked down the marble corridor toward the audience chamber, I knew what Del intended to do.

Which she did. She stood before the enthroned *khemi* tanzeer of Dumaan—the richest man in this finger of the Southron desert—and told him she was taking his daughter from him.

He flinched. He *flinched.* And I realized, looking at the expression of abject terror on his face, he'd known all along.

"Why?" I demanded. "Why in the name of all the gods did you never tell *Dario* you knew?"

He was not old, but neither was he young. I watched his

young/old face undergo a transformation: from that of a proud Southron prince with an eagle's beak of a nose, to that of a tired, aging man surrendering to something he had hidden from for too long.

His hands trembled as he clutched the arms of his throne. "I am *khemi,*" he said hoarsely. "Hamidaa'n tells us women are abomination, unclean vessels placed upon the earth by demons." His brown eyes were transfixed on Dario's ashen face. "They are the excrescence of all our former lives." His voice was a thread of sound, and near to breaking. "I will touch nothing of women, speak to no women, admit nothing of women into my thoughts. I am *khemi.*" Then he drew himself up and, with an immense dignity, stared directly at Del. "How *else* am I to cherish a daughter while also remaining constant to my faith?"

"A faith such as this *excrescence* does not deserve constancy." Del's tone was very cool. "She is a girl, not a boy; a *woman,* now. No more hiding, tanzeer. No more hiding *her.* And if you intend to force Dario from her true self, I swear I will take her from you. In the North, we do not give credence to such folly."

He thrust himself out of the throne. "You will take her *nowhere,* Northern whore! Dario is mine!"

"Is she?" Del countered. "Why don't you ask her?"

"Dario!" The tanzeer descended two of the three dais steps. "Dari—surely you *know* why I never told you. Why I had to keep it secret." He spread both hands in a gesture of eloquent helplessness. "I had no choice."

Dario's thin face was pinched. There were circles under her eyes. "Choices," she said, "are sometimes difficult to make. And, once made, you must live with them." She sighed and scrubbed at a grimy cheek, suddenly young again. "You made yours. Now I must make mine." She looked at Del. "Tell him what you told me—how it is for a woman in the North. A woman who is a *sword-dancer.*"

Del smiled a little. She faced the tanzeer squarely. Over her left shoulder, rising from her harness, poked the hilt of Northern sword. "There is freedom," she said, "and dignity, and the chance to be whatever you wish. I wished to become a sword-dancer, in order to fulfill a pact I made with the gods. I apprenticed. I studied. I learned. And I discovered that in the circle, in the sword-dance, there was a freedom such as no one else can know, and also a terrible power. The power of life and death." Again, she smiled a little. "I learned what it is to make a choice; to choose life or death for the man who dances against me. A man such as the Sandtiger." She cocked her head briefly in my direction. "I don't kill needlessly. That is a freedom I do not choose to accept. But at least I know the difference." She paused. "What does Dario know?"

"What does Dario *need* to know?" he countered bitterly. "How to kill? Needlessly or otherwise."

"In the North, at least she will have a choice. In the South, as a *khemi*—as a Southron *woman*—she has no choice at all."

Dario stared at her father. In a whisper, she asked what *he* could offer.

He stared at Del for a very long moment, as if he tried to decide what words he had that would best defeat her own. Finally, he turned to Dario. "What you have had," he told her evenly. "I have nothing else to give."

Dario didn't even hesitate. "I choose my father."

I thought surely Del would protest. *I* nearly did. But I said nothing when Del merely nodded and turned to go out of the tanzeer's presence.

"Wait," he said. "There is the matter of payment."

Del swung around. "Dario's safety is payment enough."

"Uh, Del—" I began. "Let's not be hasty—"

"Payment." The tanzeer tossed me a leather pouch heavy with coin. I rattled it: gold. I know the weight. The *sound*.

Dario stood between them both, but looked at Del. "Choices *are* sometimes difficult," she said. "You offered me the sort of life many women would prefer. But—you never asked if I thought my father loved me."

I saw tears in Del's blue eyes. Only briefly; Del rarely cries. And then she smiled and put out a calloused hand to Dario, who took it. "There is such a thing as freedom in the mind," Del told her. "Sometimes, it is all a woman has."

Dario smiled. And then she threw herself against Del and hugged her, wrapping thin brown arms around a sword-dancer's silk-swathed body.

When the girl came to me, I tousled her matted hair. "Take a bath, Dari . . . for all I know you're a Northerner underneath the dirt."

We left them together, Del and I, and walked out into the Southron sunlight with money in our possession. A lot of money, thank the gods; we could enjoy life for a while.

I untied the stud and swung up. "Aren't you even a *little* upset?" I asked, seeing Del's satisfied smile. "She made the wrong choice."

"Did she?" Del mounted her spotted gelding. "Dario told me I'd never asked her if I thought her father loved her. I didn't need to. The answer is obvious."

It was so obvious, I waited for it.

Del laughed and yanked yards of silk into place as she hooked feet into Southron stirrups. "Her father knew she was a girl from the moment she was born. But he never had her exposed." She laughed out loud in jubilation. "The proud *khemi* tanzeer *kept* his abomination!"

The stud settled in next to her gelding. "As a *khemi*," I pointed out, "what he did was sacrilegious. The Hamidaa could very well convict him of apostasy and have him killed, if they knew."

"Choices are sometimes difficult to make," Del quoted. "But sometimes *easy*, Tiger."

Valley of the Shadow

She came in on a gust of wind and rain. He saw how she struggled to keep the wooden door from being snatched out of her hands and slammed against the tavern wall. All the lanterns guttered, splashing distorted light over the faces of the men as they drank and diced and dallied with the whores. Hard faces, every one; some scarred, some lacking an eye, teeth, even an ear. But he doubted the whores cared; their faces were as hard.

A gust of wind drove rain into the room. He saw how it splattered across the two men seated at the table nearest the door. Cursing, they spun around on their stools and shouted for her to shut the door before they all were drowned. And then they saw what he did; that she was a woman, and they closed their mouths on curses and simply stared.

With two hands, she pressed the door closed and set the latch. She was heavily cloaked; black, he thought, and glittering with diamante raindrops that spilled off the wool and splashed against the earthen floor. But then she moved into the sphere of lantern light and he saw the cloak was not black after all but blue. Deep, deepest blue, the color of a night without stars, except he thought the crescent moon brooch fastening the cloak would lend enough light to them all.

The hood had slipped. Black-haired she was, with it cut straight at shoulders and again across her brows. Dry, it shone almost blue in the yellow light. Like silk. He wanted to reach out his callused hand and put his fingers in it.

Hardly a step did she take before a man blocked her way. Ugo. He knew Ugo only in passing, for upon occasion—as now—they shared a roadside tavern. Not friends. But not enemies, either. They bore one another no loyalties. In the code of their mutual profession, they did not dare to.

Ugo was an assassin.

But at the moment, Ugo was no more than a man taken by a woman, and intent upon having her.

"Drink?" Ugo asked. Big-voiced he was, to match his bulk and ego, and yet now there was an undertone of something akin to desperation. Well, he could not blame Ugo. A man had only to look at her to want her.

Not a beauty. No. Her edges were hard and sharp as glass, with no softness to them. No blurring of the lines between fragility, femininity. No pliancy. No complaisance in her, either; he knew it almost at once. But there was a keenness to her sex that put him in mind of a knife blade, honed to a sharpness that would bring no pain, none at all, even slier into the soft belly of a fat merchant who had, perchance, *neglected* to pay his creditor.

She was, in essence, more masculine than feminine, and yet—strangely—it only increased his desire for her.

And Ugo's.

Of course. Ugo's.

"Drink?" Ugo repeated, and the woman slipped by him with silence in her mouth.

Ugo turned. Heavy brows drew down, shrouding his glittering eyes. Brown eyes, peat-brown, glaring after her, with the hot light of need. And pride. Pride roused by her mute refusal; pride smashed down into pieces.

Silence filled the tavern. The men watched with their whores perched on knees and laps, watching also. "Woman!" Ugo roared.

In the echoes of his shout she stripped leather gloves from

her hands. She unfastened the moon brooch and slipped her cloak. It slid off black-clad shoulders; no, blue again. He saw it more clearly now. She dropped the wet cloak to a second stool and sat down at a small table near the roof tree. One hand dipped into a belt-purse and came up with a single coin. It glittered silver in the light.

"Wine," she said into the waiting silence of the room. "Red wine."

The tapster, like all the others, looked at once to Ugo. Ugo showed his strong yellow teeth and took three long strides to the table. In his fingers was a coin. But its patina was mere copper. "Woman," he said, "put your silver away. I will buy this wine."

She looked at the copper clenched in his thick-fingered hand. She looked at his face. She looked at the ferocity of his desire. She did not move except to set her coin down upon the table. "No," she said softly, and the word rose up to strike Ugo in his face.

He bared his teeth in a feral display of contempt. "What is it, then—a woman who lies with women?"

Silence.

"*Woman*—" Ugo roared, and reached out to trap her wrist in his hand.

Smoothly, swiftly, she rose. Silver glittered in her hand. But it was not the coin. A knife, and the blade drove home into his belly.

She let Ugo fall across the table even as she pulled the knife free of flesh and muscle. His weight buckled the table; he fell again to smash upon the floor, and she cleaned the blade upon the fabric of his jerkin.

When it was done and the silver coin retrieved, she looked again to the tapster. "Wine," she said. "Red wine."

He brought it in a pewter tankard, stepping carefully around the body on his floor, and when she offered the coin he took it. The tapster's fingers shook.

The woman, still standing by the body, drank. The others did not. To a man, they watched her. To a woman, they judged her. And found themselves lacking, no doubt.

He smiled. Quietly he rose and crossed the tavern to step into a sphere of lantern light. "Lady," he said calmly, "you lack a table. Perhaps you will share mine?"

She took the tankard away from her mouth and he saw how the red wine stained her lips. Closer, she was no more beautiful. He saw nothing of softness in her. But the intensity of her spirit was such that she overshadowed man or woman.

She looked past him to his table. Empty now, for he had beckoned no whore to join him. Even now he did not; of that he was quite certain.

Her eyes came back to him. He saw they were pale blue, almost colorless; in the dimness of the tavern they were very nearly white. Except for the black of the pupils.

She smiled. And preceded him to his table.

"Mattias," he said, and sat down. When she did not answer, he knew better than to press her. She drank her wine; he drank his, and when the tankards were empty she bought the next two with shining silver.

"Thank you," he said, "for the wine. And for Ugo's death."

Her eyebrows were straight across the smooth curve of her forehead. "Ugo," she said. "Was that his name?"

"Ugo. No loss."

"An enemy?"

"No. A business acquaintance." Mattias smiled. "His loss is my gain."

She said nothing. She drank.

He wanted to ask her her name, but he refrained. In business, names were only rarely exchanged. A name known gave a man claim on another man's life; he knew better than to lay any claim to her. Though he wanted to.

Her tankard was empty. She did not signal for another. She set it down upon the table and looked at him, and Mattias saw the smile in her eyes though it did not touch her mouth. "Mattias," she said, "have you a room?"

His own tankard, half-full, thumped against the table. "A room. Yes." His tongue felt thick in his mouth. "A room, yes."

This time the smile touched her lips. "Then let us retire to it."

He led her there, to the tiny room under the eaves, and took her clothes from her even as she took his. And there in the tiny room they made the beast with two backs as he had never known it before, in power and passion and helplessness, until he could only lie in the bed and quiver in the darkness.

"Mattias," she said. "Yes."

When he could, he smiled. And asked her who she was.

She shrugged. "Does my name really matter?"

Perhaps not. But there was a need in him to know. "And have you killed men before?"

"Oh, yes."

Her flesh was cool. He felt a chill upon his own. "Many?"

Another shrug. "I have not counted them."

Assassin, he thought. An unusual occupation for a woman but he had heard of it before. Mattias smiled. "And Ugo thought you preferred women to men."

Yet a third shrug. "Sometimes. I do not discriminate."

He stiffened. Colder still, he sat up. He looked down upon her nakedness. "Like *this?*"

She did not smile. "And do you inquire after mechanics? Or is it a question of simple passion?"

The breath was noisy in his throat. "The last," he said, and said it harshly, because he remembered how much they had shared.

She looked up at him out of the darkness. "Sometimes," she told him clearly.

He looked away from her.

"Judge me not," she said. "What gain is there in that?"

His head snapped back around. "And have you killed *women* as well as men?"

"Oh, yes," she said. "I do not discriminate."

He could not hide the curling of his lips. "At least *that* I have never done."

She shrugged. "When the Book of Life is closed, do you think it will really matter what you have and have not done?"

"And children," he challenged. "Have you killed children as well?"

"Men, women, children." Even in the shadows, he saw a strange serenity in her face. "I do not discriminate."

"Ugo," he charged, "because he wished to buy you a drink."

"I *am* sometimes capricious."

"Woman," he said, "you sicken me."

"Man," she mocked, "I am part of you."

And before he could move to get out of the bed, she placed a hand upon his arm. It stopped him. It stopped him dead.

She knelt beside him. One hand she placed against his left breast. Her palm was cool to the touch, but not cold. And yet he felt a coldness deep within.

Pain sprang up in his chest. He could not draw breath.

"Mattias," she said, "yes."

Her palm was gone from his breast, and yet he felt the grinding pain. It crushed his chest and sent numbness down his left arm, until it touched his fingertips.

She withdrew from his bed of pain. Naked, her shadow lay upon him.

"How much," he gasped, "did they pay you? And name me the name of the man."

"No payment," she said. "No man. What I do, I do for myself."

"Woman!" he cried. "Assassin should not kill assassin!"

Her answer echoed in the room. *"I do not discriminate."*

And as he began to climb down into the valley of the shadow of Death, he knew who she was at last.

BLOOD OF SORCERY

Her memories began coming back in bits and pieces, slowly.
Carefully she hoarded each one like the rarest of gems, gathering them one by one to her breast until she could judge each
one for flaws; finding none, she called it good and put it into
safekeeping. Slowly her hoard grew until she had a double handful of bright stones; looking at them all, she saw the colors of
the rainbow and more. Looking at them all, she saw a reflection
of herself. And then she *knew* herself again, after a timeless
space and place where she did not.

She was Keely. Keely of Homana. Princess-born and raised,
daughter of the Mujhar himself, who held sovereignty over the
realm. But more than that she was Cheysuli. Shapechanger. The
daughter of a man who became a wolf at will. *Lir*-shape, the
Cheysuli called it, eschewing the Homanan word
"shapechanger" with all its demon connotations, for it was an
outward exhibition of the eerie and consuming bond that linked
man and animal. Warrior and *lir*. Only the Cheysuli had the
ability. And only the warriors; male, all of them.

Save Keely.

She knew why she, alone of them all, had the ability to take
the shape of any animal she chose. Unlike the others, who were
linked only to a single *lir*, she was free to summon any form.
The Old Blood that was so fickle ran strongly in her veins, giving her the magic that allowed her freedom as had not been
known for centuries. For too long only the warriors had held

the gift, and then only in the guise of a single animal. For too long the blood had been thinned and the old magic lost. Now it was a live thing again, this magic of the gods, and it was Keely's destiny—her *tahlmorra*—to pass on the Old Blood to children of her own. That, coupled with her rank as the only princess of Homana, made her a highly desirable match. And so her father had betrothed her to the heir of a neighboring kingdom when they were both just children, before either of them knew what futures lay before them.

Keely, rebellious and defiant, had ever resented the betrothal that made her less than herself; ever resented the birth that settled her future even in the cradle. She would go to Erinn, wed her island princeling, bear him sons and then, past her usefulness, fade into the grayness of later years. It was a future that faced all women of royalty whose first duty was obedience and loyalty to the House. To be used as a gamepiece to gain land, alliances, riches. Keely loved her father well; honored her Cheysuli heritage and the magic in her blood, but she did not love and honor the fetters her sex placed on her. And so she had turned from womanish pursuits to the swordplay of men, refining her skill until it equaled that of her brothers. She was a princess but also Cheysuli, warrior-born and bred for all she was a woman, and no one dared deny her her heritage. She would follow the dictates of her *tahlmorra,* which spoke of a husband and children, but she would go to the man as herself. The spirit and arrogance that made Cheysuli warriors the finest in the land also served her well, and she would not give up her selfhood.

But her independent spirit also placed her in jeopardy even as her rank placed her in the precarious position of pawn to Strahan the Ihlini, the foreign sorcerer who practiced the dark arts learned from the gods of the netherworld. Strahan wanted only power over all men, all realms, and to achieve it he needed

267

the blood of the Cheysuli who now ruled Homana. He needed a child, a halfling, an infant taken at birth and raised in the darkness of the Ihlini, and to get that child he needed a woman. A Cheysuli woman whose blood linked her—and therefore him—to the throne of Homana.

He had taken her prisoner in Hondarth, the port city on the shores of the Idrian Ocean. She had walked into his trap with all the blindness and trust of a child. She was not a child; she was not blind and did not trust easily, and she hated knowing she had contributed to her own capture. Nonetheless Strahan held her now, imprisoned within the old castle on the Crystal Isle, only ten leagues across the water from the docks and quays of Hondarth. In all her childhood she had known the Crystal Isle as a place of mystery and whispered secrets, the birthplace of her Cheysuli ancestors who had gone to Homana to make a realm for their descendants. No one lived on the Crystal Isle now. No one went there because the breath of the gods shrouded the island in mist and magic, and the Homanans— who still feared the shapechanging sorcery of their own royal House—also feared some form of retribution if they trespassed. The Cheysuli, who knew themselves blessed by the old gods, also did not go there. Their lives were in Homana now; the Crystal Isle was of the past.

And so Strahan had made it his place, his present. He kept her there as his guest, his prisoner, and lay with her each night so the child would be conceived. The child of darkness who would slowly, carefully, patiently work its Ihlini sorcery on the House of Homana until the Mujhar and all his kin fell, and then Homana would become the realm of the Ihlini. The realm of dark magic and demons.

The trap had been sprung easily. Keely had been called to Hondarth to meet her betrothed for the first time as he arrived from his father's island kingdom. She had gone—reluctant to wed him and lose her freedom, yet recognizing the demands of her *tahlmorra*—and walked into the trap. Strahan, masquerading as the Erinnish prince, charmed her into drinking the water that took her soul. She lost her magic; lost her past, her present, her future; lost her knowledge of self. As long as her blood bore the black taint of sorcery she was helpless, stripped of her Cheysuli gifts and unable to fend off Strahan's unwanted intimacy.

But now the knowledge was coming back. Strahan's sorcery had taken her memory for countless days; now she could count them. She knew herself again, and her predicament. She knew what enemy she faced. And she knew, with all her will and strength and determination, that somehow she would get free of him.

The open casement in her room was narrow and high, but by pulling a bench over to it and climbing up Keely managed to see what lay beyond her chambers. Her prison, albeit a comfortable one. There were heathered hills and tangled forests; curving beaches that glinted silver in the moonlight and white in the day; slate-gray oceans and endless skies. Sea-spray and mist hung over the island like a veil: the breath of the gods; thick in the mornings, heavy at night, burning golden in the sunlit days. Could she put out her hand and part the misted curtain, she would draw it back and see Homana lying beyond the Idrian Ocean.

A faint breeze came in from the sea and curled through the casement, catching her tawny hair and lifting it from her shoulders. She wore it loose now, falling unbound over her shoulders to her waist, because Strahan preferred it that way. Keely, who did not, had first responded by ripping a length of fabric from the dark blue robe she wore and tying it up in a single braid. Strahan's response had been silence, and without touching her he had caused a spectral hand to loosen the plait and stroke it back into unbound freedom. Keely, shivering each time she recalled the experience, no longer braided her hair.

She stood on the bench and hugged the stone sill of the casement like a child who longs for what he cannot have. She pressed her cold cheek against the cold stone and stared out past the beaches, past the mists, and tried to see Homana.

"A caged bird," said his quiet voice. "Perhaps a linnet, or a sparrow, but certainly not the falcon, who would not countenance it, or a Homanan hawk, who knows better than to fall into the hunter's hand."

Keely did not turn. She remained on the bench, still standing at the casement, but her fingers drove so hard into the stone she felt her nails splinter.

Strahan's hands were on her, lifting her down and turning her around. Keely looked into his beautiful, bearded face and the eerie eyes: one blue, one brown, and felt the familiar revulsion stir within her soul.

"You must not grieve," he told her in his gentle, beguiling voice. "Women who grieve do not suit the men who want them. And I want you, Keely."

She closed her eyes as his hand slid beneath her robe to caress her breasts. As always, his touch raised her skin into prickles. He seemed pleased by the reaction, as if to stir any response from her was enough for him. But then he was more than a man; he was Ihlini. Sorcerer. Child of the dark gods who gave him ageless life. The only thing that kept her from being ill before him was the knowledge he might think she had conceived, and that she would never show him. It was what he wanted.

"I will keep you as long as it takes," he whispered into her hair. "Do you age before me, I will keep you young, until you have conceived by me. Until you give me the child."

She would not look into the eerie eyes that had a power of their own. To do so admitted defeat, and that she would never do. She had learned not to fight him when he took her to his bed because to fight back gave him reason to use sorcery on her, and that she hated worse than his intimacy. She was Cheysuli; Ihlini sorcery was anathema to her. Had she her full complement of arts she could withstand such dark magic, for her blood gave her a natural protection against such things, but he had made her blood black and thick and perverted. Until it ran red and rich again, she was his.

"Keely," he said quietly, "I have brought someone to you."

She did not answer. Strahan removed his stroking hand and departed the chamber; when she opened her eyes she saw the harper.

Taliesin. The white-haired man made ageless through the gift of Strahan's Ihlini father, because his harping and magnificent voice had won him fame and fortune. But the gift of immortality brought Taliesin no peace, for Strahan himself had taken his own retribution on a man he named traitor by turning Taliesin's hands into twisted, brittle, broken things, unable to play a harp. And yet Taliesin had overcome Strahan's ultimate cruelty by becoming the very traitor Strahan called him. For Taliesin the harper was also Ihlini, and a friend to Homana. And so he, with Keely, had been taken prisoner in Hondarth.

Keely, who had seen no one else save Strahan for too long, thought it was a trick of the eye. But the harper smiled sadly and came across the room, putting out his broken hands to her. She went willingly into his arms, clinging to him as if he could save her soul.

"How do you fare?" he asked at last, when she had recovered herself.

Keely's face twisted. "Well enough. I have food and wine and excellent health. He makes certain of that."

Taliesin took her hand in his twisted ones and slowly sat down on the bench. Keely, sitting next to him, thought he had begun to look old. For a man with endless life, it seemed a strange thing.

"What of you?" she whispered. "What has he done to you?"

The harper smiled a little. "Like you, he has kept me locked away. Alone. It would be a hard thing for another man, perhaps, but I have my voice. Strahan took the magic of the harp from my hands but he cannot destroy my voice, or the memory of what I had."

"I am sorry," she said softly. "You should not be here. It was me he wanted. Had you not come with me to Hondarth—"

"It does not matter," he said gently. "I would far prefer to be with you in this than think you alone with the man. And the time will come when we can win free of this place."

Keely said nothing for a long time. Finally she begged the clasp of his leather belt. At first he only stared at her, struck by her vehemence, but he complied as she asked again. Slowly he removed his belt, pulled the bronze clasp free and held it out to her.

Keely closed her hand around it tightly. She turned her left arm over, baring her wrist, and he saw the delicate tracery of scars threading the translucent skin. For a moment the muscles stood out along her jaw, then she shifted the clasp and stabbed the prong deeply into her wrist.

Taliesin cried out and grabbed at her hand, tearing the clasp from her. Keely said nothing. She sat very still with her arm upturned, watching the blood begin.

"Do you see?" she asked. "Do you see what he has done?"

The blood welled slowly out of the gash and crept down her arm. It left a trail of glistening blackness like the slime of a demon's serpent.

The harper was trembling as he closed his hand around her wrist, shutting off the blood. His face was very pale. His eyes, blue as her own, were horrified, and Keely, looking into them and seeing his suffering, felt a measure of her own revulsion rise.

"I am tainted," she said thickly. "Unclean."

"Keely—"

"I cannot stop him. The *lir*-gift is gone, lost in this foul blackness in my blood. Each night he takes me to his bed, to get a child. A child who will throw down the House of Homana." She shuddered convulsively. "I did not recall it for a very long time. It has only been the last days that I remembered, and now it is worse than before. Did he know I have recalled I am Cheysuli, he might take it from me again."

"Keely, let me bind your wound."

She smiled sadly and pulled his hand away, showing him the wound. Already the blood had slowed. "It will stop of its own accord. It does each time. Aye," she said to his start of surprise, "I have done this before. Not to take my own life, but to see if my blood is clear." She shrugged crookedly. "Then he learned what I did and took away anything I might cut myself with. It has been weeks since I was able to see my blood—to see if I was free. I am not."

"This is the Crystal Isle!" he said forcefully. "The very seat of Cheysuli power. You have only to call upon the old gods, and you will be free."

"I have called," she told him clearly. "I have pleaded. They do not hear." Keely touched the blackness on her arm. "They cannot answer." Abruptly she rose, pacing away from Taliesin like a supple cat. When she turned back, her face was very pale. "I have conceived. I bear a child . . . *his*. . . ."

"Ah, Keely—"

She shivered once, violently. "I have ever said I did not want *any* child. I am afraid. I will lose myself. I will become a breeder, instead of Keely. A broodmare, serviced by the finest stud available." She smiled humorlessly, sickened as she crossed both arms over her abdomen. "Before, the stud was to be the Erinn-ish prince; now it is Strahan. The Ihlini! And the child I bear will be a travesty of what I am." Her hands fisted. "By the gods, harper, I am afraid! I do not want this child! Before, it was because I wanted no child. Now I *must* lose it, because it is Strahan's!"

He rose and went to her. He knew her pride and strength as he knew his own, and the reflection of what made her race the finest warriors in the land. That same pride and strength had led her to learn the knife and the sword as if she were a warrior like her brothers and father. She was a princess of Homana, a Cheysuli woman bearing the Old Blood, and as fine a fighter as any man he had ever known. For her to be trapped by Strahan, trapped by the ultimate betrayal of her own body, was a prison far worse than any dungeon.

But he could not lie to her. "You cannot *wish* away a child, Keely."

She wet her lips. "Surely there is something I can do."

"It is a life, Keely. Strahan's child, aye, but do you forget you are the mother? No child who is half yours can be totally evil."

"He will take it from me," she said. "He will pervert it. He will make it a reflection of himself." She clutched at his arms. "Taliesin—I must lose it."

He took a deep breath and released it slowly. Her control was back as she waited, and finally he told her. "There are ways of ridding yourself of an unwanted child. You can take herbs to loosen it. They would have some in Hondarth, if you could get there." He sighed. "I cannot condone it, but I understand your fears. They have merit. But how do you propose to do it here, when Strahan keeps you prisoner?"

Her teeth gritted. "I will find a way. I will throw myself to the floor, if I must, time and time again, and lose it that way."

He smiled, amused by her determination even as he knew the

consequences of such folly. "Keely. It is not so easy to do as you might think."

Her breath hurt her chest as she sucked it in. "I will risk anything to rid myself of this demon's child. I must!" She stared at him. "It is my turn to serve my *tahlmorra*. My fate. My turn to sacrifice whatever I must to serve the gods. It is a Cheysuli thing, this *tahlmorra*, but it cannot be gainsaid. To do so angers the gods, who made a fate for all of us. I have accepted mine; I will go with my betrothed when I am free of this place and bear *him* children. But I will still be myself. No man may take that from me."

He was Ihlini. He was bound by his own endless future, his endless destiny, but he knew what it was that drove Keely. *Tahlmorra*—the will of the gods—drove her entire race, for each Cheysuli born lived to serve the gods. Keely's *tahlmorra*—and her father—had decreed she wed into Erinn to tie the bloodlines to Homana, but in order to do that she must first get free of Strahan.

"Which she will never do," said Strahan himself.

Keely spun around and saw him standing within the room that only moments before had held only herself and the harper. A violet mist hung around him almost like a shroud, cloaking his head and shoulders. Strahan could use a door as well as any man, but he knew his sorcery was as good a weapon as the knife he so rarely needed.

"Time for you to go, harper," he said gently. "Keely has come to value her solitude. And my company." He smiled within the shadow of his trimmed black beard, white teeth showing clearly against the fine darkness of his features. As a woman he would have been beautiful; as a man he was handsome indeed. "Do you weary of this life, harper?" he inquired.

Taliesin, white-haired and young-faced, merely smiled. "You will do whatever you wish, regardless of my answer. So I will give you none."

Keely, sensing Strahan tested her friend, moved to the harper's side. "You will not harm him!"

"I mean him no harm," Strahan answered. "Only an ending." His parti-colored eyes fastened on Taliesin. "Time ends for us all, harper. Even you."

Taliesin cradled Keely's head in his broken, twisted hands. "Do not fear for me. Do not even fear for yourself, for you are stronger than you know."

"Harper," Strahan said briefly, and Taliesin left her alone once more.

"Do not harm him," she told the sorcerer evenly.

"I do what I wish." His eyes went past her to the open casement. "I weary of this sunshine."

Keely, opening her mouth to ask what he meant, closed it as she saw him lift his hand into the air. For a moment it hung there, as if in benediction. Then he drew a hissing rune in the soundless air and when it had faded into wisping violet mist, so had he.

The storm swept in suddenly with no warning from the depths of a night so dark Keely thought she had gone blind. She sat upright in her bed and squinted against the flash of lightning outside her casement. Wind swept through the opening like a capricious demon and scattered leaves about the room.

Keely, dressed only in a thin linen nightshift, pulled the covers up around her shoulders. In another flash of lightning she saw the steady downpour outside her casement. The wind drove the spray into the room and dampened her hair with a fine mist.

Thunder slammed into the castle and crashed inside her chamber. Then she realized it was not thunder but a door instead, her own, and it stood open to the corridor. Keely opened her mouth to yell as the figure stepped into the room.

A flash of lightning illuminated Taliesin's face, showing his white hair and blue eyes, and Keely caught her breath on a gasp of relief. Taliesin beckoned with one of his twisted hands. "Keely—come quickly! This is your chance to get free!"

"Strahan—?"

"Elsewhere," he said impatiently. "Come with me!"

Hastily she climbed out of bed and gathered up the folds of her nightshift, then she grabbed one of his ruined hands and ran with him as he led her down a corridor. Her heart thudded as she realized how close she was to escape, how close she was to freedom. And how close to discovery, if they were not careful.

He took her down the winding corridor and out into the high-walled outer bailey. Keely had seen nothing of the castle save from her own chambers; she paused, stumbling, as Taliesin tried to drag her onward. The rain flattened her hair against her scalp and crept through the thin linen nightshift to the skin beneath.

Taliesin gestured. "The gates . . . *there!* Come, Keely!"

She ran with him to the tall gates, gasping as a gust of wind hammered into them both and nearly blew her off her feet. Hastily she scrubbed an arm across her face, clearing water from her eyes, but it returned as quickly as it had gone.

Taliesin pulled her against the wall as lightning slashed out of the black sky to pour light into the bailey. Keely took the chance to ask him what had happened.

"Strahan thought I was dead. When he left me he also left the door undone, thinking me with his gods of the netherworld, and I made my way to your chamber. The castle is near deserted; I thought he had more Ihlini with him, but he does not. Still, this is the Crystal Isle, and for all he uses it to his own evil purposes, he must know he is not welcome here. An Ihlini among the

Cheysuli gods? No. They will take their retribution."

"Why did he think you were dead?" she asked sharply.

His face was a blur in the darkness. "He has taken his father's gift from me."

"What do you mean?" she demanded, dreading the answer.

Taliesin flinched as a crack of thunder broke over their heads. "His father gave me endless life. The son has taken it from me."

"*Taken* it. . . ."

His twisted hands cradled her wet face. "I am dying, Keely. At long last. I have lived more than a hundred years, but my life is ending. Strahan took back the gift."

"No!"

"I cannot say how, precisely," he told her gently, "but he has done it. Already my bones grow brittle and my heart begins to fail. *I* will not go free of this place, but I will see that you do."

"Taliesin—"

"Go, my proud Cheysuli warrior-princess. Tarry no longer. I am buying your life with my own."

She stared into his aging, ageless face, and hung onto his hands with her own, as if she could give him her strength.

He smiled, understanding. "The gates are locked but unattended. I will lift you as high as I can, and then you will have to climb the rest of the way. Can you do it?"

Keely peered through the rain at the tall wooden gates with their heavy iron hinges and massive crossbars. They were not made for climbing. "If only I could take *lir*-shape," she whispered. "I would go as a hawk, a falcon, flying over the walls and on to Homana herself." She sighed and shivered, wiping rain out of her eyes. "But I cannot, so I will simply have to go over them however I can."

Carefully he interlaced his gnarled fingers, locked them together and smiled at her encouragingly. Keely, looking at the weak step he offered, suddenly threw her arms around him.

"Taliesin—"

He unlocked his hands and held her a long moment. Then he pulled away. "You must go before I weaken. Go, Keely."

She waited as he bent and held out his hands. Slowly she placed a bare foot in them, felt him brace himself, and reached upward as he lifted. She felt the trembling in his arms and shoulders as he lifted her higher, pushing her upward toward the top. Her fingers scrabbled against the wood, seeking a handhold, and she put one foot against the rough hinges supporting the right leaf of the huge gates. Her toes flinched from the splinters and the cold iron but she gritted her teeth and sought a niche.

The top was still far over her head. Keely scraped herself upward, grunting with the effort, blinking back the rain that ran into her eyes. The thin fabric of her nightshift tore and the wood scraped across her breasts. Keely's teeth came down on her lower lip as she strained to find a handhold.

One foot found the crossbar. She balanced on it carefully, wrapping one hand into the iron hinge as she dragged her weight upward. She was free of Taliesin, clinging to the gates like a spider to its web. She heard him moan below her.

Keely found the heavy iron studs with her toes. They protruded from the wood just far enough for her to hook a toe over them. Carefully she slid her foot up the line of studs, seeking one less flush, and finally felt one sticking out farther than the rest. The upper hinge was above her outstretched hand but a careful boost might put it within reach. She jammed her other foot against the stud, ignoring the pain, then pushed down against the crossbar and lunged upward.

Her right hand caught the upper hinge. She clung to it with all her might, using her momentum to pull herself steadily upward. She heard herself gasping, breath wheezing in her breast. The stud cut into her foot but she ignored the pain, scraping herself upward. The crossbar was well below her; she had no more foothold. Keely clung to the top hinge and pulled with all her strength, clawing for the top of the gate. If she fell now. . . .

She caught it at last. For a moment she hung there by both hands, feet sliding against the slick wood, then she gritted her teeth and shoved one foot into the slot between the gate and the wall. For a moment her ankle jammed; she used it and shoved upward, grunting as she jerked herself straight up toward the top. Her chin crept over the edge. Again she lifted her foot and shoved it against the wall. She gained a few more inches. Then, with eyes closed and cheek pressed against the iron lip of the gate, she swung her left leg up as high as she could and hooked her heel over the edge.

For a moment her balance faltered. Both arms and a leg grasped the top of the gate but her right foot was still caught between the hinge and the wall. Keely set her jaw and yanked it free, ignoring the sudden pain tearing through her flesh. She jerked herself up and over and balanced precariously on the lip of the gate, her belly pressed against her backbone.

Keely looked down and saw Taliesin far below. His face was upturned, watching her progress, and she saw his glorious smile in a brief flash of lightning. When another came he was huddled against the ground, and she knew he was dead.

For a moment her chest hurt so much from grief she gasped aloud. Her breath left on a faint, muted wail; her head swam crazily. Then she hung onto the gate with all her might and told herself to let the grief go, let it pass . . . her gift to Taliesin would be to escape this place. She sent a heartfelt prayer to the gods and then slid over the gate to begin her descent.

It was easier; it was harder. Easier because she had only to loosen her careful grip as she worked her way down, but if she did that she would slide, falling, and smash against the ground.

Harder because she must cling tightly, sliding down little by little, searching blindly for any toehold that might slow her descent. She used the hinges, scraping her cheek and her breasts and her knees, and her elbows were bloody shreds. The blood shone black in the lightning.

One foot found the bottom hinge, the other the crossbar. Keely clung to the gate a moment, making certain of her balance, then twisted her head around to stare down at the ground. It was wet and muddy, running with rain, but it was better than the stones of the bailey.

Keely let go of the gate and jumped.

She landed hard on her feet and fell forward to her hands and knees, then flat against the ground. For a moment she lay there, gasping in the puddles forming around her face, then dragged herself into a sitting position and pushed water from her eyes. She was alive. She was free.

Keely laughed softly, staring upward into the stormy heavens. The rain still fell and the clouds blotted the moon and the stars, but she was free. Strahan could not touch her.

The gate behind her rattled and groaned. Keely jerked around, saw the bolts being drawn and leaped to her feet. As the heavy gates creaked open she began to run.

Vines and creepers tore at her legs as she pushed her way through the thick forest. She had left the smooth grassy carpet and the beaches behind, fleeing into the depths of a strange forest. Lightning showed her the way as she ran, illuminating the path before her into an eerie greenish glow. Keely pulled her sodden nightshift up around her knees and jumped everything in her way.

She tripped several times, falling awkwardly, but each time she scrambled up and ran on. Instinct told her Strahan would be close behind her, *close,* and she had no recourse to the magic that would lend her animal shape. *Lir*-shape. If he caught her, he would keep her.

Finally she sagged against a tree, exhausted, and knew she could go no farther. Her legs shook so hard she thought she might fall and it was only because she clung to the tree that she remained on her feet. For a moment she closed her eyes, gasping painfully in the rain, then a blinding light penetrated her lids and she opened them to see a smoking purple column hiss out of the black sky.

For a moment she stared in astonishment at the coalescing column, startled by its brilliant beauty. Then she saw the form taking shape deep within it, and Strahan was with her again.

"Foolishness," he chided gently. The light slowly faded, hissing, as he put out a beckoning hand.

Keely said something incomprehensible, even to herself. Then she let go of the tree and ran again.

"You will lose the child," he called after her. She shivered as she realized he had known all along, but she also heard a note of genuine concern in his voice. If she lost the child he wanted so badly. . . .

She laughed wildly as she ran. "Good. *Good!*" The rain and foliage fell behind her like a curtain.

Lightning showed her a stone looming before her. A second flash showed it more clearly and she saw the tumbled ruins of an old chapel. Keely ducked into it and fell against the cold, wet wall, head thrown back as she tried to catch her breath. She smelled mold and age. The stone was slick beneath her hands, velveted with lichen.

Most of the roof was gone. Keely could see traces of the old beamwork, though most of it was tumbled against the ground inside the chapel walls. Timbers leaned crazily against broken stone. Part of the interior was still sheltered from the elements but most of it lay open to the wind and turbulent skies. The wet walls gleamed silver in the moonlight. Keely, realizing the storm was passing over, threw her head back and saw the moonlight and stars glowing against the black tapestry of the gods.

She moved from the crumbling doorway. A shaft of the new moonlight lay upon the remains of an altar. She crept to it slowly, half-afraid of the place. She had heard of its like before, in corners of Homana, but not on the Crystal Isle. Still, it was from the Crystal Isle the Cheysuli had come, the children of the gods, and perhaps it was her place as well.

She knelt in the wet, leaf-strewn earth before the altar. The leaning stone in front of her bore runes, shallowed and roughened by age, but runes nonetheless. She put out a hand and traced them, not noticing how muddy and bloody and scraped her fingers were. She could not read the Old Tongue but she recognized a few of the symbols, and realized she had stumbled across a chapel built by Cheysuli to honor the gods she honored herself.

A step behind her brought her upright and whirling around. Strahan stood in the doorway. She saw he wore dark leathers and a crimson velvet robe. No knife at his belt. He needed none.

He gestured with the fluid grace she despised, for it echoed that of her own race. "Pay this place homage while you may. It is the last time you will see a Cheysuli chapel. From now on I will keep you locked up like a prisoner, and you will wish you had not fled."

"I was a prisoner before!"

He smiled. The gentleness of his face made her shiver. "But a coddled one. And you will still be coddled, for a while. Until the child is born. And then I will put you away in the cells below the ground . . . until I need you again."

Keely felt the broken altar at the back of her knees. The walls seemed to close in on her. Strahan blocked the only exit and she could do no more climbing this night.

"I fell," she told him in discovery. "Before—as I ran. I fell, and I will lose this child." She felt an upsurge of fear as she realized the truth of her words, but also a fierce joy that he would not get what he wanted from her. "You will get no halfling of *me*, Ihlini!"

He glided forward. "You may lie. You may not. But it will do you little good, my shapechanger princess. If you lose this child I will simply get another on you." He smiled at her grimace of ' revulsion. "Would you not rather have it done with this first time?"

"Perhaps I will die with losing it," she said fiercely, half-hoping it was true, if only it released her from him. "Perhaps I will die, as so many women die, and then you will have nothing!"

Strahan approached. Keely tried to back away, met the unforgiving altar and abruptly fell over it. She cried out with the pain of it, hands pressing against the ground. Then she felt something sharp. Instinctively she grabbed it, counting it as a weapon as the arms-master had told her so many times—*when in danger use any weapon at hand, even that which is not a weapon*—and thrust herself from the ground, slashing at Strahan. She saw the knife go home in his chest.

Keely cried out. Strahan fell to his knees unevenly both hands clawing at the knife buried hilt-deep. His parti-colored eyes were on her, wide and wild, and his mouth opened in a horrible choking groan. He fell forward against the altar, driving the knife deeper into his chest, then slid slowly sideways and rolled onto his back.

Keely shivered. She sat among the tumbled ruins of an ancient altar and shivered so long and hard her bones ached. One hand crept to her mouth and covered it, as if she would be ill, then she clenched her teeth and closed her eyes.

I have fought before, she thought dazedly. *Fought before with knife or sword, but always in practice. Always against the arms-master. In all the years of my rebellion, when I sought a warrior's ways instead of a woman's, I never knew what it meant to truly seek another's life.* She swallowed heavily, fighting down the sourness of bile. *It is not so simple a thing to be a warrior after all!*

Keely opened her eyes at last and looked up through the broken roof. She saw the full moon clearly. The wind was fading and the thunder of the passing storm sounded more distant. Only a faint mist from the dripping trees blew through the ruin, dampening her face. Keely brushed vaguely at the spray and then looked down at Strahan.

His eyes were open. Even in death they remained eerily life-like: one blue, one brown; the mark of a demon. Keely, shuddering again, crept slowly closer to shut them, unable to let him look on her even in death. His skin was still warm to the touch. Blood had run from his mouth into his beard.

The knife stood out from his chest, smeared with blood, but Keely set her jaw and grasped the hilt in both hands. Then she jerked it from its bony sheath.

It came free reluctantly but finally she had it in her hands. She lifted a fold of Strahan's crimson robe and cleaned the blade, making certain she got the Ihlini's tainted blood from it. A good weapon should never suffer the enemy's blood to remain upon it. Then she got her first clear look at it and realized her fingers, grasping it, had recognized it even in extremity.

She saw upon the hilt the rampant lion with ruby eye. Line for line, liquid in grace and form, the image matched that on her own knife, which bore the royal crest of Homana.

"But this is not mine," she whispered in awe. "Strahan took mine from me. . . ."

She stared at the hilt, running tentative fingers over the lion. There was no doubt it was from the House of Homana; it matched those held by her father; her brothers. But what was it doing in a ruined chapel on the Crystal Isle?

A faint breeze crept down into the chapel. Keely, in damp, torn nightshift, shivered against its touch. She tried to ignore it and found she could not. Finally she stared up into the dark sky and saw the stars glitter at her, as if they sought to speak.

She flipped the knife in her hand and slid the point beneath the flesh of her left wrist, opening a shallow cut. The blood spilled freely, swift and clear, bright red in the silver moonlight.

She smiled. She looked at the blood, at the knife, and recalled tales of the kinsman who had died on the Crystal Isle some forty years before. His knife, then.

Taliesin had told her she needed only to call upon the old gods, and she would be free.

She had not fully believed. All her life she had been taught to honor the gods, but honoring them was a custom more than a true belief, and she understood why they had not answered her before. She had not needed them then.

"I give my thanks," she whispered into the darkness. "To my kinsman; to Taliesin; to the arms-master who taught me well. But most of all I thank the gods." She huddled there a moment longer, than wet her lips. "I cannot bear this child. Perhaps I will not, now, because of the violence of this night, but however it happens, I must lose it. I cannot destroy my own House."

The shadows did not answer.

Finally Keely, knowing she could not go into Hondarth wearing a torn nightshirt that showed every contour of her body, conquered her distaste and removed the crimson robe from Strahan's body. For a moment she held the garment in her hands, fighting back her revulsion at the still-wet blood, then slipped it on over her nightshift. She chopped the bottom off with the knife, took Strahan's belt and cut it to her size, then tied it around her middle.

Keely bent and grasped one of Strahan's leather-clad arms.

He was slack and heavy but she gritted her teeth and dragged his body from the ruins, so he could not profane them. She left him outside. Then she went back in and knelt once more before the altar, sliding the knife back into darkness.

"I leave this here," she said quietly. "It is not mine. I have used it, in my need, and now I leave it for the next one who may call upon the gods."

Keely hesitated a moment, wondering if they would speak to her. Then she rose and walked from the chapel without another word, and as she passed Strahan's body she thought she heard the laughter of the gods.

She stood on the white, moon-silvered beach. On the distant shore winked the lantern-lights of Hondarth. Homana. Her homeland. She had only to take *lir*-shape in the guise of a hawk or falcon, and Homana would be hers again.

She wanted to go home. She wanted to be safe and warm in her father's great palace, surrounded by her tall brothers, her kinfolk, her friends. She wanted the feel of her sword in her hand; to dance again against the arms-master; to know the freedom of spirit and soul in such work. She wanted time alone, so she could deal with the loss of a child.

She longed to fly, to feel the wind against her wings; to soar among the clouds and currents and dance among the gods. To be earthbound no more but free to drift and swoop and flirt and stoop; falling, spiraling upward to fall again. To lose her cares and concerns and her eternal *tahlmorra* upon the breath of the gods who had gifted her with life, with spirit, with pride, and with the *tahlmorra* that made her what she was.

Keely smiled. She stretched out her aching arms, reaching for the endless skies, and flew. Homeward. To Homana.

BY THE TIME I GET TO PHOENIX

I was dead-heading on I-17 southbound out of Flagstaff, swapping pines for saguaros on my way to what the tourist flacks call the Valley of the Sun. Midweek, and quiet: mostly eighteen-wheelers on the road, like mine; one or two RVs; a handful of cars.

Midsummer, midday, maybe 112 degrees, and the mercury headed higher. Waves of heat shimmered into watery mirages stretching across the pavement, but I was okay with a/c chilling the cab, Garth in the cassette player, a waxed cardboard cup shoved into the plastic holder lodged into the slot between window glass and rubber molding. Watered-down cola and melting ice sloshed as I changed lanes, crossing the lumpy reflectors mounted in gummy asphalt. A little to the right and I'd nudge Bott's Dots, those annoying metal implants meant to keep you awake if, nodding off, you ran onto the shoulder.

Dooowwwnnnn the long hill, the border between the cusp at Sunset Point where dogs and their humans got a chance to lighten their loads, and the desert canyons below. Curves like LeMans, this road, this place; but not banked for racing unless you were a college student coming down from Flag to Phoenix, stupid enough to put the stick into neutral and let 'er run. I'd done it a time or two myself; but other drivers tend to freeze up when they see a big ol' chrome grille and the bulldog filling their rearview, and I gave up the game. I blame Spielberg for that, you know: for making the truck out to be the enemy in that TV-movie called *Duel*.

Two sets of curves called the Big Hill, a few milder hummocks of undulating pavement and painted lines, Bott's Dots, then the desert flats sliding into Phoenix beyond Black Canyon City. And where pickings are usually good; with forty-fifty miles between Black Canyon and the outskirts of the Valley, drivers stop thinking about the heat, the haul from trees to cactus. Their minds are on the city, not on their gauges.

Beyond Black Canyon City there's Rock Springs; but it's not much more than a wide spot in the road and no one wants to stop there when they're so close to "civilization."

So close. So far away.

Easy pickings, when urgency and impatience lulls them into pushing the car too hard. Some of them do make it to the rest stop; but that's okay, because in high summer people just want to push on. Which means I'm usually at the rest stop alone except for the marks.

All it takes is a few minutes, usually, to fix what's broke or to break what's fixed; or to give them a lift to the nearest gas station forty-fifty miles up the road—and drop them off short. Maybe a mile or two, and about the time they're relaxing, too, thinking about repairs, about calling the road service. Never about robbery.

Easy. Take their cash, leave 'em their plastic, point them to the gas station, and wish them a happy hike. And I'm gone before they can get there to tell the mechanics to call the DPS and report a robbery. By then I'm in Phoenix where the jurisdiction changes, and in the time it takes to describe the truck, the driver, I'm somewhere else. In the truckyard, likely, swapping out the bulldog for a Kenworth, or a Peter.

No real harm done, after all. By the time the day is over they've got their car fixed, and more cash from an ATM. They don't even have to cancel any of their cards.

I squinted out the windshield. Yup, car at the side of the road, chrome blinding in the sunlight. And two ladies there with it, holding sections of tented newspapers up to shade their heads. Poor old gals. Out all by themselves with no menfolk around; they'd be pleased to see me, all right.

I smiled, cranked up Garth, started through the gears. By the time I got the box stopped and climbed down from the cab, they were aflutter with relief.

Bluehairs. Marthas and Mildreds, I call them. Maybe widows, maybe sisters, or maybe just two gals the golf-shirted, plaid-trousered husbands had let out of the house on a summer afternoon. Identical blue eyes, heat-pinked faces. Identical hair as well—too heavy on the rinse, which turned natural silver-gray to a wispy shade of gentian—shellacked into place, and the uniform of their generation: polyester knit tops and slacks, and those cheapo plastic sandals sold most often at state fairs. But nice ladies. Sweet-faced, crepe-armed, road-flat in the butts. And utterly helpless here by the side of the road, unable even to lift the table-sized hood on the big old Caddy.

Land-barges, is what those damned cars are. And I swear, they must card you before you set foot on the lot, because I've never seen anyone but bluehairs and old men driving 'em.

Usually twenty miles an hour in a forty-five-mph zone.

"Afternoon," I said pleasantly. "Where you ladies headed?"

They exchanged glances, afraid to say.

"Outlet mall?" I guessed; we were maybe ten miles away. "Guess the menfolk didn't want to come."

My ladies surrendered. "They never do," one said rather gloomily. Martha, I decided.

I grinned. "Well, some of them ol' boys get pretty bored when their women shop. They'd rather stay home and watch the golf on TV."

They exchanged glances again, chagrined. Then Mildred

straightened her shoulders and put her chin up. "What's the harm in it?" she asked defensively. "It's a way to pass the time. Why shouldn't we get out? They can stay home and watch all the TV they want—"

"—while you two ladies do the outlet mall." I nodded agreeably. "Only fair, I'd say. Now, what seems to be the trouble?"

Martha pointed. I saw the pool of sickly yellow-green antifreeze creeping out from under the car. "Uh-oh. Looks like you blew a hose." I shook my head in sympathy. "If that's so, I'd do better just to take you two ladies on into the nearest gas station. It's only about twenty miles back." I paused. "That is, if you think you can trust me."

They looked doubtful. I didn't push it; let 'em come to their own decision. They feel safer that way.

"If you want," I continued, unoffended by the lengthy hesitation, "I can try to reach the Department of Public Safety on the CB radio. If it would make you feel better."

The ladies conferred. Examined me. Looked at the truck, their car. At the spreading neon amoeba.

"Tell you what," I said reasonably, "I'll take you in to the gas station, get the guys going on fixing up your car, and I'll go ahead and take you on to the outlet mall. No reason for you to hang around a gas station bored out of your minds when you could be shopping." I grinned. "Just ask one of the gas-jockeys to come pick you up when you're done. Promise him a tip, he'll do it. Seems a shame to ruin your day because your car's being temperamental."

Hooked 'em. Shopping won out: they're women. "If you're sure. . . ." Mildred began doubtfully.

"But only if we pay *you* for your time as well." Martha declared forthrightly. "Seems only right."

"Oh, now, ladies—"

"We insist!"

I gave in gracefully. "Then allow me to help you climb up in my chariot." I gestured toward the idling eighteen-wheeler, then paused as if struck. "You don't mind Garth Brooks, do you?"

"Oh, my, no," Martha said, "He's such a nice boy."

"And rich," Mildred added.

I had to agree with that. Likely ol' Garth didn't do much shopping in outlet malls.

"Here," I said, "let me get that door for you . . . it's a big step up: if you like, I can give you a hand up, each of you."

Martha took a good look at how far up the seat was from the ground, at the inset steps, hesitated, then dropped her purse.

"Oh, here, let me—" But even as I started to bend I felt the unmistakable bite of a gun muzzle dug into the small of my back.

"If you don't want me to put a bullet through your kidney," Mildred said sweetly, "you'll do as we say."

Martha picked up her purse; or rather, took her gun out of it. Now I had a second muzzle resting against my belly.

I pulled my arms away from my sides. "You gotta be shittin' me."

"Take out your wallet," Martha commanded in her soft little voice, both hands rock-steady on the automatic jammed into my gut. "Strip out the bills; we don't want your plastic."

"No quick moves," Mildred added, prodding a flinching kidney. "We can't *both* miss you."

Likely they couldn't, not with me as a bullet sandwich. With care I dug out my wallet, pulled the bills from it—twenties, mostly, with a handful of tens—held them out.

Martha took them, disappeared them. "Check him."

I felt a deft hand digging into the rest of my pockets. Mildred found them all, all the bills folded over and rubberbanded. A good weekend's take, dammitalltohell.

"That's better," Mildred said in satisfaction. "Go ahead,

Sister. The boy wants to keep both his kidneys."

Martha nodded briefly, then climbed up into the cab without any trouble at all. She pulled the door shut, then leaned out. The gun glinted in the sunlight. "All right, Sister, you come on around now. He's mine."

"Wait a minute," I protested, "you can't take my rig!"

Martha smiled sweetly down upon me. "Of course we can."

"You can't even drive this thing!"

"Of course we can."

"My God, woman, it's got more gears than you do genuine teeth!"

"You know," Martha said, smiling, "I find that a mighty sexist thing to say. You just *assume* because we're women we can't drive a big-rig."

"I don't think you can even reach the pedals!"

"Don't tell that to our daddy," she said. "He'd be disappointed that he wasted all his time teaching us a trade."

A concussive hissing of the airbrakes told me Mildred was behind the wheel. "Wait a minute!" I shouted. "You can't steal my truck and my money just to go *shopping!*"

Martha shook her head. "I'm afraid you really are a sexist pig," she said sadly. "Too bad you never met our daddy; *he'd* have changed your mind in a hurry."

"For God's sake, woman—you can't just leave me here!"

"Of course we can." Martha smiled kindly. "But I'd like to be a fly on the wall when you try to explain to the police how you lost your eighteen-wheeler."

Something came sailing out through the open window and cracked against the asphalt: a gift from Mildred. I heard her say something; Martha laughed and repeated it for my benefit. "There's Garth," she said. "You can put him in the cassette deck there in the car. Give you some company while you wait for someone to come along." She glanced briefly at the sun.

"Hope it's not *too* long."

The truck began to roll. "Wait! *Wait!*" I put a hand on the door, and nearly got it shot off. I fell back and dodged a ricochet as it whanged off the pavement.

Martha stuck her head out the window. Blue hair glowed in the sun. "Thank you for the grubstake," she called. "It's so much more fun to gamble with other people's money!"

"Gamble—?"

"Casinos!" she shouted gleefully. "God bless the Indians for building them! Dozens and dozens of them!"

Mildred blew the horn, then put the pedal to the metal. The last I saw of the bluehairs—and of my truck—was Martha's waving hand.

ENDING, AND BEGINNING

Four had died. Killed ruthlessly. Uselessly. Three, because they were intended as examples to the others. The fourth, merely because he was alone, and Sancorran. The people of Sancorra province had become fair game for the brutal patrols of Hecari soldiers, men dispatched to insure the Sancorran insurrection was thoroughly put down.

Insurrection. Ilona wished to spit. She believed it a word of far less weight than *war,* an insufficiency in describing the bitter realities now reshaping the province. *War* was a hard, harsh word, carrying a multiplicity of meanings. Such as death. Destruction. Ending.

Four people, dead. Any one of them might have been her, had fate proved frivolous. She was a hand-reader, a diviner, a woman others sought to give them their fortunes, to tell their futures; and yet even she, remarkably gifted, had learned that fate was inseparably intertwined with caprice. She could read a hand with the hand in front of her, seeing futures, interpreting the fragments for such folk as lacked the gift. But it was also possible fate might alter its path, the track she had parsed as leading to a specific future. Ilona had not seen any such thing as her death at the hands of a Hecari patrol, but it had been possible.

Instead, she had lived. Three strangers, leaving behind a bitter past to begin a sweeter future, had not. And a man with whom she had shared a bed in warmth and affection, if not wild

295

passion, now rode blanket-wrapped in the back of the karavan-master's wagon, cold in place of warm.

The karavan, last of the season under Jorda, her employer, straggled to the edges of the nameless settlement just after sundown. Exhausted from the lengthy journey as well as its tragedies, Ilona climbed down from her wagon, staggered forward, and began to unhitch the team. The horses too were tired; the karavan had withstood harrying attacks by Sancorra refugees-turned-bandits, had given up coin and needed supplies as "road tax" to three different sets of Hecari patrols until the fourth, the final, took payment in blood when told there was no money left with which to pay.

When the third patrol had exacted the "tax," Ilona wondered if the karavan-master would suggest to the Hecari soldiers that they might do better to go after the bandits rather than harassing innocent Sancorrans fleeing the aftermath of war. But Jorda had merely clamped his red-bearded jaw closed and paid up. It did not do to suggest anything to the victorious enemy; Ilona had heard tales that they killed anyone who complained, were they not paid the "tax."

Ilona saw it for herself when the fourth patrol arrived.

Her hands went through the motions of unhitching without direction from her mind, still picturing the journey. Poor Sancorra, overrun by the foreigners called Hecari, led by a fearsome warlord, was being steadily stripped of her wealth just as the citizens were being stripped of their holdings. Women were widowed, children left fatherless, farmsteads burned, livestock rounded up and driven to Hecari encampments to feed the enemy soldiers. Karavans that did not originate in Sancorra were allowed passage through the province so long as their masters could prove they came from other provinces—and paid tribute—but that passage was nonetheless a true challenge. Jorda's two scouts early on came across the remains of several karavans that the master knew to be led by foreigners like himself; the Hecari apparently were more than capable of killing anyone they deemed Sancorran refugees, even if they manifestly were not. It was a simple matter to declare anyone an enemy of their warlord, even if that individual was manifestly not Sancorran.

Ilona was not Sancorran. Neither was Jorda, nor one of the scouts. But the other guide, Tansit, was. And now his body lay in the back of a wagon, waiting for the rites that would send his spirit to the afterlife.

Wearily Ilona finished unhitching the team, pulling harness from the sweat-slicked horses. Pungent, foamy lather dripped from flanks and shoulders. She swapped out headstalls for halters, then led the team along the line of wagons to Janqeril, the horse-master. The aging, balding man and his apprentices would tend the teams while everyone else made their way into the tent settlement, looking for release from the tension of the trip.

And, she knew, to find other diviners who might tell a different tale of the future they faced tomorrow, on the edge of unknown lands.

Ilona delivered the horses, thanked Janqeril, then pushed a fractious mass of curling dark hair out of her face. Jorda kept three diviners in his employ, to make sure his karavans got safely to their destinations and to serve any of his clients, but Tansit had always come to her. He said he trusted her to be truthful with him. Hand-readers, though not uncommon, were not native to Sancorra, and Tansit, like others, viewed her readings as more positive than those given by Jorda's other two diviners. Ilona didn't know if that were true; only that she always told her clients the good and the bad, rather than shifting the emphasis wholly to good.

She had seen danger in Tansit's callused hand. That, she had told him. And he had laughed, said the only danger facing him were the vermin holes in the prairie, waiting to trap his horse and take him down as well.

And so a vermin hole *had* trapped his horse, snapping a leg, and Tansit, walking back to the karavan well behind him, was found by the Hecari patrol that paused long enough to kill him, then continue on to richer pickings. By the time the karavan reached the scout, his features were unrecognizable; Ilona knew him by his clothing and the color of his blood-matted hair.

So Tansit had told his own fortune without her assistance, and Ilona lost a man whom she had not truly loved, but liked. Well enough to share his bed when the loneliness of her life sent her to it. Men were attracted to her, but wary of her gift. Few were willing to sleep with a woman who could tell a lover the day of his death.

At the end of journeys, Ilona's habit was to build a fire, lay a rug, set up a table, cushions, and candles, then wait quietly for custom. At the end of a journey clients wished to consult diviners for advice concerning the future in a new place. But this night, at the end of this journey, Ilona forbore. She stood at the back of her wagon, clutching one of the blue-painted spoke wheels, and stared sightlessly into the sunset.

Some little while later, a hand came down upon her shoulder. Large, wide, callused, with spatulate fingers and oft-bruised or broken nails. She smelled the musky astringency of a hard-working man in need of a bath; heard the inhaled, heavy breath; sensed, even without reading that hand, his sorrow and compassion.

"He was a good man," Jorda said.

Ilona nodded jerkily.

"We will hold the rites at dawn."

She nodded again.

"Will you wish to speak?"

She turned. Looked into his face, the broad, bearded, seamed face of the man who employed her, who was himself employed several times a season to lead karavans across the wide plains of Sancorra to the edge of other provinces, where other karavans and their masters took up the task. Jorda could be a hard man, but he was also a good man. In his green eyes she saw grief that he had lost an employee, a valued guide, but also a friend. Tansit had scouted for Jorda more years than she could count. More, certainly, than she had known either of them.

"Yes, of course," she told him.

Jorda nodded, seeking something in her eyes. But Ilona was expert at hiding her feelings. Such things, if uncontrolled, could color the readings, and she had learned long before to mask emotions. "I thank you," the master said. "It would please Tansit."

She thought a brace of tall tankards of foamy ale would please Tansit more. But words would have to do. Words for the dead.

Abruptly she said, "I have to go."

Jorda's ruddy brows ran together. "Alone? Into this place? It's but a scattering of tents, Ilona, not a true settlement. You would do better to come with me, and a few of the others. After what happened on the road, it would be safer."

Safety was not what she craved. Neither was danger, and certainly not death, but she yearned to be elsewhere than with Jorda and the others this night. How better to pay tribute to Tansit than to drink a brace of tall tankards of foamy ale in his place?

Ilona forced a smile. "I'm going to Mikal's ale-tent. He knows me. I'll be safe enough there."

Jorda's face cleared. "So you will. But ask someone to walk you back to your wagon later."

Ilona arched her brows. "It's not so often I must *ask* such a thing, Jorda! Usually they beg to do that duty."

He understood the tone, and the intent. He relaxed fraction-
ally, then presented her with a brief flash of teeth mostly
obscured by his curling beard. "Forgive me! I do know better."
The grin faded. "I think many of us will buy Tansit ale tonight."

She nodded as the big man turned and faded back into the
twilight, returning to such duties as were his at the end of a
journey. Which left her duty to Tansit.

Ilona leaned inside her wagon and caught up a deep-dyed,
blue-black shawl, swung it around her shoulders, and walked
through the ankle-deep dust into the tiny settlement.

She had seen, in her life, many deaths. It rode the hands of all
humans, though few could read it, and fewer still could interpret
the conflicting information. Ilona had never *not* been able to
see, to read, to interpret; when her family had come to
comprehend that such a gift would rule her life and thus their
own, they had turned her out. She had been all of twelve sum-
mers, shocked by their actions because she had not seen it in
her own hand; had she read theirs, she might have understood
earlier what lay in store. In the fifteen years since they had
turned out their oldest daughter, Ilona had learned to trust no
one but herself—though she was given to understand that some
people, such as Jorda, were less likely to send a diviner on her
way if she could serve their interests. All karavans required
diviners if they were to be truly successful; clients undertaking
journeys went nowhere without consulting any number of diviners of all persuasions, and a karavan offering readings along the
way, rather than depending on itinerant diviners drifting from
settlement to settlement, stood to attract more custom. Jorda
was no fool; he hired Branca and Melior, and in time he hired
her.

The night was cool. Ilona tightened her shawl and ducked
her head against the errant breeze teasing at her face. Mikal's

ale-tent stood nearly in the center of the cluster of tents that spread like vermin across the plain near the river. A year before there had been half as many; next year, she did not doubt, the population would increase yet again. Sancorra province was in utter disarray, thanks to the depredations of the Hecari; few would wish to stay, who had the means to depart. It would provide Jorda with work as well as his hired diviners. But she wished war were not the reason.

Mikal's ale-tent was one of many, but he had arrived early when the settlement had first sprung up, a place near sweet water and good grazing, and not far from the border of the neighboring province. It was a good place for karavans to halt overnight, and within weeks it had become more than merely that. Now merchants put up tents, set down roots, and served a populace that shifted shape nightly, trading familiar faces for those of strangers. Mikal's face was one of the most familiar, and his tent a welcome distraction from the duties of the road.

Ilona took the path she knew best through the winding skeins of tracks and paused only briefly in the spill of light from the tied-back doorflap of Mikal's tent. She smelled the familiar odors of ale and wine, the tang of urine from men who sought relief rather too close to the tent, the thick fug of male bodies far more interested in liquor than wash water. Only rarely did women frequent Mikal's; the female couriers, who were toughened by experience on the province roads and thus able to deal with anything, the Sisters of the Road, taking coin for the bedding, and such women as herself: unavailable for hire, but seeking the solace found in liquor-laced camaraderie. Ilona had learned early on to appreciate ale and wine, and the value of the company of others no more rooted than she was.

Tansit had always spent his coin at Mikal's. Tonight, she would spend hers in Tansit's name.

Ilona entered, pushing the shawl back from her head and

shoulders. As always, conversation paused as her presence was noted; then Mikal called out a cheery welcome, as did two or three others who knew her. It was enough to warn off any man who might wish to proposition her, establishing her right to remain unmolested. This night, she appreciated it more than usual.

She sought and found a small table near a back corner, arranging skirts deftly as she settled upon a stool. Within a matter of moments one-eyed Mikal arrived, bearing a guttering candle in a pierced-tin lantern. He set it down upon the table, then waited.

Ilona drew in a breath. "Ale," she said, relieved when her voice didn't waver. "Two tankards, if it please you. Your best."

"Tansit?" he asked in his deep, slow voice.

It was not a question regarding a man's death, but his anticipated arrival. Ilona discovered she could not, as yet, speak of the former, and thus relied upon the latter. She nodded confirmation, meeting his dark blue eyes without hesitation. Mikal nodded also, then took his bulk away to tend the order.

She found herself plaiting the fringes of her shawl, over and over again. Irritated, Ilona forcibly stopped herself from continuing the nervous habit. When Mikal brought the tankards, she lifted her own in both hands, downed several generous swallows, then carefully fingered away the foam left to linger upon her upper lip.

Two tankards upon the table. One: her own. The other was Tansit's. When done with her ale, she would leave coin enough for two tankards, but one would remain untouched. And then the truth would be known. The tale spread. But she would be required to say nothing, to no one.

Ah, but he had been a good man. She had not wished to wed him, though he had asked; she had not expected to bury him, either.

At dawn, she would attend the rites. Would speak of his life, and of his death.

Tansit had never been one known for his attention to time. But he was not a man given to passing up ale when it was waiting.

Ilona drank down her tankard slowly and deliberately, avoiding the glances, the stares, and knew well enough when whispers began of Tansit's tardiness in joining her.

There were two explanations: they had quarreled, or one of them was dead. But their quarrels never accompanied them into an ale-tent.

She drank her ale, clearly not dead, while Tansit's tankard remained undrunk. Those who were not strangers understood. At tables other than hers, in the sudden, sharp silence of comprehension, fresh tankards were ordered. Were left untouched. Tribute to the man so many of them had known.

Tansit would have appreciated how many tankards were ordered. Though he also would have claimed it a waste of good ale, that no one drank.

Ilona smiled, imagining his words. Seeing his expression.

She swallowed the last of her ale and rose, thinking ahead to the bed in her wagon. But then a body blocked her way, altering the fall of smoky light, and she looked into the face of a stranger.

In the ocherous illumination of Mikal's lantern, his face was ruddy-gold. "I'm told the guide is dead."

A stranger indeed, to speak so plainly to the woman who had shared the dead man's bed.

He seemed to realize it. To regret it. A grimace briefly twisted his mouth. "Forgive me. But I am badly in need of work."

Ilona gathered the folds of her shawl even as she gathered patience. "The season is ended. And I am not the one to whom you should apply. Jorda is the karavan-master."

"I'm told he is the best."

303

"Jorda is—Jorda." She settled the shawl over the crown of her head, shrouding untamed ringlets. "Excuse me."

He turned only slightly, giving way. "Will you speak to him for me?"

Ilona paused, then swung back. "Why? I know nothing of you."

His smile was charming, his gesture self-deprecating. "Of course. But I could acquaint you."

A foreigner, she saw. Not Sancorran, but neither was he Hercari. In candlelight his hair was a dark, oiled copper, bound back in a multiplicity of braids. She saw the glint of beads in those braids, gold and silver; heard the faint chime and clatter of ornamentation. He wore leather tunic and breeches, and from the outer seams of sleeves and leggings dangled shell- and bead-weighted fringe. Indeed, a stranger, to wear what others, in time of war, might construe as wealth.

"No need to waste your voice," she said. "Let me see your hand."

It startled him. Arched brows rose. "My hand?"

She matched his expression. "Did they not also tell you what I am?"

"The dead guide's woman."

The pain was abrupt and sharp, then faded as quickly as it had come. *The dead guide's woman.* True, that. But much more. And it might be enough to buy her release from a stranger. "Diviner," she said. "There is no need to tell me anything of yourself, when I can read it in your hand."

She sensed startlement and withdrawal, despite that the stranger remained before her, very still. His eyes were dark in the frenzied play of guttering shadows. The hand she could see, loose at his side, abruptly closed. Sealed itself against her. Refusal. Denial. Self-preservation.

"It is a requirement," she told him, "of anyone who wishes to hire on with Jorda."

His face tightened. Something flickered deep in his eyes. She thought she saw a hint of red.

"You'll understand," Ilona hid amusement behind a business-like tone, "that Jorda must be careful. He can't afford to hire just anyone. His clients trust him to guard their safety. How is he to know what a stranger intends?"

"Rhuan," he said abruptly.

She heard it otherwise: *Ruin.* "Oh?"

"A stranger who gives his name is no longer a stranger."

"A stranger who brings ruination is an enemy."

"Ah." His grin was swift. He repeated his name more slowly, making clear what it was, and she heard the faint undertone of an accent.

She echoed it. "Rhuan."

"I need the work."

Ilona eyed him. Tall, but not a giant. Much of his strength, she thought, resided beneath his clothing, coiled quietly away. Not old, not young, but somewhere in the middle, indistinguishable. Oddly alien in the light of a dozen lanterns, for all his smooth features were arranged in a manner women undoubtedly found pleasing. On another night, *she* might; but Tansit was newly dead, and this stranger—Rhuan—kept her from her wagon, where she might grieve in private.

"Have you guided before?"

"Not here. Elsewhere."

"It is a requirement than you know the land."

"I do know it."

"Here?"

"Sancorra. I know it." He lifted one shoulder in an eloquent shrug. "On a known road, guiding is less a requirement than protection. That, I can do very well."

Something about him suggested it was less a boast than the

simple truth.

"And does anyone know *you?*"

He turned slightly, glancing toward the plank set upon barrels where Mikal held sovereignty, and she saw Mikal watching them.

She saw also the slight lifting of big shoulders, a smoothing of his features into a noncommittal expression. Mikal told her silently there was nothing of the stranger he knew that meant danger, but nothing much else, either.

"The season is ended," Ilona repeated. "Speak to Jorda of the next one, if you wish, but there is no work for you now."

"In the midst of war," Rhuan said, "I believe there is. Others will wish to leave. Your master would do better to extend the season."

Jorda had considered it, she knew. Tansit had spoken of it. And if the master did extend the season, he would require a second guide. Less for guiding than for protection, with Hecari patrols harrying the roads.

Four people, dead.

Ilona glanced briefly at the undrunk tankard. "Apply to Jorda," she said. "It's not for me to say." Something perverse within her flared into life, wanting to wound the man before her who was so vital and alive, when another was not. "But he *will* require you to be read. It needn't be me."

His voice chilled. "Most diviners are charlatans."

Indeed, he was a stranger; no true-born Sancorran would speak so baldly. "Some," she agreed. "There are always those who prey upon the weak of mind. But there are also those who practice an honest art."

"You?"

Ilona affected a shrug every bit as casual as his had been. "Allow me your hand, and then you'll know, won't you?"

Once again he clenched it. "No."

"Then you had best look elsewhere for employment." She had learned to use her body and used it now, sliding past him before he might block her way again. She sensed the stirring in his limbs, the desire to reach out to her, to stop her; sensed also when he decided to let her go.

It began not far from Mikal's tent. Ilona had heard its like before and recognized at once what was happening. The grunt of a man taken unawares, the bitten-off inhalation, the repressed blurt of pain and shock; and the hard, tense breathing of the assailants. Such attacks were not unknown in settlements such as this, composed of strangers desperate to escape the depredations of the Hecari. Desperate enough, some of them, to don the brutality of the enemy and wield its weapon.

Ilona stepped more deeply into shadow. She was a woman, and alone. If she interfered, she invited retribution. Jorda had told her to ask for escort on the way to the wagons. In her haste to escape the stanger in Mikal's tent, she had dismissed it from her mind.

Safety lay in secrecy. But Tansit was dead, and at dawn she would attend his rites and say the words. If she did nothing, would another woman grieve? Would another woman speak the words of the rite meant to carry the spirit to the afterlife?

Then she was running toward the noise. "Stop! *Stop!*"

Movement. Men. Bodies. Ilona saw shapes break apart; saw a body fall. Heard the curses meant for her. But she was there, telling them to stop, and for a wonder they did.

And then she realized, as they faded into darkness, that she had thought too long and arrived too late. His wealth was untouched, the beading in the braids and fringe, but his life was taken. She saw the blood staining his throat, the knife standing up from his ribs. Garotte to make him helpless, knife to kill him.

He lay sprawled beneath the stars, limbs awry, eyes open and empty, the comely features slack.

She had seen death before. She recognized his.

Too late. Too late.

She should go fetch Mikal. There had been some talk of establishing a Watch, a group of men to walk the paths and keep what peace there was. Ilona didn't know if a Watch yet existed; but Mikal would come, would help her tend the dead.

A stranger in Sancorra. What rites were his?

Shaking, Ilona knelt. She did not go to fetch Mikal. Instead she sat beside a man whose name she barely knew, whose hand she hadn't read, and grieved for them both. For them all. For the men, young and old, dead in the war.

In the *insurrection.*

But there was yet a way. She had the gift. Beside him, Ilona gathered up one slack hand. His future had ended, but there was yet a past. It faded already, she knew, as the warmth of the body cooled, but if she practiced the art before he was cold she would learn what she needed to know. And then he also would have the proper rites. She would make certain of it.

Indeed, the hand cooled. Before morning the fingers would stiffen, even as Tansit's had. The spirit, denied a living body, would attenuate, then fade.

There was little light, save for the muddy glow of lanterns within a hundred tents. Ilona would be able to see nothing of the flesh, but she had no need. Instead, she lay her fingers gently upon his palm and closed her eyes, tracing the pathways there, the lines of his life.

Maelstrom.

Gasping, Ilona fell back. His hand slid from hers. Beneath it, beneath the touch of his flesh, the fabric of her skirt took flame.

She beat it with her own hands, then clutched at and heaped powdery earth upon it. The flame quenched itself, the thread of smoke dissipated. But even as it did so, as she realized the fabric was whole, movement startled her.

The stranger's hand, that she had grasped to read, closed around the knife standing up from his ribs. She heard a sharply indrawn breath, and something like a curse, and the faint clattered chime of the beads in his braids. He raised himself up on one elbow and stared at her.

This time, she heard the curse clearly. Recognized the grimace. Knew what he would say: *I wasn't truly dead.*

But he was. Had been.

He pulled the knife from his ribs, inspected the blade a moment, then tossed it aside with an expression of distaste. Ilona's hands, no longer occupied with putting out the flame that had come from his flesh, folded themselves against her skirts. She waited.

He saw her watching him. Assessed her expression. Tried the explanation she anticipated. "I wasn't—"

"You were."

He opened his mouth to try again. Thought better of it. Looked at her hands folded into fabric. "Are you hurt?"

"No. Are *you?*"

His smile was faint. "No."

She touched her own throat. "You're bleeding."

He sat up. Ignored both the slice encircling his neck and the wound in his ribs. His eyes on her were calm, too calm. She saw an odd serenity there, and rueful acceptance that she had seen what, obviously, he wished she hadn't seen.

"I'm Shoia," he said.

No more than that. No more was necessary.

"Those are stories," Ilona told him. "Legends."

He seemed equally amused as he was resigned. "Rooted in truth."

Skepticism showed. "A living Shoia?"

"Now," he agreed, irony in his tone. "A moment ago, dead. But you know that."

"I touched your hand, and it took fire."

His face closed up. Sealed itself against her. His mouth was a grim, unrelenting line.

"Is that a Shoia trait, to burn the flesh a diviner might otherwise read?"

The mouth parted. "It's not for you to do."

Ilona let her own measure of irony seep into her tone. "And well warded, apparently."

"They wanted my bones," he said. "It's happened before."

She understood at once. "Practitioners of the Kantica." Who burned bones for the auguries found in ash and grit. Legend held Shoia bones told truer, clearer futures than anything else. But no one she knew of used *actual* Shoia bones.

He knew what she was thinking. "There are a few of us left," he told her. "But we keep it to ourselves. We would prefer to keep our bones clothed in flesh."

"But I have heard no one murders a Shoia. That anyone foolish enough to do so inherits damnation."

"No one *knowingly* murders a Shoia," he clarified. "But as we apparently are creatures of legend, who would believe I am?"

Nor did it matter. Dead was dead, damnation or no. "These men intended to haul you out to the ant hills," Ilona said. Where the flesh would be stripped away, and the bones collected for sale to Kantic diviners. "They couldn't know you are Shoia, could they?"

He gathered braids fallen forward and swept them back. "I doubt it. But it doesn't matter. A charlatan would buy the bones and claim them Shoia, thus charging even more for the divinations. Clearer visions, you see."

She did see. There were indeed charalatans, false diviners who victimized the vulnerable and gullible. How better to attract trade than to boast of Shoia bones?

"Are you?" she asked. "Truly?"

Something flickered in his eyes. Flickered red. His voice hardened. "You looked into my hand."

And had seen nothing of his past or his future save *maelstrom*.

"Madness," she said, not knowing she spoke aloud.

His smile was bitter.

Ilona looked into his eyes as she had looked into his hand. "Are you truly a guide?"

The bitterness faded. "I can be many things. Guide is one of them."

Oddly, it amused her to say it. "Dead man?"

He matched her irony. "That, too. But I would prefer not." He stood up then; somehow, he brought her up with him. She faced him there in the shadows beneath the stars. "It isn't infinite, the resurrection."

"No?"

"Seven times," he said. "The seventh is the true death."

"And how many times was this?"

The stranger showed all his fine white teeth in a wide smile. "That, we never tell."

"Ah." She understood. "Mystery is your salvation."

"Well, yes. Until the seventh time. And then we are as dead as anyone else. Bury us, burn us. . . ." He shrugged. "It doesn't matter. Dead is dead. It simply comes more slowly."

Ilona shook out her skirts, shedding dust. "I know what I saw when I looked into your hand. But that was a shield, was it not? A ward against me."

"Against a true diviner, yes."

It startled her; she was accustomed to others accepting her word. "You didn't believe me?"

He said merely, "Charlatans abound."

"But you are safe from charlatans."

He stood still in the darkness and let her arrive at the conclusion.

"But not from me," she said.

"Shoia bones are worth coin to charalatans," he said. "A Kantic diviner could make his fortune by burning my bones. But a *true* Kantic diviner—"

"—could truly read your bones."

He smiled, wryly amused. "And therefore I am priceless."

Ilona considered it. "One would think you'd be more careful. Less easy to kill."

"I was distracted."

"By—?"

"You," he finished. "I came out to persuade you to take me to your master. To make the introduction."

"Ah, then *I* am being blamed for your death."

He grinned. "For this one, yes."

"And I suppose the only reparation I may pay is to introduce you to Jorda."

The grin flashed again. Were it not for the slice upon his neck and the blood staining his leather tunic, no one would suspect this man had been dead only moments before.

Ilona sighed, recalling Tansit. And his absence. "I suppose Jorda might have some use for a guide who can survive death multiple times."

"At least until the seventh," he observed dryly.

"If I read your hand, would I know how many you have left?"

He abruptly thrust both hands behind his back, looking mutinous, reminding her for all the world of a child hiding booty. Ilona laughed.

But she *had* read his hand, if only briefly. And seen in it conflagration.

Rhuan, he had said.

Ruin, she had echoed.

She wondered if she were right.

GUINEVERE'S TRUTH

I am not what they say I am, these bitch-begotten mythmakers so adept at patching together occasional truths and falsehoods into a wholly improper motley. They were not *there*, any of them, to say what did happen. Or also to say what did not.

They call it a tragedy now. I suppose it is; I suspect it was even then, when none of us knew. When none of us thought beyond what two of us imagined might be enough to preserve a realm. To preserve a man's dignity.

They make of it now a sacrament, some of them; others name it sin. To us, it was merely what *was*. We were never prescient, to know what would come of the moment. We were never wise, to consider consequences. We were what we were. Nothing more than that.

More, now, they would and will have us be. Great glyphs of human flesh, striding out of stories, tidbits of tales of others such as we: kings and queens and knights . . . and the follies of the flesh.

Was it folly? No. Not then. Not now. Was it flesh? Oh yes. Entirely the flesh. Wholly *of* the flesh, though they would have it be more: sacrament, or sin. The anvil upon which a realm was sundered, despite the tedious truth.

A man, first. A woman. A binding between them, magicked and ill-wrought, yet enough to get a child. And that child, bred up to be a king despite his bastardy, was made to *be* a king—be it necessary, be it required that he kill another king to gain the crown. To break what was built of heart, mortared together by blood.

And yet they blame me.

Seductress? I was not raised so, nor was given to believe it could be so; men wanted me for what I was, not who. The daughter of a man judged to be of use, of some small power in the chess game of the realm, the patchwork of a place that was not, until he came, a nation in any wise.

But he came. Was born to come. Bred to come, to take up a people as he took up the sword, to preserve what might otherwise have fallen before it was truly built; bred and brought up to stitch together out of the fragile patchwork a whole and well-made quilt resilient enough to guard the limbs of his lady, his one true lady, his steadfast Lady whose name was Britain.

A man who is king needs nothing of a wife but that she be his queen, and bear him an heir.

Whore? Some name me so. And would have burned me for it.

Yet I will burn. The priests tell me so. Afterward. God will not tolerate an adulteress in His realm.

If that be so, if it be true of men as well as of women, then surely we will play this out again, this tragedy, this travesty, this humiliating dance. And none of us wanting it.

If that be hell, we have lived it.

Such stories, in their conception, in the truths of their births, are infinitely simple. Ours was no different. But they make of it now a grand entertainment, fit to cause people to weep.

We none of us wept.

It was what it *was*, not this great sweeping epic, not this literature of the soul, binding others to it. There was no immensity to it, no bard's brilliant embroidery to win him a month of meals. Our tapestry was naught but a square of clean, fine linen, hemmed on all the edges . . . only later was it used to sop and display the blood of Britain's broken heart.

His one true lady, undone. His wife, the queen, unmasked. Seductress. Adulteress. And worse yet: barren.

Ah, but it *was* my lack. His seed was proven, though unknown by any save the woman who was his sister. His seed was sowed, was born, was bred up to be a king, even if it be necessary to kill another king.

Well, it is done.

All of it is done. And all of it also *undone;* there was no wisdom in the bastard who was inexplicably son and nephew, to see what might come of it. To see what has.

Lies. So many lies. The truth, you see, is plain, is prosaic beyond belief, and therefore tedious.

A man, and a woman. Stripped of all save the flesh, and the flesh freed of such constraints as crown, as armor. And the hearts stripped of all things save compassion for a king who needed a son, yet had none of his queen.

We did not know, then, what we came to know: that the king had bred a son. We knew only there was none and no promise of it, and a man growing older with no son to come after him, to lift the great burden and don it himself, like the hair shirt of priests. It was known only that Britain had need of an heir, and that the king's wife, after so much time in the royal bed, offered nothing to prove his manhood.

It was a solution, we thought, that might prove least painful to a man who was king, and was of himself well worth the sacrifice: his wife and his liege man would between them, in his name and the name of his realm, make a child. And call it the king's.

But no child came of it. Only grief.

It is easier, I know, to make a myth of it, to commute us to legend. But the truth is small, and of less glory than what is sung: what we did was to comfort the king. To save what the king had wrought.

Practicality. Not undying, tragic love. Not this travesty of the truth.

But it is prettier, I admit, what they have made of it.

Such a small story, ours. And a world wrenched awry.

Blame me as you will for the folly, but not for the intent. Any more than you blame the bards for making magic of what was nothing more than necessity as we viewed it then, for and in the name of a simple, compassionate man.

For king that was, and king that shall be.

ACKNOWLEDGMENTS

All stories reprinted by permission of the author.

"A Lesser Working," © 2001 by Jennifer Roberson. First published in *Out of Avalon.*

"Sleeping Dogs," © 1990 by Jennifer Roberson. First published in *Sword and Sorceress VI.*

"Mad Jack," © 1999 by Jennifer Roberson. First published in *Lord of the Fantastic: Stories in Honor of Roger Zelazny.*

"The Lady and the Tiger," © 1985 by Jennifer Roberson. First published in *Sword and Sorceress II.*

"Spoils of War," © 1988 by Jennifer Roberson. First published in *Sword and Sorceress V.*

"Piece of Mind," © 2004 by Jennifer Roberson. First published in *Murder and Magic.*

"Shadows in the Wood," © 2004 by Jennifer Roberson. First published in *Irresistible Forces.*

"In His Name," © 1995 by Jennifer Roberson. First published in *Ancient Enchantresses.*

"A Wolf Upon the Wind," © 1996 by Jennifer Roberson. First published in *Warrior Enchantresses.*

"A Compromised Christmas," © 1992 by Jennifer Roberson. First published in *A Christmas Bestiary.*

"Of Honor and the Lion," © 1988 by Jennifer Roberson. First published in *Spellsingers.*

"Fair Play," © 1991 by Jennifer Roberson. First published in *Sword and Sorceress VIII.*

"Garden of Glories," © 1995 by Jennifer Roberson. First published in *Sword and Sorceress XII*.

"Jesus Freaks," © 2003 by Jennifer Roberson. First published in *Women Writing Science Fiction as Men*.

"Rite of Passage," © 1986 by Jennifer Roberson. First published in *Sword and Sorceress III*.

"Valley of the Shadow," © 1984 by Jennifer Roberson. First published in *Sword and Sorceress I*.

"Blood of Sorcery," © 1984 by Jennifer Roberson. First published in *Sword and Sorceress I*.

"By the Time I Get to Phoenix," © 1997 by Jennifer Roberson. First published in *Highwaymen, Robbers and Rogues*.

"Ending, and Beginning," © 2002 by Jennifer Roberson. First published in *30th Anniversary DAW Fantasy*.

"Guinevere's Truth," © 1996 by Jennifer Roberson. First published in *Return to Avalon*.

ABOUT THE AUTHOR

Since 1984, **Jennifer Roberson** has published twenty-four solo novels in several genres. Her primary genre, fantasy, is currently divided among three different universes: the Chronicles of the Cheysuli, the Sword-Dancer saga, and the world of Karavans. In 1996 she collaborated with Melanie Rawn and Kate Elliott on *The Golden Key,* a massive undertaking that was a finalist for the 1997 World Fantasy Award. She has edited three fantasy anthologies. Her love of history led her to write two novels exploring the Robin Hood legend (*Lady of the Forest, Lady of Sherwood*), and a Scottish historical based on the infamous Massacre of Glencoe, *Lady of the Glen.* Works have been translated and published in Germany, France, Japan, China, Sweden, Poland, Hungary, Russia, Italy, Israel, and the UK. Roberson lives on acreage near the foot of the San Francisco Peaks outside Flagstaff, Arizona, in a book-cluttered household shared with two cats, nine Cardigan Welsh Corgis, and one goofy Labrador puppy. Her main hobbies are breeding and showing dogs, and creating mosaic artwork. Her Web site can be found at www .cheysuli.com.